Frank 'n' Stan's Bucket List

#2 TT RACES

J C Williams

ISBN: 9781719930628

First printing September 2018

Second printing November 2018

Cover artwork by Paul Nugent

Proofreading, editing, formatting, and interior design provided by Dave Scott and Cupboardy Wordsmithing

CONTENTS

Frank 'n' Stan's Bucket List #2:
Destination... Isle of Man TT Races
Again!

Chapter One

St Luke's Church sat proudly at the head of a rolling valley, flanked on either side by luscious green hillside, the still air filled with birdsong. Its remote location on the outskirts of Yorkshire caused modern navigation systems difficulty, but this idyllic church had provided solace to the remote rural communities for generations. A magnificent stone wall provided a protective arm around the quaint structure inside. Engraved stone headstones were peppered sporadically, providing a memorial for the occupants resting beneath. It truly was as beautiful a final resting place as one could have wished for. The stone bulwark, which would have taken a master craftsman weeks to painstakingly lay, was today being used for a purpose its creator could not possibly have conceived.

Stella eased up and down in a rhythmic fashion, using two protruding stones in the otherwise uniform structure as a scratching post to relieve an itch on her left buttock. She manoeuvred like a brown bear rubbing its back on a tree — except, one might say, slightly less majestically. It was challenging to see beneath her generously-applied layer of makeup, but as she slid down once again, the faintest glimpse of a contented smile could be discerned through the acrid plume of cigarette smoke emanating from her lips in a steady stream.

"Ahh," she said, rotating her hips for maximum contact. Her moment of satisfaction was, however, rudely interrupted.

"What the actual hell are you *doing?*" said Stan incredulously, stood underneath the wooden gatehouse at the entrance to the church grounds.

Stella didn't avert her gaze. "I'm having a fag, obviously," she said, stopping only to take another drag. "And scratching my arse. What's it to ya?"

Stan put his hand to his head to steady himself, before removing it to create a clenched fist which he shook like he was rolling dice. In fact, any conversation with Stella, he found, was indeed a gamble.

"Stella," he said, in as controlled a manner as the situation would allow. "He's bleeding, for god's sake."

Stella shrugged. Or, it may have been a shudder of pleasure. From the rubbing.

"Stella," Stan repeated, bracing himself against the horror. "For the love of God..."

It was rather an apt expression, considering their current location at a church.

Stella finally reacted, and looked towards Stan. "You've got orange... muck on your shirt collar," she said. "You should rub that fake tan sludge in with better care," she offered.

Stan looked over his shoulder, as if to an imagined accomplice, and paused grimly before returning his scorn toward Stella. "Why did you hit him?" he asked, finally. "He's got a bloody cut above his lip. It might need *stitches*," he added, with the tone of his voice increasing in pitch at the last word.

Stella eyed him impassively as she sucked on the final remnants of her cigarette. "He grabbed me," she explained. "So I hit him. Simples." She stated this matter-of-factly, as if the answer should have been obvious.

Stan's clenched fist returned once again. "Stella, he only asked you to not smoke inside. You can't smoke inside a church. Why would you think you could smoke inside a church?" said Stan, who was now concerning himself with containing his fake-tan on the intended area. "The only people that smoke in a church are those being cremated."

Stella's expression remained distinctly unmoved. "He shouldn't have touched me," she continued. "And sometimes there's incense."

"What?"

"Incense. You said there's never smoke in church, but sometimes there's—"

"Look," Stan admonished, before she could finish. "He only put his hands on you as you ignored his first three requests." He moved towards her. "Here. Like this," he said, raising his hand by way of illustrative example, but judging by the sudden elevation of Stella's imposing, drawn-on eyebrows, immediately thought better of it. He placed his hands firmly in his pockets, instead — where they'd remain safe.

"Well I suppose I just didn't hear him properly, now did I?" said Stella.

"Well I heard him properly, and I was stood directly next to you!" Stan replied.

"I could've been singing a tune," Stella offered.

"Singing a—?"

3

"In my head," Stella explained further. "A happy tune. So I didn't hear him get shirty with me those three times, because I was distracted. By the happy tune."

"The happy tune in your head," Stan stated flatly.

"That's right," Stella agreed, pleased with herself.

Stan was surprised that he could still be surprised by anything Stella might say. He should be used to this by now, he thought.

"The poor guy was shaking after you hit him!" he said, trying to impress upon her the severity of the situation. "He's got blood all over his... his... vestments!"

"That's still better than the muck you've got all over your vest-a-mints," she replied. "Besides, he shouldn't have touched me, like I said. Anyway, who the hell does he think he is, telling me where I can and cannot smoke? It's rubbish."

"It's his bloody church!" Stan shouted. "He's the bloody vicar!"

"Oi! Language!" Stella answered, tut-tutting him. "We're in a churchyard, Stanley, after all. Show some respect!"

"Oh, it's me that's disrespectful, is it? I'm the one? It's been me this entire time?"

"Yes, that's right, now you've got it," she said, happily lighting up another fag.

"Right. Listen," Stan carried on, undaunted. "The Big Man upstairs saw it fit to appoint the vicar as the man to look after this church, and this church's flock, and you nearly *knocked him unconscious* because he asked you to smoke outside. It's all I could do to not get him to phone the police, you know! I had to... I had to tell him..." said Stan, suddenly trailing off.

"What's this? Tell him what?" Stella demanded, her already-considerable body mass puffing out, inflating like a bullfrog.

Stan wisely took several steps back and held his hands out like a poor mime artist. "Look," he said, setting his stall out. "They were about to phone the police, so I had to think quick."

The foundation on Stella's face was starting to crack like the mortar on the wall that she'd just violated.

"Out with it, you scrawny piece of shit," she growled.

"I told them you were, well... simple," Stan admitted. "I told them that you had mental issues. Several of them, in fact. And they were very quick to believe it in the circumstances."

Stan braced himself, screwing up his eyes in anticipation of being, himself, attacked. When no assault was forthcoming, he widened his eyes, once again, and found himself unsettled when Stella was revealed to be laughing.

"That's pretty quick, actually," said Stella jovially. Then she snuffed her ciggie out and said, "Come on, then," grabbing Stan's arm. "Let's get inside, shall we?" she said, quite agreeably. "Should I talk to myself, or maybe dribble a little bit? You know, to keep the pretence up?"

Stan recoiled cautiously, his eyes scanning to see if she was being sincere. "Em... no more than usual?" he suggested timidly. When she didn't strike him, he carried on. "In all honesty, Stella, I don't think you'll need to be doing anything more than simply being yourself, and you'll be just fine," he said. "Just fine. And, I'm sure, very convincing," he added, with a tone of encouragement and a nod of the head for good measure.

Once inside the church, sombre music emanated from the dilapidated organ stuck in the far corner. The tune was difficult to decipher due to the mashing of the keys by an enthusiastic elderly lady who was, perhaps, short-sighted judging by the proximity of her nose to the music sheet. Those in the congregation already seated offered encouragement by way of sympathetic smiles and nods. It was unlikely, given the organist's lack of acuity in the vision department, that the organist was even aware of this — but the congregants were among the faithful, and presumably had hope of a miracle.

"Over here!" said Lee to Stella and Stan, waving them over, as if they needed further direction in an already intimate church. "I've saved you a seat," he told them.

As he made his way over, Stan offered his apologies for disturbing those already taken their place in the pews that he was, well, disturbing. Whereas Stella waded through the sea of seated parishioners with little concern, leaving a trail of bruised knees in her prodigious wake. She was very much living up to her newfound persona of being somewhat less than stable.

Lee, for his part, looked smart; no longer dependent on handed-down clothing, he carried a navy suit well. "There's a fair few here," he said to the pair in a gentle Irish accent, throwing his eyes over the room.

Stan bobbed his head in agreement. "He was a popular guy. People liked him," he said. "He'll be missed a great deal."

"There better be food afterwards," Stella interrupted, leaning across. "I've only had a Mars bar for breakfast and I'm bloody starving." She stood up once again, and, after a brief struggle with the buttons, removed her jacket. She looked down on her protruding midriff. "Bloody hell, I'm wasting away to nothing here," she said, shaking her head forlornly. "And I'm in desperate need of a lager as well — I've got a gob like Gandhi's flip-flops."

As if the language weren't bad enough, Stan's jaw dropped as Stella stood there in the middle of the church, pinching bits of Lycra from every conceivable fold and crevice (of which there were many). He went to speak, but couldn't. He moistened his lips, took a look at Lee who was equally as perplexed, and then cleared his throat. "Are you, eh, going for a run afterwards, Stella?" asked Stan.

Stella was occupied by a struggle with the gusset area of her attire, a struggle that she appeared very much to be losing. "A run?" she replied. "What the hell's wrong with you? Don't be bloody daft. Honestly, where do you come up with this rubbish?"

Stan looked over his shoulder, and, as usual, all eyes were zeroed in on Stella. He leaned closer to her and lowered his voice. "It's just that, you know, wearing a Lycra running suit kinda gives one the impression that you might be going for a run. As opposed to, say, attending a funeral."

Stella was still stood for the world to see, on full display, in a skin-tight Lycra running suit to be precise, with the words *JUST DO IT* emblazoned in huge lettering across the front of the sleeveless top that was doing the best it could — pulling double duty, as it were — to contain her generous, ample bosom.

"Sometimes you just don't think, Stanley," she said crossly. "You said to wear something black," she told him. "And you know full well this is the only thing I've got that's black."

"How in God's name would I possibly—?" he began, but then shook the thought away. "Look, I can see it's black," said Stan, although in parts it was, in fact, transparent due to being stretched out like an overinflated balloon. He was about to carry on when he shrugged his shoulders in acquiescence and smiled. "You know what? You're fine," he said, knowing she was causing no real harm (or, at least, no permanent damage) to anybody. "It'd put a smile on his face if he was here," Stan added agreeably, but Stella was no longer listening.

Instead, she rubbed her hand over the surface of her leggings, on the area at the top of her thigh, on the outer perimeter of her panty line. She took a grip of her stomach and moved it temporarily out of the way, peering over for a closer inspection. After a moment, she let go of her stomach and gripped the waistband with one hand and delved in with the other one. The congregation were in turmoil, whether to focus their attention on the organ being tortured on one side or the horror that was Stella, stood with her hand down her pants, foraging like a hungry tramp in a bin. Oblivious to her audience, Stella's pained expression turned to one of rapturous joy as she first retrieved a packet of cigarettes, closely followed by a partially-melted Mars bar.

"I knew I'd brought a snack!" she said with a beaming smile. She positioned herself to take a seat, but first took a less-than-discreet sniff of the chocolate treat, and, when satisfied, retired back down to the pew, demolishing its contents like a seagull eating chips.

"Is that Frank's daughter over there?" asked Lee once Stella had sorted herself out, but before a response was forthcoming the organist came to a rather abrupt halt, causing a hushed silence. The considerable wooden doors at the entrance to the church were opened, flooding the room with natural light. The instinctive reaction was to turn and look — and those that did were greeted with the sight of the hearse parked sideways, its wooden delivery sat patiently, covered in flowers, waiting for its final journey.

With the break in the music (described here, generously, as such), the vicar moved to his pulpit and cast a warm smile over the congregants. His magnanimous countenance faltered, however, as he glanced in Stella's general direction, turning to a look of suspicion. Sensing the attention, and wanting to avoid the night in a police cell, Stella reverted to her alter-ego and began twitching whilst slapping herself on the back of her own head.

As there was nothing that could be done, the vicar once again addressed his audience:

"We've had a request from the family, if you'd provide your indulgence. At their wishes, they'd like the congregated family and friends to join them outside the church and escort the coffin, and so..." he suggested, motioning with a wave of his hands to usher them all out into the sunshine.

Stan squinted his eyes as they emerged from the dark recess of the church, and, once outside, it was fairly obvious that there were fewer mourners than had initially appeared inside the intimate setting indoors.

"Shit," said Lee out of the corner of his mouth. "There's actually not that many people bothered their arses to turn up."

"I see that now," Stan answered him. "But at least we're... here?" he said, his attention suddenly drawn elsewhere.

"What is that—?" Lee began.

"Ungodly caterwaul?" Stan finished, turning on a sixpence.

A pained noise, comparable to, perhaps, a sick elephant, floated by on the breeze. Stan looked at Lee and they both moved to Stella, placing a comforting arm around her broad — *very* broad — shoulders, which now began to heave as she watched the coffin being lifted from the car.

"I'm... going... to... miss... him...!" wailed Stella, with the tears now flowing freely.

Stan was at first taken aback, as he'd always assumed that Stella was devoid of emotion. But, in that moment, she had an air of vulnerability that neither Stan, nor perhaps anybody, had seen before. Stan shared a tear, and the three of them held each other tenderly as the coffin was hoisted upon the shoulders of the pallbearers. There was a dignified silence.

Well, there was a dignified silence at least for a few brief seconds, before...

"Don't start without us!" shouted a voice through the open window of a coach that was proceeding steadily on the narrow road outside the church, nearly there. The first was followed closely by a smaller coach a short distance behind.

Rather than negotiate the narrow carpark, once reached, the coaches were abandoned, all but blocking the road to further traffic.

"Wait there!" demanded the same voice, once more, this time with even further urgency and determination.

The vicar looked warily as the occupants of the two coaches spilt onto the country lane and made their way, at great pace, stampeding through the church grounds. This was not the usual sort of service to which he was accustomed. First, it was the ungainly mentally-challenged woman's antics. And, now this.

The intention of the hordes was unknown, but as they advanced, they appeared somewhat a motley bunch. At first blush, from a distance, they looked reasonably smart. As they grew closer, however, the state of them was brought gradually into focus Their suits, for instance, were disparate affairs; most were a mismatch, with the trousers not belonging to the jacket and such. One chap was only wearing one shoe. And a number of them looked like it'd been days since they'd last clapped eyes on a bar of soap. In fact, their somewhat less-than-pleasant aroma arrived several seconds before they did, with their imminent influx causing several of the mourners to seek out a position of cover behind Stella's broad frame — with Stella presently dabbing the tears off her cheeks with a rolled-up newspaper. Not only was Stella a barrier to the odoriferous assault on the senses, but it was taken as obvious that she could handle herself in a scrap as well.

The vicar, who'd seen enough, took a step forward, his hand held aloft like he was poised to deliver a sermon.

"Gentlemen! What in goodness' sake is going on here? Don't you realise that this is a funeral?" he demanded.

The mob drew to a halt and a dubious-looking little fellow with a stooped back, errant grey hair and an unkempt, wispy, sea-spray beard, shuffled forward in what looked very much to be his favourite, most comfortable slippers. He took a cloth cap from his head and placed it under his arm.

"Yessir," he said, respectfully. "Yessir, vicar. That's why we've come."

"All of you?" asked the vicar, still unsure of their intentions.

The old man looked back towards his comrades and then again to the vicar. "Yessir, all of us, that's right," he said.

The vicar cocked his head just slightly, foreseeing an explanation.

"That man," the old fellow continued, nodding at the coffin (which was still being supported by the pallbearers, pallbearers who were in fact starting to show the onset of strain caused by the unexpected delay). "That man has helped us more in the last six months than most people have done in a lifetime. Because of Frank and Stan's Food Stamps, the majority of us have managed to have a meal each and every day — and a good meal, at that. That man cared about the people here, and did something about it. That man made a friend of each and every homeless person in his city, and we'd be damned if we didn't come here today to see him off properly."

"Ehem," coughed one of the pallbearers. "Sorry," he said deferentially. "Only Julian has got a dodgy knee. I'm worried it's going to give way?"

The vicar acknowledged him. "Very good," the vicar said, facing back to the old fellow stood cap-in-hand. "You are, of course, all very welcome, but we should get the proceedings underway. If you don't mind, we should—"

"Excuse me, sir. Just a moment," said the elderly gentleman. Without response from the vicar, he turned to those stood behind him and waved his hand. With that, twelve men, arguably the smarter-looking of the lot, stepped forward. They walked in front of the coffin and formed a line, six each, on either side of the church entrance. Judging by the stance and uniformity, it looked likely that several of the men were formerly in the military.

The vicar smiled and placed a hand on the old man's shoulder. "Let's go," the vicar said softly. "And, that really is a wonderful gesture." At the same time as the vicar instructed the coffin to move, the guard of honour that had formed stood to attention and gave their fallen comrade the respect that he deserved.

Stella was unable to contain her emotion, and the ink from the newspaper was now smeared across her face — forming a sort of cryptic Rorschach pattern.

"Come on," said Stan, escorting her and Lee into the service. "He'd have liked this," remarked Stan, admiring the men stood either side of them as they entered the church.

The vicar once again took up position in front of his congregation and scanned the room at the numbers present — swelled significantly over the preceding twenty minutes. He allowed the typical murmurings of a flock to come to natural conclusion before preparing to dive into his funereal script. He placed his notes in front of him and cleared his throat, raising one arm for emphasis, but before he had a chance to open his mouth the door flew open with one final straggler.

"Sorry, your honour. My apologies!" said the man, dripping in sweat and gasping for breath. "I had to move the coach before I could... there were two coaches... two of them, and... down the road... and I couldn't just..." He paused, suddenly aware that all eyes in the room were upon him. "Well... it's not important. Again. My apologies."

Stan craned his neck toward the man, who was looking unsuccessfully for somewhere to sit. "Over here," he called over, waving rather limply. "I saved you a seat."

"Excuse me. Sorry. Excuse me," said the latecomer, extending his regrets for the intrusion. He gave Stella as wide a berth as was possible between the narrow church pews, offering her a gracious smile, before collapsing on the hard, wooden bench seat next to Stan.

Stan gave him the order of service, offering it as a fan to relieve the flow of sweat which ran down the man's face. He looked at his watch. "Bloody hell, Frank. I didn't think you were going to make it on time," he said.

Frank wiped the sweat from his forehead, taking several gulps of air. "I know. I didn't realise half the homeless population of Liverpool were going to show up. I had to arrange a second coach at a moment's notice and have an unscheduled stop at the charity shop so I could kit them out with suits to wear. Also, it's difficult to drive when you've got your head held out the window. They're a smashing bunch, really, but, sheesh, they don't half stink, and—" He paused suddenly, mid-sentence. And, then, "Stan?" he whispered. "What's wrong with Stella's face?"

"Don't be rude, Frank," was Stan's reply.

Frank fanned himself with the order of service while the vicar made his introductions. With the arrival of the homeless hordes, it was now a very respectable turnout — with some even spilling over, out through the main doors. The moment was particularly poignant for Frank as it could very easily have been his face on the front cover of the brochure he was looking at. Fortunately, his decision to proceed with treatment for his illness meant that the arrival of his own expiry date was delayed, at least for now.

Stan used his elbow to attract Frank's attention, breaking his reverie. "You're up, buddy," he told his friend, motioning to the vicar's lectern.

"Oh, yes, right," said Frank, reaching inside his jacket pocket for his well-thumbed notes. Frank shuffled through the pew and then, lowering his head, made his way up the aisle to the front of the church. He was never one for public speaking, but he wanted to do this. He wanted to show his respect to a valued colleague who'd become a trusted friend in the short time he'd known him.

Frank looked to the vicar for approval to proceed, and then took up his pile of notes, snapping them into position. He looked at the eyes staring at him, and then back to the well-considered notes before him.

"Ladies and gentlemen," he began, with a quiver apparent in his voice. The words on the paper were swirling in front of him, blending into each other as his rehearsed speech that he'd practice-delivered so fluently in front of the mirror now eluded him. His legs started to buckle, and, to make matters worse, the acrid aroma of his passengers now followed him wherever he went, clinging tenaciously to the linings of his nostrils. His eyes started to water.

Frank stared vacantly for several seconds before taking his notes, rolling them up and placing them in his trouser pocket. He took a deep breath and placed his hands on the lectern in front of him, which also served to steady him, before continuing.

"I was going to stand up here and tell you what a remarkable man Arthur Hughes was — well, *is* — and will always be. But, I don't really need to do that, because if you didn't think that then you probably wouldn't be here in the first place. I'd only known Arthur for a little under a year, but rarely have I seen someone with such compassion, such... such..."

Frank took a moment, and dried his eyes with a white handkerchief.

"He was a special man, a man that wanted to give something back to the community. Some of you may know that with the help of my friend, Stan, we set up a charity to help the homeless in Liverpool. Fate brought us Arthur, I truly believe that. Arthur didn't rest until he'd reached out to every homeless person he could. I can promise you, he didn't give me or Stan a moment's peace. He was constantly throwing ideas and suggestions at us. Some were a bit crazy and others were genius, but, regardless, every suggestion was for the good of other people.

"They honestly broke the mould when Arthur was made. This may sound like a bit of a cliché. With Arthur, however, it couldn't be more true. Never have I had the pleasure of being with someone who was concerned more with how *you* were than himself. He was a warm, considerate man who I was very proud to call a friend. No matter how brief it was, he's made an impact on my life and those here today. These people..."

Frank gestured to the homeless in attendance, who'd now, unsurprisingly, divided the occupants of the church and were now sat on their own.

"... These people here don't own a home, and often don't know where their next meal is coming from. Arthur worked tirelessly to get these people a warm meal each day, and, often, a place to sleep — where they'd feel safe and secure.

"We all know Arthur had his own problems, but it was precisely that empathy that made him more determined to help these people. And those very people were insistent that they'd be here today. To say goodbye to their friend."

Frank looked to the coffin, and then back to the attendees.

"Arthur, you're one in a million. And I promise you this. We'll carry on with the charity. We'll get bigger and stronger and we'll help more and more people, not just in Liverpool, but all over the country. Arthur," said Frank, with his shoulders now heaving. "Arthur. You've made me a better man, and it was a pleasure to know you."

Two candles flickered as Frank placed a tender hand on the coffin. He wiped another tear from his cheek and smiled.

"Goodbye, my friend... goodbye."

Chapter Two

The smell of cheap floral air freshener was waging war against a pungent aroma of grease, tobacco, and sweat. It was a valiant effort, but, judging by Molly's reaction as the door opened, it was a battle it was not likely to win. She ducked her head suddenly in reaction to a bell attached to the top of the door frame that rang as she entered, announcing her arrival.

Frank stretched out his arm, welcoming her over to his table next to the window. "Are you okay?" he asked, once she joined him. "You seemed startled by that bell."

"No, not startled," answered Molly. "More of a conditioned response, I suppose."

"Conditioned response?" asked Frank, confused.

"It's a signal I worked out with my special clients. When they rang a bell, that meant I'd..." she began, before spotting the look of horror on her father's face.

"It's not important," Molly told him, quickly changing the subject. "Anyway. I'm not sure why you insist on meeting me here," she said, as a statement rather than a question. She scrutinised the wooden chair for detritus before cautiously hooking the handles of her designer handbag over it.

"It's good to see you, Molly," answered Frank.

"Dad, it stinks in here," Molly answered him, wrinkling her nose.

She removed her jacket, and repeated the same diligence as with her handbag, before finally taking a seat. She reached for her hair, which was tied back with thought and attention (as opposed to, say, the *I'm-late-and-have-a-meeting-in-eight-minutes* approach). "Now I'm going to have to wash my hair again. Honestly, Dad, this place is really manky."

"It's lovely to see you, Molly," Frank reiterated with a wry smile. He could have met her at work, the trendy coffee shop, or even the park — after all, it was a lovely morning — but Frank took great pleasure in meeting her here. "I thought you said you liked it in here?" he asked, feigning innocence.

Molly threw her eyes around Fryer's Café, but it only served to increase her level of contempt. "Dad, it's a complete rubbish heap. Is this not where you met me last year?"

Frank knew full well that it was. "Is it?" he said. *"Herm,* you could be right, Molly. Maybe I just misheard you last time? Anyway, so how's work?" he asked cheerfully.

"Dad, I hope you've not just asked me here to complain about my job. After all, it was *you* who told me to get a job. Remember?"

"I'm not here to judge," Frank assured her. "Only, it's just that I thought you could probably have found something more...?"

"More what?" demanded Molly. "Respectable? Are you ashamed of me, then?"

Frank held his hands aloft in protest. "Molly, I was going to suggest you could find a job with, perhaps, longer-term career prospects, is all."

"Are you saying I'm old for my line of work? That I'm past my prime??" asked Molly indignantly. "Well?"

"Of course not!" Frank pleaded. "You're perfectly fit to... look, you're perfectly fit... *cough*... I'm just saying that being a stripper has probably got a shelf life. Surely?"

Molly's mouth dropped in disgust. "Dad, I'm a *lap dancer*. Not a *stripper*. There's a *huge* difference."

It was fair to say that Frank was not overly knowledgeable on the subject, and, had it been anyone other than his daughter, he'd likely have enquired further on the subject.

Molly snapped her head towards the window and changed her expression like the flick of a switch, as two workmen in hard hats, noticing her through the window, motioned and gesticulated in a 'friendly' way. Smiling back, she held their gaze until they'd passed before adopting the expression, once again, like she was sucking on a lemon.

Frank placed his hands on the table, atop hers. "Whatever you do, Molly, you know I'll always love you. You know that, right?"

Molly nodded, her demeanour thawing a bit. "I quit my job two months ago, as it turns out," she said. "I've started taking a design class, actually."

Despite the swell of pride and self-satisfaction in her voice, she subconsciously pulled up her plunge neckline t-shirt, as if she were telling her expensive yet ample cleavage that, sadly, time was finally expired on their fledgeling career.

"That's wonderful!" said Frank, his face radiating at the news that the three of them, so to speak, were resigning.

"Yes, well I hope you're satisfied," was Molly's reply.

"Molly, you say it like you've done it reluctantly, as if you were punishing me for doing it in the first place. I've told you, I just want you to be happy. Honestly. Just make sure that whatever you do, you do it for the right reasons, that's all. Okay? And this design class sounds like a fantastic idea," he said, looking her up and down. "You're very much like your mother in that regard," he added encouragingly. "In that you've both got an elegant dress sense. I think it's a perfect fit, yeah?"

Eric Fryer, purveyor of the fine establishment that bore his name, hovered, waiting for a natural break in the conversation before pouncing with his notepad.

Fryer's checked trousers were partially covered by a black-and-white apron which had more stains than an old mattress in a brothel. Judging by the belly which flopped over his waistline, he'd evidently been overindulging in his own menu of greasy goods, and his ample bosom might well have made Molly jealous (if not for her augmentation surgery, at least).

"Get you a refill?" asked Eric, in reference to Frank's empty mug.

"Yes, please," said Frank. "And a bacon butty when you've got a moment, Eric."

"Bacon butty," Eric repeated. He then shifted his attention towards Molly, who in turn stared back at him. Hard.

"Yes? Can I help you?" she asked the confused-looking Eric Fryer sternly.

"I think, eh, that's *my* line?" offered Eric, notepad poised at the ready.

"How's that?" Molly snapped back, not at all accommodatingly.

"Can I get you anything to eat or drink, luv?" asked Eric.

Molly smiled and looked towards her father, but when Eric didn't move, her attention returned back again to the patient proprietor.

"Oh, you're being serious?" she asked. "No," she said. "No, no. Oh good god, no," she elaborated, once again casting her eyes around the room as if that should have been enough of an explanation.

Eric smiled courteously. He was either thick-skinned or Molly's reaction was commonplace, or, more likely, Eric had clapped eyes on her plunge neckline t-shirt which had returned to its original, revealing position, affording a generous, ample, breath-taking view.

"Bacon sarnie, Eric? Hello??" said Frank.

"Yes, of course," said Eric, his eyes retracting and settling back into their sockets.

"That would usually have cost you fifty pound," said Molly. "You're lucky that I don't charge for that anymore."

A bemused Eric retired to the kitchen to prepare some grease, fried in grease, seasoned with more grease.

Molly fiddled with a salt cellar on the table. Her head was bowed. She went to speak but the words didn't come. For those looking through the café window, they might've looked like they were very much bored with each other's company, right then, though that was not the case at all...

"I want..." offered Molly before trailing off, chewing her lip as she moved her attention to the pepper pot, playing it through her fingers absently.

She looked up and her huge brown eyes had welled up. Her brash exterior had suddenly deserted her, leaving her vulnerable.

"Do you know," said Frank. "Looking at you, sat there, I could close my eyes and see my little girl, sat on my knee staring up at me." Frank reached for her hand. "I miss that little girl, Molly. I miss my little girl."

Molly smiled. A tear slowly navigated its way down her cheek, over to her chin, and then onto the table. She didn't try to stop it.

"You know," mused Frank. "That tear is probably the closest thing that table's had to a clean all week."

Molly's laugh set free the remainder of her tears. "I'm still your little girl, Dad. I probably don't... well, I know I don't tell you that I love you enough, Dad. Well, I do. Love you, that is."

Frank's bottom lip covered his top lip while he nodded slowly; those words were what he'd longed to hear, and couldn't have sounded sweeter to his ear.

"I know, Molly, I know. And the treatment is going well, by the way," he said, the words drawing a sunny smile from her. He put his hands up to manage her expectations. "It's still there, Molly. It's still there, mind. But the doctors are happy with the progress. I just need to remain positive."

Molly reached for a napkin, but, distrustful of even that given their surroundings, opted for her shirtsleeve instead, wiping her cheek clean. She held her dad's hand, and with her bright smile unwavering, asked: "So does this mean I'm going to need to wait for the inheritance for a few more years?"

"It's nothing definite, Molly," responded Frank with a laugh, while reaching over and taking his breakfast from a now-returned Eric.

Frank prodded the bread, which nearly broke his fingernail, and the undercooked bacon looked like a few compressions could bring it back to life. "Although," he continued without breaking his stride. "Eating this bacon butty is probably more likely to finish me off. I think I can understand why you didn't order anything."

"Well you should listen to me more," said Molly, but not unkindly. "Oh, Mum said to say hello, by the way, and is glad things are working out. She said to call her if you wanted to talk or to, you know, go for a drink."

Frank was horrified. *"Go for a drink?"* he said, repeating the words back. "You don't think she's wanting to... *get together again* with me... do you?" he asked, aghast.

Before he even had the opportunity to digest the thought, Molly's belly laugh all but answered the question for him.

"Ha-ha! Dad, you really crack me up. You are so precious!"

Frank shared the laugh and wiped an imaginary bead of sweat from his brow.

"There's something I need to tell you, Molly," he said. "Something else."

Ordinarily, this would have sounded like a serious subject on its own, but on the basis they'd been laughing about his mortality only a few moments earlier, an inquisitive strain of her eyes is all he achieved. "Hmm?" was all she said.

"You know Stan and I went to the Isle of Man last year?" he ventured.

"*Know* about it?" scoffed Molly. "I felt like I was *with* you, the amount of times the two of you have spoken about it."

The mere thought of the previous year made Frank's eyes cloud over and stare up to the grease-smeared ceiling like a lovesick girl.

"I've bought a house in the Isle of Man," said Frank, bracing himself for the verbal assault he expected he was about to receive.

Molly gave a bit of a start, but she quickly steadied herself. She rattled her fingers on the table as she ruminated on this new development, which Eric took as a prompt for service.

Her expression caused Eric to cease and desist, instantly.

She took a moment and allowed her eyes to study her father's face. He was now blowing across the surface of his tea, carefully, before taking a sip.

"I think it's a brilliant idea," she offered, finally.

"You do?" said Frank, lowering his cup of tea.

"Of course," said Molly. "I've seen what that place has done to you couple of tossers. You've been like children since you got back."

"Oh, Molly. Thank you. I was so worried you'd be upset! The plan is, I'm going to live there all year — well, probably most — but we'll need to keep an eye on the business."

"*We?*" asked Molly, although she already knew the answer.

"Yes," said Frank. "Guess who my housemate is going to be?"

"Ohh... let me guess, now. It's got to be... Stella, am I right?" laughed Molly.

Frank shifted his mouth to one side of his face, in a comical *we-are-not-amused* fashion. "Stan has gone half on the cost of the house," he explained.

"You two are going to be like the Odd Couple," said Molly. "Are you not afraid people will think you two are... you know, what with Stan being... I mean... you know...?"

"I didn't think of that one," said Frank, rubbing the stubble on his chin in as rugged a manner as possible.

"You'll need to be overtly masculine," laughed Molly. "Butch it up as much as possible."

"That should be no problem for me," he said. "What with all this excess testosterone flowing through my veins. There's so much of it, I don't know what to do with it all!"

With that, he took up his cup once more, daintily, blowing gently on his tea again, still afraid to drink it, terrified he'd burn his delicate lips. He continued:

"This illness... this horribly shit thing inside of me... has made me take stock of things, to put things in perspective. I was never one for all that *things-happen-for-a-reason* nonsense, but this last year may just have converted my way of thinking."

"How so?" asked Molly.

"I'd always wanted to go to the Isle of Man TT races, but never did. I kept putting it off. I'm not sure why. It's not exactly far away, after all. Hell, you can virtually see the Isle of Man from our offices on a clear day," Frank replied. "So, again, I don't know why I put it off."

He paused, thoughtfully.

"Anyway, If I hadn't become ill, I would never have gone. It's funny that my bucket list is the thing that's given me a new lease of life. Honestly, Molly, the people I met over there, the things I've seen, have changed my life — and I genuinely believe that is the reason I've been able to fight this... *thing*... for as long as I have."

Frank looked into his daughter's eyes.

"You will come over and see me?" he asked.

"Of course I'll come over. Why shouldn't I? I really want to meet this Dave and Monty you keep going on about." She smirked. "Plus," she said, playing with her hair, "I might just find myself a sexy biker wearing tight leathers."

"You may encounter some stiff competition on Stan's end," Frank told her with a chuckle. "When I suggested moving over, he already had the local estate agents on speed dial!"

"So then what are you going to do with the business?" asked Molly. "Oh, and the charity?"

Frank chewed his lips for a moment before answering. "We've given this a lot of thought, actually, and one of the options was to get a full-time manager into the taxi rank."

"To manage Stella?" Molly put forward.

Frank nodded knowingly, and then sighed.

"Aye, therein lies the rub. Stella is pivotal to the business. She's the only one who can keep the drivers in line, and she's great for throwing drunks out of the office at night. If we got a manager in, they wouldn't last five minutes looking after Stella. So, the only solution is to make *her* the manager, and cut her in for an ownership stake. After all, she'll be the one running the business. Albeit, Stan and I are only seventy miles away and will come home a couple of weekends a month, you know, to keep an eye on things."

"*Mm-hmm,*" Molly said, listening along.

"And, with the charity, Lee has been a godsend. He's loving his work and run that smooth enough. He's been looking to grow the charity to extend the remit of our assistance beyond Liverpool. His aim is to have Frank 'n' Stan's Food Stamps issued to the homeless all over the country, within three years."

Molly nodded. "But, Stella. In charge? She could start a fight in an empty room."

"She'll be fine," offered Frank, finally taking a tentative sip of his tea.

"What does *she* think about all this?" Molly asked.

Frank rested his head back and looked at the ceiling once more. "Yeahhh, about that," he said slowly. "We've not told her we're going yet, actually. She was the last one we were going to tell, *erm...* actually."

"Dad. You're going to have to tell her soon, you know!" Molly told him.

"I know, I know!" Frank whined pathetically. "You wouldn't, er... you wouldn't fancy telling her *for* me, would you? Em... by any strange twist of fate?"

"Not a chance!" replied Molly. "I'm quite fond of my face, and I want to retain these looks for as long as I can."

"Ah, I don't know what I'm so worried about," Frank answered. "She's just a gentle giant, that's all she is. A gentle..."

Molly looked at him with comical scepticism, cocking her head to one side.

"Ah, bugger. Yeah, I don't believe it either," Frank said with another sigh. "I'm just going to have to simply man up and tell her that we're getting her to run the business, full-time. She'll be fine with it, I'm sure."

Molly was still giving him a look.

"I can do this! *I can do this!*" Frank said, building himself up. "I can..."

Frank trailed off, the folly of his bravado becoming clear.

"Get Stan to tell her?" offered Molly.

"Can't," Frank immediately replied. "Such was his own desire to not have to tell Stella, that... well, see, we didn't factor in the legal fees for the new house, right? And so Stan offered to pay the nearly six-thousand pounds extra all by himself, in exchange for not having to, you know... *cough*... talk to Stella."

Molly closed her eyes and shook her head in despair. "Not a pair of bollocks between you," she said under her breath, not loud enough for her father to hear.

"Even now, though," Frank continued, "I'm still not sure it was a good deal."

"Dad, for fucksake, if you're brave enough to eat that bacon butty, you're brave enough to speak with Stella! Look," she said, standing. "I have to be somewhere in ten minutes, so..." she said, crouching over to give her dad a kiss. "I'll pop around to see you at the weekend. I'm glad you're feeling positive about this. And the move to the Isle of Man? It's the right one."

As the door chimed above her head, giving her a start once again, she took a final glance over her shoulder and smiled. "Dad," she said. "I'll tell Mum that you'd love to take her out for a meal and a drink, yeah?"

"You bloody won't, or I'll throw this bread at you!" Frank called back to her, playfully.

Frank sat with a simple grin. He knew the meeting with Molly could have gone either way. She was prone to stamping her feet like a spoilt brat at times, so, on balance, it was a fantastic result. And the fact she was covering her knockers up to the paying public was an added bonus as well.

"I'm okay," said Frank, placing the palm of his hand over the top of his mug. But Eric wasn't trying to refill Frank's mug. Nor was he listening. He stood there with a faraway look on his face, and he ran his fingers through his hair. The grease from his hands gave his hair a healthy sheen that women would pay a fortune for if bottled up and marketed.

"Can I help, Eric?" asked Frank. "Eric?"

"I, eh, heard you talking about Stella?" Eric said, finally, snapping out of his reverie.

Frank tilted his head. "I did."

"Wonderful lady," said Eric, with a little too much enthusiasm for Frank's comfort.

"Ah," said Frank with a flicker of faint recollection. He'd tried to put it out of his mind, of course. Nearly succeeded, too. Until now, unfortunately. "You and her, you had a, em... *moment*, didn't you? Last year, as I recall?"

Eric's eyes floated like an empty crisp packet on the breeze. "It was one of the best nights of my life," said Eric Fryer wistfully. "Truly wonderful, it was, like something from a Hollywood film."

Frank went to speak but the words — any words — temporarily evaded him.

He thought for a moment longer, allowing Eric a further brief indulgence, before speaking. "Hang on, I thought you told me you'd bought her a can of Coke, and in return received a hand-job around the back of Tesco's? Eric, that's not exactly up there with *Casablanca* or *Brief Encounter*."

Eric threw a look of abject scorn in Frank's direction. It was delivered with the venom of a man who was about to ride into battle to defend the honour of the woman he loved.

"Right. I'll just have you know, Frank," Eric advanced, finger prodded on the grubby table. "That it was a can of Lilt. She's got a tropical side to her, that girl, like a coconut, she does. Also, it was indeed a very *Brief Encounter*, as it happened, but only because I'd been without the love of a good woman for a long while," he said indignantly. "Not that that's any of your business, mind you," he added.

"There's probably less surface hair on a coconut," smirked Frank, but his comic genius washed right over Eric.

"Anyway," said Frank, reaching for his coat. "As much as I enjoy these nostalgic reminisces about your love life, I should get going."

"Here, you're not eating your bacon sandwich?" asked Eric, now wounded, his bombast instantly fading away.

Frank looked at the table and then back to Eric. "No, Eric. The bread is stale, and the bacon is that rare it's still reciting its lines with James Cromwell from *Babe: Pig in the City*. So, no. I'm not eating it."

"Alright, Frank, fair enough," replied Eric, suddenly jolly. "Four pound, please," he said cheerfully.

"For what?" asked Frank.

"Breakfast, of course," responded Eric. "Fryer's Café is not a charity-type establishment, my good fellow," he continued, hand extended to receive payment. "I'm running a business here. And a fine business, at that."

"What?" Frank protested. "That's not breakfast, Eric," he said, pointing at the table. "Seriously, mate. I'd need a pneumatic drill to get through that bread!"

But Eric remained unmoved. "Aye, it's hearty, it is. Good bread!" was his answer. And his hand was still held out for payment.

"Bloody hell," replied Frank, reaching for a five-pound note. "I'm starting to see why Molly doesn't want to come here," he said. "Keep the change," he added, with little enthusiasm, as he marched towards the door.

As the bell chimed above his head, Frank felt Eric's firm hand on his shoulder.

"Ah, so you're giving me a refund?" Frank asked with a tinge of optimism.

Eric laughed for a moment. "No, of course not," he said, matter-of-fact. "Don't be daft. Look, now seriously," he continued. "Will you... will you put a word in for me? With Stella? I know, a woman like her, she could have her pick of men, as sure as I'm standing here. But I'd treat her right."

Frank went to move but the hand on his shoulder became firmer.

"I'll treat her like the lady she is," Eric went on. "Honestly, I would."

Sensing Eric was serious, and that his agreement was the only way he'd avoid further grease coverage on his jacket, Frank reluctantly agreed.

"Sure, mate. Of course," he said, examining his shoulder (which now had a smear like he'd been attacked by a slug). "I'll be sure to tell her that you'll treat her like the lady she is."

Once released, Frank was pleased to step into the fresh air, and his shoulders shuddered at the thought of Eric and Stella together. "*Can of Lilt,*" he said aloud, with a chuckle and a further shuddering of the shoulders. "Fucking hell."

The troubling thought was fortunately overridden by the vibration in his pocket. He rummaged for his phone and answered in his chirpiest tone. He examined the handpiece when no answer was forthcoming — a process he repeated twice more before he realised that the vibration was an alarm rather than a call.

The reminder alerted him to take his tablets — which was ordinarily a reminder of his current predicament in the health department. Today, however, he took the tablets from his breast pocket with a cheery willingness. He stared at the writing and numerous warnings about side effects — which he'd never bothered to read — and smiled, once again equating the pills to his current situation. Instead of being acutely aware of his own mortality and a reason to be full of self-pity, these pills and this illness had opened up a new chapter in his life, one that he'd be sharing with his oldest friend.

"*I'm moving to the Isle of Man,*" he sang aloud, to the bemusement of those waiting patiently at the bus stop. "*I'm moving to the Isle of Man,*" he repeated, smiling warmly at those looking back.

Frank popped the pills in his mouth and ventured up the street, with a periodic hop and a skip that Fred Astaire would have been most proud of.

Chapter Three

You need to tell her," said Frank, slumped back in his leather chair. "It's no good pretending you're busy in here," he continued, waving his hand as if swatting a fly. "If you're going to move the goalposts, then you need to man up."

Stan leaned into the compact mirror rested on the edge of his desk, directing the flossing string through his teeth with the precision of a concert violinist.

"It's important to floss," replied Stan.

"You could just take your teeth out and floss them," suggested Frank. "It'd be quicker."

"Just because I like to look after myself, Frank. And, also, they're veneers," Stan corrected his friend, rubbing his tongue against the front of his teeth with satisfaction. "Bloody expensive veneers, as well."

Stan's preening continued, with a gentle hand over his blow-dried mane of wispy hair. "Do you like my hair this colour?" asked Stan.

Frank took his feet off his desk and shifted his balance forward. "And what colour is it now?" asked Frank. "It's what, beginning of March? And you've changed your hair colour more times than I've changed my underpants."

"I forget," replied Stan, moving his head closer to the mirror for further inspection. "I think it had the word *vibrant* in it. Perhaps, *vibrant ginger*? Or something like that."

"It goes well with the fake tan," said Frank.

"I should do something with that mop on top of your head, Frank. If you let me loose on what you've got left up there, I'd get rid of that grey for you and make you look ten years younger."

"I'm not sure I—" Frank began.

"Now you're single and back on the market, Frank…" Stan carried on, undaunted, "… we need to give you every advantage, because, well, the truth of it is, at the minute, I don't rate your chances."

"The grey is distinguished," Frank protested, although somewhat unconvincingly. "Anyway, stop avoiding it. Go and tell Stella that we've bought a house in the Isle of Man."

"I will," said Stan. "Only not just now. She's busy, getting ready for an appointment."

Even though there was a wall between them and Stella, Stan had lowered his voice to a whisper and rode his chair closer to Frank. Stan took a cautious look over his shoulder to make sure she wasn't looking at them through the glass portal window which divided their office from the taxi waiting room, where Stella ruled with an iron fist. Satisfied it was clear, Stan moistened his lips to continue.

"Stella," Stan whispered. "Has got a lunch date."

"With a man?" asked Frank immediately.

"Yes, with a man!" replied Stan, after a further check over his shoulder. "As opposed to what?"

"It's not Eric Fryer from the café, is it?" asked Frank, suddenly feeling ill. It could've been the thought of that horrible bacon sarnie, or it could have been the image come to mind of Eric and Stella becoming overly familiar. Likely, it was a combination of both. Frank rubbed his upset belly, willing the contents of his stomach to remain in his stomach.

"No," Stan told him. "It's some bloke she met on a dating website, actually. He's in the armed forces, and he's in the country on leave, apparently. They've been speaking for weeks now and getting up to all sorts of—"

"Stop," commanded Frank. "Seriously. Stop. Look, em..." he said. "I don't intend this to come across as it may sound — well, perhaps I do — but has this poor fellow seen her picture? It's just, I recall she did similar last year, and she had her profile picture set as Brigitte Nielsen."

"Apparently so," said Stan. "Seen her true picture, I mean."

"And he still fancies her?" Frank asked, perplexed. "I'm sorry. I don't mean to sound cruel. But... I'm just trying to work this out... he still fancies her?"

"And she must really like him," Stan went on. "As she paid for his flight to get here."

"What? She's told you all this?" asked Frank.

Stan shook his head from side to side. "Stella? Of course she bloody hasn't. She's not exactly the sort of person to open up about her personal life."

"Then, how—?" inquired Frank.

"I read an email over her shoulder," Stan replied with a naughty grin. "How else?"

"Eric Fryer won't be pleased," offered Frank. "And he's really seen her picture, this fellow?" Frank asked, repeating himself. But Stan was now distracted by peering through the glass porthole.

"She's putting makeup on," said Stan, like a proud father watching his daughter getting ready for her prom date. "Aww, all joking apart, Frank. I do hope this goes well for her. She's been quite light-hearted this last couple of weeks, have you noticed?"

"Has she?" replied Frank. "I hadn't—"

"Relatively speaking, of course," Stan clarified.

"Ah," Frank answered.

"So perhaps a bit of romance is just what she needs to mellow her out a little bit? Plus, with her mood elevated, it might make telling her that we're buggering off and leaving her in charge a little more, I dunno... palatable?"

"But he's truly seen her picture, this fellow?" Frank asked yet again.

"Shit, she's coming!" said Stan, darting back to his desk. As the door opened, Stan mashed at the keyboard on his computer, like a teenager caught watching porn by his mum.

"Stella. You look nice," said Stan as casually as possible.

Stella had on her trademark black leggings — which were, of course, stretched out a little further than the manufacturer would have intended. They were tucked into a pair of ominous-looking leather boots that appeared as if they'd been retrieved from a corpse in a Mad Max movie. Her simple brown t-shirt had an image of two fingers, either side of her chest, pointing towards her generous bosom, with the caption emblazoned across them: *If these were brains, I'd be a freakin' genius!*

In other words, her attire was, by Stella standards, quite tasteful.

"Going anywhere nice?" asked Frank innocently, but Stella didn't offer the courtesy of a response. She reached her hand into the front of her trousers and rummaged until she retrieved her packet of cigarettes.

"I'm going out," said Stella flatly, lighting a fag. "Susie's in covering me, so you couple of massive shitgibbons stay out of her way. Especially you, Frank," she said with an accusing stare, backed up with a firm finger of suspicion.

"Wait, what?" asked Frank. "What the hell have I done?" he pleaded, but Stella was not for distracting and left, leaving a choking trail of tobacco and perfume behind.

"But what've I done?" asked Frank again, to no one at all.

"We should go out for lunch," announced Stan after a few moments. "We could go to that coffee shop on the main street, you know, the one opposite that new burger restaurant."

"What's this? You've never asked me out for lunch," Frank answered him. "Not once. Never."

"Well, then," said Stan, grabbing his coat. "It's very much overdue, isn't it? Come on, you massive shitgibbon. Let's go."

"What've I bloody done??" pleaded Frank.

Stan laughed in reply.

Frank was, in fact, eager to get away from the smell in the office and agreed to a free lunch with little resistance. "We should tell Susie that we're going out," he said to Stan. "I'm going to suggest that it's better coming from you, though. Since I'm not sure what it is exactly I've done?"

Stan only laughed at him again in response, which made Frank wonder all the more what he might possibly be guilty of.

"Why are we sat outside?" asked Frank, zipping his jacket up. "It's bloody brass monkeys. We should be sat inside."

"Nonsense," replied Stan, stirring his coffee. "A bit of bracing air will do you the world of good. Have your coffee, that'll warm your cockles."

Frank narrowed his eyes with suspicion. "You've never worried about my cockles before. First it's free lunch, and now my cockles. What's this all about?" he asked, but it was clear that Stan was looking straight through him. "Stan?"

Stan's head was angled to one side, his focus taken by events across the main street.

Frank twisted his neck like an owl and followed Stan's line of sight.

"Cover your bloody face!" shouted Stan. "Here, use this menu," he offered. "A useless spy you'd make, Frank," he admonished.

"Well I didn't know we were on a stakeout, now did I? Who is it we're—? Oh, you big soft old bugger," said Frank, suddenly catching on. He'd been unsure what surveillance operation they were on until he clapped eyes on a head covered in a tight perm surrounded by a cloud of smoke — prompting Frank to immediately seek cover behind the proffered menu.

"I'm certain I don't know what you're on about," protested Stan in mock ignorance. "I just wanted to take my oldest buddy out for a coffee and a bite to eat. Can't I even take my—?"

"She's a grown woman," responded Frank. "And she can seriously look after herself. Better than you or I, in fact."

"I know she can," Stan said eventually, conceding his obvious true intentions. His gaze across the street remained unwavering, however. "I just don't want to see her getting hurt, or hooking up with some absolute psychopath," he admitted. Stan turned to Frank. "Do you know what I mean, Frank?" he said, and his eyes betrayed genuine concern.

Frank nodded. "I certainly do, me old mate. And I think that it's nice that you care like you do. It warms my cockles."

"Told you," Stan answered him with a discreet chuckle (because they were, after all, on a stakeout).

The pair of them sat outside that coffee shop, freezing their bollocks off for the next forty-five minutes. The muscles in Frank's neck had given up the ghost twenty minutes or so earlier, so to continue his surveillance he had to sit snugly next to Stan. To those passing by, the two of them likely would've looked very much like intimate lovers enjoying a coffee date — albeit a slightly odd sort of date, what with them both peering intently, off into the distance, over the top of their shop menus.

"I'm getting hypothermia," said Frank. "I don't think I can feel my feet anymore. Is that the first sign?"

"You're confusing hypothermia with frostbite," Stan responded. "And they're still there, at the bottom of your legs where they've always been," he said, kicking out at Frank's feet for good measure. "Here. Do you feel that?"

"Feel what? *Ouch*, that hurt! No, I can't feel a thing, actually," came Frank's reply.

"Dementia, most likely, is my prognosis," Stan said. "Though of course I'm not a doctor."

"That really hurt," Frank complained. "Through the numbness and lack of feeling, I mean."

"Do you get the impression that Stella's date is running late?" Stan asked, getting back to the subject at hand. "She's been sitting there alone this whole time."

Frank gave his old pal a sympathetic glance. "Stan, I hate to say it, but maybe the guy's shown up, seen Stella — in the flesh, as it were — and continued on his way, forthwith."

Stan's head dropped. "Maybe, Frank. Maybe. I hope not, for Stella's sake. Let's give it another half hour and we'll call it a day, okay?"

Two more cups of coffee were had, a pork pie for Frank, and a cucumber sandwich for Stan, and a half hour had turned into an hour and a half — with still no sign of a man in uniform at Stella's table across the way. Frank and Stan, on the other hand, were cosied into each other for warmth, enhancing their appearance of being an adoring couple.

"What's she doing now?" asked Stan, straining his eyes.

"She's got her head in her hands," replied Frank.

Stan pushed his chair back and stood up. "Right, then. Come on, let's see to her," said Stan, beginning his march across the street without so much as looking back.

"Slow down, Stan!" Frank replied, hobbling after. "There's no blood left in my feet," he said, whinging. "The circulation's completely gone..."

"Nothing a good amputation won't sort out," Stan assured him. "Now come on!"

The pair of would-be spies navigated the street, weaving their way through busy traffic — resulting in several horns tooted and a handful of two-finger salutes. A waiter stood at the doorway of the burger restaurant with a concerned — or possibly frightened — expression on his face, as he glanced back inside, apparently unsure what to do.

"We've got this," said Stan to the waiter.

Stella had her head placed on her hands, which were planted on the table. She'd have looked like a child at primary school having a nap if it were not for her outsized form and the spine-chilling wailing noise emanating from her person.

Frank and Stan approached Stella with purpose, from opposite ends of her table — safer that way — and sat down next to her on either side. Stella raised her head briefly and broke down in tears when she caught sight of them. They both leaned into Stella's substantial frame and shared a rare moment of tenderness with her.

"I've... been... a... complete... dickhead," sobbed Stella, the tears now flowing uncontrollably. "I thought he really liked me," she said, as Frank and Stan held onto her.

The waiter signalled to his colleague, assuring him there was no need to phone the authorities regarding the mad scary woman.

"Come on, Stella," Stan said softly. "Let's get you back to the office."

Stella sat in Frank's chair, sucking the very life out of a cigarette.

"If you mention any of this, I'll remove your bollocks with rusty shears," she said, their shared moment of tenderness well and truly left behind.

"We won't say anything," Stan assured her. "So what happened to your date, anyway?"

"Who said anything about a date?" she replied, steely-eyed.

"What?" asked Frank. "So why were you sat outside the restaurant for nearly three freezing-cold hours?" Frank knew immediately, as soon as he said it, that he'd put his frozen foot right in it.

"And how would you lot even know I was there?" growled Stella.

Frank backpedalled. "I, *erm*, drove past earlier and noticed you — by pure coincidence — and when I drove past again later... again, by pure coincidence... you were, *em*... still there?" he offered unconvincingly, fooling no one.

Stella's eyes continued to bore into Frank's, mercilessly, but then, suddenly, she completely deflated.

"I met a man on the internet," she said, all her piss and vinegar depleted. "And he was supposed to meet me today. Only he didn't."

"Maybe he was just late? Or got the wrong day?" suggested Stan in an effort to massage her ego back to life.

Stella raised her eyes skyward. "No, I've been stitched up like a kipper," she said. "I've already paid over three thousand pounds to this guy as he said he couldn't afford his flights. He texted me when I was sat there, with some bullshit story about his flight being cancelled and that he needed another two thousand pound sent over to him. I've been such a tit," she said, her shame now turning to anger. "I've sent some bloody thieving, lying bastard over three thousand pounds! And I had to borrow that three thousand pounds from my sister, as well!" she exclaimed, smashing her fists into the desk.

"We... might be able to help you out with that, actually," Frank proposed, taking a position of safety near to the main door.

"What?" barked Stella. "You'll find him and kill him for me? I can do that myself!"

"No. With the money," replied Frank. "We'll give you the three thousand pounds back," he told her, waving his hand between him and Stan for, presumably, illustrative purposes.

"And why exactly would you do that?" she asked suspiciously, but pulling herself together well enough, at this point, to light another fag.

"Yes," said Stan, echoing her words. "And why exactly would we do that?"

Frank moved forward a pace, feeling it safe enough now to do so.

"Look, Stella," he began. "We've got something to tell you and it may come as a bit of a surprise." Frank took up a breath, before continuing. *"Me-and-Stan-have-bought-a-house-in-the-Isle-of-Man-and-we're-moving-over-there,"* he rattled off on the exhale, without stopping.

"Whassis?" Stella replied, eying him queerly.

"This is a gesture of our goodwill," Frank told her.

"It is?" Stan said, interjecting. And, then, giving in, "This is a gesture of our goodwill," he said, repeating Frank's words with a shrug.

"As well as a pay rise," Frank continued. "And a share of the business if you'll run things for us."

All that was missing from his delivery was a roly-poly and a couple of jazz hands to conclude.

Stella looked at Frank through the corner of her eye. "So let me be sure I'm clear on this. You'll be giving me a three-thousand-pound up-front bonus, a pay rise, *and* a share of the business?"

"Yes, that's right," Frank confirmed.

"Yes, that's right," Stan reiterated, not wishing to be left out and not given credit.

"How *much* of a share?" Stella enquired.

"Two percent," offered Frank, who looked at Stan for approval.

"Ten percent," countered Stella, fag hanging from her bottom lip.

"Five!" replied Frank, once again looking at Stan, who had abruptly distanced himself from this negotiation.

"Seven!" panicked Frank, talking the figure up further even though Stella hadn't responded to the previous offer.

"Done!" snapped Stella, spitting in her palm before reaching out her chubby hand to cement the deal.

Frank smiled. "So, you're not upset that we're going?"

"Why the hell should I be upset?" Stella answered. "I've known this for days. Molly told me when she came in looking for *you*," she said, looking at Frank. "And the sooner you two Bellend Boys are gone, the better, as far as I'm concerned!"

"So you knew we were going all along?" asked Stan, glaring over at a suddenly-gone-quiet Frank.

"Yup," said Stella. "But the cash will come in very handy, as will the seven percent. Of course, I'd have settled for the two percent," she told him. "But *he*," she said, pointing at Frank. "Is shit at negotiating. And I knew I could get him up. Besides," she added, "... you two have been about as much bloody use as a packet of rubber nails around here lately."

"Well done, Frank," said Stan. "Well done. I'll be the chief negotiator of this team from now on." He turned to Stella. "Anyway, Stella, we'll be back most weekends, so you don't need to worry."

"Why would I worry? I'm not worried," she said, placing her packet of fags back into the darkest recess down the front of her trousers. "In fact, I'm quite looking forward to it."

"Great," interjected Frank, finding his voice once again. "Now all that's sorted, Stanley, we can get the boat booked!" Then he remembered something. "Oh, Stella, one more thing," he added. "Aside from spying on you with Stan — looking out for you, I mean — what's this nonsense about something I've done? What have I *done*?" He implored pathetically.

"Jesus, Frank, are you still—? She's just having a—" Stan began.

Stella stared hard at Frank. "You know full well what you've done, you great wazzock. *You know.*"

Frank turned to Stan for aid.

"Don't ask *me*," Stan laughed. "This is *your* problem you've gotten yourself into. I certainly can't get you out of it."

Frank was left both helpless and nonplussed.

"Well, then," Stan said with finality. "That's everything sorted, isn't it!"

"But—" Frank protested, to no avail.

"Right. So," Stan continued, smiling with some satisfaction. "I'll let Dave and Monty know that we're all sorted and we're on our way! I can't wait to see those two lovely knobs again!"

"I know!" Frank chimed in happily, the subject having been successfully changed. "The thought of having our sidecar team at the TT races has been keeping me going all year! I just hope that after their crash, they're ready for this, both mentally and physically."

"They'll be fine," Stan assured him. "From what Dave's been saying, they're as excited as we are. He said that they've been working on a punishing fitness regime all winter to make sure they're ready, no less. We're really going to put Team Frank and Stan on the map this year, just you wait and see!"

Chapter Four

A gentle breeze carried the salty spray from the Irish Sea that lapped gently against the sea wall. Douglas Promenade was, well, a large promenade that stretched beyond two miles — from the ferry terminal at one end, over to the electric railway station off at the other end. For a small child on their new bike, the prospect of clear tarmac ahead was the stuff of dreams. (Yet a formidable challenge, as to cycle to the other side, you had to then cycle all the way back!) A diminutive girl of seven, maybe eight, had a determined expression on her face. Head buried into the handlebars, pigtails poking from under her helmet — and arse pointed skyward — her legs were going like the clappers, and she wasn't stopping for anybody.

"Move it, fatso!" she shouted, with a timely application of the bell for good measure. She raised her head, only breaking her stare when it was no longer safe to hold it.

"Are you going to let her talk to you like that, Monty?" said Dave with a hearty chuckle.

"What?" asked Monty, distracted by the effort in his lunge. For a man of his current capacious girth, the angle he was precariously balanced was impressive — front knee bent, and with his trailing leg stretched out behind.

"I can't hold it, Dave. Dave, I'm struggling here," Monty pleaded. His knee was shaking like a shitting dog and he reached out for support — to which there was none on offer — from Dave, who stood, arms folded, observing his soon-to-be-fallen comrade with an amused grin.

With a pathetic whimper, Monty succumbed to the inevitabilities of gravity and collapsed unceremoniously in what could be best described as a heap, where he proceeded to flail his limbs — like a turtle on its back — in an effort to right himself.

A group of elderly joggers slowed to give Monty a wide berth, eyeing him with a mixture of alarm and dismay. "Should we—?" one asked, tentatively. "Best not to get involved," another of the group counselled. And the pensioners renewed their pace from *very slow* back to their usual *slow*.

With no assistance forthcoming, Monty rolled over onto his rotund stomach, and, using every last ounce of strength still in his possession, pushed himself with great effort back into a vertical position. "Bloody hell, Dave. You could have at least helped me up!"

"I *could* have," Dave agreed cheerily. "But where would the fun be in that?"

"Oh, I see how it is, then," chided Monty, with a half-smile.

"Where did you get those shorts from?" inquired Dave.

"Why? What about my shorts? What's wrong with them?" asked Monty, dusting himself down.

"They're tight, Monty. Very tight. They're in danger of cutting off your circulation," Dave answered.

"Nothing wrong with these, Dave," replied Monty, pinging the elastic waistband. "I am, perhaps, carrying a little holiday weight, is all. Otherwise, fit as a fiddle!"

"More like a cello," Dave observed. "No, wait. What's the biggest one? Upright bass. More like an upright bass."

"Dave, you missed your calling," Monty sniffed with exaggerated umbrage. "You should've been a—"

"You two must be Dave and Monty?" said an enthusiastic voice moving at pace toward them. Monty puffed out his chest and commenced a series of star jumps in an effort to disguise how knackered he actually was.

"I'm Sam," said the slim, athletic owner of the voice. He reached out his hand and flashed a perfect, white smile. Dave accepted the handshake and struggled to keep his eye off Sam's arms, which were sculptured like those of a Greek god — a look highlighted all the more by the lack of fabric in his vest top.

In that moment, Dave and Monty had never felt as emasculated as they did right then.

"I saw you when I parked the car up, Monty," related Sam. "Impressive angle on the lunges," he continued.

"Lunge," Dave corrected.

"Pardon me?" asked Sam.

"Lunge," explained Dave. "Singular, rather than plural. There was only ever the one."

Monty slapped Dave and scowled like he'd just been shown up in front of his new girlfriend.

"Well," offered Sam, full of encouragement. "One is better than none. We all need to start somewhere!" he said, in a kind of sing-song fashion.

Monty sneered back at Dave, with a *that'll-tell-you* expression.

"So," said Sam, looking Dave and Monty up and down, though not in an overly-critical fashion — rather, like an artist eyeing up two slabs of clay. "Just so I'm clear, you two didn't hire me directly, is that right? Your friends Frank and Stan did, correct?"

Dave agreed with the enthusiasm of a child told to clean his room. "Yeah, you've got it right, alright," said Dave, looking down to the ground.

"Well, that's a different sort of arrangement," chirped Sam. "Still, we'll have fun working together!"

This Sam was perhaps a little too eager and cheerful for Dave's comfort. He found himself exhausted already, just from Sam's excessively lively demeanour.

Sam continued: "Do you mind if I ask why Frank and Stan are—?"

"We're professional sportsmen," said Monty proudly, shoulders flexing (and bones cracking in protest). "You've been hired to fine-tune us."

Sam laughed, waiting for the punchline. But Monty appeared deadly serious. It was difficult for Sam to get the measure of Monty, what with Monty's crossed eyes and everything. Sam's gaze darted back and forth, unsure which of Monty's eyes he should focus on, all time he was conscious about offending his new clients.

"Ah. You're sportsmen," declared Sam, trying to make it sound like a statement rather than a sincere question. "What, eh, sport, are you guys involved with? Bowls or darts, or — oh, I bet it's darts," said Sam, chucking an imaginary arrow for further impact. Sam busied himself, while he waited for an answer, taking a tube of something from his compact backpack and rubbing it into the back of his legs in a practised, automatic fashion, without thought — like someone else might absently scratch an itch.

"Why would we need to be fine-tuned to play darts?" asked Dave, with a deadpan expression. "Darts is not exactly an energetic sport where you're required to be at the peak of physical prowess. Is that what you're saying, Sam? Are you saying Monty and I are not what you'd call athletes?"

Sam's cheeks flushed. "I... em... didn't mean..."

"I'm pulling your chain, Sam," said Dave, allowing Sam time to remove the shovel from the hole he'd been digging himself.

"Ah," Sam replied, looking slightly relieved.

"Of course we're not athletes, that should be obvious," Dave continued. "Here, look at this," he said, jumping on the spot. "Look at my boobs! I should be wearing a bra with these bad boys, yeah? Whaddaya reckon?" he said, laughing. And, then, "Hey, what's that cream you're rubbing in there?"

"Cream?" Sam asked, suddenly becoming aware of the tube in his hand. "Ah. It's Deep Heat. I've had a twinge in my hamstrings. It's great for warming the legs up. Want to try some?"

"I'm good, but thanks," Dave answered him. "That quick bit of exercise I just had will warm my legs up soon enough, I expect."

Monty didn't break his gaze at Dave's ample bosom, which was still wobbling, hypnotically, not yet come to rest. "Dave," said Monty, entranced, eyes unwavering. "I think I'm getting a little aroused over here, and don't forget I've got tight shorts on."

Dave briefly provided a further moment of titillation (as it were) but sensing Sam was on the verge of running, he quickly brought things back to order.

"We're sidecar racers, Sam," he explained. "I drive, and this chunky monkey is my passenger. The problem with two full-figured gentlemen such as ourselves in a sidecar, as you can imagine, is that the extra weight means loss of speed. We want to go quicker — as do our sponsors — which is why you've been hired. To help us lose weight."

"Lose weight," repeated Monty for no discernible reason.

Sam had a flicker of recollection. "Ah! You're the two fellows who crashed last TT, but saved the other outfit from—"

"That's us!" Monty interjected. "If it wasn't for us slowing the other outfit down, they'd be..." he said, trailing off and pointing skywards to the heavens.

"We weren't exactly what you'd call *svelte*, even then," admitted Dave. "But the recovery from the crash has taken its time. And without too much physical activity, of course, the pounds have just piled on."

"And curry," offered Monty.

"Yes," agreed Dave. "Curry probably hasn't helped matters."

"And beer," continued Monty. "Loads of beer. Loads and loads of beer." He patted his belly contentedly, which, in turn, produced a rather handsome belch.

Sam raised a motivational finger. "Okay, well, no problem! You're motivated, so—"

"We're really not, actually," said Dave. "Motivated, that is."

"Motivated," repeated Monty, again, for no particular reason.

Sam managed half a smile, unsure exactly what he was dealing with, unable to ascertain if this were, perhaps, some sort of wind-up and he was actually on one of those hidden-camera types of TV shows, for instance.

With no camera crew presenting themselves for the big reveal, assuring him it was all for a laugh and thanking him for being such a good sport, he continued on. "Anyway, we're just going to start off with a gentle jog. Nothing too strenuous, just get the blood flowing."

"What, right now?" Dave asked, horrified.

"Okay!" Sam said encouragingly, ignoring Dave's protest and taking the lead and heading up the length of Douglas Promenade. "Let's do this! You lads will be fine-tuned athletes ready to tackle the TT course before you know it!"

Precisely Twenty-three seconds later:

"Something's snapped!" screamed Monty, clutching his hip. "I've overdone it. Man down!" he wailed, falling abruptly to his knees. "Man down!"

He placed the palm of one hand on the concrete surface, with the other clutching at his leg. "It's gone," he insisted, rolling onto his back, knees in the air, like a dog wanting its tummy tickled.

Sam ran to Monty with genuine, professional concern etched on his chiselled face. "What's wrong?" he enquired, looking Monty over thoroughly for signs of broken bones. "Don't worry," he said. "I'm trained for this."

"My leg," replied Monty. "Somewhere in the hip region. I heard it snap! Bloody hell, it's my old war wound acting up, I just know it!"

"Goodness, you were in the war?" Sam exclaimed, full of sympathy and newfound respect for the disabled man before him.

"A large scuffle at the local pub, some years back," Dave explained.

"I still have post-dramatic stress syndrome!" Monty cried.

"Give him some of that Deep Heat," remarked Dave, who was busying himself eating a pork pie.

Sam looked at the pie, unsure from what recess Dave had retrieved it. "No, the Deep Heat is for muscle pain," he cautioned. "If he's pulled something, we need to—"

"Give it here!" screamed Monty, his face wracked with agony. "I need it *baaaad!*"

It wasn't worth the battle for Sam, so he immediately handed the tube of muscle relief down to Monty.

Monty was breathing like a woman in labour. "No, not *that,*" he said through gritted teeth. "The *pie.*" He pointed over to Dave. "That greedy bastard's eating my pork pie!"

Dave took a step back, raised the meaty treat to his lips and seductively extended his tongue, leaving a trail of saliva all over the surface. "Still want it?" he taunted.

"*Yeeesss,*" Monty pleaded, extending his free arm skyward like the final last-gasp gesture of a dying man.

Dave, unmoved where food was concerned, dispatched the pie effortlessly, in one go, like a gannet swallowing a fish.

Monty closed his good eye; he'd seen enough. "Bastard," he whimpered. "Bastard," he said again in a hoarse whisper. "Goodbye, my dear friend," he moaned in despair. It was unclear, at this last lamentation, if he was referring to Dave or the pork pie.

"You two gormless idiots are on your own," proclaimed Sam, staring with disgust, his professionalism effectively dashed to bits. "I'm sending the cash back to

Frank, or whatever his name was. *Fucksake, who'd even bring a pork pie with them on a training run? I mean, why?"*

"Two," offered Dave by way of correction, wiping a crumb from his second chin. "I ate the other while we were waiting."

Sam turned on his heels and was on the point of setting about returning to his car. Some things were more important than money. His sanity was one of those things.

Dave placed his arm across Sam's shoulder before Sam could escape.

"Sorry, Sam. Look, we need you, we really do. Well, we need to get in shape. And, as you can see, without your help, that's unlikely to happen, ever."

"You'll get no argument from me there," replied Sam, still surreptitiously looking Dave up and down in an attempt to work out where the previously hidden food had originated.

"Don't go," said Monty from the concrete floor. "My leg seems to be easing up now," he offered. "And this cream seems to be hitting the spot," he added, his hand stuffed down his unbuttoned shorts, where he was presently applying the cream quite liberally to all areas therein, various and sundry.

Sam's face contorted in abject consternation as Monty tried to return the tube to him. "That's fine. Keep it," Sam told him, without thinking twice. "But please tell me you've not rubbed that on your… you know—?" Sam asked. "Because, honestly, you're not meant to—"

"Everywhere," replied Monty with a satisfied waggle of his eyebrows. "I can feel the soothing heat, just like you said. It's quite nice."

"Dear god," Sam said, shaking his head in dismay; he knew what was coming.

"I'm just sorry I never tried this stuff sooner," Monty remarked happily.

"Monty," asked Sam. "Did you say you *felt* something snap? Or *heard* something snap?"

"Heard," replied Monty. "But this cream is really doing the trick. I can hardly feel a thing now."

"Oh, you'll be feeling something very soon, I'm afraid, I can assure you. Anyway," Sam told him. "I'm fairly certain it was your shorts you heard," he said, pointing.

Monty craned his neck. "What about them?" he asked.

"You didn't pull anything. You've ripped your shorts," Sam proclaimed.

Dave chuckled. "I told you they were too tight, Monty, me lad."

Monty's relieved expression was souring, rather abruptly, and he seemed less concerned about the torn fabric between his buttocks than...

"This, eh, cream, Sam. It's, actually, erm... it's pretty hot."

"Deep Heat," Sam stated. "Clue's in the name," he suggested, his patience levels waning.

Monty shuffled on the spot like he was desperate for the loo. "Something's not right," he said, a look of sheer panic contorting his jowly face. "I'm being serious," he went on. "Something's really not right. My testicles feel like they've been dipped in acid. Help me!" he pleaded. "It burns!"

Sam shrugged his shoulders. "There's not an awful lot I can do," he said. "That stuff," he continued, in reference to the tube. "Is meant for muscle pain. It is in no way meant to be applied anywhere near or on to your gentlemen's area."

"I know that now!" screamed Monty. "You could have imparted those pearls of wisdom on me two minutes ago!"

"Well, most people wouldn't have even *thought* to, much less..." Sam began, but then gave up, there being little point in trying to reason with one such as Monty.

"*Ow-ow-ow!*" yelped Monty, with his vocalisations accompanied by an impressive-looking piss-jig. He cupped his groin over his shorts and used the fabric in an attempt to massage the pain away underneath. "This must be what it feels like to be bitten by a snake!" screeched Monty, causing concern to those passing by. "A really *big* snake! A really big, *poisonous* sake!" And, then, "I need water," he appealed, looking at the water bottle in Dave's hand.

Sam was now glad he stayed. "Water will make it... You know what? Never mind, crack on," he said.

"Please," said Monty, reaching out for Dave's bottle.

Dave moved his arm back and flipped the lid open. "What, this?" asked Dave.

"Give me the bottle, please. The burning is spreading down my tackle."

Dave grinned. "It won't have far to travel, then," he said, before placing the bottle to his lips and draining the remaining contents, washing the remnants of the pie down. "Oh, but there's none left," he said, with the faintest glimmer of what, from a distance, might possibly have appeared something similar to an apology. "Sorry, old son."

For a man who didn't often run, the speed at which Monty travelled to the ornate Victorian fountain on the promenade was impressive. He struggled through the pain to remove his shorts, and, most unfortunately, the decorative aqua-flowing apparatus was playing a role that its designer could not possibly have envisaged.

Monty placed his considerable arse cheeks on the cold surface, lapping the cooling water onto his inflamed skin. The pain initially intensified as the water reacted with the cream, but soon the look of sweet relief on Monty's face gave a clear indication that the burning was starting to subside.

Parents nearby shielded their children's eyes from the sordid spectacle.

"Is it always like this with you two tosspots?" asked Sam.

"Like what?" asked Dave, stood in his familiar pose, arms crossed, one hand rubbing his chin.

"*This*," Sam said, with a broad gesturing wave of his hand.

"Pretty much," chuckled Dave. "Though this is a quiet day. Stick around, kid, things with me and Monty get pretty exciting."

"It gets worse than this?" asked Sam in disbelief.

"Or better, depending upon your point of view," Dave replied. "So, what about it? Are you going to get us two fat bastards in shape so we can fit in our sidecar?"

Sam's shoulders dropped as he considered Dave's request, but he was soon distracted by the sound of police sirens, sirens that were getting ever nearer to Monty — who was presently flailing in the water like a beached manatee.

"Or," mused Dave. "You could suggest to Frank that his money may be better spent on liposuction?"

Sam licked his lips and looked sideways, with eyes narrowed, and a *that's-not-a-bad-idea* expression.

Fortunately for Monty the sound of the sirens continued onwards, and, once his testicles had returned to their optimum surface temperature, the two 'athletes' that were Dave and Monty continued on their first training run. Cosmetic surgery to remove their excess fatty tissue was always an option, but, for now, a gentle meander up Douglas Promenade was not a bad way to start. Sam knew he had his work cut out for him, when, after fifty metres or so, his new charges were blowing desperate bursts of expelled air more than surfacing whales.

Still, progress was being made, and this one small, exceptionally slow and laboured step was progress to decreasing their mass and increasing their lap times at the Isle of Man TT.

Chapter Five

Early summer — 1968

Frank Cryer!" shouted Mr Prenderghast, who marched straight for Frank's desk. Once there, he smashed his hands down, causing Frank's assortment of stationery and writing implements to tumble to the floor. *"Do you think I'm an idiot?"* Prenderghast screamed, with saliva spraying over those seated nearby, and a visible vain throbbing intently on his forehead.

"No, sir, not at all," replied Frank, "I was just—"

"I know what you were doing, you useless little gobshite. You were staring out of the window and ignoring every last word I've bothered to impart on you, same as you've done all year."

Ordinarily, an outburst of this degree would evoke some form of shock, but, this being Mr Prenderghast's class, it was taken as business-as-usual.

"I know you've only got three weeks left at this school," Prenderghast continued, not yet done with Frank. "And trust me, we'll be as glad to see the back of you as you will of us." He stood over Frank with his gaze unwavering, through ugly, thick-rimmed glasses supported over the bridge of an impressive Roman nose. In point of fact, it was the *only* thing impressive about Mr Prenderghast.

"But, sir," Frank protested. "I *am* going to miss this school. And I'll *especially* miss you and these little chats we have from time to time," Frank went on. "They're very dear to me," he said, much to the amusement — and astonishment — of the class. "They're very dear to me," he repeated. "And I shall miss them when they're gone."

Frank spoke in such a gentle, sincere tone that it was difficult to think he were not being genuine. Which of course he wasn't. But it was precisely this that intensified his teacher's ill temper and lack of decorum.

"Well I won't miss *you*, you smarmy little git, you can be certain of that. In fact I won't miss any of you uninspired idiots. And trust me, from what I've seen this year, not one of you vacuous little shits will amount to anything, mark my words."

Frank waited politely for a moment before raising his hand. "Sir?" he enquired, but no acknowledgement or permission to speak was given. "Sir?" he persisted, this time with a deliberate overemphasis and drawing-out of the *er* in the word *sir*.

"*What??*" screamed Mr Prenderghast.

Frank's solemn expression didn't flicker. "Sir. Is any of that going to be in the test?"

Frank, as it happened, was not stupid. He just wasn't interested, and he was counting the days till he could walk out of school for the last time. It was challenging growing up in a less-than-salubrious section of Liverpool. Violence in the community was rife, and the school walls were, unfortunately, no safeguard. A disagreement in school, for example, could soon escalate and retribution on the streets was commonplace. Frank was fortunate in that his sharp wit and personality made him popular with all ranges within the social spectrum, and he was therefore able for the most part at managing to keep those who could do him serious damage at arm's length.

One of those who relished serious damage — inflicting it, that is — was Wayne Stanhope. Being kind, he would be best described as scum, scum bred from a long line of scum, and one who if heaven forbid was able to find a girl stupid enough to oblige, would surely breed additional scum. He was abhorrent. And he couldn't blame how he was by how he was brought up, either, because like most in the school nobody had anything apart from a shared sense of community. This sense of belonging meant little to the Stanhopes, however, who would think nothing of stealing from their own.

In no way did Frank consider Wayne Stanhope a friend, but, on balance, it was better to be stood behind him than in front of him.

As Frank made a sharp exit from Mr Prenderghast's class, it was no great surprise to see the aforementioned villainous cur in the corridor, resting on one knee, pummelling some poor unfortunate who had, perhaps, looked at Wayne on a jaunty angle.

The easiest way to get schoolchildren to congregate at a moment's notice, of course, was not the use of the school bell but rather the chant of *fight-fight-fight!* If any further evidence of Mr Prenderghast's caring nature (or lack thereof) were required, he leaned out through the doorframe at the sound of the commotion, shook his head dismissively, and retreated from whence he'd come — leaving the unfortunate wretch on the floor at the mercy of the skin-headed brute atop him.

Frank wasn't one for taking enjoyment in other people's misery, but such was the popularity of this one-sided bout that easy access toward the canteen was not possible and he had no alternative than to watch on from a distance. Frank felt a pang of guilt, taking heart that, since it was someone else on the receiving end of the Stanhope boy's violent overtures, then at least it wasn't him. This was a sentiment likely to be shared by the rest of the crowd, though, unlike Frank, this bloodthirsty horde appeared to relish the cruelty on display before them. He cringed at the sheer delight shown on their faces. These were the sort of people that would be cheering the lion on as it ripped the throat out of a Christian slave.

"So who pissed in Wayne's chips this time?" asked Frank, with a sigh, to no one in particular.

"Sidcup," said an enthusiastic voice belonging to a pasty-looking kid with half-mast trousers and a haircut forged by a mother's love.

Frank nodded with a vacant expression as he'd seen it all before, but then there was a sudden recognition and realisation. *"Fuck, what?"* shouted Frank, to be heard over the baying mob. "Stan Sidcup??"

The pasty kid shrugged his shoulders and grunted without averting his eyes from the spectacle unfolding on the cold concrete floor. Entertainment such as this, after all, was a welcome relief and broke up the day quite nicely.

"Shit," said Frank, dropping his schoolbag. Without a moment's hesitation, he lowered his head and barged into the crowd without any clear plan as to what was coming next. As one obstacle was pushed aside, the gap was simply filled by another — it was like wading through quicksand — but, with a dogged persistence, he soon had a ringside view of the melee.

Wayne crouched over Stan, throttling or punching — whatever stage of his repertoire he was currently delivering. It was a mismatch of epic proportions, with the aggressor being at least two foot taller than the other, much-smaller boy. Stan, being as slight as he was, would have struggled in a fight even with the pasty kid Frank had encountered a moment earlier.

From Frank's vantage point he could not at first get a visual on Stan, but he could hear the dull, meaty slap of flesh being pummelled. Frank looked closer and caught sight of a pair of shoes poking out from under the huge frame above. If Stan were wearing ruby red slippers, he'd have made a perfect facsimile at that moment of the Wicked Witch of the East with Dorothy's house having come down to squash him.

Frank took one step forward with his arm extended. He took a grip of Wayne's beige school shirt, a once-white shirt which looked like it'd been worn by a fair few generations of Stanhopes before him. Frank applied the appropriate degree of force, and, with a quick jerk and shove and with leverage to his advantage, caught Wayne off-balance — as Wayne was unaccustomed to *conflictus interruptus* — tipping him onto his side and splayed out on the floor.

Frank glanced up from the melee for a brief moment — perhaps looking for divine inspiration — but was met with only a sea of confused faces: *What was he playing at? Why was he ruining the afternoon's festivities?*

Frank was equally as perplexed, but for a different reason; he was unsure how this situation might pan out.

Stan, for his part, held a hand to his damaged face and tried to comfort himself. With the onlookers now quiet, unsure what to make of this new development, and the heretofore sound of knuckle-on-face now abated, all that could be heard was Stan's involuntary whimpers of pain.

"What the fuck?" demanded Wayne, now risen up again on one knee. He was not used to being humiliated in such a fashion, and, eager to redeem himself, was now keen to impart a second beating of the day.

Frank raised his hands in submission, standing with mouth agape. It had all seemed like a dream sequence up until this point, happening in a strange sort of alternate reality, moving through air made of treacle. But he was snapped back to the present, sharply, as a sudden flash of silver dashed out from Wayne's rear pocket.

"I'll fuckin' do you, Cryer!" screamed Wayne, cocking his arm back.

This dispute had deviated from the path of a simple beating — a difference of opinion, if you will — and turned rather more dire. For fear of being caught in the thick of it, and wishing to avoid injury, the crowd of spectators quickly retreated. Blood and eviscerated entrails and grievous bodily harm were all well and good in theory, of course, but this was becoming all too real.

Prenderghast appeared once more, briefly, before also taking up a position of hasty retreat.

Frank knew the best course towards immediate self-preservation was to run. But he also knew that, if he did, Wayne and his cronies would simply smash his front door through that night and exact their revenge.

Frank swung his right foot in Wayne's direction and with remarkable precision (and quite to his surprise) kicked the implement — now identified by Frank as a screwdriver — from Wayne's grasp and sending it skittering up the corridor, spinning.

Frank continued his offensive with a decisive advance. "Mr Price," he said through gritted teeth.

Wayne gripped the front of Frank's shirt and used it to pull himself up to full standing position. "You absolute wan—"

"*Mr Price,*" repeated Frank with greater urgency. "*He's walking up the corridor,*" he continued, with his eyes now partially closed.

Wayne glanced over his shoulder, and, when greeted by the appearance of the school headmaster and two security guards, he released his grip on Frank.

Thinking on his feet, Frank had an idea. "I saw him coming," he said, nodding in Mr Price's direction. "And wanted to warn you," he told the Stanhope boy.

The use of burly security guards in a school was testament to the calibre of some of the more unsavoury pupils found therein, and they soon flanked Wayne, preventing further assault.

Mr Price looked at those stood, down to Stan and then back to Wayne. "Right! What's all this, then?" he demanded, his eyes darting back and forth between them.

"Wayne was helping him up," offered Frank, pointing down to Stan, still there on the floor. "I think he must have fallen over?"

Mr Price looked down at Stan, whose face was a bloodied mess. "Sidcup, did he do this to you?" he asked, pointing at the Stanhope boy.

Frank gave Stan a furtive look, which left no illusion as to what his response should be.

"No, sir," said Stan weakly. The word 'sir' was pronounced *shhhir*, likely due to one tooth missing from the beating and another one dangling like an over-ripe pear from a tree. "As Frank *shhhed*. I fell."

Mr Price's face was pinched with anger. "You *fell*? Into *what*? A bloody revolving door??" He gave one further look of suspicion before marching off. "Present yourself to the nurse, then, Sidcup," he said over his shoulder. "And don't forget to put them teeth under your pillow for the tooth fairy. Bloody pillock."

Wayne dusted himself down and scanned his knuckles for damage. They were bloodied, with the skin torn open. He looked them over, and he nodded with satisfaction. Then he squared up to Frank and Stan, who were now standing together. He was still unsure as to what had just happened, exactly.

Wayne Stanhope was stupid. Of this, there could be no doubt. Still, he knew enough to realise that if Frank had not cast him off the Sidcup boy, he'd be in rather a spot of bother. Being suspended or expelled caused Wayne no concern, of course. However, being caught in possession with a screwdriver for nefarious purposes, on the other hand, would have been a matter handled by the police rather than the headmaster. The likely destination for Wayne, in such case, would have been a young offenders' institution, and, no matter how much swagger you had, a few months locked up in there was not something that held much appeal.

Wayne held his stare for a moment, likely as the cogs in his brain were clogged up by the aroma of glue, which he and his brothers were rumoured to partake in. Which, on reflection, really could explain a great deal about his general disposition.

Frank stared back, as if he were not the slightest bit bothered. But, on the inside, he was shitting enough bricks to build a moderate-sized row of houses. People, Frank knew, have ended up in hospital at Wayne Stanhope's hands for a lot less than he'd just done.

"Frank," stated Wayne, flatly — which was taken as a *thank you*. Then Wayne turned to Stan. "Look at me again, Sidcup," he said. "I fookin' dare ya."

Wayne's rage was now in check, but only barely. The pressure had to be relieved somehow, it seemed. A pimple on his spotty, greasy face burst of its own accord, its contents of pus spewing forth in sudden, sweet release.

"If you look at me again, you bleedin' poofta, I'll take the rest of your teeth out," he warned the Sidcup boy, but he said this almost placidly, as he was now unexpectedly rather calm.

Wayne flexed his shoulders and cracked his neck, casting an eye over those in the crowd that had remained, to ensure there were no signs of dissent. With his reputation of being the school's premier arsehole apparently intact, he picked up his partially-ripped bag, gestured to his like-minded — in that they were also mentally challenged — posse, and receded back into whatever cavity or shadowed recess bullies reside in when they're not actively engaged in bullying.

"Move on," instructed Mr Prenderghast, who'd finally appeared from the safety of his classroom now the confrontation was over. "You should get that mouth looked at, Sidcup," he added, with no genuine concern.

Frank put his arm around Stan's shoulder and steered him towards the gent's toilet to clean himself up and stem the flow of blood from his open wounds. Frank looked back to Mr Prenderghast and shook his head. "I'll be really sad to see the back of you, Prenderghast," he called out. "Really sad." The pretence of politeness in Frank's voice that he'd employed earlier in class was now entirely gone. "You think I didn't learn much from you this last year, but I have. I've learned what a really shit teacher is like. Oh, and some of the words you've taught us by your example over the course of the term have definitely stayed with me. Every time I hear the word odious, for instance, I shall think directly of you, sir."

Prenderghast gave in response something between a grin and a grimace, unsure of what to say. But, as there were still a few bystanders lingering, he mustered some incoherent threat involving detention and achieving nothing in life, before, like the Stanhope boy, retreating back from whence he came.

Growing up, Frank and Stan were inseparable, like brothers. In fact, the majority of people assumed they were related. They shared a love of football, cycling, anything in the great outdoors. Frank was the one who'd be first up the tree, charging forth, all safety instructions from their mothers forgotten in an instant, whereas Stan was rather more cautious, and more likely to be the one holding the coats.

The street they grew up in was an intimate affair. Two rows of terraced houses sat either side of the road — or the football pitch, as it were, since it was often commandeered by the neighbourhood youth who'd strategically placed a range of inanimate objects so as to prevent vehicular access from disturbing their game.

There wasn't a lot of money to go around, but the two boys' families managed nevertheless. Whilst the meals they had, for instance, may not have been gourmet, they were substantial enough ("Eat some bread with that, lad!" was a familiar mantra) and, importantly, warm. There were also annual holidays to the Isle of Man, which they simply adored. Generally, they'd be in each other's houses most days, and if they hadn't returned home by bedtime the parents knew they needn't worry since either boy would simply end up sleeping at the other's house. It was a wonderful, carefree time and nothing would ever get in the way of the bonds of their friendship...

That is, until the intimacy of the street was taken a stage too far. It wasn't just Frank and Stan who were hopping over the fence to play. Stan's dad, as it turned out, was also happy to pop over to play whenever Frank's dad went out to work. Sadly, through no fault of their own, Frank and Stan came to be separated for reasons unbeknownst to them at the time. They knew something was afoot, but what exactly that may have been was not explained to them. Two families were destroyed and uprooted and whilst Frank and Stan never fell out, that special bond they'd enjoyed for so long was cruelly snapped — presumably like the elastic in Frank's mother's knickers.

Presently, Stan leaned over the sink and spat blood into the porcelain bowl. "Thank you," he offered. "I think he'd have killed me if you hadn't stepped in."

Frank didn't immediately answer, instead, just watching over his old friend cleaning himself up. "Here,"

73

he said, providing a towel which someone had presumably left behind from a gym class. "Use this to wipe the blood."

Stan looked in the mirror and pulled his lips back, baring his teeth, to review the extent of the damage. "Shit," he said, disgusted at the sight he was presented with. He turned away from the mirror and fell back against the wall. He looked at Frank, broken. He went to speak, but the emotion caught up in his throat had other ideas. He used the towel in his hand as a shield to hide the tears that ran down his face.

Frank walked over and placed the palms of his hands on Stan's shoulders. "It'll be okay, pal. Don't let that arsehole worry you, Stan."

Stan took several deep breaths to compose himself. "You didn't ask why he was kickin' the crap out of me," Stan suggested.

"I didn't need to, mate," Frank replied. He smiled at his friend reassuringly.

"You know?" asked Stan.

"Of course I know, you silly sod. I've always known. I think I knew even before you did."

Something approaching a grin worked its way through the pain on Stan's face. "How?"

Frank stroked his chin thoughtfully, as if it were covered in a beard. If he'd been smoking a pipe, now would have been the perfect time to take it from his mouth before speaking. But, just before he could say, "Why, elementary, my dear Watson," the door opened and a younger pupil appeared. "Bugger off!" Frank growled menacingly.

Now, Frank and Stan weren't exactly physically imposing, either of them. But the sight of Stan covered in blood, with teeth missing, was enough to convince this young chap that finding another toilet was not so bad an idea at all.

"How did you know?" pressed Stan, once they were alone again.

Frank placed his finger to his lips and thought for a moment before answering.

"Right, well you know when my sister used to try and paint my nails, and I'd go mental?" he said. "The fact that you didn't go mental if she wanted to do yours, and often suggested it? I suppose that may have been a clue."

"I wouldn't call that conclusive," tendered Stan.

"No, but I just knew. I'd be trying to climb trees, for example, yeah? Whereas you'd be wondering what flowers would prosper in autumn."

Stan screwed up his aching face. "There's nothing wrong with that!" he insisted. "It's science!"

"No, I know," replied Frank, hands now up in submission. "I'm just saying that you were perhaps a bit more sensitive than most, and not your typical boy more intent on climbing things and breaking things and mischief-making and such."

"I can so make mischief!" Stan protested. "Surely there was that time... *erm*, there was that time... that one time..." Stan thought hard for a time, but came up with nothing.

Frank laughed amiably. "Yeah, so I'm not saying there was anything wrong or anything. And it's not one particular solid thing I could place my finger on, as such. It's more all things considered together, and just an overall feeling I had. I'm just explaining that's how I knew."

"*Herm,*" Stan said, taking this all in.

"And, Stan, you should know, it never bothered me then and it still doesn't bother me now. So long as you don't try and kiss me or nuthin, that's all I'm sayin."

"I can promise that," said Stan with a chuckle, despite the pain.

"What, are you saying I'm ugly, then?" Frank replied, messing about.

"I couldn't anyway, even if I wanted to," Stan explained with a laugh. "I think part of my lip is caught under Wayne's nail."

The days couldn't pass quick enough for Frank. He was fed up to the core of high school. The exams were now all complete, and, for many, a nervous wait for results was the topic of conversation. Not for Frank, though; if he passed he passed, but if he didn't, he wasn't bothered because he had a plan. He'd saved every penny he could and was going to buy his own taxi. He didn't want to just drive a taxi like his dad — it had to be *his*; he didn't want to give away most of his cash to someone else. Frank, unlike most, had a plan.

The beatings for Stan didn't ease up, unfortunately, despite Frank's efforts, and each day Stan would shuffle through the school corridors like a broken man. Frank did what he could, but there was only so much. The beatings were relentless. "You have to stand up for yourself," Frank encouraged him on numerous occasions, but Frank knew that would likely only make matters worse. It was an impossible situation. The school couldn't care less, the police were more concerned with Wayne's wider family who were responsible for the crime rate in the area, and Stan couldn't punch his way out of a wet paper sack.

Frank was in celebratory spirits leaving Prenderghast's class for the last time. There may have been some less-than-discreet hand gestures offered by Frank as the school bell approached, but his joviality was interrupted when he left the school building.

"Your mate, the gay boy," said a pupil from the year below. "He's just had a proper kicking from Wayne." There was some concern in his voice, and 'gay boy' wasn't so much an insult as it was a simple descriptor.

Frank's shoulders dropped. "Fuck. Where is he?" asked Frank of the younger child.

The boy shrugged and turned to be on his way.

"Where did he go?" shouted Frank, gripping hold of the boy's shoulders.

"He ran towards Albion Wood about twenty minutes ago. Now let go of me!" said the boy, shaking loose of Frank's grip.

Frank caught sight of Wayne running through the school grounds, presumably making some other child's life a misery. So one small mercy for Stan, at least, was that Wayne was not in pursuit of him.

Albion Wood was only a short walk away, but was a vast expanse of trees covering several acres. Frank and Stan had spent countless hours playing there when they were younger due to it being a paradise for children eager to explore. There was one tree, Frank couldn't help but recall, that Stan was receptive to climbing. It was a soaring oak tree, but the branches formed in such a way as to act almost as steps. For someone not overly adept at climbing trees, this one was an ideal compromise and served as a wonderful base of operations for the two intrepid explorers.

There were thousands of trees in the Wood, but Frank was certain that's where Stan would be: in their old, familiar base, where nobody could hurt him.

"Stan!" shouted Frank once amidst the trees, but there was no answer. It'd been years since Frank last visited there, and the overgrowth made progress more difficult than he remembered. He reached for a sturdy branch on the forest floor, fallen from one of the huge trees above. Frank swung it back and forth to clear a path, and, for a moment, imagined using the branch to clear a path straight through Wayne's skull.

"Stan!" he shouted, walking towards their customary tree. "It's me! Frank!" he said once more, but, again, nothing.

Perhaps he's not here? thought Frank, scouring the area. A few more thrashes of his arm and a grin crept across his face. He looked at the tree they'd spent so much time together in, and, there, at the base of it, he could see a pair of shoes in view, attached to the ends of two outstretched legs. Frank approached the tree reverently, and played his fingers across the coarse bark, looking for the various markings they'd carved as small boys. "Remember this one?" asked Frank, as much to himself as to Stan, and with his nose a few millimetres from the trunk. *"Frank and Stan's – Keep Out!"* Frank laughed, caressing the grooved letters, each one in turn, not really looking at them, his eyes far away, as if he were reading Braille.

"Stan. I heard that massive fuckstick Wayne Stanhope gave you another thrashing. Are you okay, pal?" he said. "How badly are you hurt?"

"Do you remember when we did this carving, Stan?" he asked again, making his way around the tree's considerable foundation. "Stan," he repeated. "Stan?"

He froze, staring down at what he saw once Stan was in full view.

"Fucking hell, Stan. Stan, what the hell have you done, mate?" he said, dropping to his knees. "No. Oh, no."

"Stan! Fucking Stan!" Frank cried, searching for any signs of life from the limp form slumped against the tree.

Frank looked desperately around him. "Help me!" he shouted. *"Fucking help!"* But it was useless — they were too far away from anyone for them to hear. Frank placed his hand against Stan's cheek. "Wake up, Stan. Please, wake up!" he pleaded.

Stan's cheek was clammy and cold. He didn't rouse, in spite of Frank now shaking him like a horrid, frustrated parent shakes a fussing baby. "Wake up!" shouted Frank again, gripping Stan by his arms now, pulling on him. Stan's head lolled back like a lifeless doll.

Frank couldn't make sense of the image he was presented with. "What's wrong with you??" he demanded. "Wake up," he said, but this time weakly as the emotion ran through him. It was then that Frank noticed his hands were covered in blood, and his grip on Stan was slipping. His eyes raced across his friend's body to determine the source of the injury, and he recoiled when he caught sight of Stan's wrists.

Frank fell back, looking about, hopelessly, for someone to assist. "Help," he asked faintly, to no one. "Help me."

Frank wiped his hands on his shirt. He could scarcely comprehend the extent of blood marking the leaf-covered floor where Stan lay. He ripped his school tie off and placed it around Stan's left wrist. In a moment of clarity, he grabbed Stan's tie and repeated the process on the other wrist, pulling the ligature tight. Frank felt the presence of a pulse, thank goodness — weak, but still there.

With no other option, Frank wrestled Stan away from the tree and with every last ounce of strength in his body forced Stan over his shoulder in a fireman's lift. His knees were bursting, struggling to right himself, swaying back and forth under the increased load. How he managed to make it back to the school grounds with the dead weight of Stan on his shoulders, he didn't know.

(Frank wasn't exactly an athlete at any stage of his life. They didn't often speak of that dark, dreadful day, but whenever a snide comment would be made about Frank being unfit or carrying a few extra pounds around the midriff, Frank was always quick to give Stan a knowing glance — one that, in the end, always brought a tender smile to Stan's face.)

The issue of the human maggot known as Wayne Stanhope was not going to go away. "Fuck it," declared Frank on the day that Stan was being released from hospital. He'd made a decision. Frank knew that by remaining, Stan's life would continue to be a misery. And so, with a week or so of school remaining and no plans for the future, Frank made the proclamation that the two of them were going on a road trip around England.

Frank used the money he'd been saving for a taxi, investing it instead in a yellow VW Camper which he'd gotten cheap on account of it having had its engine stolen. (They did live in a classy neighbourhood, after all.) After procuring an engine — with the one purchased likely being the very engine stolen from the van in the first place, such was the nature of things — Frank and Stan buggered off on their road trip.

They hadn't dwelled on it at the time, but that road trip probably saved Stan's life. Another legacy from that time in Stan's life was his penchant for cosmetic alteration. Then, it was fixing his broken teeth and the jagged skin on his wrists. But the habit stuck, and, years later, when money was less of an obstacle, it was hair plugs and Botox injections.

They never did have the honour of Wayne's company again, but when they heard, during their time of travelling, that he was spending fifteen years at Her Majesty's pleasure (Wayne and his collection of half-witted brothers had decided, as it happened, that robbing a post office would be a good idea), they certainly slept a little easier, under the stars, in their cosy little yellow campervan — which they'd named Daisy. Frank had called it that simply because daisies were yellow, but Stan was keen to point out the daisy was also a hardy aster that, as it happened, bloomed well in the autumn.

Chapter Six

Four sugars?" asked Susie, with teaspoon poised. "Is that right, Stella? I just want to be certain." She strained her eyes through the cigarette smoke, seeking confirmation.

"Only four sugars," barked Stella. "I've told you before, Susie. I'm trying to cut down on calories so I'm starting with my sugar intake. You probably haven't noticed, because I carry it so well, but I'm sporting a bit of excess poundage. More of me to love, granted. Still. I need to think about my health," she went on, flicking her fag in the general direction of the overflowing ashtray. "A girl needs to look after herself," she said, removing the wrapper from a pork pie.

"Only four sugars it is," said Susie, hovering, mug-in-hand, looking for an area of Stella's desk which wasn't coated in ash. "I like the mug, by the way," remarked Susie, nodding in approval. It was black with an embossed image of their company logo — a smiling cartoon face of Dr Frankenstein's famous creature (a pun on Frank & Stan) — and with simple wording underneath (*Stella. Shareholder.*) in reference to her newfound company ownership. "Very smart," Susie added.

Stella chomped down on her meaty treat. "Matches the shirt," she said between bites, extending her chubby thumb to the same logo on her shirt.

Susie smiled. She had a genuine affection for her work colleague (and now, it would appear, boss). She was polar opposite to Stella: demure, reserved, petite, and, well, yeah, everything opposite to Stella. But while Stella was brash, vulgar, aggressive, and very often hungry, Susie was able to chip away the abrasive exterior (granted, an exceptionally large chisel was required), and reveal the nearly-identical though still-slightly-less-abrasive layer underneath. And, so, what had been genuine fear when she first joined the company had turned to fondness. She wasn't sure if that fondness were reciprocated, but life, at least, was never dull in Stella's company.

Susie took a KitKat from their biscuit barrel shaped like a London taxi, but then placed it back in. Ordinarily, she'd offer Stella a biscuit with her coffee, but in view of Stella's current health-conscious attitude, Susie didn't want to appear to be placing temptation in her way. "It's a bit quiet, Stella," she remarked by way of conversation. "You know. Without Frank and Stan."

Stella turned five degrees to her right, in her well-worn leather chair. She had a solemn expression, and, for a moment, Susie was concerned she'd somehow caused offence.

Stella cleared her throat and wiped the remnants of the pork pie from her chin. "Are you taking the piss?" she said with a voice akin to a gravel crusher.

"What? No. Sorry, Stella, I just thought it was a bit—"

"Oi. Where's my KitKat?" Stella interrupted, pointing to her coffee. "You know I never drink coffee without a KitKat," she grumbled. "What are you playing at? I need that KitKat, to fortify me for the day ahead."

"Oh, yes, sorry, Stella. I just thought, you know, about the sugar and all..." Susie answered, trailing off.

"Are you mad?" Stella replied. "That doesn't apply to KitKats. Obviously. On account of their health benefits."

"Here you are," said Susie, handing over two biscuits — one extra to redeem herself.

Stella accepted her customary single biscuit but put the additional one firmly back in the biscuit barrel. "I told you, I'm cutting down on sugar," said Stella, shaking her head, causing her tightly-wound perm to wobble. "Bloody hell, what's wrong with you today?"

"It's quiet around here," Susie remarked again, tapping her pen against the rim of her mug absently. "Quiet without them two," she reiterated, now using the pen to point out Frank and Stan's part of the office. "Do you miss him?" asked Susie. "Arthur, I mean."

Stella lowered her head, and for a moment Susie worried she'd overstepped the mark.

"I do miss the soppy old bugger," said Stella, picking up the framed photograph next to her phone. She had a not-often-seen expression of tenderness in those beady eyes — beady eyes that nevertheless still looked like two piss-holes in the snow.

"Aww," said Susie, circling into Stella's airspace. "At least you guys made his final months memorable and gave him a sense of purpose, what with the charity work and everything."

Susie laughed, staring over at the picture of Stella and Arthur.

"You know, Arthur almost looks like he's in some sort of distress in that picture," Susie offered. "His face is all blotchy and his false teeth are about to drop out," she said with a chuckle. Susie strained her eyes. "Hang on. Stella..." she said, moving closer. "I've never noticed it before now, but it almost looks like you could be choking Arthur in that picture."

Stella nodded. "I was," she replied dispassionately. "Arthur," she said, with a brief pause to light another cigarette. "Thought it was a good idea to borrow my stapler and not return it. Discipline, Susie. If you don't nip these things in the bud, they fester. Today it's a stapler, but, if you don't do anything, before you know it they're taking your underwear off the washing line."

"What...?" replied Susie, thoroughly confused. "I don't—"

"But that's another story," said Stella. "Frank took that picture and I like it. Happy times," she said. "Happy times."

Susie tried to smile encouragingly, but, given what she'd just heard, her expression came out more like she had trapped wind. Even that, however, disappeared from her face quicker than Stella's pork pie when she spotted one of Stella's pens that'd somehow made its way over to Susie's side of the desk. Fortunately, Stella's attention was taken by a ringing phone, allowing the pen to be returned to the correct side of the desk and sparing Susie from a potential headlock or other form of unpleasantness. Aside from that, unwanted images of stolen undergarments were, mercifully, removed from Susie's mind as the main door to the office burst open and a figure appeared.

"How do, ladies?" crooned Lee in a soft Irish drawl, holding a single red rose in each hand, peering over the countertop. "How are the two best-looking taxi operators in the entire county doing today?" he went on. "And you, Susie. When are you going to make an honest man out of me, my dear?" he asked, handing over one of the red roses to her.

Susie giggled like a schoolgirl, wafting her hand like she was swatting an imaginary fly. "Oh, Lee. You're full of it. Still, I *will* take that rose," she told him, having a sniff of the floral gift.

Lee slid up the counter like a drunk moving in on another pint. He rested his chin on the counter and looked down on Stella at her desk with puppy-dog eyes. Stella was immune to his charm — or utter bollocks as she liked to call it. Lee, undeterred, made the outline of a heart with his fingers, staring over like a lovesick horse peering out of its stable.

Stella ended her call with professionalism, taking a moment to raise her middle finger dutifully and offering it in Lee's general direction.

Undeterred, Lee handed over the other rose to her. "I brought you this, dear Stella. And I feel compelled to say, its beauty is matched only by—"

"The fuck do you want?" asked Stella, her middle finger remaining resolute.

Lee feigned a look of shock, as if this sort of behaviour from Stella were something completely unexpected. "Frank and Stan in?" he enquired, peering through the porthole window.

"They're gone to the Isle of Man, Lee," said Susie, with rather more civility. "I think they're exchanging contracts on their new house."

"What?" said Lee, marching over to their office to confirm their absence for himself. "I thought they were going tomorrow," he said, dejected, placing a carrier bag on the floor.

"*I'm management*," said Stella, resting her mug on the countertop — logo clearly present — to confirm her stature. "Shareholder, yeah? Just like it says," she told him, tapping the relevant bit with her fingernail.

"Thanks, Stella, but it's to do with the charity, not the taxi business. Balls, I really need to talk to them about something. Well done on the ownership, by the way. Good on ya," Lee said, opening the office door, hoping Frank and Stan might actually be inside there yet, perhaps only in hiding.

Stella held her attention a little longer than expected in Lee's direction. Susie didn't miss a trick, and was straight onto this, raising one eyebrow in her colleague's direction — resulting in a distinct reddening of Stella's cheeks and a coarse rebuff.

Lee cleaned up well, it must be said. It was impressive what not living on the streets could do for a man. His gut had disappeared as a result of eating a healthy diet, and he looked fresher from not sleeping in a wheelie bin. Overall, a bed, a flat, and a job had really perked Lee up. (And had certainly perked up his arse as well, if Stella's staring was any indication, what with her eyes gorging themselves on it as they were.)

Having been on the streets for so long and coming out the other side had really spurred Lee on in the charity work. Largely a result of his diligence, Frank and Stan's Food Stamps had gone from strength to strength. There was plenty of money in the bank to cover it, and an ever-expanding army of volunteers, eager to deliver assistance to the homeless, spreading out across the country. Also, their sponsorship of Dave and Monty at the previous TT had worked wonders for the charity, and whilst their team hadn't finished the race, they were plastered all over the national press due to their gallantry. The publicity the charity received from sponsoring them was priceless.

"What's with that carrier bag, Lee?" Stella queried, now in a standing position and hands on her hips. "And what are you doing carrying your empty coffee mug around with you? You do realise you're not homeless anymore?"

Lee's shoulders dropped. He knew from Stella's question that Frank and Stan had bottled it. "Those two didn't say anything to you, then?" asked Lee.

Stella didn't speak, just shook her head gravely, side-to-side, ever so slowly.

"Bastards," Lee spat out, slapping the wooden doorframe. "Those couple of bloody cowards promised me that they'd told you and it was all alright."

"What *all* was alright?" enquired Stella, her eyes narrowing with suspicion.

Lee sighed. "The Chuckle Brothers—" Lee began.

"You mean the Bellend Boys?" suggested Stella.

"If you like," said Lee. "Yes. They told me that I was okay working from here and that they'd cleared it with you. Look, Stella," he pleaded with her, all his previous swagger well and truly having deserted him by now, and taking a breath before continuing. "I won't get in your way, honestly, and I promise that once a day I'll—"

"It's fine," Stella commented.

"—make the tea, and then..." Lee stopped speaking, looking to Susie with confusion, and then back to Stella. "It's fine?" he said, repeating Stella's words back to her.

"It's fine," remarked Stella once more. "Whatevs."

Lee and Susie both stood there, hesitant to react, and waiting for the other shoe to drop. But it never did, and they had no choice but to take Stella's words at face value.

With Lee's confidence restored, and his ego inflated back to optimal level, there was a melodic lilt to his voice once more. "Besides," crooned Lee. "You two couple of lovely ladies could probably do with a man about the house, so to speak, especially after the robbery last year, yeah?"

Stella laughed (or cleared tar from her throat — they sounded essentially the same). By the time her bum had touched the leather of her chair, she'd retrieved one knuckle duster, a miniature baseball bat, and what appeared to be some sort of small, portable mediaeval torture device.

Lee goggled at the items on display, unsure what to make of them.

"If you're ever going to borrow an umbrella," she said. "Don't take that one," she told him, pointing to the corner of the room. "It's a sword."

He stared back at her, confused.

"Let me put it to you like this, Lee. If anyone came in here to try and rob me again, I'd bloody well castrate them." She wasn't joking when she said this. She was dead serious. "Don't worry, I've got things well and truly under control," she said, stroking the mysterious-looking torture device affectionately.

Lee retreated into the office like a frightened hermit crab, wondering if the innocent-looking umbrella was indeed a lethal weapon.

Lee took a final glance through the porthole, though he wasn't sure why. Perhaps to make sure Stella wasn't in pursuit? But that was entirely irrational — after all, why should she be? He reasoned the arsenal on her desk must have spooked him more than he first realised.

He hadn't walked two paces away from the window when he spotted a handwritten note on Stan's desk, obviously written by Stan, as Stan had the better handwriting of the two:

> Lee. Welcome. If you're reading this note it means we're chickenshit and didn't tell Stella you were coming to share her office space. If you need us, just phone.

> Stella. If you're reading this, we'll hopefully be flying high above the Irish Sea and out of range. At least for a while. p.s. We love you, and remember who pays your wages. XXX

> Stan and Frank

> p.p.s. Oh, Lee. Just be warned about the umbrella outside our office. It's not all it seems. If it's raining and you use it, you might very well lop your own head off.

Lee made himself comfortable in Stan's chair, placing his foot on the corner of the desk for good measure. He rolled up the note with a grin. "Bloody jellyfish," he said, lobbing the paper expertly into the nearby bin. He reached into his trouser pocket, placing the piece of A4 paper he retrieved therein onto the table, flattening it out, and considering what he saw printed upon it. After a moment of deliberation, he dialled a number and placed it onto speakerphone:

Frank: *Hello, this is Frank.*

Lee: Frank, it's Lee. I'm phoning from your office.

Frank: *Ah, are you okay? Are you still in one piece?*

Lee: Yes, no thanks to you two.

Frank: *Yeah, sorry about that, but, you know, we're cowards. So... yeah. Hope you're settling in?*

Lee: All good, thanks. Look, where are you two?

Frank: *Just on the way to the airport. We're exchanging contracts on the new house later. Is everything okay?*

Lee: All good, Frank. This guy I met who's an estate agent was talking about the Isle of Man and knew I worked with you. He'd read about the TT sponsorship you did last year.

Frank: *Okay...?*

Lee: There's a property being auctioned tomorrow and it looks pretty special. Apparently it's smack bang in one of the fastest parts of the TT run. The views are to die for. Not literally, of course, but you know what I—

Frank: *You do know we're about to buy a house already?*

Lee: I know. But this house I mention isn't for you.

Frank: *Lee, are you absolutely certain Stella hasn't smacked you over the head several times? Because, if you had a head injury, you wouldn't necessarily know it. And you're not making much sense.*

Lee: I'm fine. This house is derelict. It's in a desperate state and needs to be gutted. But it's huge, see? It was used as some sort of hostel, previously.

Frank: *No, I don't see. Lee, what are you banging on about? Why would that interest us?*

Lee: It's up for auction and this guy thinks it'll go cheap, right? I know how much you love the Isle of Man so wondered if you wanted to do something, you know, from the charity angle. It's got a load of farmland attached, so—

Frank: *I don't think there are many homeless people in the Isle of Man, Lee.*

Lee: I know. I wasn't thinking for housing them. But maybe some sort of rehabilitation or something?

Frank: ...

Lee: You know what? Forget it. Sorry, Frank, it's a stupid idea. Don't worry yourself over it.

Frank: *No, no, Lee, thanks for this. I was just thinking. Can you scan the details over in an email and I'll take a look? I'm not sure what we could use it for just yet, but if it's as good as you say it is then it's certainly worth a butcher's. Besides, we'll have some time to kill while we're on the Island. Right, we're pulling up to the airport presently, Lee. So I'll be sure we stay in touch. Oh, Lee. Lee, one thing...*

Lee: Does it involve Stella?

Frank: *No. Well, yes. In a way. The umbrella by the door? Don't touch it, yeah? It nearly took my hand clean off.*

Lee eased himself back into the seat and admired the rolling Manx hillside on the estate agent's handout. It did look impressive, and Lee could see himself, quite comfortably, as landed gentry on this sprawling estate. As far as turnarounds go, eating from a skip a few months earlier to landed gentry was something out of a movie, or even a book. It was always good to dream, and that's exactly what he did, closing his eyes, imagining the country air ruffling his hair as a voluptuous farm girl kicked the barn door to one side, demanding that Lee immediately—

There was the sound of a throat clearing. Alas, it was not that of the farm girl.

"Shit!" said Lee, jumping out of the chair like he'd been electrocuted. He rubbed his eyes. "How long have you been stood there, Stella?" he asked. "You're not armed, are you?"

"Only with a cuppa," she said, placing a cup of tea on his desk before him, as well as one of her precious KitKats.

Lee's eyes darted over the items, looking to see if it was some sort of trap being laid, but they looked innocuous enough.

"Thank you," he said. "That's... very kind."

"Yeah well don't get a swelled head or nuthin' and expect this every time," Stella replied, and leaving him to it. As she exited the office, a rattled Lee was left checking his underpants for seepage, owing to the dramatic manner in which he was awakened. Stella was certainly more effective, in her way, than was his alarm clock.

"Lee," called Stella, poking her head back through the door.

"Yuuuursss," Lee responded, now expecting the punchline.

"You're taking me out for a drink," she said. "You decide when and where, but I'm free on Friday night." This wasn't an invitation but rather more a statement of fact. "Right," she said in closing, the matter settled.

Lee's eyes shifted around the office like he were looking for salvation, or, more likely, an escape route. There was none. He took a slug of tea and nodded his head. "Eh, right ho, Stella. A drink it is. Do you mean like a date?"

Stella shrugged her unnaturally broad shoulders. "Call it whatever you like, but if you're calling it a date, be warned that Stella doesn't put out on the first," Stella told him, chuckling to herself at the last statement and giving him a wink, leaving Lee to reflect, or to quite possibly phone a travel agent.

"What the fuck?" he asked rhetorically once the door was closed and when sure the coast was clear. He slapped himself several times, wondering if in fact he might still be in the land of slumber and just dreamt — or nightmared — the last conversation.

But he was indeed awake, and he had to face the truth of it.

"I'm going on a date with Stella? Jaysus, Mary, and Joseph. I'm going on a date with Stella."

Chapter Seven

Frank and Stan had a spring in their step walking into the airport terminal. They were evidently proud of the charity they'd set up, what with the huge logo on each of their matching navy polo shirts.

"We're buying a house in the Isle of Man," said Frank, beaming ear to ear, and saying it aloud to convince himself it was actually happening and not just a fantasy. "I only wish we'd gotten the boat over, like last time. I really enjoyed that."

"This is certainly a new experience," agreed Stan, pulling documents from a plastic wallet. "We'll get the boat next time, though," he promised, as if placating an excitable child (which, essentially, he was).

"Where are you flying to today, sir?" asked the check-in lady accommodatingly, the check-in lady sporting nearly as much tan as Stan himself (though hers appeared to be, in fact, genuine).

"Isle of Man!" replied Frank on Stan's behalf, appearing eagerly from the rear. "We're buying a holiday home over there!" he explained, despite no explanation being required.

"Excellent," replied Shelly (that is, as evidenced by her name badge). "And will this be your first time visiting the Island?" she asked amiably.

It was a question asked as a matter of routine, simply as a pleasantry, one would expect. For those unfortunate enough to find themselves in the queue behind Frank and Stan, however, this would result in a good ten minutes added to their wait time in that queue, with Frank jumping into action relaying their previous year's experience of Dave and Monty, the TT races, and so forth. Such was the passion in Frank's voice that Shelly — good-natured soul that she was — was drawn in. Much to the frustration of those stood behind.

One gentleman, in particular, was exceptionally effective in letting his frustration be known, coughing at regular intervals, and tapping his watch on several occasions. After one final strategic cough, Shelly relented and reluctantly ushered the two eager travellers on their way. "Have a safe trip!" she bade them. "And I'll be looking out for Dave and Minty at the TT!"

"Monty," Frank corrected her kindly, smiling and waving his boarding pass.

"About bloody time," said the coughing man. He tapped his watch once more, for good measure, so all could see that his time was valuable and important. He was well-dressed, with neatly-pressed slacks, polished shoes, and dark hair slicked back. A navy blazer hung over the handle of the travel bag at his feet.

"I've somewhere to be," the man said, throwing a look of callous disapproval.

Though Frank had a very low tolerance for pompous gits, he nevertheless disliked causing offence and preferred to settle matters in as polite a manner as he could whenever at all possible (he was, after all, British) and so turned to offer his apologies and lament on the cause of their excitement.

As he looked the man in the eye to speak, he failed to notice the fellow's bag stood at knee height.

"Sorry about that," said Frank. "As I was just telling young Shelly here—"

But Frank's tale was cut short by him stumbling on the travel bag, sending it forth with a sharp kick. The man's blazer, after a short travel through the air, came to rest unceremoniously in a crumpled heap, sending the sunglasses formerly stored in its breast pocket sliding along the floor.

The commotion caused an inquisitive Stan to step forward, but his progress was halted by the sickening crunch of breaking glass. Stan picked up his foot as shards of expensive sunglasses lenses dropped from his rubber sole and tinkled down to the floor.

"You blithering idiots!" shouted the man, causing the armed security to glance over in their direction.

Frank and Stan offered their services to rectify the situation, with Stan offering several times to make financial recompense, but the man badly wanted nothing more than to rid himself of their company and insisted they just *"Piss off!"*

The two travellers took their leave and left the grumpy stranger to his own devices.

"Charming fellow," whispered Frank, once at a safe distance. "You dodged a bullet there, Stan. Those glasses looked very dear."

Behind them, back at the ticket desk, the unhappy gentleman whose travel bag Frank had accosted was being taken care of...

"Name, sir, and destination?" Young Shelly asked, ever the consummate professional, though with her smile now painted on.

"Franks," he replied, shaking his blazer clean. He was not smiling, nor even attempting to smile. In fact he was not even looking at her, his attention solely on his blazer and deeming her not worthy of direct interaction.

"Rodney Franks," he continued, as if that in itself should mean something to her, or anyone else, for that matter, who heard the name. "And I'm travelling to the Isle of Man as well. So be sure to not sit me near those two imbeciles," he demanded from her, pointing to the receding figures of Frank and Stan.

"Here you go," said Stan, placing two pints of beer on the sticky airport bar table. "They actually stock beer from the Isle of Man," he continued, taking a grateful sip. "Lovely."

Frank didn't lift his head from his phone. "Cheers. You know, Lee might be onto something with this auction." Frank pinched the screen to expand the image displayed on the phone.

"It's a bit... rough around the edges?" Stan offered, in reference to the questionable-looking farmhouse.

Frank nodded, taking a mouthful of beer. "I know. It's in a sorry state, which is why I'm guessing it's cheap. But look at the view of the course. That's only about two hundred yards up from where we were standing last year watching the race, and remember what the countryside was like around there? It was pretty spectacular."

Frank's mind was racing with the possibilities.

"And why would we want to get involved with this, again?" asked Stan doubtfully. "Aside from giving tours of it at Halloween as a haunted house?"

Frank nodded once more. "I know. That's what I said to Lee, but look, it's got a load of farmland and outbuildings."

"I see that," replied Stan. "But, once again, what's that got to do with us?"

"I'm not sure," admitted Frank. "But I've got a feeling about this place. Look, the auction is this afternoon, and we're only going to be hanging about waiting for the lawyers to phone and give us the keys to the house anyway, right? So let's go and see it," he wheedled, like a child pleading with his parents to go to the fairground.

"It's a waste of time, if you ask me," replied Stan.

"I'll buy you another pint of Isle of Man beer," offered Frank. "Isle of Man beer!" he repeated, both for emphasis to make his point and because the thought of another pint of Isle of Man beer was getting Frank himself excited.

"You're an idiot," Stan told him. "But go on, then. And the bar's over that way," he said, pointing the way.

Pints of beer drained, and now boarded, they sat patiently on the plane that could be best described as a puddle jumper — an intimate contraption with two rows of seats on one side and a single row on the other.

"It's all right, this. I think we're only in the air for half an hour or so," said Stan. "Oh-ho," he whispered, his finger pointing out the window. "Here come's that miserable sod from earlier."

Rodney Franks marched with purpose across the airport apron, squinting from the midday sun and with one hand up to shield his eyes.

"He should get himself some sunglasses," chuckled Stan, prodding Frank in the side.

"Silly of him not to have any," Frank agreed with a smirk.

The plane was all but full, apart from a single seat one row forward from Frank and Stan — and close enough for Rodney Franks to audibly express his disapproval at his proximity to them with an incensed clearing of the throat.

Frank, sat next to the window, had his eyes closed, feigning sleep, leaving Stan to offer a half-arsed smile in an attempt to remain cordial. Rodney placed his bag in the overhead locker and removed his navy-blue blazer, spinning round as he did so, with the motion causing the hem of the jacket to catch Stan full in the face. In view of the expensive loss of eyewear their fellow traveller had suffered at their hands, Stan opted to retain a conciliatory position and take the indignity of the minor assault to his person in stride — taking one for the team, as it were.

Rodney sat bolt upright as the plane hurtled down the runway, rigid and unyielding in his indignation.

Frank, for his part, truly was asleep now, and snoring.

Legroom was a little neat and Stan — who didn't have the most fluid of knee joints — stretched his left leg out to gain relief. His foot caught a plastic bag holding several tablets. Stan could see handwriting from his seated position, and he leaned down, reading the handwriting which said simply: *Franks*. Since it was sat on the floor in the middle of the aisle, Stan could only assume it'd been jettisoned from Rodney's blazer during the moments-earlier introduction of jacket-to-face. Not wishing to engage Mr Franks in further hostile conversation — or any conversation at all, for that matter — he sat up and simply slipped the package furtively into the man's blazer pocket which sat, presenting itself, draped over the armrest of his seat.

"You're snoring," announced Stan to Frank with a gentle nudge, waking his friend from slumber.

"Was I?" Frank said, not really understanding the problem. "It must be those two pints. Grab us a coffee, would you, Stan?" he asked, in reference to the hostess approaching.

The hostess dutifully obliged, and placed two plastic cups of coffee on their seatback tables.

"Oh, miss," said Stan. "Sorry, could I trouble you for some milk?"

The trolley rolled back a pace.

"It's just there, sir," the woman explained, pointing.

Stan looked confused. This is because he was, in fact, confused.

She lowered her arm further and extended her index finger towards the plastic tube which Stan was now holding, quite by accident. "That's it, sir," she said, pleased to assist.

"What's it?" replied Stan, none the wiser.

"That's it. In your hand," she answered patiently. "There. Just there. In your hand... no, now you've taken your hand off it... yes, that's... no, now you've taken your hand off of it again... there. Yes. There you are. Lovely. And there you have it."

"Amazing," said Stan, now confident enough to be left to his own devices, to a rather underwhelmed Frank.

"Look, Frank. Frank, look. The milk is in this little plastic tube," he said in wonderment. "What'll they think of next?"

"They?" asked Frank, not entirely interested in the answer.

"Yes," replied Stan.

"They, who?"

"You know," said Stan. "They. *Them.*"

"Them?" Frank answered, enjoying this now.

"Them that think of things," Stan explained.

"Ah," said Frank, taking a sip of his coffee.

Stan's initial enthusiasm quickly evaporated. There was a problem with the milk, it seemed, judging by the colour of his coffee, which had not changed. "Hang on, it's not working. Nothing's coming out," he said, continuing to squeeze the tube. "Maybe I've got a defective one?"

Stan kneaded the receptacle like he was milking a cow's udder. Despite his vigorous effort, it produced no result. "Why is it not working?"

"Stan, that's not the way you're meant to…" Frank began, before adding, "You know what? Carry on." Since there was no in-flight film, the flight being too short and the plane being too small for that sort of thing, Frank was happy for any entertainment provided, however modest.

The milk tube's contents were, in fact, reducing, if but very slowly. And yet, somehow, Stan's coffee remained black as a moonless night. Eventually, there was nothing left to eke out.

"What the Dickens?" Stan muttered to himself. Eager to solve the mystery of the vanishing milk, he held the tube up to his eye for a proper look. Peering into the tip of the device like a scientist into a microscope, he caught a glimmer of an opening no wider than a flea's arsehole in the plastic.

"I'm sure that's not the way it's supposed to be," Stan mused. "Still, the milk must've gone somewhere, surely?"

Frank sniggered, tapping Stan on the arm. "Over there," he said, softly enough for only Stan to hear, pointing the way for Stan's eyes to follow.

Rodney Frank's immaculate navy-blue blazer now sported an erratic line of milk that resembled the trail of a drunken slug.

"Oh, bugger," Stan remarked. "How long before this bloody plane lands?"

Stan drank the rest of his coffee black and was grateful when, in due course, the flight ended and the plane landed without further complications.

"Hang back, will you, Frank?" Stan told Frank as the rest of the passengers began to disembark. "I don't want him to see that jacket and put two and two together."

They watched as Rodney put his blazer on and dusted off the shoulders of his jacket, failing to notice the staining on the back. Frank and Stan delayed their departure and skulked into the airport, maintaining a safe distance between them and their milk-covered adversary.

Ahead, a jovial customs officer appeared to be acting more of a guide, extending a cordial welcome and handing out tourist information leaflets, while competently assisted in this task by a hefty German shepherd sat obediently next to its master.

"Welcome," said the generously proportioned official, handing a brochure to one Mr Franks — which was promptly ignored.

The German shepherd lurched forward, virtually dislocating the arm that gripped onto its lead, and unleashed a bark that echoed through the arrivals hall. Rodney jumped back with a start. "Fine! I'll take one of your rubbish brochures, then!" he snapped.

Frank and Stan stopped in their tracks. "*Uh-oh,*" said Stan. "Do you reckon the dog must have smelt the milk? He's going bloody mental."

"Dunno," Frank replied, because he didn't know. He looked on, anxious to see how this scene would unfold.

The customs officer handed the dog, now back at his side, a treat. Then he placed a hand on the unhappy traveller's shoulder. "Probably nothing to worry about, sir," he said. "But the dog's indicated to your pocket. Could you kindly empty the contents into the tray on the counter? Thanks ever so much."

"This is absurd," grumbled Franks. "I've got nothing in my..."

Rodney retrieved a plastic packet from his pocket and dangled it in abject confusion.

"Don't suppose those are yours, are they, sir? What's your name?" asked the official, his amiable tone now suddenly somewhat less amiable and slightly more imposing.

"Franks. Rodney Franks. And of course they're not bloody mine. I've never seen them before!" he protested.

"That is a familiar refrain," the officer said, taking possession of the package. He was smiling again, though this time for a different reason. "*Franks,* it says here on the label," he noted. "Fancy that. Come with me, sir. If you'd be so kind?"

With their nemesis now unexpectedly dispatched, Frank and Stan made their way through the line and took their leave, with Frank throwing Rodney — waylaid on the sidelines — a look. "It takes all kinds," Frank remarked loudly, shaking his head in exaggerated dismay, whereas Stan lowered his head and kept on walking.

With no checked-in luggage to collect, the pair moved swiftly through the luggage carousel area. "We should get a taxi outside," suggested Frank.

"No need, my friend, no need," replied Stan, taking his friend by the arm. "It looks like Stella has come good for once."

"What are you on about?" asked Frank.

Stan moved in the direction of an immaculately dressed man in a sharp, grey suit.

"Ah," said Frank, spotting the little board held up for his benefit with the word *FRANKS* written on it. "Good old Stella," he said to Stan in agreement, and then, "I think you're here for us, my good man," he told the driver, completely oblivious to the missing apostrophe in the word written on the board.

The impeccable dress sense of the driver was matched only by the sumptuous leather on which Frank and Stan now found themselves luxuriously sat. "Stella's done a proper good job," marvelled Frank.

"Where to, gentlemen?" asked the driver.

"Would it be possible to take us here?" asked Frank, showing the auction description on his phone. "We just wanted to check something out. Should be ten minutes or so. If you could hang about? And then we'll need to go into town to our solicitors. We'll pay you extra for your time, of course."

The driver gave a confused yet respectful glance in the rear-view mirror. "Of course, sir. I was booked to take you there, and this is all on account. You're able to have use of the car for the duration of the stay. If you'd like a glass of champagne, sir? There is a mini fridge located underneath the armrest."

"Excellent," said Frank, patting his pockets like he was putting out a fire. He leaned toward Stan and whispered out the corner of his mouth, "Stella's pulled a masterstroke with this driver. I really must phone and thank her later." Frank continued patting himself down, taking a moment to look down to the footwell. "You wouldn't happen to have seen my tablets, have you, Stan? I think I've misplaced my medication. They were in a little plastic bag. How odd. I could've sworn…"

Stan shook his head no, in what he hoped was a convincing manner, his earlier mistake now confirmed without a doubt. "You, eh, aren't going to die or anything, you know, immediately without them, are you?" he asked.

"What? No," replied Frank, continuing to explore himself. "I'd put today's tablets in a plastic bag. I must have left them at home," he assured himself. "I've got some others in my travel bag, but that's really bizarre. I was certain I—"

"But, you're definitely not going to die without them?" enquired Stan once more.

"No," replied Frank. "Why do you keep—?"

"Excuse me, sir," said the driver. "May I trouble you with a question?"

"Of course," Stan answered, with mouth half-full of peanuts, and a glass of expensive champagne in hand at the ready.

"My instructions... you see, I was expecting only one passenger. Of course this is no problem at all. I just wondered how I might address the two gentlemen?"

"Sorry?" Frank asked.

"Who is who?" said the driver, making it plainer.

"Ah! I'm Frank!" said Frank. "And that's Stan."

The driver went quiet for a moment. "Apologies, sir. But would you prefer I called you by your surname, Franks, or by your Christian name, Rodney? Or, simply, Mister Franks?"

Frank looked blankly at Stan, who was occupying himself filling his glass flute yet again. "Oi," whispered Frank. "Stan, we're in Rodney Frank's bloody taxi."

"Busy at the moment," Stan demurred, looking at his glass sideways and then pouring in another dram of champagne to get the fill level just right, as if this were a delicate operation that required careful supervision.

Frank coughed nervously and leaned forward in his leather chair. "You can call me Rodney," suggested Frank. "Rodney would be just fine."

Frank and Stan stood in the middle of a substantial field as the car waited patiently for them. It was only a few hundred yards from where they'd had their first TT viewing experience the year before. Rolling Manx hillside flowed in every direction they turned. They filled their lungs with the fresh country air, walking casually towards the main house, which sat proudly a few feet back from the busy Douglas-to-Peel road. They peered over the shallow stone wall, and, as if on cue, a motorbike passed them by. Granted, it was going at a rather more sedate pace, but it afforded them an indication of what the view of the TT Races would be like.

They hadn't even stepped foot inside the property when Frank told Stan, "This place is unbelievable. Truly amazing. What a view and what a location."

Stan nodded in agreement. "I can't argue with you there, Frank. But, like I said earlier, I cannot see a practical application for us, personally, or for the charity?"

Frank rubbed his forehead. He did that, sometimes, when he was trying to produce thoughts. Occasionally, it actually worked.

"I think there is, Stanley," Frank said, gesticulating with enthusiasm. "I think there is, actually." Frank paced on the spot, his hands now waving around like little windmills. "Okay, remember Lee correcting us when we wrongly assumed that most of the homeless folk were male?"

"Not really, no," replied Stan.

Frank was like a wind-up toy. Stan couldn't tell if the hands, waving continuously in circles, were generating the motion of Frank's legs as he paced back and forth, back and forth, or if it was the other way around. Stan thought it best, whatever was happening, to let it run its course.

"Oh, wait, now I do. Alright, go on."

"The charity is doing well, yeah?" Frank continued. "Follow me, now..."

"I'm trying," Stan replied. He was getting dizzy.

"We've got money in the bank to fund the food vouchers. And more comes in as the word gets around, right? Henk, from last year, said that he'd employ some of the homeless who wanted to learn new skills, remember?"

"Okay?" Stan replied, unsure what direction this was all heading.

"We need to think about the next stage in their evolution. We give the homeless food stamps, yes, But then what? Here..." said Frank, introducing the house with a theatrical arm gesture, like a gameshow host, "... is a huge house which can be used as a hostel. And out here..." he continued with another grand wave, "... is the remnants of a working farm."

Stan's eyebrows perked up. "So," he confirmed, following Frank's logic. "A hostel for people to stay, and a farm for people to learn new skills?"

"Exactly!" said Frank, pacing that quickly he was taking up a layer of grass. "We can use this as a creative community — crafting, farming, classes for the local children."

"Ohh," Stan opined, a thought forming in his own noodle. "And with this prime location, in TT week, we could sell tickets to watch the TT — all proceeds going to the charity."

"Yes," said Frank. "Excellent. Yes, yes." In addition to the locomotion of his legs and the waving of his hands, Frank's head was now bobbing up and down like a car dashboard nodding dog.

"What about the females?" asked Stan.

"What about them? I didn't think you were keen on them, Stan?"

"No, you idiot. You mentioned about the homeless being not just male, and with a large number of them female. What were you on about!"

"Ah, yes!" said Frank, finger in the air, either testing the wind, or about to make some point, or perhaps both. "Yes, that."

"Yes?" said Stan expectantly.

"Yes!" Frank said again, trying to catch up with his thoughts. "Right. Well. Yes. Lee told me that a fair few of the homeless women he met were homeless as a result of domestic violence, and lived in fear of being found by abusive partners."

"I remember now," Stan verified.

"Well, how about this place?" said Frank, giving the house an encore. "That could be a good option for them? Away from the main island?"

"I suppose so," shrugged Stan. "We'd need to look into the practicalities, but I like what you're saying. There's the opportunity to raise money for the charity, help the homeless, and give something back to the local community. This place won't be going cheap, though. I mean, look at this land."

"Yes, but the house needs a boatload of cash spent on it," Frank pointed out. "So there's that."

Just then, a spritely fellow in a tweed jacket waved his arm from an open window like he was painting a ceiling. "We're starting up in five minutes!" he called out, extending his five digits to emphasise the point.

"Very good!" Frank answered, waving in return. And then, to Stan: "Come on buddy, let's see how much this place is going for."

The same man in the tweed jacket appeared to also be the auctioneer for the day, judging by his position of prominence at the head of the room. Frank and Stan hadn't really looked around inside, their eyes having been drawn to the multiple natural shades of green on beautiful display outside. "This place is alright," said Frank, once his eyes had adjusted to the indoors. "It's a bit dated, alright, but aside from that..."

Stan surveyed the room, politely, but suspiciously, trying to read the faces on those assembled. "There aren't actually that many here. Less than ten, including us," he whispered to Frank. "Do you think it's quiet because every other bugger knows something that we don't know?"

Before Frank could answer, the auctioneer began.

"Now, you'll have all registered, and have all had the legal pack in advance, so to the business of selling this magnificent property by auction — which is my distinct pleasure. If you've not previously participated in an auction, fear not. I'll make this as straightforward as I can, and I will not be speeding through it like I'm auctioning cattle. So! To business."

"I guess this is it," Frank said, exchanging glances with Stan.

"I'm starting at two hundred. Do I have two-hundred-thousand pounds?" asked the auctioneer. "Two hundred I have," he said, answering his own question, pointing, presumably at the initial bidder.

Stan followed the direction of the auctioneer's hand, sceptical that he'd find a genuine person there.

"Do I have two-fifty? I do. Thank you, madam," the auctioneer went on.

Bidding continued, up beyond three hundred thousand pounds and into the four hundred thousand range. "This is out of our depth now," said Stan. "Let's get out of here."

For Frank, however, time seemed to be moving at a different speed. Or, it could merely have been Stan's perception of it, as an observer, as he witnessed the events unfold before him. Either way, Frank's eyes appeared wide, like he'd been smoking something he shouldn't have been smoking. And, then, in a motion best described as languid yet inexorable, Frank's hand raised from its resting position.

Stan watched, paralysed, powerless to prevent Frank's limb heading skyward.

"Four-fifty. New bidder. Thank you, sir," said the auctioneer.

Stan looked behind them, praying they were in a parallel universe and that there was another Frank and Stan seated there, with *that* Frank raising his hand instead of *his* Frank.

"*What in the hell are you doing?*" Stan hissed through gritted teeth.

"I've got a feeling about this place, Stan," Frank replied without even looking at him, so mesmerised was he. "Go with it," he said dreamily. "I promise, it'll all work out."

"And I've got a feeling as well," was Stan's answer. "Only you're lucky I've forsaken violence."

Aside from their brief exchange, the room fell quiet after Frank's bid, with the auctioneer desperately surveying the room in an attempt to resurrect the bidding activity. After several arduous seconds, it was evident from the hushed silence that Frank was the highest, and likely final, bidder.

Frank gave Stan's shoulder a giddy squeeze as the gavel smashed down.

"Thank you for the highest bid, sir..." announced the auctioneer.

A little squeal of delight escaped Frank's throat. He couldn't help himself.

"... but I regret to advise, per the legal pack, that there is a reserve price that unfortunately has not been met this day. I'd like to thank you for your interest today."

Stan breathed a sigh of relief.

"Ladies. Gentlemen," the auctioneer said, addressing the small crowd as a whole, and, with that, he buggered off, quick smart.

"Did we win? I don't understand," said Frank, blinking, confused.

Frank had done what every novice has done at an auction, and got suckered into the atmosphere, bidding at will. For better or worse, the outcome was not as he expected it.

Stan shook his head, wiping a bead of sweat from his forehead. "No, mate. No, you didn't, but as far as impulse purchases go, that one would have taken some beating. Now put your registration card down, slowly. We need to go and buy the property we *actually came here to buy*, for fucksake."

Frank blinked again, and waited. The auctioneer, however, did not reappear.

"Frank. *Frank!*" said Stan, clicking his fingers in an attempt to snap his friend back into the present. Frank rose, but he was still in a daze. "Come on, we'll get you a beer when we're all finished," Stan said, coaxing him along and ushering Frank through the hallway.

Their progress was halted by the sound of an all-too-familiar voice in the dining room, near to the entrance.

Stan stopped in his tracks and peered through the door, which sat slightly ajar.

"We could be in a spot of bother here," whispered Stan.

Frank — now back in the present — moved closer to gain a better view. "Is that not the bloke from the airport?" he whispered back, although, due to the volume of the angry voice emanating from inside the room, discretion on Frank's part may not have actually been a requirement.

"What's he doing here? What the hell does he want?" asked Frank.

Stan looked ashen. "Eh, to be honest, Frank, it could be any number of reasons given the events of the day."

"Yes, but..." Frank began, but, then: "Oh, bugger! Shit, Stan, he's coming. Do something so he doesn't see us!"

"Something like what?"

"Just something!"

Stan — who didn't cope well under pressure — took a step forward, wrapped his arms around Frank, and set to work kissing him passionately about the mouth. He kept this up for a few long moments — long enough for one Mister Rodney Franks to walk past them and into the room they'd just vacated.

"What the hell was that??" asked Frank, gasping for air once set free. "You kissed me!"

"You told me to do something!" protested Stan.

"But you promised you'd never do that!" protested Frank, in turn.

"When did I promise that?"

"You promised!" Frank sputtered.

"Look, you said to do something, and that's what I did, Frank. I stepped up, and it worked, now didn't it?"

Frank couldn't argue with results. "Come on, let's get out of here, before they chuck us out," he suggested.

Stan arched his neck. "Hang on, Frank," he said, clearly eavesdropping.

Rodney Franks was currently berating a demure young lady, by the sound of it, who was trying her best to articulate that the sale had ended, and the auctioneer had left.

"Yes, yes, I understand that," said Rodney. "What *you* fail to understand is that I've come specifically all this way to the Isle of Man with the sole purpose of buying this bloody property, and you're telling me that it's too late?"

"You should have been here on time?" replied the young lady, some strength in her voice.

"Yes! Give it to him!" Frank said, secretly cheering her on. Stan shushed him so they could continue their earwigging.

"But I *was* here in plenty of time, I can assure you," Franks went on. "But thanks to some *idiot* at your airport, I've been stuck in a room having an argument with two men armed with *rubber gloves*."

"I'm sorry, sir," answered the young lady, though from the sound of her voice she likely wasn't all that sorry, actually. "You'll have to phone the office to see what the next step for the property is. It really is out of my hands, I'm afraid."

Stan couldn't help but chuckle to himself, and he grabbed Frank and ran for the door.

"We can't take the poor bloke's taxi. Not again," said Frank.

"Can and will," said Stan. "Poor bastard doesn't know we've taken it, now does he? And as far as the driver is concerned, you're Franks."

"Now I think on it, that little slate the driver held up?" Frank said. "It said *FRANKS*, didn't it?"

"Apostrophe abuse is so rampant these days," Stan giggled. "People are always either forgetting to add it in where it belongs, or leaving it out entirely."

"True, true," agreed Frank with a grin. "And besides," he said. "The real Franks is a complete knob."

"And not in a good way," Stan added. "Come on, let's go and get the keys to our little holiday home on the Isle of Man."

"I'm right with you!" Frank said, obligingly.

As Frank and Stan eased away in luxury, Rodney Franks stood at the doorway of the property he'd missed out on buying, presumably phoning for a taxi.

Stan chuckled once more. "Rubber gloves, *ha-ha*. Couldn't have happened to a more deserving fella."

"You'll get no argument from me," said Frank.

Stan shuffled closer across the back seat of the car. He had something private to share.

"Frank, can I just tell you? That kiss was special. You'll make some lady very happy one day, you surely will."

"You promised!" was all Frank could manage to say.

Chapter Eight

Jurby Airfield in the north of the Island had a proud heritage as a Royal Airforce training base during World War II. The old runways and taxiways now regularly played host to a very different sort of powered vehicles: motorbikes and sidecars.

It'd been a few months since Frank and Stan had been able to scratch their racing itch at the previous year's TT races. For two people who'd never paid much attention to motorsport, they were now well and truly hooked. In fact, DVDs of the TT action from previous years had been their entertainment of choice over the preceding winter months; indeed, they'd both inadvertently bought each other the most recent copy as a Christmas present.

Frank often reflected on his first trip to the TT races to pretty much anyone who'd listen. He spoke with passion, vigour, and admiration, all the while reflecting on the eclectic characters that they'd both met on their pilgrimage the previous year. Yes, the weather had been kind, but regardless, they'd fallen in love with this special little rock in the middle of the Irish Sea.

Frank's bucket list was, however, the subject of some derision. Not with malice. Rather, as gentle teasing owing to the fact that there was only one item on that list — well, two, technically, as they were back once again: the Isle of Man TT Races! Considering the sheer spectacle of the greatest sporting event on earth, there simply was no relevance in adding another item to that list. To do so would have been a bitter anti-climax for Frank, and of course for his able travelling assistant, 'Passepartout' Sidcup, as well. Both of them would have simply compared any future experience with the one they'd had the previous year, and they knew that was impossible.

Everything about their previous trip had been an assault on their senses. From the palpable anticipation they'd experienced by those waiting to board the ferry to the sense of loyalty, friendship, and community that they'd never experienced before. And all that before they'd even set their peepers, wide-eyed, on the first bike erupting down Bray Hill at 180 miles per hour.

It was each to their own, but the thought of watching tennis on Centre Court, sitting in front of the Taj Mahal, or even looking on in wonderment at the scale of the Great Wall of China was not compelling in the slightest. Why? Because it wasn't the TT races. It was impossible to articulate or convey that the TT wasn't just about the racing. It was, truly, a way of life. From the second they'd returned home it was all they could talk about, counting down the days until they could return once more.

The thought of travelling across the world to watch a sporting event would once have sounded like lunacy but now they could understand, for they would surely do exactly the same if not for their already-close proximity. And the sense of brotherhood wasn't confined only to the Island for those two weeks each year, either. Frank and Stan were like twin boys wearing their Isle of Man TT shirts at home at every opportunity. If you wore the shirt of your local football team, chances are you'd be approached by someone who wanted to either kiss you or knock the living daylights out of you, depending on where their loyalties lay. The TT engendered a different sort of reaction, however, one that was entirely positive. Strangers would see Frank and Stan's TT attire and would approach them, eager to talk about their own previous TT experience. Or, they'd have a thirst for knowledge since they'd planned their first trip and were desperate to get some foresight into whether what they'd heard could be true — that there was simply nothing better on earth and the only way to experience it was for yourself.

Once experienced, you'd see those stood on the deck of the ferry, waving as the landscape of the Isle of Man slowly disappeared from view, for at least another year, and these grown men would be in tears. It was then that they had a chance to reflect on what they'd just lived through. Frank knew that the thought of anywhere else for item number two on his bucket list was sheer lunacy; it would've been the ultimate anti-climax. There was nowhere else he was going. He was back in the place he loved.

Presently, Frank and Stan had replaced the luxurious mode of travel from the day before for a slightly-more-humble rented Fiat 500. It was sad to say goodbye to the chauffeur-driven limousine, but they were able to console themselves with the thought of the invoice dropping through Rodney Frank's letterbox.

"How the devil can we be lost?" asked Stan, with his head out of the window like an excitable dog lapping up the breeze. "It must be somewhere around here."

As for Frank, he was unflappable at present. After all, as far as drives in the country go, this was pretty special.

Their last visit was during the mayhem of the TT festival, so to see this sedate Island in rather a more relaxed manner was, well, appreciated. And that's exactly what Frank was doing: appreciating. He drank in every glorious second as they negotiated narrow country roads, taking the time to exchange pleasantries with those whose paths they crossed.

Frank did take a moment from his cultural dalliance to remind Stan of the fact that it was Stan himself who had garnered the directions to take them to Jurby.

"Ah," replied Stan, bringing his head back inside for a moment. "The Sulby Glen Hotel," he said, in a moment of recollection.

Frank slowed, awaiting further instruction. "Yes?" he prodded, when instruction was not forthcoming.

"Turn left right here," directed Stan. "Yes, left, the fellow said. I'm sure of it."

"You could have told me that before I'd already gone straight past—?" Frank started to say. But then he smiled, again relaxing. There was no rush. It was a perfectly agreeable drive, after all. "Never mind," he said. "We'll get there in the end."

"I think I can hear engines," enthused Stan, with his ears moving in all direction in an attempt to triangulate the noise. "Yes, young Frank, it must be this way. Lead on and don't spare the horses!"

"As many horses as this little Fiat can muster, mister!" was Frank's giddy reply.

Dave and Monty's machine stood out like a blind cobbler's thumb. Their sidecar outfit — which had been totally destroyed in the accident — had been rebuilt with exactly the same livery: blue & yellow like a big boiled sweet, with the number *forty-two* emblazoned proudly at the front. It was impressive. The logos of their chief sponsor — Frank and Stan's Food Stamps — were festooned all over the bodywork, including the considerable 'bodywork' of those riding onboard.

"What are you waving at?" asked Frank of Stan. "They must be doing a hundred and thirty. There's no way they can... Oh, wait. They did," Frank corrected himself. "How on earth can they even see us at that speed?" he said, gobsmacked.

Frank and Stan stood in awe, watching as their sporting heroes navigated their outfit around that circuit like masters. They were like high school cheerleaders fawning over the football jock in the big game. The smell of petrol and oil carried in the wind, as did the screaming of engines. They were both excited about signing the contract on the house, but this, what they were watching right then, was what really buttered their toast. It was magnificent. It was a real community feeling to the qualifying-stamps club event, with dozens of families with children cheering on their favourite rider, or, for the younger audience, perhaps, the most colourful outfit. The local Scout troop was also in attendance, doing a sterling job with crowd direction near to the car park.

With the action drawing to a close, Frank and Stan trudged over to the familiar-looking van to wait for Dave and Monty. They'd been in regular contact during the pair's recovery, but, as they'd not been to the Island since the previous June, it was like rekindling an old friendship.

"Let's sit in Dave's van, yeah?" suggested a weary Frank. "My legs are bloody killing me being stood up for so long."

Stan opened the door and they both jumped in. "So worth it, though, eh, Frank? That noise. That smell. It's unbelievable. It makes me feel like a man!"

"But you're already a man?" Frank answered with a cheeky grin.

"It makes me feel like a man would feel if he weren't already a man!" Stan exclaimed. "You know," he said, changing subject, "I wouldn't mind a cup of tea just now, or something. I've not had anything since breakfast."

"Here, what's this?" said Frank, taking up a lunchbox that looked more like a suitcase. "We're bloody paying for those two chubby bastards to lose weight and they're eating like pigs," he remarked, examining the contents of the portable tuckshop now on his knee.

"It's a tragedy," Stan chimed in.

"They've even let their van go, by the looks of it. I remember it being in better shape than this," Frank remarked.

"So true," Stan concurred. "Such a shame," he said, wiggling his fingers in anticipation. "Now give me that sandwich, I'm famished!"

"Dig in, Stanley," Frank replied obligingly, handing over a sandwich and two biscuits. "We'll help them get fighting fit!" he insisted, availing himself as well. "I'd say it's our duty!"

"They'll thank us for it later," Stan agreed.

It took an age for Dave and Monty to appear. Well, several sandwiches, countless biscuits, three cans of Coke, and one bottle of Irn-Bru's worth of time, to be precise. Stan was just tucking into a jam doughnut as Dave sauntered towards them.

It was strangely compelling to watch Dave and Monty — in unison — unfasten their leather suits, seductively easing the zip, revealing the sweating torsos beneath. Frank and Stan instinctively began humming the theme tune to *Baywatch*, both visually assaulted by the jiggling of male breasts on full view.

"I'm not overly convinced that fitness trainer we hired is having the desired effect," suggested Frank.

Stan nodded, wiping sugar from his chin. "I would say not, judging by their man boobs. All this rubbish cannot be helping, surely," he added with a glance into the tuck shop.

They sat in the van, fully ready to admonish, but also looking forward to seeing their friends. However, Dave and Monty reached the van and simply carried on. Stan wound down the window. "Oi!" he shouted. "Are you two ignoring us?"

Monty's face lit up when he turned around. He wiped the sweat from his forehead before offering the same hand through the window to a now rather reluctant Stan.

"Here they are," said Dave, also grinning. "The Isle of Man homeowners. Great to see you both," he said. "We've really been looking forward to you two coming over. We've missed you sincerely, no bollocks."

Dave took his head back out of the window and looked up the length of the van. "So this is your van? I mean, what's with the dodgy wheels?" he asked. "I thought two classy guys like you would be driving a better vehicle than this rolling dung heap."

Frank released an awkward laugh. "Our van? Dave, I thought...?" But Frank's voice fell away as, over Dave's shoulder, he spied a trail of bright-eyed Scouts walking across the car park, their work apparently over for the day. Like ducklings, they followed their pack leader, and that leader was guiding them directly towards the van in which Frank and Stan were sat.

"Oh, bugger," said Frank.

"This doughnut is quite good," said Stan, unaware of what was very shortly to come.

The pack leader, a considerable unit with excessive facial hair, opened the driver's side door of the van and peered in. "Right! You lot! What are you doing in my van?" he demanded. But then seeing what was in Frank and Stan's hands, along with the remnants around their mouths, his initial fury only intensified. "*Are you two bell-ends eating the children's lunch??*"

There was some giggling amongst the Scouts. "Mr Harding said *bellend*," one of them said, which set off another round of giggling.

Frank went to speak but the half-eaten sandwich in his mouth prevented communication, which, for him, was fortunate considering he had bugger-all redeeming to say for himself.

A small tow-headed boy with sky-blue eyes pushed his way to the front. His flawless, angelic face was contorted into a mask of grief and despair. Staring up like a waif from a Charles Dickens novel, he looked as if he might burst into tears at any moment. "Mr Harding," his tiny voice begged, and it was a voice that perfectly straddled the line between adorable and cloying.

"Yes, Timothy," answered Mr Harding.

"Mr Harding..." repeated Timothy, this time choking out the words between sobs.

"Remember what I've told you, lad," Mr Harding encouraged him, trying his best under the circumstances to be patient. "Stiff upper lip, boy. Stiff upper lip, eh?"

Timothy pointed into the cab of the van. "B–b–but Mr Harding. That orange man," the young urchin cried, pointing in Stan's direction. "He's eating my g–g–gluten-free d–d–doughnut."

"Right. I've seen enough. You two. OUT," Mr Harding ordered. "Before I *drag* you out. And don't think for a minute the children being present will stop me from giving you two moochers a damned good thrashing!"

"Look, no," replied Frank desperately, and holding up his open palms in an *I-give-up* gesture. "Look, apologies, we thought it was *their* van, honestly," he protested, referring to Dave and Monty. "Tell them, Dave. Dave?" Frank pleaded, but there was no answer. "Monty...? Anyone...?"

In fact, Dave and Monty, apparently feeling discretion the better part of valour, had already legged it, fleeing the scene.

"How about pizza? For everyone?" shouted Frank with a clap of the hands — attempting to diffuse the situation and avoid the aforementioned thrashing — prompting an immediate, enthusiastic response.

The collective cheers prompted Mr Harding to accept on behalf of the children, but there remained one bit of unfinished business. "GET. OUT. OF. MY. VAN."

"Very good," said Stan, who didn't need asking twice, and both he and Frank vacated the vehicle fairly lively.

Standing in slumped submission before Mr Harding, Frank reached for his wallet, pulling out a pile of notes. His finger bobbed around the collective congregated heads and he groaned when he counted thirteen of them. Still, it was better than a beating, or, even worse, a criminal record for breaking and entering, along with the stigma of stealing children's lunches.

Frank looked at Stan for financial assistance, but was met with the shrug of shoulders. "I've not had a chance to get any cash out," Stan insisted.

"Great," said Frank, turning back to the Scout leader. "Thirteen boys," he said, taking a pile of notes. "This should cover pizza for them all?"

"Very hungry boys," came the reply, accompanied by impatient toe-tapping.

Frank handed over a few more notes.

"And me?" replied Mr Harding, arms folded. "You think I don't have a mouth on me?"

"Right, sorry," said Frank through gritted teeth. "Pizza for fourteen it is," he added, handing over still another few notes, draining the contents of his wallet. "It's been an expensive snack we had," said Frank. "*Very* expensive," he emphasised for Stan's benefit.

Frank and Stan retreated, leaving behind them a group of very happy Scouts. Except, of course, for Timothy, who had a gluten intolerance.

Speaking of which...

"You've still got that bloody doughnut?" asked Frank, gripping Stan's arm.

"Yes," said Stan, taking a final bite. "It was actually pretty good. You'd never have guessed it was gluten-free. And, besides, I didn't want to waste it," he continued. "After all, it was expensive!"

And a few minutes later...

"Ah, you two!" said Frank, giving a warm embrace to Dave and Monty once reunited with the pair. "We've missed you two. Thanks for your help in that whole mistaken-van situation, by the way. Nice to know you gents had our backs back there."

"Come on, Frank. They were Boy Scouts, we weren't exactly going to wade in there," said Dave with a laugh. "Anyway, you looked like you had it all in hand. And, look!" he continued, pointing at the van approaching.

Chants of *"Pizza! Pizza! Pizza!"* emanated from the van as it passed by, presumably on its way to procure said pizza.

"You've made a load of little friends happy," Dave declared, in reference to the waving hands coming out of the vehicle — all apart from young Timothy, who extended his middle finger.

"So you're homeowners on the Isle of Man?" asked Monty of Frank. Frank didn't respond, believing the question was directed to Stan due to the lazy aspect of Monty's eye.

Once you were used to it, the eye, it was fine, but after an absence of several months, it was a challenge to recalibrate your own vision to account for it again. Frank eventually reacted with a glorious grin. "Oh! Yes, indeed! We are! All signed, sealed, and delivered. We've got a house up by the grandstand with a spectacular view of the course. We've also got that crazy Dutchman, Henk, as a neighbour, so that'll be a bit of fun."

"Tell them about the farm," said Stan. "And how we were nearly landed gentry!"

"Yeah, that was an experience," said Frank. "Shame, though. It was in a fantastic spot, Stan, wasn't it?"

Frank paused for a moment, recalling the view from the back windows over the broad expanse of land. "It was spectacular. I'm a bit gutted, to be honest. It was on that leap where you come out of Cosby—"

"Cosby is an actor-slash-comedian you probably wouldn't want giving your sister a lift home. Do you mean *Crosby?*" asked Dave.

"Oh, yeah. That's the one. What a tremendous spot. It had a farm attached and we had loads of plans," said Frank, fondly reminiscing.

"*Frank* had loads of plans," Stan interjected.

"Hang on," said Dave, scratching his nose. "The house on Crosby Leap? The big bugger on the left?"

Monty was also scratching his nose, though from the inside. He got hold of a large nugget, extricating it from his left nostril. "Big booger on the left? What...?" he asked, absently, before realising they were talking about something else — at which point he carried on with his successful mining operation.

"Yeah, that's the one," confirmed Frank. "I looked at a video on the internet and, by god, the bikes are virtually taking off when they go past. It would have been amazing."

Dave looked confused, closing one eye to emphasise the point. "How did you nearly buy that?"

"Auction, yesterday!" said Stan.

Dave was rubbing his cheek now with the palm of his hand. He was in danger of setting fire to it, he was rubbing his unshaven stubble so hard. "There was talk they were going to turn that place into a TT-themed hotel a few months ago, due to that very location," he said. He went on: "I thought it'd all fallen through, but obviously not...? There were quite a number of people interested in it."

Frank shook his head. "Not judging by the amount of people at the auction. There must have been, what, Stan, a dozen at most?"

"Ten people, including us, I counted," Stan answered. "Well, eleven, if you add Rodney Franks," he said with a chuckle.

"Oh, yeah," said Frank, joining in. "I wonder if he managed to get a taxi, by the way?"

"Hang on. Rodney Franks?" asked Dave.

"Yeah, this tosser we met at the airport. Generous chap, mind you," said Stan. "He paid for a chauffeur-driven limousine for us, though he doesn't know it yet!"

"Rodney Franks was one of the people trying to buy that farmhouse," said Dave, giving Monty a quick glance.

Monty held up the tip of his finger, loaded with nose candy, nodded to Dave, smiled, then plunged the finger into his mouth.

"Monty sez yeah," Dave confirmed.

"I know," replied Frank. "That's what we're saying, he was at the auction. Though he didn't make it in time to bid due to... complications."

Dave's eye remained quizzically half-closed. "No, I don't mean yesterday. He was one of the ones trying to buy it the last time, but it fell through. There was interest from all over the world, so I'm surprised to see it at auction with hardly anybody there."

"That's right," said Monty, thrusting his finger — now shiny and clean — into the air for emphasis. "Two brothers inherited the place when their old man died. One of them wanted to cash in and turn the place into the Isle of Man Las Vegas, but the other wanted to sell it as a farm, didn't want the countryside turned into a theme park."

"I don't know why, Stan," said Frank. "But knowing Rodney Franks is so keen to buy that place just makes me want it even more."

"You'll struggle there, boys," Dave offered, rubbing his thumb and forefinger together in a rapid motion for illustrative purposes. "I know you two aren't exactly skint, but Rodney Franks is loaded. Proper minted. He throws his cash into the top racers like his money is going out of fashion."

"What's this?" asked Stan. "He throws his money into the TT?"

"No, not the TT as such," replied Dave. "I thought you two read the motorcycling press?"

Dave's question was met with only vacant stares.

Dave continued: "Rodney Franks is a multi-millionaire and throws a load of cash into the top motorcycle riders and the sidecar world champions. You do remember how I said the sidecar races would be very interesting because the world champions were going to be racing? You do remember that, Frank, because we spent about thirty minutes talking about how it may bring extra coverage for the charity?"

"Oh, yes," said Frank, who if he was Pinocchio would currently have a nose the size of a baby's arm. "I thought the ones you were racing last year, the McMullan brothers, were world champions?"

Dave shook his head. "They were, but Rodney Frank's team took it off them. His boys, Jack Napier and Andy Thomas, are unbelievable. I've only met them a couple of times, but they are absolute tools. I thought Harry McMullan was a twat, but these boys are on a different level altogether. Rodney Franks isn't much better, though.

I mean, to give you an idea, even Dutch Henk cannot stand him, and Dutch Henk loves everyone and everything. But you can't knock Napier and Thomas' ability as racers. Which is why the sidecar race this year is going to be special."

Dave waited for a reaction, but once again he was met with slack jaws and vacant eyes. So he reiterated, slowly, in terms they could understand:

"The current world champions are coming to the TT for the first time. They will be racing the former world champions, so the sidecar races are very eagerly anticipated by the world's sporting press. You guys sponsor us, and we're in those races, so there will be a lot of publicity for the charity. Understood?"

"Oooh," said Stan, like an apprentice ghost. "That'll be good."

Dave wasn't often serious, but he took a step forward, placing a hand on both Frank and Stan's shoulders. "Guys. I've said it over the phone, but I need to say it once more. When we totalled the sidecar at last year's TT, I thought that was it. Not just the injuries to us, but the money to get a new bike. We could have never afforded to replace it, so thank you. I mean that. We now have an outfit we can challenge the top boys in."

Frank smiled. "Dave. Monty. The money we've paid is nothing. Well, okay, it was a lot. But what you've brought into our lives is immeasurable. Before I met you, the Isle of Man, and the TT last year, I was focused on dying. Thanks to you I'm now focussed on living."

"Jaysus, this is all too maudlin to bear," Monty interjected, rolling his eyes. "Throw me the bloody sick bucket here!"

"So the bike is quick?" asked Stan.

"As lightning," nodded Monty. "That engine is capable of a one-hundred-and-ten average lap. We could get a top-ten finish on that thing. It's *rapid*."

"We just need to make sure we're fighting fit," added Dave.

"Yeah, how's that going?" asked Frank, unable to remove his eyes — with a sort of morbid fascination — from Dave's heaving bosom, which was framed perfectly by the unfastened leathers.

Dave sighed. "I'm not going to lie, Frank. So I won't," he said, drawing that line of questioning to a close. "But I promise you this, Frank and Stan, we'll not let you down. We're serious about that fitness trainer chap and we'll be lean athletes come race day. As Monty said, that bike can do one hundred and ten miles per hour and I'm guessing that our extra weight could cost us three or four of those. We'll lose some weight even if it means amputation."

Frank inadvertently looked over at Monty's leg, presumably factoring in lap time if it were surgically removed. "That reminds me. Are you still on for a BBQ tonight at Casa Frank and...?" He looked over at Stan. "What are we going to call the house, Stan?"

"We need to call it Frankenstein's Castle," suggested Stan. "We can get a big bust of Frankenstein's creature carved out of wood and place it by the door. Use it to scare the children."

"I think your fake tan will do that well enough, Stanley," said Frank. "But Frankenstein's Castle it is, and it's having its debut BBQ tonight. You'll have to forgive the lack of essentials, guys, such as furniture, but the new stuff we ordered doesn't arrive till the weekend."

"We'll make do," Dave assured him. "As long as there's plenty of—"

"David Quirk!" travelled a firm voice on the breeze. It was the sort of shrill tone that all men knew. As a child, it meant that it was time to pack up your football and head home, and as an adult it usually meant that you'd been in the pub for too long.

"David Quirk," came the voice again, getting closer. "You're bloody useless."

"Sounds like my old teachers," chuckled Dave. "Same tone."

"Or your girlfriend, about you in bed," replied Monty, eager to get in on the act.

"That's just wrong, Monty," said Dave, shaking his head. "That's no way to talk in front of my mother. Have some respect, man."

Monty lowered his head. "Hi, Jessie," he offered, apologetically, as Dave's mother appeared.

"Hello, Shaun," she answered Monty, and then marched up to Dave, poking a firm finger into his chest. "I've been trying to speak to you all week, you never return my calls. I was worried about you!"

"You don't need to worry about him eating," said Monty, eager to retrieve some kudos, but it was not forthcoming.

It was Dave's turn to lower his head in submission. "Sorry, Mum, I've been busy," he offered.

"Nonsense," insisted Dave's mum. "A loving mother shouldn't have to travel to the other side of the Island to see her son because the lazy bugger won't return her calls."

It was amusing for Frank and Stan to see this woman, a little over five foot, tearing strips out of someone twice her size.

Dave leant down and left a kiss on his mum's face. "Sorry, Mum," he said. "I'll try harder."

Dave's mum removed her finger from her son's chest. "You better had! I worry about you, David. That's a mother's job!"

Duly chastised, Dave regained his composure and offered an introduction. "Jessie Clague, or *Mum*, as I call her. This is Frank and Stan who I've told you about. And that cross-eyed womble is Monty, as you know."

"Lovely to meet you boys," said Mrs Clague, with deep sincerity. "Dave and Monty have told me all about you. The work you both do for charity is truly humbling."

Frank was first to react, offering a warm handshake. "Lovely to meet you as well," he said, lowering his head to kiss her cheek. But there was some confusion as to which cheek would be on offer, and Frank spent the next few moments vacillating between the two, finally ending up rubbing noses together with her, like amorous Eskimos. *"Ehem, excuse me,"* mumbled Frank apologetically, taking a step back, and wondering how he'd managed to violate a woman he'd just met.

"Clague?" asked Stan, breaking the awkward silence, and in reference to Dave being a *Quirk* rather than a *Clague.*

"She's been married a fair few times," explained Dave with a mischievous grin. "Elizabeth Taylor, they call her around these parts. Father's Day was always a bit confusing when I was a kid, and we may as well have had a revolving door for all the men she brought home."

Mrs Clague's face was a picture. "You cheeky sod!" she scolded him, the finger in danger of being released once more. "I've been married *twice*," she assured Frank and Stan, and, then, "I've only just met these two lovely gentlemen," she said, admonishing Dave once more. "And now they think I'm a—"

"Nice bike," interrupted Dave, recovering it at the last moment by pointing to the new Ducati being eased out of the car park.

"We're having a BBQ tonight, Jessie," proposed Frank.

Stan had to suppress giving Frank a look — not at the invite offered, but by the voice Frank had currently adopted. It was as if the local vicar had popped by for afternoon tea and Frank was trying his best to impress, over-enunciating every word.

"That's very kind, Frank. Thank you, but I already have plans tonight. Another time, perhaps?"

Frank took the opportunity to follow the route of the TT course, heading towards the northern town of Ramsey and then heading up the staggeringly beautiful climb to the mountain section of the course. On a clear day, the view up top was mesmerising.

"I nearly shat myself in this very position last year," recalled Stan, contributing what he could to their moment of culture. "Remember, on that trike tour we went on? Honestly, I was seconds away from following through. It wouldn't have been pretty, not wearing those leather trousers."

"I don't think it'd be pretty whatever type of trousers you had on!" Frank told him.

Stan went quiet, looking across to the drivers' seat with a simple grin on his face.

"What?" said Frank. "It wouldn't."

For the next several minutes, the grin remained on Stan's face and did not falter.

"What??" Frank asked.

"You do," said Stan.

"I do, *what?*"

"You know."

"Are you still on about that?" laughed Frank. "I've told you, I do not."

"You do," Stan repeated, nodding. "You most certainly do. You like Dave's mum. I saw you blush, and you did this really goofy, weird voice thing. And what the hell was that nose kiss thing? I don't even know what that was. But, yes. You do." He was trying to get a rise out of Frank. It was working.

"Okay, she seemed nice!" conceded Frank, eventually, before clarifying, "I mean, a nice person. She's nice, that's all, alright?"

Stan smiled; he was quite happy with himself. "She's not your usual type," he teased.

"Maybe I'm fed up with the Barbie-doll look," snapped Frank. "I'd like to meet a woman who is happy with the skin she's in, not filled with more plastic than an Easter egg box."

"I just meant brunette rather than blonde," said Stan. "Besides, there's nothing wrong with a bit of assistance to prevent ageing," he insisted, stroking his head — which had more plugs than an electrical shop.

"I know," replied Frank. "But I don't mean to have a go. I think the experience with my ex-wife has made me appreciate natural beauty rather than collagen and Polyfilla. No offence, Stan!"

"None taken," said Stan, who was busying himself styling his eyebrows.

"Stan," said Frank after several minutes of comfortable silence, with the both of them enjoying the picturesque scenery.

"Whaaat?" asked Stan.

"There's something I can't stop thinking about."

"Dave's mum?"

"No!"

"You mean besides Dave's mum?"

"Yes!"

"Frank, there's no need to shout," Stan said in a soothing, tranquil voice — though with a cheeky grin.

"That house with the farm."

"Ah. So we're back to this."

"With that low turnout at the auction, I can't help but think we could maybe get that place cheap," mused Frank.

"You already tried," Stan reminded him. "Remember? And you bid quite a lot, and it still wasn't enough. And now that Rodney Franks is in the game..."

Frank strummed the steering wheel. "I know, but there is so much potential. Imagine the opportunity for people to learn new skills, regain confidence, or even to provide a safe haven to help people escape violence," Frank went on, filled with enthusiastic exuberance. "I can just see the working farm with a craft centre, selling products and produce — a real community."

"Sounds a bit like a cult?" said Stan.

"I don't mean like a bloody cult!" Frank protested. "Seriously, Stan. These last twelve months have really opened my eyes. I'm really enjoying putting something back, and this is something we can make a great success!"

"You're using the word 'we' quite a bit, I notice," remarked Stan.

Frank's eyebrows drooped. "You wouldn't want to get involved?"

"Of course I would," Stan assured him. "We're joined at the hip. And it would be quite nice to annoy Rodney Franks. If Henk hates the guy, it might be worth speaking to him next time he's over!"

"You know what, Stan. That's a bloody good idea. I've got a good feeling about this. I can see me and you in our hunting jackets surveying the land."

Stan gave a lingering gaze out through the window.

"God I love this place," he said, after some time.

"I know," said Frank. "It's special. We're going to be very happy here."

Chapter Nine

Summer 1974

Nomadic life, wandering from town to town, wasn't for everyone. There was time enough to make new friends, but permanent roots were never planted. Those who encountered Frank and Stan were often envious as to their ability to up sticks, and, as they called it, 'go for an amble' whenever the mood dictated. It wasn't that they were unhappy where they were, but more that they were eager to see what their next destination had to offer.

Sadly, there'd been one casualty on their travels; Daisy the campervan had served them admirably, but the strain had been showing for a number of months and the outcome was inevitable. Accommodation, however, was never a problem owing to the amount of money they were pulling in. They were a double act with an ability to bounce off each other, gifted with natural personalities that people warmed to; whatever they were selling, people were willing to buy.

Whatever they sold — hoovers, washing machines, TVs, and, for a time, encyclopaedias — they were hugely successful. Frank's Northern humour was especially popular with some of the housewives, eager to sample things he wasn't technically selling. On several occasions, in fact, their decision to move to pastures new was driven by irate spouses not overly impressed by Frank's extended warranty! Still, they had fun. Money was coming in quicker than they could spend. They were young, free, and single, with an insatiable appetite to experience the nightlife on offer.

Whilst Frank had a personality that was adept at snapping knicker elastic, Stan was arguably the better-looking of the pair. Stan was immaculate — a proud man who clearly gave a lot of time and money to his appearance. In a time where homosexuality was legal, it was nevertheless a taboo subject and the subject of much derision. Stan wasn't particularly camp, so it was easy enough to explain his single life as being the result of a difficult break-up. Besides, if anyone did have an inkling, it wouldn't be long before they'd moved on.

One such time was instigated by Frank. Sat around the table with several work colleagues, the familiar topic of conversation, queer-bashing, reared its ugly head. Stan was used to it — water off a duck's back, you might say — but Frank was fed up of hearing it. It made him sick to the stomach how ignorant people were, offering an opinion on something they knew nothing about, and he snapped. Frank wasn't ordinarily one for violence, but the right hook he landed on that obnoxious cretin's chin was one he wouldn't forget about — mainly due to him having two nights in the police cells to think about it. And they were soon on their travels, once again.

London was the centre of the cultural universe. It wasn't deliberate that Frank and Stan had never previously visited; they'd just never ventured that far down south. Now, though young, they were seasoned travellers. Still, when they did finally make their way to

London, even they couldn't have prepared themselves for what met them in the capital. The scale of the place was overwhelming and at times daunting. They didn't know anybody, had nowhere to stay, and their cheeky wit was matched by hundreds of other young wannabes who were equally as hungry to succeed. Also, they soon realised that their budget for accommodation would need to be revisited. For what they'd once been able to secure a spacious house, they were now lucky to get a one-bedroom flat.

There was an undercurrent of discontent in London they weren't expecting to find. The economy, so buoyant at the start of the decade, had turned flat. Industrial action was an everyday occurrence and the three-day working week was, until recently, a reality.

While there may not have been much spare cash around, those who had it — and a large number who didn't — were eager to forget about their money worries, ironically, by spending their money. The musical landscape, as an example, was thriving and diverse, with glam rock artists, for instance, on the same bill as reggae bands.

With a decent amount of dosh tucked away — in relative terms, at least — Frank and Stan were eager to absorb everything that this strange new world had to throw at them.

Frank turned his nose up at the tatty interior as they entered the building. Patches of plaster render were missing from the brick walls, with additional fragments looking as if they might break away at a moment's notice, thick oak support beams, that would once have been resplendent in some distant past, were now largely rotten — adding to the overall sense of despair.

"This is it?" asked Frank, arching his neck. "This is the place you insisted I absolutely couldn't miss?"

Stan slapped his old friend on the back. "Yes, granted, it's not the nicest pub in London. But, we're not here for either the ambience or a pint."

"Well why the hell are you dragging me here?" Frank replied.

"Frank, have faith," Stan told him. "All will be revealed. If I told you in advance, you wouldn't have come. When have I ever let you down? Come on. First round on me."

The place was surprisingly spacious, considering its modest exterior frontage (much like a Tardis, in that respect) and busier than one would expect for such a murky dump. As far as pubs went, this one was tired, grim, and considerably past its sell-by date — rather like the plump, partially-dressed stripper, in fact, plying her wares to anyone in the crowd happy to drop a few coins into the velvet red hat in her hand.

"Here you go," said Stan, once at the bar, handing over a pint of lager that was less than lively. Sensing Frank's enthusiasm was flatter than the pint in his hand, he sought to deliver a modicum of enthusiasm. "You'll like this, Frank," he began, taking a sip from his own glass. "We're here to see the entertainment," he went on, "… because we're going into the talent representation business."

Frank's face scrunched up like curdled milk. "Please, please tell me you don't mean *her*?" he said, in reference to the stripper they'd just seen, and who was now on all fours trying to retrieve a misplaced coin (and which would have been a more successful endeavour, perhaps, if only she'd put her cigarette down).

Stan shuddered at the thought. "Don't be bloody daft," he said, crouching down to pick up the coin that'd rolled by his feet. Ever the gentleman, Stan held the coin out to return it to its rightful owner. The exotic dancer, unfortunately, took that as an invitation and began to gyrate, fag-in-mouth. To Stan's horror, she moved ever closer, with a gentle, rhythmic stagger. It was unclear if this was part of her dance, and meant to be enticing, or was merely the result of a midday drinking session.

Frank pushed his own seat back a few inches, leaving his friend directly in the firing line.

"I'm Shelly," said Shelly, presenting herself to Stan, and jiggling her udders. Her pale breasts hung low, with blue veins running generously throughout them. Stilton cheese would now be ruined forever for Stan.

"Thank you, Shelly, but I'm fine. I was just returning your..."

But Shelly was now in full flow, her arse now centimetres from Stan's face. Stan tried desperately to shift his chair back, but Frank had extended his foot against Stan's chair leg, preventing his friend's timely escape. Stan reached into his pocket and held out his hand, this time offering up notes.

Shelly's eyes lit up when she spotted the notes. "I get off work in ten minutes," she told Stan excitedly. "That'll be more than enough," she added, with a casual wink.

Stan shuddered once more as the smell of tobacco on her breath hit him. "You don't understand," he said, trying to retain his composure. He was acutely aware that the focus of the pub was currently directly on him. "Listen,"

Stan stuttered. He motioned her closer and leaned into her ear. "Take the money and bugger off, luv," he said casually. "I don't want anything in return. I'm gay, you see." *And if I weren't already, I would be right now,* he thought to himself.

Shelly didn't judge. She took the notes, and, as requested, happily buggered off — notes in hand.

Stan gave a wry smile of liberation; Shelly was only the second person he'd told about his sexual persuasion, and it felt good. Strange. But good.

"I think I've seen enough of this place," remarked Frank.

"Wait," said Stan, grabbing his arm. "They're up next."

"Who are?"

Stan held out a pointed finger to the stage, as three bedraggled-looking youths in long green trench coats trudged towards microphones being hastily erected.

"*They* are!" Stan announced excitedly.

"I think I was more impressed by the stripper," Frank replied dryly.

"Just watch," insisted Stan.

"Who are they?" asked Frank once again.

"They, young Frank, are *The Garden Tools.*"

"You're having me on, yeah?" Frank protested, but then the young musician on the left took hold of his guitar and burst into life.

Frank stood down, easing back into his chair. The sound system was laughable, and it was clear they were playing at a venue where the regulars were, perhaps, not their target audience, but the band were captivating.

Stan kept one eye on Frank as the act moved through their setlist, watching and waiting for a reaction.

It took three full songs before Frank was able to break his full attention away from the stage, turning only briefly to throw Stan a look of awe. "Wow," he mouthed over the din.

Stan didn't try to respond, only giving a knowing nod in return. Today was a gamble — calculated, yes, but still a gamble. The contented expression on Frank's face was all Stan needed to see to know, satisfied, that they were about to start a new chapter in their lives.

"Come on," said Stan, draining his tepid lager. "Let's get out of here."

Once outside, Frank winced in pain as the natural daylight once again made contact with his retinas. The two of them walked for a time, in quiet thought, before Stan could no longer contain himself, fearing he might burst.

"Well?" he asked, stood in front of Frank, his hand up on Frank's chest, temporarily preventing further advance.

"Well what?" asked Frank.

Stan tilted his head, with eyebrows heading north. "Well what do you think?"

Frank shook his head. "I think," he offered in return. "That I'll not be returning to that pub again."

"Me neither, but what about—?"

"They were very good," said Frank. "I'm not a massive music fan, but they were good. Who were they again? The Garden Fools?"

"*Tools*," corrected Stan.

"Ah," nodded Frank. "Then that makes at least a little more sense."

"Frank, I've got a good feeling about this — you know, me and you, in the entertainment business."

"What, you were serious about that bit?" Frank gave a half-smile. "What do we know about the entertainment business? We'd last five minutes."

"No, listen," said Stan, putting his arm around Frank's shoulder now, and pressing down slightly for effect. "Entertainment is just another commodity to sell. You've said it yourself, Frank. We're the best salesmen in the game. It doesn't matter what we're selling, the underlying principle is the same. It doesn't matter if it's a hoover, washing machines, or whatever. You're trying to sell a product to an end user, and in this case that product is entertainment, or, to be more precise, music!"

Stan guided Frank into a shop doorway, pulling him in, where they stood like moonstruck lovers.

"Come on, Frank, me and you. Imagine it. Me and you, best friends, working together as music agents! Frank," Stan went on, moving closer like he was preparing a tender kiss. "Frank," he repeated. "We can do this. I can feel it in my water, we're going to make our fortune!"

An elderly couple passing leisurely by eyed Frank and Stan with suspicion. "Disgusting," the man commented.

"The times are changing, Bertrand," his wife told him, kindly. "It's not like it used to be."

"It's rubbish. I don't like it one bit," the man answered her. "Not one single bit!"

"Mind your blood pressure, dear," she told him. "Remember your condition."

"Things ought to stay exactly as they've always been," he said.

"Oh, I shouldn't like that at all, things always staying the same," the woman remarked. "Not at all."

Their voices faded away as they continued on their way, until they could no longer be heard.

"Well, Frank? Are you in??" asked Stan.

Frank rolled his eyes skyward. He knew he was going to lose this battle. Still, he soldiered on:

"So. These Garden Tools. What if they don't want us to manage them after all? Especially when you tell them we've got bugger-all knowledge of the music industry. What then?"

"Ah," offered Stan, finger in the air. "But I do have musical knowledge. I was a former assistant stagehand!"

Frank laughed. "You're talking about the school production of *The Wizard of Oz*, aren't you?"

"Maybe," admitted Stan. "But it's all about the details, isn't it? And in this case, I didn't go into details. It was a minor point that wouldn't have helped my negotiations."

"This is all going to go tits-up, Stanley, I can guarantee it. But, what the hell, maybe we should give it a go. What's the worst that could...?" Frank paused. "Hang on. *What* negotiations? You've already spoken to them??"

Stan's finger was in the air once again, like a flagpole. "Ah!" he said, pausing for thinking time. "Ah! Well, see, I knew you'd see things my way, so—"

"*Stanley?*" Frank demanded.

"I knew you'd say yes in the end, so I've already taken the liberty of paying them a small retainer to, you know, secure our position as their exclusive management and such."

Frank's eyes narrowed. "What! And exactly how *small* is this small retainer?" he asked, not at all amused, and slapping the floating finger to one side.

"Only two hundred pounds," Stan replied. "Not that much," he quickly added.

"Bloody hell, Stan! Two hundred pounds!"

"Right. Not that much," Stan said again.

Frank, for his part, appeared unconvinced that £200 was not all that much.

Stan, however, was full of bravado. "It'll be fine, I promise you. This time next year we'll be millionaires! You've seen how good they are, and they're just the beginning of our empire. Just picture it!" said Stan, thrusting his arm aloft and sweeping it majestically across an imaginary horizon. "Besides, you said I was the money man!"

"I meant you were good at *spending* it, not good *with* it, as is now very evident," Frank sighed with despair. "*Two hundred pounds. Bloody hell, Stan.*"

"It'll be fine," Stan assured him once more.

"Stan," said Frank, with eyes fixed. "That was *our* money, Stan. I appreciate why you've done it. I do. But, in future, promise me you'll talk to me before you spend what is our collective money? Yes?"

Stan bowed his head like a naughty schoolboy. "I promise, Frank. I just got caught up in the moment, that's all. It was too good an opportunity for us. We're going to be rich and famous by the time we're twenty-five," he said, brightening up again and slapping Frank across the shoulder as if that should be all the assurance Frank required.

"I'm going to hold you to that, Stan. Now come on, let's get out of this doorway. It smells of piss."

Stan didn't move. His head was down again, and he was examining his shoes by the look of it.

"Stan? I said let's go," Frank reiterated.

"Ah," replied Stan. "Well here's the thing," he said. "It's just that..."

"It's just that what? What is it now?" asked Frank, but there was no immediate response.

"What've you done, Stan?" Frank asked again, casting him a hard look. "Or, should I say, what else have you done?"

Stan took a deep breath. "Well, you know the saying about getting hung for a sheep than a lamb?"

"Yes," replied Frank. "But I never really understood it. I have a feeling, though, that in this particular instance, it's not good news."

"Just the opposite!" Stan answered, feigning more confidence than he actually possessed. "Come on," he said, placing his arm around his friend's shoulder again, and gently ushering him out of the doorway and over in front of the shop window.

Stan gave Frank's shoulder a playful squeeze for good measure.

"Okay... I don't get it," said Frank. "Are we waiting for performing monkeys to appear or something?"

Stan pointed to a piece of frayed rope which ran down the left-hand side of the window. "Grab that, Frank," he instructed. "And give it a tug."

"Not the first time you've said that to me," chuckled Frank.

"I'm serious," replied Stan. "Give it a pull."

"Okay, okay," said Frank, looking up to see what it was attached to. "Does a bucket of water come crashing down when I pull it?"

"Just pull it!" repeated Stan.

Tentatively, with a cautionary glance over his shoulder, Frank tugged at the rope, instinctively retreating a step as he did so. He was expecting more fanfare, with the resulting action being no more than a plastic sheet — still, for the most part, affixed — rustling in the wind.

Stan was mortified. "It worked in rehearsal, honestly!"

Frank looked like he might be losing his patience.

"Pull it once more, a bit harder!" Stan said, in his finest Benny Hill styling.

Anxious for any sort of resolution to this affair, Frank gripped and pulled, this time releasing an invisible clasp, setting the plastic sheet free to reveal...

Stan hovered, with jazz hands poised. "Well?" he asked. "Do you like it?"

Frank took several steps back for a proper look, placing his thumb and forefinger to his chin and cocking his head to one side.

Above the dingy, bordering-on-derelict shop was an immaculate gloss-white sign that ran the length of the glass frontage. Either side of the sign were two huge portraits of Frank and Stan, radiating a prideful confidence, like two marble lions stood sentry at the gates to a splendid country residence. The bold images were matched only by the impressive wording that gave the impression the lettering had been applied by hand with painstaking precision.

Frank freed his chin from his grasp and read aloud what he saw:

Frank Cryer & Stanley Sidcup
Theatrical Agents
Est. 1962

Frank looked at the sign, over to Stan, and then back over to the sign. "I bloody love it," said Frank, much to Stan's visible and audible relief. "And I'm assuming you've leased the shop as well, and not just appropriated the face of it to hang the sign? I'm not even going to ask the cost—"

"You probably shouldn't," interjected Stan. "But we've got enough — well, *had* enough — without going into debt or borrowing anything."

Frank patted his belly like he'd just enjoyed a good meal, then shrugged his shoulders.

"What've we got to lose, Stanley? You have to speculate to accumulate. But that whole sheep and lamb thing? If you spend my money without telling me, ever again, the only thing that'll be getting hung, is you, by your testicles! Now, come on, you need to buy me a decent pint of beer and assure me that dump of a pub we've just been is not going to be our local!"

With that, the two of them skipped off to begin a new chapter in their lives. Certainly, for Frank at least, it was a chapter he didn't see coming. But he figured, *what's the worst that could happen?*

"Stan," said Frank, pausing for a moment. "That sign you've put up?"

"It's good, isn't it," replied Stan, rather more a statement than a question.

"It's brilliant," replied Frank, pushing out his bottom lip in appreciation. "But one small point, if I may?"

"Of course," said Stan. "Go on."

Frank used his finger, counting imaginary figures, before continuing:

"Established nineteen sixty-two? We were at primary school in nineteen sixty-two. I'm not convinced you could tie your own shoelace in nineteen sixty-two?"

"Details, Frank. I said this earlier, it's all about the details, or, once again, the lack of them. I didn't want people to know we were beginners. And if anyone pushes the point, we'll just say we're second-generation."

"Okay," replied Frank, seemingly content with the strategy proposed. "Stan," asked Frank, in a manner which indicated he wasn't entirely certain he wanted to know the answer. "Do we actually have any money left?"

Stan chuckled. "Of course we do," he said. "Just not an awful lot. But you remember this conversation next year when we're swimming in a bathtub full of cash!"

"I may get you to sign something to that effect!" countered Frank. "Now, come on, you can buy me a pint that's actually got a head on it."

Stan picked up the pace and broke into an enthusiastic skip, gambolling down the pavement whilst singing the Cole Porter classic "Who Wants to Be a Millionaire?" — to which Frank joined in.

"I've got a good feeling about this!" shouted Stan over Frank, who was now in full voice. "Here's to the Garden Tools!" he proclaimed, shaking his fist in delight.

"The Garden Tools!" repeated Frank, before adding, "What the hell have we got ourselves into!"

Chapter Ten

The curtain-raiser to the Isle of Man TT was the eagerly anticipated launch event. Held several weeks before the action on track commenced, it was the ideal showcase for the teams to talk about their ambitions, show off their new machinery, or perhaps to introduce the latest riders to their team. For those fortunate enough to secure tickets for the sell-out event, you had the opportunity to mingle with your sporting heroes and be immersed in the majestic atmosphere that is the TT Races — the greatest sporting spectacle on earth.

The general feeling in the queue outside the Villa Marina was one of cheerful, patient camaraderie. Those waiting were eager to share their own experiences of the TT and, perhaps, offer an opinion on who'd be at the top of the podium come race day. Conversations got only more animated as the queue progressed, with spirits high all around.

There were, however, two people who were not as jovial as those in their immediate vicinity, with their admittance into the event hitting a bit of a snag.

Security at the entrance was minimal — after all, this was the TT, not football — and entrance to the evening's proceedings was granted by a slight youth wearing a white shirt a size too big for him. Adrian, was his name, according to the name badge he proudly sported. He was a polite young man, wielding his tally counter with a practised ease and great facility, and giving it a confident click with each passing ticket holder. Despite his pleasant demeanour, he was, nevertheless, a boy who took his job very seriously.

And Adrian, in the case of the two ne'er-do-wells before him, had apparently seen enough.

"I've told you two. And I shan't tell you again, I'm afraid. If you do not have a ticket, then I cannot let you in. It's really as simple as that," Adrian admonished the pair, puffing out his pigeon chest as he did so. "You'll need to step away from the queue, please," he instructed. Adrian wasn't for coercing, but his tone was rather firm and he was in no doubt of the important authority bestowed upon him as gatekeeper.

Dave finally relented. "Fine!" he said, with a petulant stamp of the foot, and then taking Monty by the arm and leading him away.

"One bloody job, Monty," Dave whinged while stepping out of the queue, as instructed. "One job to not forget the tickets..."

"You can't blame *me* for this," Monty protested, with a shrug of his shoulders. "It's hardly my fault."

Dave held out his empty hands. His hands were quite large, making their emptiness only that much more apparent. "Monty," he said. "Did you have the tickets?"

"Yes!" replied Monty happily.

"Monty," Dave continued, extending his hands closer to Monty's face so as to make their lack of contents indisputable. "Do I have anything in my hands?"

Monty examined Dave's palms very carefully, even though they were now only inches from his face and plain to see. He shook his head. "Nothing there!" he said, enjoying this game, and waiting for the magic trick he was sure would come.

"No, Monty, there isn't. There is nothing in my hands because you didn't bring the tickets!" Dave answered.

It was the most rubbish magic trick Monty had ever seen, and naturally he was disappointed.

"I do have a day job, you know!" he protested. "Besides, I didn't think they'd have that bloody jobsworth on the door!"

"Insults won't get you anywhere, gentlemen," Adrian replied, overhearing. He turned to them and gave them a stern look. "No ticket, no show. You need a ticket to see the show," he told them. "Those are the rules."

Dave took an impatient breath, looking to the watch on his chubby wrist for emphasis. "Adrian," he implored, adopting a more conciliatory tone. "Adrian, I can see you're a man of power and influence. But we don't want to *attend* the show. We're *in* the bloody show, you see."

Monty, pleased that they were all on a first-name basis, took a step forward and happily joined in the conversation. "Adrian, my friend," he said. "Dave and I are sidecar racers and we're due to be interviewed in the Q-and-A in about twenty-five minutes, he explained," with so much pride in his voice he was fit to burst.

The queue — which was accumulating in number due to the current delay — looked Dave and Monty up and down in unison.

"You're racers?" asked Adrian, asking what everyone was thinking, rather quite incredulous. "I've heard some unlikely excuses in my time," chuckled Adrian, as if his experience were vast and spanned ages. "But if you two are sidecar racers, then I'm Vin Diesel." Adrian was proud of that comment, looking to the crowd for laughter, but got no reaction. Everyone was too busy staring at Dave and Monty. *"Vin Diesel,"* Adrian said again for emphasis, undeterred.

Enough was enough for Dave. "Right. Get it out of the bag, Monty," he instructed his partner.

Monty stared at Adrian for an intense few seconds. "Right-O. You asked for this," he told the boy, before ever-so-slowly reaching into the cheap supermarket plastic bag, partially torn near the handle. Monty kept his eyes locked to those of the gatekeeper, his hand plunging into the depths of his receptacle...

And fished around...

It was there somewhere...

Fucksake, it was a small bag...

Shouldn't be that hard to find...

Where could it have...?

Adrian placed the clicker in his pocket. This is the moment he'd been waiting for. This is where all his training would finally be put to use. It was his moment to shine.

"Tooled up, are we?" the boy — all of about four-foot-two, and ninety pounds soaking wet if he were very lucky — asked with a cocky grin.

Before Monty could respond, Adrian, in one fluid motion — a motion presumably practised in front of his mum's mirror — whipped out a solid piece of wood secured to his ankle. Given the oriental design on the cosh, it was evident that Adrian was quite the kung-fu aficionado.

"Bring it!" demanded Adrian, now prancing on the spot like a featherweight prizefighter.

"What the hell? I thought we were friends now!" pleaded Monty, taking a step back behind Dave for cover.

"Thou shall not pass!" Adrian called out, in no uncertain terms. His lungs may have been small but his will was indomitable.

"Look at this," Monty whimpered, finally producing from the shallow depths of the flimsy plastic bag the sought-upon object. "This is why we're here. *This*."

Monty held up the object in his hand like one would brandish a crucifix to ward off a creature of the night.

"Right. Did you lot steal that?" asked Adrian, gazing reverently at the gleaming trophy in astonishment, as if he were staring at the Holy Grail itself. "Because if you did, I warn you, I'll be forced to open up your head like a tin of beans!"

"To be fair, I can see why you'd think that," Dave intervened. "But, no. We won that Spirit of the TT award. Last year."

"You must recognise us, surely?" suggested Monty, bravely stepping out from behind Dave once again. "We're heroes," he added, arms thrust back, chin — well, at least one of his chins — raised skyward.

Adrian took a lingering look at Dave and Monty, and smiled as a glimmer of recognition filtered in. "Ah!" he said. "You know what, now I think on it... yes, you two... you two are legends, aren't you? I remember reading about it." Adrian put his weapon away, his stance finally relaxing. "But... but what happened? Only, what happened to you between then and now? Because..." he asked, looking them over with visible consternation. After all, this wasn't the way heroes were meant to look. "... I mean, did you let yourselves go?"

159

"Wow. Bit harsh, mate," said Dave. "Anyway, they say that being in the paper puts ten pounds on you. Don't they, Monty?"

Monty nodded. "Ten pounds," he offered. "At least."

"Is it not the TV?" asked Adrian, looking at the frustrated crowd who were thoroughly uninterested, just wanted to get inside.

Dave's patience was wearing thin. "Oh, for the love of... Adrian, now you recognise us, could you kindly... y'know...?"

"*Ha-ha*, sorry, guys," came the reply. "But it's like I already said. No ticket, no entrance."

Dave was in danger of using the Spirit of the TT Award to beat the doorman, *the doorman to the TT showcase event itself*, to death. (There had to be an irony there somewhere.) However, salvation came in the form of a familiar figure marching through the Villa Marina gardens at a fair rate of speed. Chris Kinley, host for the evening, had a severe expression, tapping his watch as he moved forth. Chris, whose silky dulcet tones graced the TT coverage as one of Manx Radio's presenters, was better known for oil-stained overalls, marching through the pits gathering expert opinion from the riders, and the occasional expletive. Tonight, he was immaculate in full black tie, and with no oil stains visible to the eye — though his underpants were anyone's guess.

"Dave. Monty. They're all looking for you in there. What are you doing? Come on!"

"We're trying," moaned Monty. "But Bruce Lee here won't let us in without tickets."

Kinley put the palm of his hand on top of his immaculately-shaven bald head and looked up to the sky.

"Do I have to do *everything* around here?" he asked of no one in particular. "Adrian, do me a favour and let these two gentlemen in, will you? There's a good lad."

"Very good, Mr Kinley. Certainly, sir," replied Adrian, stepping to one side.

"Tin of beans, was it?" said Monty, with a sideways glance, as he walked past Adrian. To be fair, however, with his eyes pointing in two different directions such as they were, he couldn't help but give the boy a sideways glance.

"Right. I can't hang about, I've got people to talk to on stage," the presenter said. "Dave, press photographs are over there," he said, and you're on stage with me in about one hour. Please don't be late, or you don't want to know what I'll do with my microphone."

"I'm hungry now for beans on toast," remarked Monty idly to Dave.

"Later," Dave had to assure him, as they finally made their way into the event.

Frank and Stan gushed like proud fathers, stood next to sidecar Number Forty-Two. There were several outfits lined up next to each other, mostly the factory-sponsored machines, but the big blue & yellow boiled sweet — Number Forty-Two — was an equal to any of them. She was immaculate. The stage lighting overhead bounced off her bodywork like a polished diamond.

Every man or woman, on either two wheels or three, petrol or electric motor, was a hero. It didn't matter if you were parked up the top of the paddock in a sumptuous motorhome or holding up the rear in a rusty transit van. Each and every one of them had their own motivation, their own challenge and reason for tackling the famous TT course.

Dave and Monty had for years done everything themselves and one of the biggest challenges for them, unfortunately, was money. The prize money on offer was, relatively speaking, chicken feed. The racing for these people — Dave and Monty included — was about more than the money, but, money is what paid for the engines, tyres, and petrol. So, to have two sponsors like Frank and Stan was a godsend. No longer did Dave and Monty have to get bank loans, borrow from friends, or offer sexual favours for cash to visiting TT fans. (Most believe the latter was an urban myth, started by Dave about Monty, but as most know, there's no smoke without fire, and Monty's awning was, as it happened, particularly popular.)

In addition to a new engine — which was more than capable of producing a top-ten finish — Frank and Stan were providing matching leathers and helmets, festooned with advertising for the charity. If their boys, Dave and Monty, were going to start high school, so to speak, proud parents Frank and Stan wanted them to have only the best school uniforms, as it were.

Presently, Stan was busying himself, applying his handkerchief in circular motions above Number Forty-Two's wheel arch; there would be no imperfections on the bodywork left unchecked.

"And here they are," announced Frank.

Stan turned and stood, awestruck, pride etched all over his face as Dave and Monty emerged from the makeshift dressing room. The yellow leather suits were resplendent, as were their helmets held under their right arms. They waited in that doorway, poised, with an air of unmistakable confidence, perhaps even bordering on arrogance, surveying the vista before them. They looked like astronauts preparing to embark on a voyage of discovery, to the moon, or possibly beyond. They looked at each other, sharing a knowing nod, before bravely progressing towards their adoring public (which, in this particular case at least, consisted of Frank and Stan). The only thing missing from their dramatic arrival was the plume of dry ice for them to walk through with a fanfare of dramatic, stirring music. They even walked in an exaggerated slow-motion; they were fully embracing their role. The glamour and romance evaporated, however, when the reason for the slow-motion became apparent...

"My testicles are chafing!" shouted Monty, well and truly shattering the heroic persona they'd presented for a few short seconds.

The leather suits were visibly too tight for them, and their ambulatory progress was fraught due to the restrictive nature of their attire. Consequently, they hobbled like they'd been repeatedly violated by King Kong.

"It... leaves little to the imagination," said Dave, pulling at the seams by the gusset. His face was a puce colour, with every laboured breath a struggle. "I may pass out, actually," he gasped, with a stream of sweat running down his face.

Stan's gushing pride was soon replaced with that of vexation. "Those suits were professionally fitted," he insisted. "And at a cost that was very dear, I might add. Have you two put weight on?"

"That's what Adrian asked as well," Monty replied morosely.

"Who's Adrian?" Frank interjected.

"Someone who was giving us guff, but then was our friend, and then... I'm not sure," Monty answered.

"No. No, we didn't put on weight," said Dave, before an exceptionally long pause. He bowed his head, rubbing the sole of his new boots like he was putting out a cigarette. "We were optimistic," he confided. "We told them at the fitting to take a couple of inches off, as we were looking to lose a few pounds."

Stan approached, rubbing his hand to feel how taut the smart-looking leathers were (or that was the excuse he was using, at least). "We're the only ones who'll be losing a few pounds if those don't fit you come the TT," he admonished. "Especially if we need to buy you another set each."

"It'll be fine, Stan. We're still with the fitness trainer. I promise these leathers will fit like a glove," Dave assured him. He tried to place his confident hands on Stan's shoulders, but with minimal give from the leather, he could only get his arms to just above waist height. From this, coupled with a pained groan from the suit restricting his crotch, he resembled a zombie — a leather-clad zombie, or, more specifically, a leather-clad zombie astronaut.

Frank smiled broadly. "They do look bloody good, though, don't they?" he said. "I mean, apart from the overstuffed-sausage appearance? Here, stand next to the bike," he guided them, waving his arm in case Dave and Monty should need direction. The press photographer appeared with precision timing, right on cue, plying her wares with a series of snaps.

"Smile," she prompted, but all Dave and Monty could offer were constipated grins of pain. "Perfect!" she said. "I'll send you a copy for your publicity campaign."

He had no idea it was coming, or even where it came from, but Frank was overwhelmed by a wave of emotion, resulting in watery patches just under the eyes. Perhaps it was the question on his own mortality, or maybe the idea that Dave and Monty may not have walked away from their crash the year before, but, stood there, looking at what he was a part of, was something a bit special.

Stan smiled, offering a tender pat on the back. "It's good, this. Isn't it?"

Frank nodded. "The best."

"Right. I'd like that beans-on-toast now, Dave," Monty suggested.

No matter how many times you'd watched the onboard footage of man (and woman) and machine negotiating the 37.73 miles of twisting tarmac climbing from sea level to nearly fourteen hundred feet in a matter of a few exhilarating minutes, it was still mesmerising. It was incomprehensible for the brain to absorb the speed at which the Isle of Man countryside, for the riders, approached and then disappeared. These guys weren't riding on a generous, purpose-built track, with gravel traps and run-off areas. These guys were riding past people's houses, bus shelters, shops, and even telephone boxes temporarily covered in padding. There were severe crosswinds over the mountain that could blow you the width of the road, bird strikes were common, and to think the bikes would reach speeds of over 200 miles per hour on this course was difficult to fathom. Common sense told you it couldn't be real, but, oh boy, you better believe it's real, and one of the main reasons these riders were held in such high esteem.

Presently, the auditorium reverberated with the deafening tone of a BMW S 1000 RR screaming through the Bungalow section of the Mountain Course. The crowd sat in awe, slack-jawed, soaking up the onboard footage — which was on display from a previous TT so as to whet the audience's appetite for the current year's race.

"What about *that*??" said Chris Kinley, taking the stage as the video ended, and applauding the massive screen at the back of the platform. He'd seen the footage before, of course, but was still captivated. "And wasn't it great to see Dave and Monty earlier with their Spirit of the TT award! Worthy winners last year and we wish them every success with their Team Frank 'n' Stan's Food Stamps outfit!"

Kinley strutted on stage at the Google Villa marina venue like a peacock; the audience were well and truly in his hands. He rubbed his palms together in excitement. "We're onto the final section of the evening, so take an opportunity to top up your glasses!" he encouraged them.

But the sound of snoring was causing a distraction.

The presenter strained his eyes against the harsh lighting. "Only not you, Peter Last," he chuckled, in reference to the sleeping man, head on table, surrounded by an array of empty beakers. "I think my old mate Peter has perhaps had enough!"

Chris's quip fell largely on deaf ears, apart from one laugh that started off slow, gradually increasing in tempo, very much like an old engine sparking up on a cold morning, until finally it was roaring at high idle — and then, the pipes clearing out, a loud *BANG!* expelled:

"*HE'S DRUNK!*" said the booming voice in between the roar of laughter. "*HA-HA-HA!*" it continued. "*I MUST TAKE THAT MAN OUT FOR A DRINK!*" it continued, once more, all eyes in the room now focussed on the round table near to the stage, slightly to starboard.

Dutch Henk had landed on the Isle of Man, and the Isle of Man now knew it from the foghorn-esque laugh. He was built like Richard "Jaws" Kiel from *James Bond*, with a personality as equal in stature. He was unconcerned that everyone was looking at him. In fact, he took it as a compliment, raising his own beaker of ale as a friendly acknowledgement.

Frank and Stan were honoured to call Henk their new neighbour, and the hospitality Henk had shown them at the previous TT was one of the reasons they'd enjoyed themselves so much. He oozed from every pore an infectious zest for life that you couldn't help but be swept along with. (Granted, that's a lot of oozing.) Henk may have appeared a puzzle; looking at him, you mightn't think he had two pennies to rub together, dressed as he was in tatty denim with a leather waistcoat emblazoned with motorsport badges, though Henk was, in fact, loaded. But while he was reserved about his wealth, that's where the modesty ended: he was loud and a lot of fun. And it was precisely for this reason that Frank and Stan made sure they were sat with him, in addition to a relieved, now-leathers-free Dave and Monty.

Henk, as it happened, loved the bejeezus out of the TT — everything about it — the people, the racing, the location. Everything. He put his money into motorsport across Europe; it was the perfect advertising for his motor showrooms. The TT had a global appeal, which was one of the reasons he was delighted to become chief sponsor for Harry and Tom McMullan.

Currently, Chris Kinley was tapping his forefinger on the stage microphone in an attempt to redirect the focus of the room.

"Okay, ladies and gentlemen, if I could have your attention? Thank you. Now, I'm not alone in admitting my affection for the sidecar racing at the TT races. The level of competition has always been gripping, but this year, it's going to take on an entirely new intensity. It's not been widely known, until now, and I'm delighted to announce that this year we welcome not one but two regular competitors in the greater World Sidecar Championship!"

The crowd responded accordingly, and, once the cheering and applause subsided, the presenter continued.

"We've got Harry and Tom McMullan. Harry, you will recall, was involved in the incident for which Dave and Monty received the Spirit of the TT award. Tom had an injured wrist last year as a result of this, so it's fair to say they're champing at the bit to get racing. And, if that wasn't enough motivation, we're also going to welcome their main competitors in the World Championships, Jack Napier and Andy Thomas! Ladies and gentlemen, let's give them a huge Isle of Man welcome!"

Dave took a mouthful of his pint, shoving his elbow into Monty's shoulder. "Get your video ready on the phone, Monty, because this could get very interesting very quickly. Whoever thought of getting them four on the stage at the same time needs their bloody head examined."

Chris Kinley sat back in the comfortable Sherlock-style chair placed in the middle of the stage for him. Two intimate sofas sat either side, where the crew of each outfit took their places.

The presenter smiled, using his hand to lower the cheering from the audience before proceeding.

"What a welcome. Wow. Guys, you can tell from that reception that the Isle of Man are looking forward to seeing you battling it out for the top step of the podium. Jack, Andy, if I can come to you first. You're currently topping the leaderboard in the championship, with, not surprisingly, these two," he said, pointing to the other sofa, before continuing. "In your hot pursuit, it's really been about you both in the championship for the last three years, with currently one World Champion win apiece. What made you decide to come to the TT now, and was it a difficult decision?"

Jack Napier gave a snide grin to those sat opposite him. He flicked back a shock of black curly hair, causing an elderly woman on the front row to whistle admiringly.

"Well, Chris," replied Napier. "The TT is the greatest test for a sidecar outfit, anywhere, in the world. Andy and I are winning the championship... again," he said, picking at his fingernails nonchalantly, feigning indifference to the competition. "We know we're the finest racers in the sport, which is why we're top of the championship leaderboard. So we need to win the two sidecar races at the TT, you see, in order to remove any doubt that we are, in fact, the best."

Chris Kinley nodded slowly. "And you think you can win both races?"

"We wouldn't be here if we didn't," offered Andy Thomas. "Besides, those two," he said, pointing his thumb to the other team, though not even acknowledging them with the courtesy of a glance, "... are the favourites. And they're shit, aren't they? So, if that's the best on offer, then it's a given that we'll take both races for ourselves."

Kinley sat back in his chair, giving a nervous grin. "I'd heard you didn't get on with each other, but I thought it was just down to sporting rivalry — you know, playing up to the cameras?" he said. "But you really don't get on, then, do you," he added, more an observation than an enquiry.

Tom McMullan laughed sharply. "Chris, if you spent ten minutes in their company — that's all it'd take — you'd want to punch their lights out. They're arrogant sons of—"

"You're confusing that with a winner's confidence," interrupted Thomas.

"They're arrogant," continued Tom. "Which is fair enough, but their biggest problem is that they're dangerous. They take unacceptable risks on the track. I know I'm one to talk, in that respect. I know people didn't really take to us, for that very reason. Well, more Harry," he said, casting an accusatory nod towards his brother. "But we never put other professional racers lives in danger. Not like *them*. *They* do," he finished off, with an accusatory finger point.

"Piss off," said Napier with a contentious shake of the head, looking straight ahead. "We're winners and we give it one hundred percent whenever we race. Perhaps if you two losers did the same, you wouldn't be second in the championship. What you call *dangerous*, most would call *competitive*."

Chris Kinley was not big in physical stature and he really did not want to be getting in the middle of a brawl between these four, should they resort to fisticuffs. "Okay, moving it away from the race, if we can," he said, pushing his chair back a few inches for safety. "Tom, if I may, your outfit, sponsored by this... *herm*, and how should we describe you, Henk?" he asked, with a furtive glance over to Henk's table. "I think we'll go with *enigma!* That okay with you?" offered Kinley.

The booming laugh, in response, indicated that Henk was happy with the characterisation.

"I'd go with loser, also!" shouted a very loud and exceptionally brave voice from the rear of the hall, brave in that Henk was not the sort of chap you wanted to annoy — rather like throwing stones at a brown bear, it wasn't conducive to a long and healthy life.

"Well," said Chris Kinley, wiping his forehead. "This is all getting a bit... lively?"

The owner of the heckling voice sauntered forward with a cocksure arrogance, and as its owner emerged from the darkness it was revealed that the voice belonged to none other than Rodney Franks.

"It's that wanker again," whispered Frank to Stan. "And it looks like he's bought himself some fancy new sunglasses!"

Further round the table, Dave was also whispering — to Monty. "I hope you've pressed *Record* on that phone?" he said.

With Franks' approach, the presenter once again attempted to maintain order. "Gentlemen, please," pleaded Kinley, tapping the microphone once more.

Rodney proceeded forward, taking a trajectory that left two rows of tables between him and Henk; he was a gobshite but he wasn't entirely stupid — Henk could crush his head like a pimple.

"My team and my boys," Franks carried on despite Kinley's appeal for civility, pointing up to the stage. "Are champions! They have the best machinery, pit crew, and management. The McMullan brothers are a joke. A joke! I mean, look at their main money-man — he's an oaf. A giant oaf and a laughingstock!"

On each table, a small rubber ball with the TT logo was left for each guest — a memento of the evening, as it were. It wasn't the soft sort of rubber; rather, it was of the denser variety, like a stress ball. And it was one of these balls, at that moment, which hurtled through the air like a comet, connecting perfectly with the side of Rodney Franks' forehead, sending the new sunglasses nestled there flying into the darkest recess of the room.

Back at the table, Dave placed a congratulatory hand on Monty's arm. "Tell you what, Monty. For a man with wonky eyes, that was a shot a bloody military sniper would envy."

"Years of practice working up that right arm," replied Monty with a contented grin.

"I won't ask for what purpose," Dave replied with a chuckle.

"I had to do something," Monty went on. "This whole scenario is like the plot from a *Rocky* film — I felt like it needed some sort of resolution."

"You did the right thing," suggested Dave.

Henk erupted into uncontrollable laughter. Franks, for his part, crawled on the floor, rubbing his head with one hand and reaching out with the other in search for his glasses. It was a most undignified look for such an arrogant man, which meant Henk couldn't stop laughing, with the result of infuriating Franks only further.

"Put your money where your mouth is, Rodney!" said Henk, draining the contents of his glass. "My team against yours!"

"They've definitely been watching too much *Rocky*," said Monty, not bothering to whisper now.

"*Rocky Four*?" asked Dave, but Monty couldn't be sure.

Henk stood, and his sheer mass caused several of the attendees to gasp.

"Rodney!" Henk said in his booming voice. "I'll bet you my Vincent! The one I took from you at auction! I'll bet you my Vincent that my boys will win both sidecar races!"

Franks stood. He had not found his sunglasses. He didn't like his eyes showing, especially in negotiations, but a challenge like this had to be accepted nevertheless.

"Not a chance!" Franks called out. "And, deal! What do you want from me, cash?"

Henk waved his hand, so vast, it blocked out the light for many in the audience. "I don't need your money, Rodney!" he chuckled. Franks disliked being addressed with such familiarity, using his Christian name. Which is of course precisely why Henk did so. "Tell you what, Rodney!" Henk continued, moving forward. "I beat you to the Vincent at auction, so you put up what you won at auction today!"

"W–what?" replied Franks. "W–what auction?" he stuttered. He wasn't the sort of man that ordinarily stuttered.

"The auction for that farm you won today! The auction you somehow managed to get rearranged without anyone else knowing about it!"

Rodney paused for a moment, before answering, "That farm is worth more than the bloody Vincent, and you know it."

"I'll throw in the Aston Martin!" replied Henk without hesitation.

"Deal," Franks answered. "My sidecar will beat your sidecar in both races. I'd shake your hand on it. But I don't know where it's been," he added, acting the maggot, because, yes, he was that much of an arsehole.

Monty leaned back into Dave. "This is fucking embarrassing. You'd think two men as rich as them would be a bit better at this whole threats-across-a-crowded-room thing. Look, even Chris Kinley's had enough — he's buggered off," he said, in reference to the empty chair on stage. "Dave," said Monty, tapping Dave's hand. "Two things. What's a Vincent, and what bloody farm?"

"I'll tell you later, but can you do me a favour with this just now? I'll tell you when," he said, handing Monty his rubber ball.

The four people who were pivotal to this bet were sat on stage equally as perplexed as those sitting in the crowd. Egos had been deflated, and, with Kinley having legged it, it appeared as good a time as any to draw the evening to a close.

Jack Napier had leaned over the sofa to retrieve his bag, and, once his back was turned, Dave tapped Monty's knee. And Monty, like a catapult, released the rubber ball in the direction of the stage per Dave's instruction.

Dave was deeply impressed as the ball caught Napier square at the base of the skull. "That really is some arm you've got," he said admiringly.

With no clear indication of where the assault originated, Napier could only assume it'd come from the sofa opposite, and, without thought, leapt at Tom and Harry McMullan with fists flailing.

Security was non-existent, so this was, once again, a certain waif-like boy's time to shine. Those hours scrutinising martial arts movies were clearly about to pay dividends.

"Look! There's Adrian again!" exclaimed Monty. "Frank, that's Adrian," he told Frank.

"Let's crack on," said Dave, turmoil ensuing behind him. "Leave them four to bash each other to pieces. Hopefully they'll put each other out of action in the process, and that means we'll get on that top step."

"Nice!" said Monty enthusiastically, apparently enjoying the thought of that prospect. "That's the spirit! One might say you're full of the TT spirit. They should really give you an award for that..."

"They've already done, if you recall," said Dave in answer, unsure if Monty were being serious or having him on. It was often difficult to tell.

Monty smiled. "I know, Dave. I know," came his reply. "Now, let's go get them beans-on-toast!"

Chapter Eleven

Glencrutchery Road was an iconic stretch of tarmac. It had a dual purpose: a main arterial route for the Island's commuters, and, then, during racing, home to the Grandstand — the world-famous scoreboard, and, of course, the start/finish line of the most famous and challenging race anywhere. Those last few hundred metres could be the difference between heartbreak, or of the fulfilment of a lifelong dream: hurtling towards the chequered flag to be immortalised as a winner of the most challenging high-speed road race on the globe.

Many riders over the years, to their great regret, had miscalculated their fuel stop only to find the engine stuttering to an agonising stop at Governor's Dip and be forced to push their machine the final few hundred yards of Glencrutchery Road to bring her home. The margin for error over multiple laps of this circuit was nil; the machines and riders took a brutal physical hammering, and all that effort could be for nought if you'd not filled the tank to the brim or, for instance, one wire had unhelpfully shaken loose.

The saying, *"To finish first, you must first finish,"* was never more relevant than it was on the TT course.

One person who'd never tire of his view of Glencrutchery Road was Stan. It'd been a late night, but he awoke fresh, surprisingly enough, considering the time they'd gone to bed. He stood in just white underpants, watching the commuters on their way to work from his bay window, a contented expression on his face. Such was his delight at the absence of a hangover that he greeted the new morning enthusiastically, with a series of star jumps to get the blood flowing.

"Frank!" shouted Stan, mid-star jump. "Frank, I think Henk is in the garden, and he looks like he's crying! How did he not make it home? I know he was drunk, but he only lives next door!"

Frank peered around the bathroom door, toothbrush in hand. "What? Why is he crying?"

"I'm not sure, but I think he's strangling a tree. You should go and see him, for the sake of the tree if nothing else," suggested Stan.

Frank hadn't taken one step out the front door when Henk pounced. Henk wasn't wearing the same clothes as the night before, so must have at least made it home at some point, which only presented Frank with more confusion.

"I've been ringing that bell for twenty minutes!" exclaimed Henk, poking his finger desperately into it again to illustrate, recreating the act over and over again. "You didn't answer!"

Frank retreated a step. He was frightened.

"I don't think we've got a battery in it yet," he offered, tentatively. "Is, eh, everything okay, Henk? You look a little... unhinged."

Henk had the look of a complete nutter about him, eyes wide and feverishly darting in this direction and that. He looked box-of-frogs loony.

Henk fell to his knees, which, considering his height, was a considerable journey. "Frank!" he pleaded, arms reached out as if in prayer. "Please tell me I didn't bet the Vincent! Frank, tell me it was all a dream!" he beseeched, in his broken Dutch drawl.

Frank took a moment or so, out of respect, before nodding in acknowledgement. "I'm afraid so, Henk."

It was too much for Henk, who pitched forwards, head now rested against Frank's waist. Frank was new to the neighbourhood, and caught sight of the middle-aged man in the house opposite, briefcase in one hand, small girl in the other. Frank offered a salutary wave, but couldn't escape the fact he had a seven-foot crying Dutchman's head inches from his crotch. And, unfortunately, to push Henk to one side, in his current condition, would be about as wise as throwing stones at a hornet's nest.

Frank looked down on Henk serenely, placing a comforting hand on his shoulder, like a vicar blessing one of his flock.

"Henk, can you not buy another Vincent? I mean, if need be?" he put forward mildly.

"Nooo!" Henk moaned. "Do not be an *achterlijke gladiool!* That motorcycle was the object of my dreams when I was a boy! It was all my father spoke about — he loved that bike more than he did me! I had posters of it when I grew up and I swore that one day I would own one! My Vincent Black Lightning is one of the finest and rarest machines ever made! It is irreplaceable! And what made it even sweeter still was that I purchased it right from under Rodney Franks' *neus!*"

"His what?" Frank asked.

"His *neus!*" Henk reiterated, pointing to his nose. "His *neus!*"

Frank was a little underwhelmed. After all, as lovely as motorbikes were, it was still only a motorbike.

"You must be confident, though, Henk, yeah?" Frank asked. "Look, mate, sorry, but any chance you could, you know... stand up?" he suggested gently, offering a further awkward wave to another neighbour who would likely never speak to him again after this.

Henk rose and, now, at full height, loomed over Frank once more, before Frank continued.

"Look, you must be confident in Tom and Harry, right? After all, you know how good that machine is," Frank told him. "And so surely you'll win the bet?"

Henk put his hand to his head. "I *was* confident! Until I got a call from Tom this morning telling me he's fractured his wrist, fighting with Rodney's boys last night!"

"Is that the same wrist that kept him out of the TT last year?"

"Yes!" wailed Henk. "He's broken it all over again!"

Frank climbed on his toes, offering a series of friendly *it'll-all-be-okay* pats across the arm, but Henk was beyond consolation.

"There's still a few weeks till the TT, Henk," said Frank. "He'll be fine," he assured him. "Em... just out of interest, how much would a Vincent Black Lightning set one back?"

That question sent Henk's bottom lip aquiver. "I do not know, maybe five-hundred-thousand pounds! It's one of the finest and rarest motorcycles! Anywhere!" Because of the booming nature of his voice, even when Henk was quietly sobbing, it sounded as if he was shouting.

At Henk's reply, if Frank had been a cartoon character, his eyes, in response, would have extended from out their sockets and smacked into Henk's chest with an *AHH-OOO-GAH* horn sound effect. As it was, he chewed the back of his own hand, instead, to resist a reaction that would likely finish Henk off.

Frank was running out of comforting words. "It'll be okay, Henk. Tom and Harry will win both the sidecar races with ease, you'll see, and you'll have bragging rights over that wazzock, Rodney Franks, for life, and you'll own a farm on top of it all."

"I do not want a farm!" Henk answered. "Do I look like a farmer?? I only threw the farm into the bet because you mentioned it earlier in the day! If I win that farm, the pair of you are buying it off me! You and Stan were the ones putting the idea inside of my head! Do you have any beer??" he said, before realisation kicked in once more.

"*Godverdomme*, if I lose this bet I am going to lose my beautiful Vincent!"

Frank took his gnawed-up hand from his mouth. "Are you certain you want a beer, Henk? It's only nine in the morning," he said, looking at his watch. "Don't forget the Aston Martin!" he offered.

"What??" replied Henk. "What about my Aston Martin??" he asked, doubling his body mass, clearly unaware that his beloved car was at stake as well as his cherished bike.

The blood in Frank's face drained.

"Eh," he said, looking for inspiration, or a trap door to fall through. "Do you want a glass with your beer, Henk?"

Chapter Twelve

An excitable girl with an orange gingham dress and yellow bunches squealed with delight when a chocolate cake with seven flaming candles arrived on the plastic table in front of her, followed by a chorus of "Happy Birthday." Others, in for a quick meal, smiled politely, or with sympathy, at the man — presumably the girl's father — who tried, without success, to keep control of several high-energy children fuelled by burgers, chips, Coca-Cola, and, imminently, sugary cake.

Ordinarily, Stella didn't let anything disturb her Big Mac meals; she'd think nothing of smashing her fist into the heart of that cake. But, today, she sat at her usual booth, distracted, with her eyes glazed over, head bowed. She gave an expectant glance towards the sound of the door opening, but it was only the arrival of another group of giddy children — and was met with disappointment rather than frustration.

"Are you not eating tonight?" asked one of the braver members of staff, cleaning the adjacent table.

Stella took a further look at her watch, followed by a cursory glance at her phone. "No," she said, picking up her half-empty bottle of water, and shuffling across the bench. "Not tonight. I'm on a, er..."

"An ay-yure?" the staff member asked, confused.

"Ah, you know what, it doesn't matter. I'll see you tomorrow, Hayley."

Stella took one final glance around the restaurant, sticking her head into the booth behind hers, and, with the shake of her permed head, moved in the direction of the exit.

Hayley followed close behind. "Stella," she said, with what for all the world appeared to be a sincere smile. "I hope you don't mind me saying this. But I just wanted you to know you look really nice tonight. I don't think I've ever seen you in a skirt before, and it really suits you."

Stella scrutinised Hayley's face, and Hayley didn't know it but she was about nought-point-eight of a second away from being punched directly in the windpipe.

Stella soon deduced that there was no sarcastic undertone. She was caught off guard by the compliment, unsure what exactly to do with it. Stella pulled a fag from somewhere — from where, Hayley couldn't be sure; it was retrieved and dispatched to her mouth with the kind of skilful sleight-of-hand a seasoned magician could only aspire to.

Stella offered a nod of the head to Hayley, pulling up the collars on her leather jacket to protect her from the bracing chill air outside. Once outside, the rain that had threatened earlier now settled onto Stella's tightly wound perm, before spilling over, taking a layer of her mascara with it, and running down her face. The butt of her cigarette was coated with an application of cerise pink lipstick, matching the colour of her fingernails — which Stella had spent an age perfecting.

"Stupid bitch," she cursed, with a gruff, breaking voice. Another glance at her phone screen invoked a further reaction of hostility. She used the back of her hand to rub the pink lipstick from her mouth, gently at first, before rubbing like she was attempting to start a fire.

"Stupid, stupid, bitch," she repeated, causing those in her path to step gingerly to the left-hand side of the pavement.

For most of those in town the rain was an unwelcome visitor, but, for Stella, the raindrops were the perfect alibi to mask the tears that flowed freely. They weren't tears of sadness but rather tears of anger.

Her cigarette — like her hairstyling — succumbed to the heavy shower, and so a vacant bus shelter was a welcome respite.

The driver of a silver Vauxhall slowed like a kerb-crawler. The passenger window wound down as the driver leaned over. "Give you a lift, Stella?" came a familiar voice from within the taxi. The taxi was one replete with Frank 'n' Stan's logo plastered all over its rear quarter.

Stella shook her head. "No, Bert. Thank you," she replied.

"Why are you getting the bus? You okay, Stella?" pressed Bert. "You look nice tonight, Stella, by the way."

"What's it to you, Bert?" she said, rearing up, normal service resumed. "If you're taking the piss out of me, Bert, I'll run you over with your own bloody car!"

Bert offered a hand out in submission, "No, Stella. I'm not taking the piss." Bert, like most who possessed sense, was not brave enough or stupid enough to do such a thing.

Stella paused for a moment and a rare tinge of guilt ran through her. "I'm sorry, Bert. Thank you for the offer. I was supposed to be having a, eh, meeting with Lee tonight. But I must have gotten my days mixed up."

Bert scratched his chin. *"Hrm,* I'm sure I heard his name over the radio, earlier. You want me to check on this here thing?" he offered, pointing to the box-like modern technological device stuck to the inside of his taxi's windscreen.

"No," said Stella. "Actually, yes," she said, changing her mind instantly.

Bert mashed his fingers on the screen; it was fairly evident he'd not embraced this new-fangled gadgetry. "Are you sure you didn't want a lift? It's a shitty night and this rain's going to get heavier later," he said. "Ah, wait, here we go, Stella. Tommy dropped him off at a quarter to eight at MacArthur's."

"Is that the expensive steakhouse?" asked Stella.

"Yeah. That's the one. I can take you there, if you like?" Bert suggested.

Stella dropped her freshly-ignited fag, jumping into the back of the taxi. "Yes please, Bert. And turn that rear-view mirror this way, would you? I need to sort out my makeup."

"Are you wearing perfume?" asked Bert. "It's nice!"

Stella was more accepting of the second compliment of the evening. She forgot herself, almost releasing a titter, before remembering herself once again. "Keep your eyes on the road, you cheeky old get," she demanded. "And you can turn that meter off, for starters!"

Bert averted his eyes, and, wishing to remain in good health this night, the meter was duly switched off as instructed.

"Did you go to the wrong meeting place?" he asked, once his daring had returned.

"What?" snapped Stella, before taking a severe slug from a hip flask.

"Where did you wait for him?"

"McDonald's," she replied, with a *that's-not-stupid-though* look on her face. "That could explain it," she said, less abruptly, her expression softening. "He mentioned food, and I heard *Mac*, and my mind defaulted naturally to a burger. Do you want a slug?" she offered, waving the hip flask like a flag.

"Thanks, Stella, but, eh, I'm good," he said, eying the flask with caution. "Is that some sort of test, by the way?" he enquired. But, with the arrival at their destination only moments later, Bert would never know the answer.

"No tip?" he asked, catching more than an eyeful of the departing Stella as she exited the vehicle.

"You want a tip? Right, then. Never trust a fart," she offered with sage-like assurance. "You'll lose, eventually."

Stella wasn't overly gushing with praise, as was her nature, but Bert knew the rattle on the side door was her way of expressing her gratitude.

With Bert off on his way again, Stella sheltered under the awning of the shop next door to the MacArthur's restaurant, checking her phone once more. "I'm sure he said *McDonald's*," she said to herself, aloud, before taking another mouthful of Dutch courage.

The high street was, sadly, not as it once was. The independent shops there had long since vacated in favour of betting shops, charity shops, and takeaway outlets. To find an establishment the calibre of the newly-opened steakhouse was welcome — although likely a misjudgement on the part of the owners, considering the run-down nature of the street.

Stella ran her hands over her hair, removing the excess water in a manner akin to squeezing a sponge. That sorted, she turned her attention to another matter: unfortunately, the combination of walking and sitting had played havoc with the hosiery and lingerie departments on her person. Her knickers were in a pitched battle with her tights to see which could make further progression up her gluteal divide; it felt like cheese wire cutting her in two. She looked left, and then right, before taking the plunge.

She gripped the back of her skirt with her left hand and ran her right hand down the contours of her posterior cheeks, removing unwelcome fabric like a plough through a field. But her knickers were nothing if not tenacious, and the last hurdle wouldn't budge. This was to be a two-handed job.

And so she hitched up the rear of her skirt, using the glass window to secure it in place. She now had free reign to delve in with both hands, and, no matter how obstinate, her knickers would not have standing to resist a sustained assault of this type for long. With inevitable victory thus secured, she whisked her tights down, taking the opportunity to restore order where once there had been none.

Such was the well-practised military precision of the operation — Stella having fought this same campaign many times before — that those passing in the road were none the wiser. The same could not be said, however, for the unfortunate cleaner who'd just reported for duty in the shop behind which glass frontage Stella was stood. The grey-haired gentleman holding a mop wore a solemn, haunted expression, with his lower jaw swinging loose.

This poor chap had just seen things that would be impossible to unsee, the horror of which would plague him for the remainder of his now sad, hopeless existence. And, to add salt to the wound, it was his job to have to remove the symmetrical grease patch left behind from Stella's tremendous behind.

At Stella's end, with her mission officially and successfully accomplished, green rope and mood lighting directed Stella towards the entrance of MacArthur's restaurant. She eased open the door, releasing a burst of warm air, stinging her reddened cheeks (those located in the upper bodily quadrant, that is). The quality of the décor was matched only by the glorious aroma emanating from the kitchen, though the patrons on several of the tables offered her a less-than-discreet glance over the rim of their wine glasses.

Stella examined each table in turn — to the apparent discomfort of those seated — but there was no sign of Lee. Stella put her hip flask back in her bag — now was not the time for a quick nip — and ventured further up the restaurant where it became clear it was an L-shaped floor plan with an additional room at the rear, housing several more tables.

An impressive fish tank built into the wall served as a partition between the two sections of the eatery. Stella pressed her nose to the thick glass but her view into the other room was contorted by the movement of the water. She heard a laugh she recognised. Her entire face was pressed flat against the cold glass; it would have been quite the vision had those on the other side possessed the inclination to look in that direction.

But no one in the room beyond the fish tank looked in her direction. Stella's heart sank. The room was empty apart from the owner of the familiar laugh and the brunette lady sat opposite. Although Stella's view was distorted, it was clear what was going on.

She felt a fool.

Embarrassed, she took a step back, followed by several deep breaths. *Get out of here, you stupid cow,* she instructed herself.

"Can I help?" asked the woman who'd come up behind Stella. It was delivered, however, in a tone which didn't suggest that any help was actually on offer. In point of fact, there was a distinct *what-the-fuck-are-you-doing-in-my-restaurant* connotation to the tone.

The woman was a good five inches shorter than Stella but carried a certain air of authority, with her jet-black hair tied tightly back, and, on her nose, brown-rimmed glasses perched — which she looked down through. For someone so lacking in height, it must be said, she did a remarkable job of looking down on someone.

"Well?" the woman demanded.

Stella went to move around her. "I was just looking for... I'm sorry, it's a big mistake. My mistake," she said, uncharacteristically conciliatory.

The woman — the owner/proprietor — put her hand across Stella's path to prevent her exit.

Ordinarily, this course of action would have resulted in broken bones, a serious choking, or often both. But there was no wind left in Stella's sails, and she went to move again, offering a whimpered "sorry" as she did so.

The proprietor was not content to accept an apology, raising her voice to an extent that all eyes in the restaurant were now on Stella.

"I'm fed up with people like you!" bellowed the woman. "We've invested money into this community to try and make it a better area to live, and the thanks we get is your sort in here every night trying to use the toilets, or, more than likely, steal purses from the cloakroom. We've had enough of it! Coming in here looking like that, it's not on! Now you mind yourself, and you tell the rest of your lot that you're not welcome in here. Ever!"

Stella stared for a moment. But she didn't have anything to offer in return. Not this time.

Audible murmurings of disgust were issued forth by those seated, with Stella opting for as dignified an exit as she could muster under the circumstance. She was dumbstruck; her legs like jelly. It took every ounce of strength to make it down the stairs without the floodgates opening. Once outside, she sat on the bottom step, allowing her head to drop to her knees.

The cleaner from the nearby shop had now ventured outside as well, busying himself sorting out the remnants of Stella's earlier contribution. He'd wrapped a tea towel around his face like a cowboy in a sandstorm. A wet cloth hung from a broom handle, which he used to remove the violation on his window from a suitably safe distance. And then he noticed Stella.

"Can I help you there, miss?" he asked, clearly not recognising Stella from a frontal trajectory, but Stella just shook her head.

"I've got this," said a voice from the figure now trailing down the stairs behind Stella. "But thanks," the owner of the voice called over to the workman.

Lee sat next to Stella and put his arm around her shoulder. "You're quite the topic of conversation in the restaurant, you know," he said.

She didn't look up. "You didn't see me. How did you know it was me?" she eventually replied.

"The waitress said there'd been a kerfuffle with a prostitute trying to use the toilets again. She said she was glad it wasn't her that chucked you out because you were pretty scary, with hair like Velcro. I pretty much figured it was you at that point."

Stella grunted in response.

"The owner realised her mistake," Lee went on. "She's very sorry and says you're welcome back in, if you'd like, for a complimentary meal."

Stella lifted her head, wiping her face. "I've been sat in McDonald's all night. I thought I'd got the date wrong. Or something."

"McDonald's?" Lee said. "Honestly, now. Do you think I'd take you on a date to McDonald's? Not on yer nelly. Stella, come on, I've got a bit more class and you deserve a bit better than that for our third date. I haven't a notion how to work this bloody phone properly," he said by way of explanation. "It must have autocorrected or *I-don't know-what*, and here I've been sat all night thinking you've stood me up!"

"So they thought I was a prostitute?" said Stella with a grin.

"That's a good thing?" asked Lee.

Stella pondered that thought for a moment. "When you're often referred to as a bloke, a prostitute is at least heading in the right direction. At least prostitutes are female."

"Not always," replied Lee in an instant.

"Not helping, Lee. And you seem to know a lot about the subject."

"I've bought you something, Stella," said Lee after a moment, handing Stella a white plastic bag. She sighed, giving her cheek a further wipe with the back of her hand. "What is it?"

"Open it and see, whydontcha."

She pulled out a large piece of black fabric which she gently unfolded before holding it out in front of her. "It's a picture of a motorbike?" she said, surprised.

"And so it is," replied Lee cheerfully.

Stella's face turned to thunder. "Are you calling me a bike, you cheeky bastard? The town bike?? Because, if you are, I'll do to you what I should have done to that stuck-up cow in the restaurant!"

"Jeez, no! No, of course I'm not," protested Lee, gently easing Stella's clenched fist back to a resting position. "It's an Isle of Man TT shirt. Take a gander, that's the map of the island around the motorbike."

"I don't get it?" said Stella, not getting it.

"Look, Stella. I know we've only had two and a half dates, but it's the Isle of Man TT next month. I wondered — well, hoped — that I could take you over to the TT? I've spoken with Frank and Stan and we can stay with them. It's all sorted."

"Sordid, you mean?" she replied.

Stella retained a look of suspicion, certain that Lee was having her on, and going to punctuate his sentence with *"just kidding"* or similar. But he didn't. Instead, he stared kindly into Stella's eyes and used the back of his hand to wipe the remaining tears off her face.

She coughed, clearing her throat. "I'd... you know, quite actually, em... like that. And I can wear the t-shirt," she added, holding it out once more, now divining its purpose.

"That would be grand," Lee answered.

"Lee, who was the girl you were sat with? Not that it matters, but, you know... I just..."

Lee leaned forward and placed the simplest of kisses on Stella's cheek.

"That was the waitress! I told you I was rubbish on the phone. I'd texted you three times to see where you were, but I got some error message. I think I was sending you a message over the internet when I didn't have Wi-Fi. Something like that. So the waitress was showing me how to send a—"

Ping-Ping-Ping

With impeccable timing, Stella's phone lit up with three consecutive messages.

"Come on. Let's go and eat her free sympathy meal," said Lee, pointing back up to the restaurant. "I hope you're hungry!"

Stella chuckled. "You needn't worry there. She's going to need to get more staff on in the kitchen!" she replied, patting her stomach. "Lee..." she said, yanking on his arm as he rose. "Only that entire restaurant thinks I'm a prostitute."

Lee gently lifted her up, helping Stella to her feet.

"It's better than being a bloke, Stella, you said it yourself. Besides, so what if they think you're a working girl. It's a posh restaurant, so at least they'll suppose you're a classy one. They might think you're high-rent!"

"High-rent, that's me all over," replied Stella with a generous portion of sarcasm. She stopped again before they reached the door.

"What is it?" Lee asked.

"Look, when we open this door..." she told him. "They're all going to be staring at us."

"Let them?" he replied.

"No, listen," she explained. "I'm going to tell them you came out for a quick hand job, right?"

"Let's crack on, then!" replied Lee, laughing, and without the slightest bit of concern. "And considering some of those women had faces on them like burst trout, you might pick up some new 'customers' from the gents in here!"

"Excellent," she said, taking one further slug from the hip flask.

Outside the shop, the cleaner had a tender smile on his face, pleased for the young couple starting out on a new romantic chapter in their lives. Okay, it wasn't quite Mills and Boon, but sweet nonetheless. His starry-eyed distraction came crashing back to earth with the realisation that the arse grease on his window wasn't budging and he'd have to redouble his efforts. He held out his arms to measure the length of the imprint, rather like a fisherman explaining the size of his catch, as his brain struggled to interpret what he was seeing.

He shuddered. "That's a whole lot of loving," he said, putting his back into the job at hand.

Chapter Thirteen

June 1979

"The Garden Tools are a rusty shadow of their former self."

"Someone please put The Garden Tools back in the shed!"

The tabloid press were the makers of men, and, sadly, also the breakers. Just like the seasons, fashions changed as did tastes in music. The Garden Tools rode the crest of their wave, with money coming into one pocket hand-over-fist, but going out the other just as quickly. Sold-out concerts and in-demand TV appearances, once common for TGT, were now a thing of the past.

The band had earned and spent more than most would see in a lifetime, but, for Frank and Stan, they could see the writing was on the wall and their business model was to make sure all of their eggs weren't stored in the same basket. Sure, they'd done their best for the lads, but ultimately the band's overindulgence in drugs, alcohol, and other excess — along with the capricious nature of public favour (or lack thereof) — had undone all Frank and Stan's hard work in the case of the Tools.

Still, with Stan's dramatic flair and Frank's charismatic persona, their talent agency had grown to one of the largest in London. There were new premises, new staff, a new townhouse, and the latest cars. Their acts filled the dance halls and music venues and seeing first-hand how fickle the public could be, they ensured they had acts on their books that covered all genres and age groups. On any given day they'd be arranging country & western acts, punk bands, or even classical musicians, for instance.

What they were selling, people wanted, and on the uber-trendy London social scene, Frank and Stan were very much "A-list," counting celebrities, sport stars, and politicians amongst their social circle. One tabloid that'd been so eager, early on, to stick the boot into their first signing, were now equally keen to laud them as two of the country's most eligible bachelors under thirty.

Frank was happy, it should be said, to reap the benefits of that 'eligible bachelor' title — often, in fact, more than once in the same evening — but, for Stan, it was a different story. He was adept at concealing his true persuasion and whilst tolerance had increased over the course of the decade, there was still an undertone which made leaving the closet door carefully closed the preferred choice. There'd been romantic dalliances, but nothing of merit, certainly nothing constituting anything meaningful. This played heavily on Frank's mind, but, his friend was content — at least on the surface.

Meanwhile, business in the seventies was very much about who you knew, and talent alone would not a career make. This was overwhelmingly the case in the music management business where competition was fierce with the financial stakes considerable. Palms were often greased with those expecting their cut for facilitating an introduction, or, perhaps, turning a blind eye when required. It was the acceptable way of doing things; those adept at playing the game prospered, and those that didn't, well, didn't.

Charged with bringing financial order to Frank and Stan's empire was Craggy Sally — as she was affectionately known — a spirited lady of a certain age. Her once-proud mane of shoulder-length blonde hair was now kept yellow by a coating of nicotine residue, rather like the index and middle fingers of her left hand. Her skin gave the appearance of someone who'd used butter rather than suncream in her youth, and years of sucking one fag after another resulted in an outer epidermal layer that could well use the benefit of an iron.

... And so it was, one day at the office, that Stan clapped the side of his face, and then examined the palm of his hand for a trace of blood. "What the hell was that?" he said, looking for a wasp or some other tiny-but-vicious winged assailant.

"It was me, you daft shit!" shouted Sally, pointing her gammy arm at the projectile on the floor with such force that her bingo wings flapped like a flag in the breeze. "Get your arse in here, and bring my pen in!" she commanded.

Stan did as he was told, as it was unwise to make Craggy Sally even more cross than usual.

With Stan in supplication before her, and without looking up from the erratic pile of papers strewn over her desk, she thrust one with a barely legible scrawl written on it in his direction.

"What's this?" she demanded.

"That would be a receipt, Sally?" replied Stan, in an overly cheery inflexion. "You told me to always keep receipts, so that's what I've done."

"This isn't a receipt, this is a piece of scruffy paper with a name I've never heard of." Still holding the paper out, she took her cigarette out of her mouth, and, with it between her fingers, tapped the front of the document sharply. Ashes dropped to the carpet in the process.

"*This*," she said. "*ABC Talent Management*," she continued, without having to look. Then, she placed her fag back in her mouth and lifted her head up, looking at Stan directly. "Who the hell are they?" she asked, flicking the paper like a matador taunting its wounded quarry.

Stan moved to close her office door, looking cautiously over his shoulder as he did so. "*Ah-ha*, Sally!" he said moving closer, holding his hand aloft as if all was well in the world. "They're a consultancy company we're working with."

The furrows on Sally's forehead deepened further than they were already, further than Stan thought possible for a forehead.

"Consultancy!" she yelled. "You're paying a consultant I've never heard of a hundred pounds a week! What the hell are they consulting on??"

Stan fanned his hands at Sally, which was never a good idea. "It's fine, Sally. It's a company that's been doing some work for us."

"And Frank knows about this?"

"Of course he does. Well, he will when I tell him. Look, Sally," he said, moving to a position of rest on the corner of her desk. "In our line of work, we sometimes have to pay out a little bit to people who are able to help us expand our reach, or perhaps—"

"Do I look bloody stupid, Stan? Do I? You've paid — whoever this is — over two thousand pounds in the last six months. If this money is for consultancy payments, then I haven't got a hole in my arse."

"Lovely imagery there, Sally. Thanks for that. Look, it's a facilitation fee," he offered, with more hand-waving. "In our line of business, we need to work with people who can, you know, get other people to take our calls, or, perhaps, as importantly, not take the calls of our competition."

Sally was not so easily swayed. "You can't afford this sort of money to be going out," she said, devoid of humour.

"It'll be fine, Sally. We've never been busier!" Stan said, trying his best to reassure her.

"Are you stupid?" asked Sally. "Seriously, just how stupid are you? Do you or Frank have any idea what's going on? I've been telling you this for months. You're spending too much!"

Stan opened his mouth to speak, but Sally didn't give him the chance.

"*This* is the *incoming* receipts," she went on, pointing at a small pile in the tray on one side of her desk. "But *this* is the *outgoings*," she said, pointing at the much larger pile sat in the tray on the opposite side.

Stan shifted his weight from one foot to another. This time he did not try to speak. It was clear Sally wasn't finished.

"You don't have to be a mathematical genius to figure out that more going out than coming in does not make for a healthy business. You two, the pair of you, have been haemorrhaging cash. And it's not sustainable. You'll be bankrupt if you carry on as you are, so sort this shit out!"

Stan thought it was his turn to speak, but it wasn't, as it turned out, not quite yet...

"I'm too old and angry to get a position anywhere else, and I need this job, Stan," she said. "Promise me one thing, Stan?" she went on. "That bloke you had in here a few weeks ago? Tommy Banks? He's bad news. Trust me, I've been in this town longer than you, and I know it for a fact. I hope for your sake you've not gotten into business with him. Now, I say this with all sincerity," she added, her anger replaced with genuine concern. "You lot need to get your affairs in order."

Stan smiled, offering up a cheeky wink. "Sally, I appreciate your concern, honestly I do, but all is well. Everything's right as rain, I promise!" he said, blowing a kiss in her direction.

Seven weeks later...

"You must be mistaken?" said Frank, taking his feet off the table. He put a finger in the ear not glued to the receiver. "I can hear what you're saying... sorry, Mitchell, was it?" And, then, "Sorry. Michael. I misheard. Very much like I'm not hearing you correctly now."

Frank listened intently, the shades of red in his face progressively intensifying, before he closed with, "Thank you, Michael. I will speak with Stan." He got up and strode out of his office, with grim and determined purpose.

"*Saaaaaally!*" he hollered, drawing out the letter A in her name for at least the length of the corridor separating their offices, only stopping when he'd all but taken her door off its hinges.

"I've just had Mitchell on the phone from the bank!" he announced.

Sally drew on her cigarette with pursed lips, leaving a rim of vibrant red lipstick when removed.

"It's *Michael*. And I know. I just spoke to him and advised him to call you directly."

Frank paced back and forth like a frenzied, caged animal, gripping the hair atop his head every time he came to a halt.

"Two things, Sally. One, *you're* the accountant, so why's he phoning *me*? And, two, *where the hell is all of our money??*"

"Yes, I *am* your accountant, but you don't listen to me, do you?" Sally replied. "You never have. Also, don't swear. I've got my granddaughter with me today."

Frank gave a conciliatory glance to the child sat on the sofa behind the door, initially out of view, holding a hand to his mouth in reference to his cursing and to his tone. "I'm sorry. What's your name, sweetie?" he asked.

"Stella," the little girl answered, putting her toy down on her knee.

Frank smiled. "Your bear hasn't got himself a head. Did it fall off?"

"I ripped it off," said the girl matter-of-factly and without further explanation.

"Oh, okay, then," said Frank, returning his attention to Sally.

"You don't listen to me, Frank. I've been telling you for ages that you're pissing your money up against the wall — well, Stan, mainly — so I thought I'd have the bank talk to you directly rather than through me. I thought you might listen to *them*, if not me. And, by the fact you're stood here, mission accomplished, I might add."

Frank tried to answer, but, like Stan, had to wait his turn because Sally was not finished with him yet.

"Did you actually read any of the reports I left on your desk?" she asked. "Or register any of the times I told you that the finances were not in rude health?"

"Stan's the money-man, Sally. You know this. I look after the acts, I don't do money."

"You like spending it, though," was her reply.

"I do," said Frank, pacing once more. "But I didn't think that would be a problem as we had so much coming in. Em... don't we?"

"We do," replied Sally, picking up the small stack from the one tray to illustrate, and then setting it back down and picking up the larger stack from the expenditures pile. "But you've got much more going out. See?"

"Are you skint, mister?" asked the child, once she'd taken the bear's head from out of her mouth.

"What? No!" Frank replied. Then he turned to his accountant. "Wait. Sally. Are we? We can't be... can we? Not if we have all of this money coming in, surely?"

"Cashflow, Frank," said Sally, smashing the pen tip into the desk like a pneumatic drill. "Cashflow is everything! You're nearly at the limit of your overdraft. And, if the money goes out before it comes in, you are, as Stella pointed out, broke! Or at least will be, very soon. If the bank doesn't extend your credit line, you'll lose everything."

"You're broke," repeated Stella.

"Does she need to be here?" asked Frank.

Stella, in response, merely popped her toy bear's head back in her mouth.

"But where is it all going?" Frank continued. "The money, I mean. I've not signed a cheque or been to the bank for months. Is Stan ripping me off??"

Sally shrugged her shoulders. "I can account for every single penny that's been spent for the last five years. Every penny. But you'll need to ask Stan why so much of it has been going to certain areas, since my own enquiries put to him in that regard have yielded very little information," she said, pushing a slip of paper in Frank's direction.

He picked it up. "Is this right?" he asked. "We've paid this ABC company thousands? What the hell?"

Sally placed her head on the desk. "Frank, I've told you this at least five times already. And, it was in the report I left on your desk as well. Again, did you bother to read it?"

"Maybe, *erm*...? Actually, ah... no. No, I haven't," he admitted. "I'm not so good at reading things."

"Or at handling money. What *are* you actually good at?" Sally asked, her patience failing. "Anything at all?"

"Mucking things up?" suggested Stella from her perch on the couch.

"She's quite the charmer, your granddaughter, isn't she? Simply delightful!" Frank remarked, apparently not appreciating the young girl's keen insight.

"She's got a point, Frank. You're shit with money and you're shit at reading. How you've come to any success at all is a mystery to me."

"Charm?" Frank proposed feebly.

"Imagine how successful you could be if you were *actually good at things*," she told him.

Frank was about to protest. He hadn't come into Sally's office to suffer abuse, after all. But, he needed her.

"What do we do now, then?" asked Frank.

"You want my opinion?" said Stella.

"No, I don't want your opinion, Stella! I'm asking your gran, my *accountant!*" Frank cried. "Although... if you've got any ideas...?"

Sally, interrupting, punched her calculator with a flurry of sharp jabs and then thrust it in Frank's face.

Frank curled up his lip in shock.

"We need to find that much?? By when?"

Sally put her hand to her head. "You poor, sorry, stupid bastard. You don't need to find that amount only *once*," she told him. "You need to stop spending that amount *each month*. Otherwise, you're done for. You'll lose the houses, cars, everything. And you can go a good way to meeting that target by not paying this *ABC-Whotsis* company," she said, pen rat-a-tat-tatting once more on the desk. "Who are they?"

"I haven't got the faintest idea!" declared Frank.

"That's hardly a surprise," said the child in the corner, removing the bear's head from her mouth and shaking it in Frank's direction.

This garnered a coarse laugh from Craggy Sally, along with a look of affection and pride at her granddaughter.

"I need to speak with Stan," Frank decided aloud. "Where the hell is he? Oh, I know. He'll be with his boyfr–" He stopped himself abruptly, midsentence.

Sally rolled her eyes. "Do you think I'm dead from the neck up? I know Stan doesn't like women."

"Everybody knows," Stella added.

"Anyway, he's been spending too much time with his friend lately," Frank groused. "What's his name again?"

"Harold," Sally told him. "Though god knows why he should spend so much time with him, what with me here on offer every day," she added, whilst using her cigarette lighter to dislodge a foreign body from her ear canal.

"Right. Harold," replied Frank. "Stan's been too preoccupied lately. He's taken his eye off the ball."

"And onto a pair of them," remarked Stella.

"She's quick, this one!" said Frank, ruffling the girl's overwhelmingly curly hair.

Stella, in turn, eyed him with suspicion.

"You'll go far, young Stella. Just don't smoke like Granny, okay? and you just may stick around a bit longer. "Now, here," he said, producing a few coins from his pocket and trying his best to get rid of her. "Take this and buy yourself some sweets. May as well, before the bank takes it all from me. Just not too many sweets, you don't want to get fat, yeah? Right, off you go, then."

Frank moved back to Sally. "If we cut this ABC payment out, we should be okay?"

"It'd help."

"Can you give me the total amount we've paid to them? Everything, all told?"

"It's in the report. On your desk," replied Sally.

"Great. Young Stella," said Frank, turning to leave. "It's been a pleasure to meet you. I do hope your bear gets better?" he offered.

"I don't," said Stella, though not very clearly, because the bear's head was back in her mouth once again.

"If you see Stan before I do, tell him I'm looking for him!" Frank called over his shoulder as he exited.

"Alright," said Stella.

"Not you!" Frank answered her, exasperated. "Your granny! But... you know what? Fine. If you should see him. Yeah. Thank you."

Back in his own office, Frank fell into his chair once again. It was an office he shared with Stan, and he glared with contempt at the empty seat opposite. The glimmering framed gold discs hung on the wall — a symbol of their acts' chart successes — brought him little comfort due to the mood he was in, and he blurted out several incoherent expletives as he reached for the bottle of aged whisky stored in his bottom drawer. There was no requirement for the glass, with Frank opting to take a generous slug directly from the bottle — liquid courage, perhaps — preparing for the review of the file from Sally that'd sat on his desk for days.

Reading spectacles were retrieved and placed on a nose screwed up with anger. A further slug from the bottle and with his index finger tracing along the lines of the document, he tried to make sense of the figures he found there. Thirty seconds later, he threw his hands up in defeat. He couldn't work out what he was seeing. After all, that's what he paid his accountant for!

"*Sally!*" he screamed without moving from his chair.

"Just look at the numbers I've highlighted in yellow!" returned a response echoed down the hallway after a brief lull. This was followed promptly thereafter by a child's laughter.

"Ah!" he said, calculator at the ready, but it wasn't required. He followed the accounting line for *ABC*, and such was the span of it that he had to moisten his finger to turn the page.

"Shit," he said, tapping his thumb quicker than a woodpecker's pecker. "Bollocks... what the...? Aww, shit... bollocks..." he said, continuing the theme of incoherent fury.

"Right!" he said, pushing himself from his chair. "Where's the key for the safe?" he said, shouting again.

After another brief lull, a garbled response returned which Frank couldn't decipher, apart from a few choice unrepeatable words.

He rummaged through Stan's drawers and felt a pang of guilt for doing so, but he had to know. He was also wracked with the frustration that he should have been asking these questions months ago.

There was no key to be found.

It seemed unlikely the safe would be left unlocked, but, without the key, there was little else to be done but to check anyway.

It had been that long since he'd been in the safe, Frank had forgotten which gold disc it was hidden behind. In fact, now he thought on it, he couldn't remember ever going into the safe at all. Nevertheless, for some reason, he thought it must have been hidden behind one of the gold discs hung on the wall.

There were a baker's dozen, and one by one he peered behind each. Some were easier to reach than others, at eye level, while others required a fair bit of stretching to get at. The last of the lot, lucky number 13, would require something to stand on. He placed Stan's desk chair in position and stepped up on it, rising to the challenge. The chair took his weight with ease, but the wheels — and the several whiskeys — made ascent rather precarious, with Frank's legs wobbling like those of a new-born foal. Sweat ran down his spine, and he could feel his back tense up both from his efforts to keep his balance as well as the stress of the current situation.

"You're bloody kidding me!" he shouted as the last disc revealed nothing, shaking his fist to the heavens. Unfortunately, his balance being precarious as it was, that wasn't the best thing to do, as it turned out, and he tumbled to the floor like a large sack of potatoes. "Bastard!" he said, because there was little else to be said at this point.

"What's all the ruckus? The safe isn't in—" began Sally, but she stopped short as she entered Frank's office and surveyed the scene, with him laid on the floor on his back and Stan's chair spinning round in circles.

"What are you...?"

"I'm, eh... doing some exercises? Exercises, that's it. Got to stay fit," Frank put forth.

"Fucksake, you really are a daft bugger," she replied, shaking her head in dismay. "I came to tell you the safe's not in here. But here's the key," she said, holding it out for him. "Not that it'll do you any good."

"Help me up, will you?" Frank pleaded.

After he'd dusted himself off, he held the key in his hand, unsure what to do with it. "Hang on, what do you mean it won't do me any good?"

"Because it's unlocked already. And there's nothing in it, besides."

"There's nothing—? *Have we been robbed??*" Frank wailed.

"You great pillock," Sally sighed. "There's never been anything in the safe."

"Pillock," a young voice reiterated.

"Didn't I give you some money to bugger off and buy sweets??" Frank replied at the sound of the higher-trebled voice.

"The safe has always been kept open, with nothing inside of it," Sally explained to a confused Frank. "To fool burglars into thinking there was nothing to steal. At least that was you and Stan's reasoning at the start. Don't you remember?"

"What? But that doesn't even—"

"Make sense?" Sally answered. "Yes, I know. But this is the sort of absolutely sterling logic to which I've grown accustomed from you two bellend boys whilst working here."

"Bellend Boys," Stella giggled.

"Not helping, Stella," said Frank, shooting the girl a look.

"I presume you're trying to figure out what Stan's been up to? Have you tried his filing cabinet?" suggested Sally.

"He's got a filing cabinet?"

"You both do!" replied Sally with despair. "I don't know why I bother, really I don't. Here," she said, removing a key from her chain. "Here's the spare key to both cabinets. Have at it!"

Frank foraged through the first cabinet, aware that Stan could return at any time. "Empty! I'm guessing, er... I'm guessing this one must be mine, then," he said, sliding it shut, before returning his attention to the second cabinet.

"Here we go," he said as the key opened the lock. This one gave the appearance of belonging to someone with a greater degree of organisation. Frank thumbed through several files, but he didn't know what to anticipate. He half expected to find a file marked *ABC*, but life wasn't often that generous. Still, fortune, as it would happen, seemed to be on Frank's side. He looked over his shoulder before removing a tatty-looking white envelope and removing the contents.

His left hand hung loose, the envelope dropping to the floor, as Frank gawked.

"Stella, can you please do me a favour and go to the shop? There's a good girl."

Frank's hand trembled, with the photograph firmly in his grip.

Sally could see from Frank's face the graveness of the situation. She pressed gently on Stella's back. "Go on, luv," she instructed. "Do as he says, dear."

Frank rubbed his eyes with thumb and forefinger, and then opened them again to confirm what he'd just seen was still, in fact, what he'd just seen.

"Sally..." was all he said, passing the black & white photo over to her.

"Oh my," came her reply. "Hell's bells. Stan, you very naughty boy. Frank, how's he managed to even get himself into that position? I don't even..." she said, turning the photograph several different directions.

Frank shook his head. "Sally, forget about what they're doing, and what position they're in, or what that aubergine has endured," he said. "Just look at the person that he's doing it all with."

Sally looked at the photo, up to Frank, and then back down once again. "Holy fuckballs, Frank. Is that who I think it is?"

Frank took the opportunity to retrieve his bottle of whisky. "It is that, Sally. That is indeed who you think it is," he said, taking a generous mouthful from the bottle. "Oh, Stan. Stan, Stan. What the bloody hell have you gotten yourself into?"

Chapter Fourteen

In a little over a week's time, pit lane would be home to organised chaos. Precious seconds on a fuel stop, or, a shaking hand on a tyre change could be the difference between TT glory or a trip home on the boat wondering if next year, perhaps, might instead be your year. There was no margin for error if you wanted to be on the top step of the podium. One mistake, no matter how slight, and someone else as hungry for victory as you was then snapping at your heels.

Teams had started to arrive on the Island for what was the pinnacle of their racing calendar; it simply didn't come any bigger than the TT. Parc fermé and the paddock — empty for months — were, once again, welcoming their guests for the better part of a month. Gargantuan race trucks were equally as welcome as the rusty transit vans which would be home to these warriors of the tarmac. The Island, so tranquil and sedate for most of the year, was about to come alive, yet again, with the unadulterated sounds of majestic horsepower of mechanical steed. The atmosphere was changing — it was charged with tension, optimism, hope, a daring to believe, and, for most, a healthy respect and desire that everyone arriving would make it back home, when all was said and done, unharmed.

A gang of wide-eyed children were circulating around the race trucks, hopeful of a glimpse of their sporting heroes, or, more likely, in hopes the teams with their merchandise would throw a t-shirt or cap their way — which they most often did.

"Excuse me, mister. Are you Dave Quirk?" asked one small boy, resting on the crossbar of his bicycle.

Dave eyed him warily, waiting for a barbed comment or maybe an egg to be thrown at him. Dave nodded in confirmation that he was indeed himself and no other, but kept one eye out for a covert attack.

The little boy — ten or maybe eleven — reached into his pocket, resulting in Dave taking a precautionary step back. The boy shouted over to his friends, "I told you it was him!" With the others gathering round, the boy then presented his mobile to set up a shot. "Mister Quirk, you're our favourite rider. Can we have a photo?"

"Did Monty put you up to this?" Dave laughed, but didn't wait for a response, rather jumping in the middle and going with it. He was three times the size of his fan club members, but gave a genuine and not-at-all affected grin. His ego was bolstered further when another child mentioned a snapshot he'd taken of Dave and Monty the previous year, asking if Dave would sign it. The boy thumbed through his pile of unsigned pictures excitedly until reaching the image in question.

"Sure!" said Dave, obligingly. "I think this is the first picture I've been asked to sign, actually. If you hang about, maybe I can find Monty to sign it for you as well."

Dave crouched down on one knee, placing the picture on the top of his thigh. "Writing implement, my good man?" he asked of the child, receiving promptly, upon request, a biro in return. This kid was clearly an accomplished autograph hunter.

"This is a cracking picture," remarked Dave. "Did you take it?"

"Yes!" came the reply, with the boy swelling with pride. "My dad took me out to watch."

"It's cracking," said Dave again. The reason for the chatter was that he had no real idea what to write or what sort of signature to do. "Do you want me to dedicate it?" he asked.

"Yes, please," came the polite reply from the golden-skinned child. "My name is Theodopolis."

"*Bless you,*" said Dave, but received only blank faces in return. "Oh, you're being serious. How do you spell that?"

Familiar with that question, the boy — ever the consummate professional — produced a pre-written card with his name on it, presumably to avoid erroneous entries on his prized photographs.

Dave drew a small line on the card, ensuring the flow of the pen was fluid. "To T-H-E-O-D-O-P-O-L-I-S," he said, announcing every letter as he wrote. "Yours faithfully," he said, admiring the neatness of his handwriting. He pressed down to deliver a seamless signature that would adorn the wall of his young admirer for life. A final glance up to absorb the pride in the boy's face spurred Dave on, but as he pressed down he heard the sickening sound of a tear.

The pen had sunken straight through the picture, coming to a halt when it met the surface of his jeans. The boy, unaware at this point, continued to smile.

"This picture," said Dave, clearing his throat, nodding down as if the child needed a reminder of what the picture looked like. "Is, eh, this picture the only copy you have?"

"Yes!" said the boy. "The only one in the world! That's why it's so special. I took it on my dad's camera before he returned to Greece with work. He would be so proud of me to know I've managed to get it signed." The boy's face beamed, radiantly, as pure as extra-virgin olive oil.

Dave cupped the pen with his other hand, engaging the child in further chit-chat. He slid his hand down the shaft of the pen, using the tip of his finger to feel for the damage without moving his eyeline. *Bastard*, he thought.

"Theodopolis. You know how this picture is the only one? In the world?" continued Dave. "Well, I think this is the very best picture of me that I've ever seen. I think it would look absolutely fantastic in my van. Would you like to see my van? No, no, forget about that, Theo, that came out all wrong," he said, holding out a pacifying arm. "I think I'd really like to buy your photograph for my van. Would you like to sell it to me?"

The boy thought for a moment. "I guess," he said with a shrug of his shoulders. "Fifty pound," the boy dispatched without delay.

"Fifty pound??" shouted Dave, rearing up somewhat.

That was not a good idea, the rearing, as it was met with the sound of a further tear.

"Twenty pound," countered Dave.

"Fifty," came the swift reply. "It's the only one in the world, and I took it right before my father returned to Greece..."

Dave uttered something incoherently, in feeble protest.

"... right before he passed away," Theodopolis added.

"Right, fine," said Dave, giving in. "Fifty it is, for the greatest picture in the world," he agreed through gritted teeth. A wallet was produced, and five crisp ten-pound notes were handed over in return for the violated picture which Dave managed to keep concealed. "You should work in finance when you're older," said Dave. "You'd be an excellent banker."

Dave went to ruffle the child's hair, but then thought better of it in view of the earlier *do-you-want-to-see-the-interior-of-my-van* suggestion.

"I hope you have a great TT, Mister Quirk!" said the boy, gleefully fanning the fifty pounds.

Dave put his empty wallet back in his pocket. "Me, too! I need the prize money!"

Two of the other boys stepped forward. "Could we also have our picture signed, Mister Quirk?"

Eager to make amends, Dave agreed, but also took their cardboard-backed envelope to use as a writing surface, lest he make the same (costly) mistake twice. The two boys handed over three pictures in total, which Dave held like a poker hand. He looked at the three pictures in turn, then over the top towards Theodopolis, who was poised to make good his escape.

"These are all the same bloody picture, you little bugger! You told me yours was the only one in the world!"

"It's the only one in the world with a hole poked through it!" laughed Theodopolis, now waving the notes in Dave's direction. "Thanks for the money, Mister Quirk!"

"What just happened?" said Dave to nobody in particular, before he then started to chuckle. "Little bastard, that's brilliant," he said to himself. "Fair play to the cheeky little monkey."

Although his wallet was lighter, he walked in the direction of pit lane with a spring in his step. After all, all things considered, the children knew who he was, and even had his photograph.

"Where've you been?" asked Frank, tapping his watch, at Dave's arrival minutes later. "The film crew were getting twitchy."

"I've just been waylaid," said Dave. "But I'm here now."

Frank, Stan, and Monty were stood at the entrance to pit lane, joined by an exceptionally attractive female journalist testing her volume with her cameraman.

"What's that?" asked Dave, while waiting, spotting the package in Monty's hand, but he was afraid he already knew the answer.

"Frank got them for us!" replied an enthusiastic Monty. "It's an action shot from last year's TT. We can hand them out for a bit of publicity for the charity. Have a look!" suggested Monty.

"No need, my old mate. I think I've just seen them three or four times already."

"Okay, guys, I think we're good to go," said the cheerful blonde-haired presenter, microphone in hand. "I'm Jenny," she told them. "And you may feel a little bit nervous, but you should just try and relax. Just be yourself and you'll be fine," she assured them. "Okay, I'm going to stand to the right of the camera, so can I ask you all to look towards me rather than directly into the camera? It comes off more naturally that way. Is that all right?" she asked, without waiting for a response. "Right, are we good to go, Neil?" she asked of the cameraman, and then started.

"I'm here with two very special guests today. We have the winners of last year's.... wait, Neil, pause it," she said.

Neil paused it.

"Could I ask you to look towards me, rather than at the camera?" she asked Monty.

Monty nodded in agreement, though didn't move a muscle.

"You're, *em*, you're still doing it," said Jenny, offering a forced smile.

Monty smiled back, unsure what exactly he was being accused of. "*Erm...* what?" he eventually asked, confused.

"Can I ask you not to look at the camera?"

"Ah! Sure!" Monty replied, now that was sorted.

"Great, thank you. Okay, Neil, if we can..." She paused again. "Mister Montgomery? You're still... only you... it's just... if you could..."

"Ah," offered Dave after a few minutes of this. "If I may? He's not looking at the camera, not exactly. He's looking at you. But, it also looks like he's looking at the camera. When he's not."

Jenny the presenter lowered her microphone. "What...?" she said, her bubbly demeanour now slightly muddled, and lessening in effervescence with each passing second.

Dave was used to this line of questioning. "Well," he said, hands now being used in an animated fashion. "Do you know when you see a chameleon on the television, and their eyes move independently of each other? Right. Well, that's our Monty."

"He can move his eyes independently?" she asked.

"Well, not precisely," explained Dave. "But it kind of looks like it. He has one eye that's looking *at* you, and one eye looking *for* you. Do you know what I mean?"

"I can't say I do, no," came the reply.

"They're stuck that way. He's looking right at you, but also at the camera. At the same time," Dave explained. "All at once. See?"

"Could we... perhaps turn him around a bit?" she suggested.

"I *am* here, you know," protested Monty. "I'm stood right here."

"Spin round a bit, won't you?" said Neil over the ridge of the camera, before returning to the viewfinder. "That's done it, Jenny," said Neil, with a thumbs-up.

And they started again:

"I'm here with two very special guests, the winners of last year's Spirit of the TT Award, Dave Quirk and Shaun "Monty" Montgomery. I'm sure you need no reminder, but their selfless act in response to a fellow racer's troubled sidecar mitigated a tragedy that could have been much, much more serious. Dave, if I can come to you first?" she said, deliberately keeping Monty standing in the same spot. "Dave, you were both injured last year in the crash. How are you feeling now?"

Dave cleared his throat. "I'm excellent now, Jenny, thank you for asking. If I'm being honest, I'd struggled for years with my knee, but the crash seems to have knocked something back into place! Which is an unexpected but happy outcome. Monty, however, is still on the mend, and struggles with his hip and ankle. Don't you, Monty?"

"I do!" said Monty merrily, but he was rigid, like a poker had been inserted up his bum. He was afraid of moving.

"But you're okay to race, Monty?" pressed Jenny.

"You couldn't stop me!" said Monty. "My leg would have to be hanging by a bit of gristle for me to not race!"

"Your machine was, of course, destroyed last year. What's the plan for this TT, Dave?"

"We're very fortunate to have our sponsors from last year back on board," said Dave, pointing to an out-of-shot

Frank and Stan. "They've given us the financial backing to put a package together that's beyond our wildest dreams. The new machine is like a rocket! Our sponsors are involved in a charity called Frank and Stan's Food Stamps, which raises money to feed the homeless."

"Excellent. So, your new outfit. What sort of result are you hoping for?"

"Top ten!" replied Monty. "This machine is capable of getting us a top-ten finish, alright. We just need to make sure we're fit enough to hang onto her!"

"About that," said Jenny. "I couldn't help but notice, you're both looking a lot leaner and meaner than last year. Does this help?"

"Are you flirting with us?" laughed Dave, receiving a dour death-stare in return. He cleared his throat before continuing:

"It's kind of you to say so, Jenny. Thank you. With the help of our personal trainer, we've lost about three stone each, and I've lost a further fifty pound only a few moments ago, but that's another story."

"So the weight loss will help the lap time?"

Dave nodded. "Absolutely. These sidecars only have little engines, and we're wringing the hell out of them for three laps, which, over this circuit, is unbearable stress. So it's certainly not helping things out by being overweight."

"It should be worth three or four miles an hour of our lap time," suggested Monty. "What with the new engine and the weight loss an all, I'm confident we'll be in the top ten."

"I very much hope I'll be reporting on you indeed finishing in the top ten. If I move to the wider field, there's been even more speculation on the sidecar race than I've ever seen. We've got the reigning world champions, Jack

Napier and Andy Thomas, competing against their closest rivals — and previous world champions — Harry and Tom McMullan. People are drooling at the prospect. What are your thoughts, Dave?"

Dave's arm crossed his chest, with his other hand caressing his chin. "They're all tossers," said Dave after a moment of thought.

Jenny lost her composure for a moment, presumably wondering if the expletive would make it through editing.

"Is that you stoking up the competitive fires, Dave?" she said, once she'd righted herself.

Dave shook his head. "Not at all. It's just me being honest. Don't get me wrong, those boys will be racing an entirely different race to us, whereas we're hoping to simply get into the top ten. I respect what them boys can do. They're remarkable, they truly are. But as men, they're all complete tools. In my opinion."

"I thought, after saving Harry's life last year—?"

Dave cut across her. "Okay, I suppose a better way of saying it is I dislike Harry McMullan less that I once did. I think he's making a concerted effort to be less of a knob. But, would I go for a pint with him? Not a chance. As for the other two, Napier and Thomas, well, you must have interviewed them and know for yourself what they're like."

Jenny raised her eyebrow in a *you're-not-half-wrong* fashion. "Okay, but if I was going to press you on who'd be taking the honours?"

"I'd have to say the McMullan brothers," said Dave. "Yeah."

"Agreed," pitched Monty. "Thomas and Napier, I would say are quicker, and on a quicker machine. But you cannot underestimate course knowledge. The McMullan brothers, on the other hand, have dozens of laps around this circuit, and that's got to be worth a few miles an hour per lap, I'd say. I wouldn't be surprised if the McMullan brothers won both races, comfortably. Either way, excluding mechanical failure, it's going to be between them, and with the rest of the field fighting for the third spot on the podium."

Jenny turned back to the camera. "Well, I think it's fair to say there's no love lost on the starting grid this year, but what is not in question is that we're in for a spectacular treat in the sidecar races this time around. We may see lap records tumble, and I don't know about you but I cannot wait! Join me next week, where we'll keep you up to speed on all the action at the greatest show on earth!"

She waited for a few seconds, until Neil's familiar thumb was raised once more, and then her camera-ready voice gave way to a more relaxed, everyday tone.

"Hey, thanks, guys," she said.

"I liked the up-to-speed bit," Dave ventured. "Nice wordplay."

"*Heh*. Thanks. I added that in last-minute," she replied, pleased with herself. "You really did a good job of getting that competitive drama across, by the way. You really don't like them?"

"No," said Dave. "Not the least bit. You can't tell me that you do?"

She cast a glance over her shoulder before confiding, "Complete tosspots. Glad to see it's not just me that thinks so. Thanks, guys, and I hope you get your top-ten finish," she said. "Bye, Monty," she added with a cheery wave, tilting her head, covertly trying to figure out if she were, in fact, in his line of sight.

"Bravo!" cried Frank, clapping his hands after the camera crew were on their way. "That was first-class, and great publicity for the charity!" he said.

"Frank, what's up with Stan?" asked Monty. "He's got a face like a slapped ass."

"He wanted to be on the interview, but Jenny made it abundantly clear that wasn't happening." Frank lowered his voice, before adding out the side of his mouth: "He's had his eyebrows done, and a top-up of the tan, also."

"He does look more orange than usual," remarked Dave, glancing at his watch. "Right, we need to go, lads. We've got another session with that ruthless little dictator you hired to get us fit."

"It's working!" suggested Frank. "I might need to get him to take me out for a fair bit of exercise as well. Well, maybe not a fair bit. But at least a little— hang on, are you limping, Monty?"

"Bit of a twinge, I think, Frank. Nothing serious," Monty replied, bursting into an on-the-spot jig-like gentle jog to emphasise the point. "See?" he continued. "Fit as a fiddle, me!"

After they'd gone, Frank gazed down the length of pit lane: to the grandstand on the left, over to the fuelling stations on the right, and across Glencrutchery Road to the iconic scoreboard. He closed his eyes, allowing the gentle breeze to caress his face. In a few short days, machinery would be hurtling by where he stood, slowing desperately, applying the pit lane limiter to ensure compliance of the 60 kph pit-lane speed limit for fear of attracting an unwanted thirty-second penalty for breaching this regulation.

Legends of the sport had ridden by just there, many on their way to TT glory. He spared a moment to think of those who set out on their journey but never made it back. He was humbled; it wasn't difficult to understand why, for many, a pilgrimage to the TT Grandstand was the first port of call for visiting bike fans, or even novice riders whose first experience of the course may begin on this very spot, in a hire car, learning the course first-hand rather than through onboard footage on the internet.

Frank pushed himself up onto the wall where Stan sat, the pair of them swinging their legs back and forth like schoolchildren at the park. "I'm sure you'll get interviewed next time," he told his mate with an encouraging pat on the leg.

"I've even had my teeth whitened. Look!" said Stan, grinning inanely. He went quiet, lowering his head. The two friends sat, listening to the sound of the passing traffic which was rather more sedate than it soon would be.

"Frank, may I ask you something?" said Stan, finally.

Frank smiled. He had an inkling what was coming. "Of course," he said.

"This morning, in the kitchen. I pretended not to notice when you were coughing. But I saw it, Frank. I promised you I wouldn't go on about, you know... the illness... but I saw the blood in your handkerchief."

"I had a feeling you did," confided Frank. "Stan, I'm on a journey and I don't think the road is always going to be smooth."

"Does the doctor know?"

"He does, yes."

"You promise? You're not just saying that to shut me up?"

Frank gripped Stan's knee, looking him straight in the eye. "I promise," he said.

"You know I don't mean to pry, Frank."

"You? Pry?" laughed Frank. "You're just looking out for me, I know that."

"Have I ever truly thanked you, Frank?"

"For what?"

"You know what! Frank, you've done more for me than any friend I could have ever wished for. I'll never forget how you've had my back, all my life. Not just at school, but in business as well. All the way from when I was a child, right through to adulthood and to the present. Frank, genuinely, without you in my life I don't think I'd be sat here now."

"You'd be sat somewhere else, that's all," Frank replied with a chuckle. Despite this, Frank dabbed with his thumb the moisture near to his eye. "Don't get all maudlin on me, you silly old bugger."

"Frank, I mean it. I want you to know what you've done for me in life. You're more to me than a friend," Stan said, with his hands raised. "Frank, from the bottom of my heart, thank you for everything you ever did. Now you're going through all this... this smegging unpleasantness. It may be ridiculous, but I see this, in some small way, as my chance to give you something back. I wish the circumstances were different, but, whatever you need from me now, and from here on, you just ask me. I mean it. Promise me!"

"I promise, Stan. We've had quite a journey together, my old friend, and I'll be damned if this is the final chapter!"

Staring vacantly seemed to be the order of the day, and the two of them were amongst the most adept.

"I could sit here for hours," offered Frank. "Just watching the world go by."

"One more thing," said Stan.

"You sound like Peter Falk," laughed Frank.

"What?"

"Columbo. Hello? Peter Falk? Falk!"

"There's no need to swear, Frank."

"Never mind. What's the other thing, Stan?"

"You know how I said I don't mean to pry?"

"Apart from earlier today?"

"Yes," confirmed Stan. "Well, seeing as though I'm on a roll. When are you going to tell Dave?"

"About...?"

"You know what about!" exclaimed Stan. "The fact that you're taking Jessie out for a drink. You're taking *Dave's own mum* out on a date."

"Oh, that," Frank replied with a laugh. "I bloody knew you were listening, you nosey old sod! Besides, it's not a *date*, necessarily. It's just two people of a certain age going out to enjoy each other's company, that's all."

Stan's eyebrows were arched skyward, which was impressive, on account of all the collagen. "I'm sure Dave will be pacified by that description, though you've never been a very good liar."

"You know me too well, Stan."

"I know you well enough!"

"That's what I said."

"Come on, let's go for a stroll," Stan suggested, jumping down from the wall.

Stan put his arm around Frank's shoulders, escorting him down pit lane where they imagined the electric atmosphere that would soon descend upon them.

"Frank," said Stan.

"*Whaaat?*" Frank replied, feigning annoyance.

"Frank and Jessie, up in a tree, K-I-S-S-I-N-G!" Stan sang like a seven-year-old.

"Bugger off!"

"Frank. Frank, can I be a fly on the wall when you tell Dave?"

"Bugger off!"

Chapter Fifteen

Are you being shot out of a cannon, Stella??" shouted Bruce from the safety of his porch.

Stella took the fag from her mouth. "I'm going to the TT, Bruce. Keep an eye on the old place, will you?" she said, pointing to her modest bungalow.

"Nobody would be stupid enough break into your house, Stella. Trust me. Are you going over on a motorbike, Stella?"

"You're not half stupid you, are you, Bruce," she said, as a statement, looking down at her leather trousers, jacket and helmet. "Nothing gets past you, does it?"

Stella was dressed head-to-foot in leather, which was not typically the most comfortable attire for late May. If it wasn't for the helmet, you wouldn't be blamed for having mistaken her for a leather couch, resting on its end, awaiting the bin men.

"I couldn't help but notice you don't have a bike, Stella?" Bruce put forth.

"Don't you have somewhere to be, Bruce?" said Stella, rearing up, before taking a breath. "I'm getting picked up by my boyfr– by my *friend*. He's bought a new bike for our trip to the TT."

Now, Stella was no expert on motorbikes, and her outfit was on loan, but even her novice ear could tell that the approaching machine — negotiating the winding road of her estate — was not what one might describe as throaty. Rather, it was more high-pitched and whining — like a scalded cat. Stella looked over her shoulder, willing Bruce to retreat to his house.

"This it, Stella?" Bruce shouted. "Sounds like you could enter that thing in the races!" he said, with the slightest hint of sarcasm.

"Bruce, do I need to come up there? Because I will," Stella threatened, but her attention returned to the noise getting closer and considerably louder. The smoke the bike left in its wake formed an impressive visual effect, like a pop star walking through dry ice, although this thing didn't sound quite so good. The neighbours' curtains were twitching as Lee brought the bike to a controlled stop, accompanied by a toot on the horn.

"Looking good, Stella," said Lee with a leisurely wave.

Stella circled the bike like a dog looking for a place to sleep. "This is the bike you've purchased, is it?" she asked, conscious that her question was as obvious as the one asked by Bruce a moment ago.

"Sure is!" enthused Lee. "Not quite what I imagined, but, still, we'll have a blast."

"Lee, it may have escaped your attention that I am a woman with a fuller figure? And this backpack isn't exactly light, either."

"That's just the way I like it!" replied Lee, assuming she was fishing for a compliment. "A full pack!"

Stella pointed at Lee's partially-rusted, somewhat-less-than-impressive red steed. "Lee, that thing couldn't pull a tea biscuit, so how's it going to get me and you to the Isle of Man?"

"It'll be fine, jump on! The boat goes in a couple of hours."

"Bruce, if you don't sod off I'm going to crack your skull when I get back!" she shouted to a head poking from behind a rubbish bin.

She lifted one leg to mount the bike, causing the leather trousers to creak under the strain like a ship's rigging during a heavy gale. She got her foot as far as the passenger seat, but her leg simply wasn't flexible enough for the final hurdle.

"I think I'm stuck, Lee," she said, currently looking like a letter 'T' with her leg extended. "It's these leather trousers, is what it is. They're not flexible enough," she continued. "Lee, little help, please?"

"I can't," replied Lee. "Only you're in the way of the sidestand, and if I get off the bike it'll fall over."

Bruce sauntered over. "You stuck, Stella?"

She was poised for a barbed response but in view of her precarious position and left leg shaking under the strain, she adopted a rather more conciliatory reply.

"Yes, please, Bruce. If you wouldn't mind."

"Happy to help," said Bruce, and tugged at her heel. "You were nearly there, Stella. Your boot caught on the strap you need to grip on when you're riding."

With her foot free of constraint, Stella hopped the final few inches before collapsing in relief on the back seat. The rear suspension welcomed her arrival like a fart in a spacesuit, and with Lee rising up an inch as if on a seesaw.

"Cheers, Bruce," Stella told her neighbour.

"All aboard!" said Lee. "It's exciting, this! Lee and Stella, on a road trip! Next stop, the Isle of Man TT! Well, the ferry crossing first..."

Bruce gave them a smart salute to see them off.

Lee engaged first gear and let go the clutch, increasing the throttle in the process until the bike shrieked in pain. In a leisurely manner, the bike edged slowly out, like a ship leaving port. Lee kept the throttle pinned and they were soon on their way — albeit sluggishly — leaving, in their wake, another impressive cloud of smoke.

The cool breeze in Stella's face brought welcome relief from the earlier exertion, drying out the moisture on her forehead. The steady increase in velocity meant that smoking became a challenge, however, and so Stella flicked her fag to the ground and lowered the visor on her helmet. A smile spread across her face; despite being fagless, she was quite starting to enjoy this.

Progress towards the Port of Liverpool was best described as steady. Several rather more muscular bikes — likely heading to the same destination — slowed, extending an arm to offer a jovial tow. It was liberating, this bike lark; Stella eventually built up the courage to lean forward, placing her hands securely around Lee's waist, taking a firm grip.

Lee turned his head, shouting to Stella, but his words were lost on the breeze. Stella gripped tighter, moving forward an inch, craning her neck.

Lee shouted once more. "Stella, your hands! they're on my crotch!"

It took her a moment to translate what she was hearing. With her thick gloves and his jacket, it was an easy mistake to make. She raised her hands to the correct position just as Lee dropped down a couple of gears, negotiating the sharp right-hand turn which offered them their first view of the Isle of Man fastcraft, *Manannan*. She was certainly an impressive sight, framed perfectly at the end of the road beneath the famous Royal Liver Building, but it wasn't that which took their breath away — at least not entirely.

Lee pulled the bike over to the pavement, engaged the sidestand, and offered Stella an encouraging arm. She was more flexible this time; the journey must have both loosened up her ligaments and stretched out her leathers. They both removed their helmets and stood without saying a word, jaws open like early Man must've done once fire was discovered.

"Jaysus," said Lee after a while. "I mean, just, holy Jaysus. Frank has been wittering on about the Isle of Man TT all year. And to be honest, Stella, a lot of it just washed over me. Sure, I've seen videos and stuff, but until I turned that corner," he said, pointing back up the road. "I didn't really have a clue what he was on about. He told me it was like that. But even then, I still didn't understand it. If this is what it's like here, *waiting to get there*, what the hell is the actual Island going to be like?"

Lee and Stella stared down the stretch of road at the spectacle of several hundred people waiting patiently for their carriage across the Irish Sea. It was orderly chaos with the semblance of a queue, but it was the sound of engines revving and the smell of horsepower that hung in the air. People of all ages mixed politely, with most taking a moment to admire the machinery of people they'd met a mere few seconds earlier.

And language appeared to present no hindrance; it was as if the TT was able to transcend all barriers, even that of communication, as demonstrated by a portly gentleman pointing with exuberance at a bike resting a bit further up the pavement: "MV Agusta," he said, adoringly, in an exceptionally heavy accent. He walked up to the bike and bestowed a tender kiss to the top of its petrol tank. "Giacomo Agostini," he said reverently, blowing a further kiss towards the machine as he took a step back to admire it. He took a picture on his phone and then returned to join the hoards nodding or shaking their heads in appreciation, same as him.

As they waited, Stella took a lead from the other more seasoned riders, loosening her leather jacket to welcome the sea breeze to her armpits.

She fidgeted at the sight of three men staring over in her direction. It was getting unnerving.

"Nice ride!" said one, with a laugh and a nod of the head.

"She's been around the block, mate?" said the other.

The third man took a step closer, adjusting his glasses. "She's got to be, what, fifty years old? She's had a hard life, but plenty more action in that beast!"

Stella was in her rucksack looking for a kosh or some other form of blunt-force weapon — she rarely travelled without such — and two, possibly three spectators were about to have a detour to the local hospital. The closest of the men, in fact, reached into his own bag. Stella took this as confirmation that things were about to get ugly. But it didn't happen like that at all...

"May I have a go at her?" the fellow asked, looking to Lee for approval, and, once granted, knelt down on one knee, carefully applying a soft cloth to the tired-looking chrome.

"I thought so!" he said, triumphantly. "She'd come up a treat, mate," he offered, looking down on the small patch of bodywork — now gleaming.

"I never imagined!" replied Lee. "I'll have a go at her myself when I've more time, I surely will."

"She's a classic. Definitely worth the effort," the fellow replied encouragingly. "Oh!" he said, looking at Stella. "Lovely t-shirt!" he commented, without the least hint of sarcasm or malice at all.

Stella stood down, pulling her hand back out from her rucksack. "Thank you," she said, blinking several times — she was unaccustomed to receiving compliments, no matter how modest.

Shortly, the engines of dozens of bikes burst into life in unison: an audible invitation that the Seacat ferry was ready to depart. Lee took the opportunity to casually extend his hand to Stella. She hesitated for a moment, not wanting a further error or faux pas like the earlier crotch incident.

Lee wasn't moving his hand away, however, so Stella placed her gloved hand in his, allowing herself the faintest of grins to appear.

"I think we're going to have an amazing time, Stella." Lee smiled, turning to face her once he was seated on the bike. "Stella," he said. "Thanks for this, you coming with me. It's just grand, so it is, and, truly, it means the world. Now pull yer socks up, it's time to go! Do I need to be helping you to get a leg over?" he asked, in reference to the bike.

"Cheeky sod!" said Stella. "You need to buy me a steak dinner before I'd even consider that! Now hurry up. We don't want that thing down there leaving without us."

Chapter Sixteen

Saturday – Practice Week

What a difference a year makes!" remarked Frank, caressing the blue bodywork of sidecar Number Forty-Two. Do you remember, Dave? The first time we met you, you were beating the hell out of the engine because it was knackered?"

"Happy times," said Dave, cracking open a can of lager. "Monty?" he asked rhetorically before throwing a tin over, as well, to the partially-sleeping Monty on the leather couch.

"Remind me why you're drinking alcohol?" asked Stan.

"Because we like to. You want one?"

"You're not going out for practice?"

Dave nodded. "Of course we are. Aren't we, Monty? We like a beer or two to steady the nerves before we hurtle down Bray Hill at one-hundred-and-forty miles per hour, that's all."

Dave held his stare, but Stan wasn't on board. Which was fine, actually, because Dave wasn't sure how much longer he could keep a straight face.

"Stan, of course we're not going out for practice, mate. Tonight is mainly about the newcomers, solo and sidecars."

Dave and Monty were parked up at the rear of the grandstand for the full two weeks. Even though they lived less than ten minutes away, they wanted to be right there, part of the action. They didn't want to miss a moment of it. When they weren't racing or practising, the paddock was a campsite for friends, who, in large part, may not have seen each other since the previous year or for perhaps just the occasional qualifying race. There were rivalries, sure, but for most they were with like-minded people sharing a collective passion. Racers would happily oblige if a competitor needed the loan of a spare part or perhaps needed a second opinion about suspension set-up. Dave and Monty had a succession of newcomers to their awning throughout the day, with a desperate thirst for knowledge about the track they would soon face for the first time. The experience of more seasoned campaigners was vital to the newcomers and they sat like a child listening to its grandfather as Dave spoke about a particular apex or optimum racing line. These guys needed to figure most of this out for themselves, but they'd be foolhardy to not soak up any of the available knowledge around them.

Further up the paddock where the motorhomes expanded in size, the same sense of comradery was in the main shared. The factory teams may have had more money and more mechanics, but, ultimately, they were also joined by the desire to race — with the only difference, on the whole, being that such guys had more of a chance of actually winning.

Two sumptuous race trucks who were not joined by the mutual respect of their owners, however, were that of the McMullan brothers and the Napier/Thomas teams. The trucks appeared somewhat larger than those of their contending peers, perhaps as a very visible dick-swinging contest. The press were partially to blame, stoking up the flames whenever they had the chance, though one person who was far from impressed with this — as he called it, "childish bolloxology" — was the man in charge of the proceeds. The two team principals had been put on notice by the Clerk of the Course that he wouldn't tolerate any repeat of the nonsense that'd been witnessed at the pre-launch event, and any physical altercations would be dealt with immediately. Ultimately, these guys were fierce competitors, but there was never any question that they'd allow this to spill over into the racing. Yes, they hated each other, but once they planted a wheel on the track, that's where any shenanigans ended — they all knew how serious the ramifications could be if they didn't.

Of course, this didn't stop them winding the hell out of each other at every opportune moment...

"Are you Tom Macamoooliman?" asked a pretty little girl, with her hair in bunches and a face as pure and innocent as one could ever imagine, evidently struggling with the pronunciation of the rider's name.

Tom McMullan put down his spanner in the forensically-sterile preparation area where their sidecar lay in several pieces. He could hear the voice but, as yet, saw nothing.

The little girl stood on highest tippy-toe, like a ballerina dancer, affording Tom a temporary glimpse of her, before disappearing from view once more as her feet fell back to the ground. He moved over to the awning wall, peering over, where he saw the girl looking back up at him, race cap in hand.

"Hello, darling," he said gently. "You want me to sign the cap?"

She smiled at him in return, and then shook her head from side to side, her pigtails swaying back and forth as she did so.

"No, but thank you," she said, clearly struggling to remember what she was going to say next. It seemed as though she'd rehearsed her lines, but in spite of her best efforts the words escaped her. She looked at the back of her hand where she'd scrawled a reminder note before continuing:

"Mister Macamoooliman," she said, again pronouncing the McMullan brother's name in her own adorable, inimitable way. "My dad has got a Citroën 2CV and says his car would go around the TT course quicker than your sidecar."

Tom leaned over the awning to get a closer look at the girl's cap, which, he now noticed, sported one particular signature.

"Did Andy Thomas sign your cap a minute ago, wee one?"

She nodded, unsure what her previous recitation actually meant, concerned only by the two gold coins rattling around in her hand. She returned to the custody of her father, who was busying himself admiring the array of high-tuned machinery on display.

Tom McMullan offered a particularly half-arsed wave as she departed, allowing his eyes to fall on that of another awning a short distance away. There stood Andy Thomas with a proud grin on his face, offering a vertically-extended middle finger for Tom McMullan's kind consideration.

Tom collapsed in a canvas chair, putting his head in his hands. "I'm needing to smash that face in," he said, virtually sobbing with anger.

Harry, composed and practical — though ordinarily the instigator — calmed his brother down. "Tom, I need you to focus," he said, gripping Tom's shoulders. "I want you to close your eyes and think of that chequered flag waving as you're bringing that machine home," he told him, pointing to their sidecar. "Across the line for a victory. And don't just imagine the one, either. Picture it, for a moment, next Saturday, and then *again*, on the following Friday. Visualise us climbing up to get presented with the trophy, perhaps spraying champagne down on the adoring crowds below. You never know, maybe a drop spills over onto the face of a pretty girl stood next to you on the podium, you both laugh, and you proudly show her the trophy. *Your* trophy, yeah?"

"And where's Thomas and Napier in this scenario?" asked Tom, more relaxed now.

Harry patted his cheek. "Who cares, Tom? They're not on the top step and that's what's important. No matter what he says to wind you up, whether it's about the size of your appendage, how slow you are on the track, or even that he slept with your girlfriend, just let it all wash over you and imagine you're sat on the boat going home with a large cheque and two trophies."

"Wait, hang on, I didn't know that he'd said that?" Tom answered him, the anxiety back in full measure and then some. "When did he say that??"

"Which bit?" asked Harry.

"About my girlfriend!"

Harry adopted his most soothing tone, kneading Tom's shoulders. "Don't let it worry you. Just think of the chequered flag... the chequered flag... the chequered flag...

that's right, the chequered flag..." he repeated, like a two-bit hypnotist.

Eighteen-twenty to the second and the solo newcomers made their way furiously away from the grandstand on their speed-controlled lap; the TT fortnight was officially underway.

"My god, I didn't realise how much I missed that noise!" said a delighted Frank, raising his hands to emphasise the point.

Dave had very thoughtfully secured them two pit passes, and, coincidentally, where they were watching the opening practice session just now was where they'd sat, contemplating, only a few nights earlier. It was exhilarating to watch pit lane, now a hive of activity, loaded with petrol cans and mechanics ready to pounce on their riders' machinery at a moment's notice.

Stan nodded. "I know. It's a bit special. I was somewhat worried the novelty might have worn off this year," he confided. "You know? I mean, how do you better something that's perfection in the first place, right? I thought it wouldn't have the same impact."

"And has it?"

"I think I'm even *more* excited this go-round, Frank, I've got to be honest with you. I can't wait to see Dave and Monty out there. Imagine if they got a top-ten finish!"

Frank didn't need to respond, the proud look spread all over his face like Marmite-on-toast said it all.

"Frank, did you ask Henk?"

"What, about buying the farm? No, he's been fairly preoccupied when I've seen him. Well, that's being polite. I think he's bordering on *psychotic*, is what it is. He always wants to win, but this stupid wager with Rodney Franks has really gotten to him. That bike of his, the Vincent, means more to him than life itself. It's a shame, because I think it's going to ruin his enjoyment of the TT. The more I think about it, anyway, that farm would be good but it's too expensive for what we need. We'd end up bankrupting the charity."

"Well, you do some stupid things when you're drunk," Stan replied. "My old dad, god rest his soul, always told me two things — never gamble when you're drunk, and never go to bed on an argument. It's served me well. Hold on, is that a new shirt?" asked Stan, changing the subject and reaching out to feel Frank's collar. He ran his hands over Frank's cheek. "And you've had yourself a shave!"

Frank blushed, trying to use the now-departing sidecar newcomers as a temporary distraction.

"And you've got aftershave on," continued Stan, sniffing at Frank's neck.

"Bugger off, will you?" said Frank, swatting Stan away. "If you must know, I met a friend for a drink earlier."

"What friend?"

"Just... a friend."

Stan smiled. "Does she happen to have a son that races in the TT?"

"I didn't say it was a *she*, now did I, Clever Dick?"

"Did you meet Jessie for a date?"

"It wasn't a date."

"Why didn't you invite *me* along, then?"

"What? No chance."

"If it was just a friend, you wouldn't have minded me coming along," teased Stan.

Frank merely pouted in response.

"I wondered where you might have disappeared to this afternoon, you sly old dog. So what has Dave had to say about all this?" asked Stan with a grin, undeterred.

Frank cringed. "It's not been discussed."

"Why? Because you need him to concentrate on the racing?" Stan suggested.

"No, because I'm a coward," Frank answered. "But I like your reason better, and I'm going to nick it to use on him when the time comes."

"So?" pressed Stan.

"So, what? Look, can we watch the practices, please?"

Stan looked up the empty road. "There's nothing going on right at the moment."

Frank shrugged his shoulders, and then sighed in resignation. "If I tell you I like her, will that shut you up?"

"Yes. Maybe. We'll see. Carry on..."

"I quite like Dave's mum, okay?"

"Okay. I won't say another word about it."

"Fine."

"So where did you go for a drink?" asked Stan.

"You weren't saying another word!"

"I didn't totally commit."

"But you said yes!"

"And then I changed my mind."

"This is going nowhere."

"Just like your explanation to Dave?"

"Fair point."

"On the subject of romance..." continued Stan.

"I thought you were shutting up?"

"I said we'd meet Lee and Stella for a pint in town later. They seem to be getting friendlier," Stan insinuated, with his insinuation eyebrow stood to attention.

Frank nodded in approval. "I'm really pleased by that. God knows it'll take a man of a certain temperament to cope with Stella, and hopefully that someone is Lee. We've known her a good long while, our Stella. About time she found someone."

Stan wore an expression of consternation. Or perhaps constipation. "Frank, can you imagine Stella wearing—?"

"Don't even go there, Stan!"

"What? I was only trying to imagine Stella in her wedding dress — I don't know where *your* gutter-mind was. She'd probably wear hobnailed boots with her dress. Do you think she'd ask either of us to walk her down the aisle?"

"I'm watching for the bikes, Stan. Why don't you ask her yourself?"

"Because I'm not brave enough. Or foolish enough."

"My entire body is in pain," moaned Stan, opening his eyes in stages like the shutters of a shop doorway. He went silent for a moment, presumably taking an inventory of what exactly was causing him difficulty. "Frank, if it was anybody else I'd be questioning why you were in bed with me. *Ahhh*," he continued with increasing volume. "I hurt. Even my eyeballs hurt. What happened? Who would do this to me?"

"I think his name was Jack Daniels. And judging by how many we had, the bastard must have brought all his friends with him."

"Bastard," agreed Stan.

"I think you invited half the patrons of the beer tent back here for a party," Frank went on. "It was a great night, though. Dave and Monty are somewhere about. Stella's in one room and I think Lee has, being a gentleman, taken the couch. As for everyone else... I've not a clue."

Stan eased himself upright, with the back of his hand pressed against his forehead in dramatic fashion.

"Knock-knock, hope you're decent?" boomed Dave's voice, entering the bedroom, and his large frame following shortly thereafter.

"Aren't you supposed to wait for an invite?" asked Frank, rolling over.

"Funnily enough, I just had the same response from across the hallway — although not quite as polite. That was the wrong room, as it turned out. You'd think I'd learn. But, no."

Frank squinted through the sleep in his eyes. "Dave. You seem too chirpy. Why are you chirpy," he said, not having the energy to raise the last word into a question.

"I feel fine. And, besides, any hangover I might have had would've been effectively obliterated when I walked into the room across the hall."

"That's Stella's room," Stan replied gravely.

"I know that now," said Dave. "And I saw more of Stella than I needed to at this time of the morning — or *any* time, for that matter. Never am I entering a room again without knocking first."

"Only you just did," Frank replied.

Stan put his hand up, like a child asking a question at school. "Hello? I've got an image of Lee and Stella climbing onto a rodeo bull. Did I dream that?"

"Nope, it happened," replied Dave.

"Dancing with a policeman at the beer tent?"

"Happened," replied Dave. "And don't forget about the dodgems."

"Aww, fucking hell," continued Stan, hand remaining aloft. "Was I topless?"

"Yup! Swinging your shirt like a lasso!"

Stan buried his head in his hands. "Dave, you were the sensible one. You were supposed to be making sure I behaved."

"That's the first time anyone has ever said those words to me," Dave answered. "But, thanks. I'm not exactly a bastion of sensibility. And I've gotten a tattoo... I think?"

"You think?" asked Frank, now more interested in the conversation.

Dave pulled up his sleeve, revealing a white bandage with the words, *In case you forget, leave me alone for 24 hours* written in thick black marker pen on it. "I've also got a text telling me exactly the same message. I must have told the shop to text me, just in case I forgot?"

"What sort of tattoo?" asked Frank.

"No idea. My mate did it. I gave him my phone and he swiped through. He finds a picture he likes, and he does the rest. I didn't ask questions. He's only done the outline, apparently, as he didn't have too much time, so I need to go back to get it finished up."

Frank joined Stan sat up in bed looking perturbed. "Hang on, Dave. If you've just had a tattoo will that not hamper your arm movement, especially if you're wearing leathers?"

"Nah, she'll be fine," replied Dave, with a thumbs-up. "Not a problem."

"But how can you be sure until you get out on the track?" pressed Frank.

"It's fine, Frank. I did the same thing last year," Dave explained, revealing his other arm.

Frank clambered for his reading glasses to confirm he had indeed seen what he thought he'd just seen. "Bloody hell!" he laughed, moving in for an even closer look. "And you say your mate did this?"

"It's a belter, isn't it!" Dave replied, with an admiring glance at his arm. "I'd been mucking around with photoshop and this picture was the one that caught his eye. It's quite the conversation piece!"

"I'll say!" said Frank. "Never did I think I'd see a tattoo of a voluptuous mermaid in a bikini top, scales and all, with the head of one Shaun Montgomery. I'm not sure if I'm horrified, or—"

"Aroused?" said Dave, cutting across.

Frank's voice went up a pitch. "Aroused? That's not the word I was looking for. At all. You're not right in the head, mate. You really need to have that looked at... your head, I mean... by a licensed therapist..."

"Oh," said Dave, voice tinged with disappointment. "Most people say aroused."

"Anyway," continued Dave. "Stan, you need to lay low around the paddock. If they watch the CCTV, you'll be in a spot of bother."

"A spot of bother?" enquired Stan.

"In deep shit," Dave clarified. "Anyway, I need to get going, chaps."

"Wait, what?" said Stan, pulling his trousers on. "What do you mean about the CCTV?"

"You've got to be kidding me?" said Dave.

"No, what?" pleaded Stan, reaching for Dave's forearm.

"Oi! Mind the tattoo," said Dave, taking a step back. "Now, you're saying you don't remember the huge penis from last night, then?"

Stan blinked.

"The enormous cock?" said Dave.

Stan looked over to Frank for help.

"What are you looking at *me* for?" said Frank. "I'm not the one that's done it!"

Stan turned his attention back to Dave. "*What about the CCTV??*"

"You," said Dave, with a prodded finger. "Drew a penis — the size of a grown man, no less — on the side of a race truck."

"No. I didn't... did I?" Stan asked, looking back towards a shoulder-shrugging Frank. "Why the hell would I do that?"

"Well. Because I dared you," Dave explained. "But you weren't interested. It was only when Monty got involved and double-dared you that the spray paint came out."

"Where did I—?" began Stan.

"It's the stuff they use to mark out camping pitches on the grass," Dave told him. "How you got hold of a tin of it, I've no idea, but I've got to tell you, Stan, you're quite the talented artist."

"Whose truck was it?" asked a panicked Stan.

"Not entirely sure. Possibly the McMullans'? Can't say for certain."

Stan's face was ashen. "I'm never going out with you lot again. I'll bloody kill Monty when I catch up with him!"

"*Ehm*, Monty didn't exactly come out of this whole thing unscathed himself," offered Dave.

"My ears are burning," said Monty, peering around the door. "Dave, by the way, don't go in that room across the hall," he added, thumb pointing. "I've just seen things no man should see. That way lies madness."

"If only you'd told me that ten minutes ago," replied Dave.

Frank was now on his feet. "Monty, what the hell? Where's your hair?"

Stan nodded, shaking his hand in a moment of recollection. "Ah. Monty. I shaved your hair... I think?"

Monty ran his hand along his shaven bonce. "And a cracking job you've done, as well."

"Remember the giant cock from last night?" asked Dave to Monty, to which Monty cast a glance in Frank's direction.

"Will people stop bloody looking over at me about this?" Frank protested.

Monty chuckled. "Oh, yes. Yes, now I remember. Napier and Thomas are going to be mad as a bag of ferrets."

"Was it not the McMullans' truck?" asked Dave.

Monty shrugged. "Maybe. Now you mention it, you could be right?"

"Oh, dear god," said Stan. "This is a nightmare. I'm a team principal. I'm supposed to be responsible, not running around at stupid-o'clock-in-the-morning defacing our competitor's truck."

"They're not really our competition, though?" offered Monty. "I mean not really."

"Yes, but you take my point, Monty. It's not exactly role-model behaviour. The TT hasn't even started for us and I'm in danger of getting us kicked out!"

"Nothing to do with us," said Dave, holding his hands out. "If you go down, you're going alone!"

"Great team spirit, guys, thanks!" Stan moaned.

"Don't stress it," said Monty. "I'm pretty sure there's no CCTV there. Trust me, if there was, we'd have been in serious trouble over the years. Who do you think they're going to blame, anyway? Whichever truck you vandalised, they'll just assume it was the other team. Don't worry about it. Anyway. Doughnut?" asked Monty, holding out a box.

Stan sat on the edge of the bed, nursing his throbbing head. "That's it, I'm never going out again, and I bloody mean it!"

"I'll take one of those doughnuts," remarked Frank.

Chapter Seventeen

June 1979

Frank was known for many things, but being an early riser was not one of them. He was slightly embarrassed to realise he didn't know where the light switch was to the reception area of his own office — which he consequently fumbled through, tripping over several chairs in the process. Sleep had eluded him the previous evening; every eventuality ran through his mind, and with Stan away on business he hoped that his imagination was running away with him, but there was one nagging thought he just couldn't shake.

"Bloody hell, Frank, what are you doing up so early? Did you wet the bed or something?" asked Stan, en route to his office.

"Good trip?" asked Frank.

"It was good. Brilliant, in fact. Let me get rid of my bag and I'll tell you all about it."

Keep calm, Frank, keep calm, he said to himself, but the reddening of his cheeks suggested he wasn't adhering to his own instruction.

Stan fell into the seat on the other side of his desk, running his hands through his hair. "You should come up to Manchester next time, Frank. There's a lot we can do up there, a lot of switched-on people."

Frank didn't respond, instead, taking several deep breaths.

Stan waited for a response that didn't arrive.

"Everything okay, Frank?"

Frank reached into his drawer, pulled out the file Sally had prepared, and slammed it down on Stan's desktop.

"Where's the money, Stan?"

Stan was caught unawares. His grin turned to laughter. He was unsure what he was laughing about, but he assumed it was a joke he didn't quite at the moment get.

Frank's solemn demeanour was unwavering.

"You're being serious?" asked Stan.

"Very," said Frank, opening the folder. "Who are they?" he asked, prodding the highlighted spreadsheet. Stan didn't seem overly concerned, which only served to increase Frank's frustration.

"Who are ABC Talent Management, Stan?" he continued. "Stan, are you ripping me off?"

Stan raised his hands in a *don't-shoot-me* pose. "Wait a minute, Frank. You're actually being serious here? Bloody hell, Frank, I can't believe you think I could possibly be ripping you off."

Stan stood, closing the door. It was still early, but he didn't want any of the staff to overhear. Stan placed his forearms flat on the surface of the desk, leaning closer, but not in a threatening manner.

"Frank," he said, shaking his head. "Look at me. I swear I've not ripped you off. I never would. Ever. *Ever.*"

"Who are ABC?" Frank reiterated.

"It's Tommy Banks' company. I told you about this, Frank. I've not kept you up-to-date with every transaction because you kept telling me you weren't interested in the money side."

"Stan, that's when I thought we had money," replied Frank, dropping a bank statement in front of him. "Stan, we're nearly broke!"

"It's not that bad," said Stan, although he recoiled somewhat when presented with the balance on the bank statement. "It's all about cash flow, Frank. We have to spend money to make money, don't forget. Frank, everything we do is cash up-front. These music halls we hire cost money."

"But they sell out!"

"Frank, I know. But we have to pay most of these places in advance. Sure, we'll get the money back. But we have to speculate to accumulate. Everyone we deal with has got their hand out for their slice of the action, and that includes the bloody tax man who wasn't shy about asking for his bit, either. Frank, this is an expensive business. Perhaps I should have been a bit more upfront with you, but I genuinely thought you just wanted to concentrate on finding the talent."

Stan reached over and placed his hands over Frank's.

"Frank, I'd never rip you off. I promise you."

Frank's demeanour softened. "Okay. I believe you, Stan. But why are we paying Tommy Banks all of this cash, still?"

Stan put one hand to his forehead. "Frank, in this business there's a lot of competition, as you know. We were small fish, two nothings in an established town. The music venues didn't want to know us and most of the decent acts had a countless number of agents just rolling the red carpet out for them. We were the bottom of the pile. Tommy Banks sold himself as a consultant that could smooth our progression into the business — grease a few cogs, as it were."

"Are we being shaken down?" asked Frank.

"Is that even a thing?" scoffed Stan, but Frank was deadly serious.

"Stan, I'm not brilliant with money, but I'm not bloody stupid either. I don't care what you call it, but is this money a retainer for Tommy Banks? Are we being shaken down? In other words, Stan, if we were to stop paying Tommy Banks, would his heavies be kicking our door down and rearranging your perfect white teeth?"

"Yes," said Stan.

"Fuck! How much do we owe him?"

Stan's façade of confidence was replaced with that of vulnerability. "I'm not sure," he confided. "It's not that simple."

"If we owe him money, how much for him to piss off?"

Stan thought for a moment.

"Frank, he helped to secure music halls when we started out. He helped us to be at the top of the queue when acts were looking for representation. He got involved when every wise guy wanted to take what was ours. It wasn't one amount — he sees this more as an ongoing investment."

"I can't believe I'm hearing this, Stan. How much is his ongoing investment costing us?"

"Five hundred a month."

"Five hundred a month! That's a bloody fortune! For how long do we have to pay this?"

Stan's head fell. "Ongoing," he replied.

"Frank," Stan continued. "I'm not throwing any of this at your door, but we were both more than happy to spend the cash on flash cars and champagne. Look, it's fine, we just need to get through this slump and we'll be fine. It will all be okay."

"Stan, listen to yourself. We're not okay, we have no money. The bank has been bouncing our cheques and they've called in our overdraft. You said the tax man has been paid, but he hasn't. Sally's sat on a final demand which she says you've known about for weeks. I can't believe I've been thinking about this, let alone saying it out loud, but, Stan, I think we need to wind the business down. We need to call it a day."

Stan shook his head furiously. "Frank, we can't! We've still got all the acts. We'll get through this."

"Stan, you're kidding yourself. We've got nothing. Anything we have is as a result of Tommy Banks, not our hard work. We just need to settle what we can and bugger off."

"There was a loan, also," Stan admitted after a pause. "Tommy lent the business ten thousand pounds to take it to the next level."

Frank laughed. But it wasn't the happy sort of laugh.

"This gets better by the minute, doesn't it? Stan, you can tell Tommy to stick his money where the sun doesn't shine. Here!" he said, throwing his keys over. "Tell Tommy it's his. Everything. But everything is not as substantial as I once thought it was, is it?"

"Frank, I know what you're saying, but we can't... I just can't. It's not that simple. Frank, I need to come clean with you. What I just said, I've lied to you. Well, not lied, exactly. But, not told you the complete truth."

"You *have* been stealing?"

"No! I wasn't lying about that, Frank. Frank, look, Tommy Banks did loan us money and open a few doors, but... but he's also blackmailing me."

"What? What do you mean he's blackmailing you? Fucksake, Stan!"

Frank took to his feet and slapped the office wall, causing a gold disc to wobble precariously. "Does that explain this, then?" said Frank, sliding a white envelope towards him.

Stan pulled out the photograph and collapsed back. "I'm not going to ask how you found this," he said.

"Stan, I had to do something. I had to know what was going on. Do you know who he *is*?" asked Frank. "What are you doing with him? He's a bloody politician. He's a politician with a family, and an outspoken critic on homosexuality on top of it. I say again, what are you doing with him?"

"I love him," said Stan, voice breaking. "And he loves me."

"I can see that from the photo. There's a lot of love going on there! If the papers got hold of that they'd have a bloody field day, which is why I'm guessing you're paying the money to Banks?"

"I don't know what to do Frank, please help me," said Stan, unable to keep back the emotion. "This picture will finish him off."

"How?" asked Frank. "How did this happen?"

"They knew he was leading another life and followed him for long enough until they had the pictures they wanted. Tommy Banks didn't know I was involved with him, for him it was a happy coincidence for him to have a hold on me. Frank, you need to understand one thing. Any money I gave to Banks came out of my share of the business. Anything I gave to him meant I took out less money from the business so you were not out of pocket. The business is still in good shape, we just need to get through the next few months!"

"Stan, you want my help? We need to pack up and disappear. This Tommy Banks thing? It'll never end. He'll never go away, he'll bleed you dry until you have nothing left, even if it takes a lifetime. You need to break it off with this fella of yours and we'll go back to Liverpool."

Stan's tears flowed uncontrollably. "Frank, I love him. I really love him."

"Stan, you need to get out of my office. I need you to not be around me at the moment. So, please. Just go."

Stan didn't move, until Frank gripped the arm of his shirt. "Stan, get out. I don't want to be near you just now," Frank said again, ushering him out the door.

After Stan was gone, Frank snatched up the closest gold disc and threw it across the room. "Shit!" he screamed, before lowering his voice to a whisper. "Shit."

"Good shot," commented Sally, taking a position resting against the door frame. "This is why you shouldn't come into the office early."

"I'm sorry about the noise," Frank told her.

"Nevermind that. Do I need to start looking for another job?" asked Sally with a grin. "All good things must come to an end, I suppose."

"Sally, I've got a couple of affairs I need to sort out," Frank said, as much to himself as to Sally.

"Yes," Sally agreed.

"Sally, how do I get hold of this Tommy Banks?"

"Frank," she said, moving closer. "This guy is serious business. Do not underestimate him."

"I won't, Sally. I promise," he said, placing a gentle kiss on her cheek.

"What do you mean I'm too old?" barked Sally down the phone. "You cheeky bastard, I've been an accountant for over forty years! Some would call that *experienced!*" she said, before listening for a moment, and then replying: "Is that so? Well I'm not too old just yet to come down there and smash your face in, you scrawny son of a—"

Sally slammed the receiver down. "Frank, where the hell have you been? I've been phoning around everywhere looking for you."

"I had things to do. I told you I was going out, and... it sounds like you were trying to get another job?"

"Call it a contingency plan. Did you go to see Tommy Banks?" she asked.

"I was going to but changed my mind in the end. Where's Stan?"

"That's why I've been trying to get hold of you," she said, clutching for a cigarette. "He's gone to see Banks. He said something about getting the police involved."

"What, is he bloody stupid? When did he go??"

"Not long after you left. Frank, you need to be careful with this guy, like I said. Seriously. Do you want me to come?"

"Thank you, Sally. It's a kind offer, but, well, I don't want you to put yourself in harm's way. But thanks!"

And, with that, he was off.

Frank sped through the streets of London in his prized Jaguar. Ordinarily a very careful driver, he figured it'd be repossessed by the end of the week anyway and so threw caution to the wind.

Presently, Frank had precisely not one single clue what he was going to do next. However, the thought of Sally volunteering her services to come along as protection brought him a momentary grin. He took the crumpled note — which he'd discarded earlier — retrieving it from the footwell and cross-checking the name of the bookmakers with the one he was currently parked outside for confirmation.

"I'd like to see Tommy," he asked of the surly cashier, once inside. Her demeanour indicated that she did not like her job very much, did not like people very much, or both.

"Wait there," she said flatly, disappearing through a door at the darkened recess of the shop.

It was a difficult environment in which to wait in comfort. Frank tried his best to look inconspicuous by reading a newspaper about greyhounds, but the truth of it was that he stood out like a polar bear with diarrhoea. He'd well and truly stepped into the city's criminal underbelly and wherever he looked, ignoble, battle-scarred blaggards covered in tattoos stared back at him with contempt. And that was just the women.

"Go through," said the cashier, once returned, in the same monotone delivery as before.

Frank took a deep breath, gathered himself together, and walked into the office.

Tommy Banks waved him in. "Please," he said, offering Frank a seat. "You're Frank Cryer, if I'm not mistaken? A pleasure to meet you."

The cordial welcome was unnerving and unexpected. Frank nodded, taking a seat as instructed. Tommy was short, built like a boxer. His hair was shaved to the scalp and his deep-set blue eyes had a fierce intensity. He exuded confidence.

"I've been meaning to speak with you, Frank — may I call you Frank? — so your timing is impeccable."

"Ah," said Frank. He'd meant it to come out with a deeper timbre than it did, but it sounded instead like he'd inhaled helium. "Ah," he repeated, once he'd cleared his throat, but he knew the moment was lost.

"We're both busy men," said Banks. "So I won't do you the discourtesy of treating you like an idiot, Frank. Fair enough?"

"Yes, fine," squirmed Frank.

"You and your friend, Stan Sidcup. It's a nice little business you had there."

"Had?" asked Frank.

"Sure," said Tommy. "Stan came to see me and told me all about the money problems. Cashflow, as he explained. Shame, really."

"Do you know why I'm here?" asked Frank. "Seeing as how we're not treating each other like idiots?"

Tommy waved his hand, inviting Frank to continue.

"We can't operate in this town without you on board, Tommy. I know that."

"Your friend Stan and I have an agreement. I'm sure you, being partners, know all about it?"

Frank took another breath to compose himself.

"I do. And that's why I'm here. I'd like to buy Stan out of his commitment to you."

Tommy laughed. "And why would you want to do that, Frank?"

"How much?" said Frank.

Tommy Banks didn't speak, resulting in Frank filling the silence. "Tommy... Mr Banks..."

"*Tommy* is fine. We're friends here, Frank," Banks assured him. But Frank got the impression there was no such thing as being friends with Tommy Banks any more than a hare could be friends with a jackal.

"Stan's source of income was the business," Frank went on. "That's gone pear-shaped. So he'll have no money to give you."

Banks nodded but said nothing at this.

"Right. So there's three thousand there," said Frank, pushing over an envelope. "That's all I have."

Tommy pushed the envelope back.

"I understand you're the talent man, Frank? I'm not entirely sure what Stan brought to your operation if I'm being frank, Frank. So you must be the brains out of your little partnership?"

"And what if I am?" asked Frank, getting a little braver.

"Well, if you're the brains, then you're the asset of the business. What's say we work together, Frank? I'll give you the money to get the business back on track, and I'll introduce you to whoever you need to know. You'll be the biggest in London. And don't worry, I'll stay out of your way — as long as I get my cut, that is — and you won't even know I exist."

"And what about Stan?" Frank countered.

"Stan, who?" said Tommy, but Frank knew exactly what he meant.

"I've got a feeling your friend Stan has been working a bit too hard lately," Banks went on. "In fact he'll really be needing to take some time off to rest and recuperate, actually."

"What've you done to him?" asked Frank. "*Where is he?*"

Tommy Banks leaned over the table, resting on his knuckles. "Frank, forget about Stan. We'll work together, you and I. You'll be the biggest agent in London. Frank, I can make you a wealthy man. You just need to forget all about Stan."

"So Stan was here?" Frank demanded. "*Where is he now??*"

Banks' face gave away the faintest smirk. "Frank, people don't take too kindly to being threatened with the police. It's not particularly nice, and it's not especially polite, either."

"TOMMY, WHERE IS STAN? WHAT HAVE YOU DONE TO STAN?"

"You can't park there!" protested an overzealous attendant, broom in hand. "It's a *No Waiting* zone!" he shouted after Frank. "You'll get a parking ticket!"

Frank stood in front of the arrivals board, but the words and figures melted in front of his eyes. A passing nurse applied the brakes on the wheelchair she was piloting. "Are you all right, dear?" she asked, compassion evident in her voice. "You look like you need help?"

"Ward seven," said Frank, struggling to catch his breath.

"End of the corridor, turn left, then the third ward on your right," she said, using her arms to draw a virtual map, but Frank was already gone.

Frank sprinted, but traction was always difficult in a hospital; it must be something to do with the wax used.

"Sally!" he shouted. "Sally, I got your message, I came as soon as I could!"

Frank didn't want to ask for fear of the answer. His eyes darted over Sally's face, looking for a glimmer that everything would be okay.

Sally's bottom lip trembled, she went to speak, but the emotion choked her.

Frank gently gripped her shoulders. "Sally. How is Stan?"

She put her shaking hand to her mouth. "Frank, he's in a bad way."

"He's alive?"

"Yes, but he's got internal damage and something about a possible bleed on the brain. The doctor said the next twenty-four hours are critical."

Stan's family were small in number, and those he had were up north. Frank didn't leave his side for three days, before finally relenting due to the smell — his own, that is, from lack of a shower — and the friendly complaints from the nursing staff. Not once did Stan's friend from the photograph — though informed of Stan's injuries — visit, phone, or apparently give Stan a second thought.

Stan eventually roused almost six days later, and the first thing Stan saw when he opened his eyes was Frank.

Frank shouted for the nurse, barely able to contain himself.

"Hiya, pal," Frank said. "Don't try and speak because there's damage to your jaw and it's wired shut."

Stan just looked at him. Nothing needed to be said for Frank to read his face.

"You had me worried there," said Frank, wiping the snot from his nose and then daubing at his eyes with the back of his hand. "I thought I'd lost you, you daft old sod. Again."

Stan gently gripped Frank's thumb but no words were spoken. Those few days were the only time in Stan's life when anyone could actually get a word in (a fact Frank was often eager to remind him of later on).

Stan would spend three months in that hospital and even after several rounds of major surgery, the thing that concerned him most was his teeth — or rather the lack of them. Once the hospital surgeons had finished with him, his next appointment would be with the cosmetic surgeon.

"I've got a plan," said Frank one wet Sunday afternoon when some of Stan's strength had returned. By this time, he was able to urinate on his own terms, and the wiring on his teeth had come off.

"Remember years ago, when we bought Daisy the campervan?" Frank asked, a twinkle in his eye.

"Of course," Stan replied. "Daisies, by the way—"

"Bloom well in the autumn, I know," Frank answered, and they both shared a laugh.

"Do you remember what I'd originally intended to spend the money on?" Frank continued. "Before Daisy?"

"A taxi, wasn't it?" responded Stan.

"A taxi, yes. I can see it now, Stan. When you get out of here, let's go back to Liverpool and buy a taxi, yeah?"

"There's no money in that, is there? Or is there?" Stan wondered aloud.

"Well of course there is," said Frank, reeling off the business plan he'd conceived during the long nights in the hospital waiting rooms. "We can pick up and start again, right? But maybe I'll keep one eye on the money *with you,*" Frank added. "Assuming you don't mind."

"You can have that, Frank. I just wanted to say I'm…"

"We don't mention it again, Stan. It's over and done. You don't need to worry about Tommy Banks, either. He's sorted. I'm ready to get out of London. We'll make a new start. I can see it now, Stan," he said again, this time driving an imaginary car. "We'll have one car, and then two, and, hell, before long, we'll have a whole *fleet* of taxis."

"With the name Frank-and-Stan plastered all over them," said Stan, embracing the idea. "Oh, our logo could be Frankenstein, see, as in—"

"Yeah, I think I get that one, Stan, no further explanation required," Frank replied, stretching his arms out and doing his best impression of the famous monster — which got another good laugh out of both of them.

"I've got someone primed to help us in the office as well," offered Frank.

"Who?"

"Craggy Sally. She'll be fantastic! She can help us out with the accounts, of course. And she says she's got some money saved so if we don't pay her for a few weeks it's not the end of the world."

"Brilliant," said Stan. "Frank, thank you. You're a very singular friend."

Frank dismissed him. "They may have to stay with us for a while — you know, until they get settled."

"They, who?" Stan asked.

"Craggy Sally. You do know she looks after her granddaughter, right? So the little one is coming along for the ride. She's an unusual kid, but she seems..."

"Seems what?"

"Well, she's an unusual kid. Yeah."

"What's her name?"

"The kid? Stella, I think it was. Yes, Stella, that's it."

Chapter Eighteen

Dave ambled down pit lane, taking an appreciative glance at the outfits queued up waiting patiently for the ultimate test of any racing machinery. His leathers were immaculate; he felt like the kid at school daring to unveil his new trainers for the first time.

Over the throbbing clatter of revving engines, he couldn't escape a squeaking noise that appeared to be following him. He took a glance over his shoulder... but nothing. It sounded as if he were trodding on a duck with each step.

Confused, he looked down, appearing for all the world like he was bowing his head offering a last-minute prayer to the big guy in the sky.

"Ah," he said, the answer revealed: the noise emanated from the inside of his thighs every time the fresh leather met with the opposing leg on each stride forwards.

Mystery solved.

Monty was already aboard sidecar Number Forty-Two. Dave offered a firm slap on the back, and climbed himself aboard the bike they'd both spent countless hours building, stripping down, and rebuilding. It'd been their obsession for months, and, now, for the first time, it was about to be revealed if their determined efforts would produce the results they hoped for.

Dave pulled at his crotch, where it felt constricted now he was sat down. It could well have been the new leather, not yet broken in. An alternative explanation, however, was that his testicles had necessarily increased dramatically in size: after all, he was about to pilot this precision-tuned contraption down Bray Hill.

The outfits higher up the starting order were dispatched at ten-second intervals. Dave ran his tongue over his lips and took a deep breath to counter the increase in his heart rate as he pressed down on the electric starter. He winced in anticipation, but he needn't have fretted as the engine burst into life at the first time of asking with a glorious roar. He gave a series of short twists to the throttle to get the oil circulating, and looked back at Monty, who was now crouched, prepared for action.

He rolled forward as another machine set off towards the traffic lights at St Ninian's crossroad. He tried to keep focussed but his mind raced with nagging doubts about gearing ratios and suspension set-up. Ultimately, the only way to know if he'd chosen the correct combination was to test them on the TT circuit — something he was about to do, just now as a matter of fact, as a hand pressed down on his right shoulder gave him the permission to go.

Dave released the clutch, applying the power as they burst away from pit lane. The outfit, full of composure, was lively off the line before settling as Dave moved up the gearbox — second, third, and then fourth — as they tore steadily towards St Ninian's. He had to remember to breathe as he knocked into fifth approaching the top of Bray Hill, doing one hundred and thirty. He'd been sat still only a few brief seconds earlier, and was now virtually hurtling off the face of the earth on one of the most daunting descents in road racing.

If this were the *U.S.S. Enterprise*, then Dave and Monty had just entered warp speed, you could say, as they passed through the popular vantage point at the foot of Bray Hill, where the suspension was provided its first challenge as the outfit bottomed out — creating a haze of sparks caused by metal hitting tarmac at one-hundred-and-fifty miles per hour.

Breathing was a little easier as he tucked in, keeping the throttle pinned over the iconic Ago's Leap — named in homage to the TT legend Giacomo Agostini — a short distance up Quarterbridge Road. Houses, telegraph poles, and garden walls flashed by in a blur, the occasional glimpse of a marshal's orange tabard visible in Dave's peripheral vision: all representations of the speed he was travelling.

His brain was starting to catch up with the images being thrown at it as Dave dropped back down the gearbox and applied the brakes, gently at first, as he came up on the landmark of Quarterbridge — by day a daunting series of roundabouts, but now a fierce right-hander that required a rapid reduction of velocity — before easing around the sharp bend in second gear on relatively cold tyres with minimal grip. It was another popular vantage point, where there could be several hundred people to witness a careless tumble by competitors perhaps braking too late or perhaps having been overly confident in the grip their tyres would offer.

No such problem for Dave, accelerating away from those enjoying a cold beer on this warm evening at the Quarterbridge Pub. He was getting a feel for the bike; it wasn't perfect, but he was pleased, and the new engine was seriously rapid. He caught sight of the outfit that set off ten seconds before him, but he didn't have time to register if he was going quick or they were going slow.

A short burst of acceleration brought him towards the oak tree at Braddan Bridge, where he applied the brakes just after the rugby club on the right — its fields peppered with tents from the visiting fans.

Dave dropped to second gear for the sweeping left and right-hander at Braddan Church — slow in, fast out — thirty, maybe thirty-five miles per hour in front of the temporary grandstand. His confidence about the grip increased as the tyres were surely getting warmer by this point. He felt Monty clambering over on the right-hander; agile for a man of his build, this was truly a team effort.

Dave was motoring east, and the sky was clear. He winced, for he knew the sun's rays would bore into his eyes as he passed the industrial estate to his right. His tinted visor provided protection, but he was still momentarily blinded — which is not ideal when traversing at the pace he was. Time enough to recover before calling upon his brakes, once more, on the left towards the Railway Inn, followed by a right which caught out many a rider too enthusiastic with the throttle.

Dave accelerated in third gear, the suspension softening for a moment as he caught the dip in the road over the defunct Douglas-to-Peel railway line. Those riders catching air was the reason it was so popular with the congregation of photographers blocking the view of others waiting patiently at Union Mills Church. And it was here the ferocity of the glaring sunshine hit, coupled with a flock of birds taken to the wing by the commotion of the race. It was obstacles like this that the novice rider would have to experience to understand.

The next section — the ascent up the Ballahutchin — was quick, and then flattened out for what seemed like an age. It gave Dave a brief opportunity to shake his head and clear his senses before being thrown into the infamous Ballagarey right-hander, which was a serious test for how the bike handled and also for how brave you were feeling.

Dave's hand was in conflict with his brain but he powered through without lifting off, quite smartly, and he carried this valuable momentum onto the straight. In races which could be separated by hundredths of a second, it was corners such as Ballagarey — or Ballascary, as it was affectionately known — which separated positions on the podium.

The hedges and walls were scattered with faces, and, whilst Dave couldn't make out any precise detail at his rate of speed, he could appreciate the volume of people desperate to exploit any viewing opportunity.

A constant stream of wee winged creatures, meanwhile, paid the ultimate price, with their remains enjoying a lap of the course plastered all over the front of Dave's visor.

Dave was focussed, listening out for any noise or vibration that would provide him feedback on the bike's performance — and the flat-out Glen Vine section was a worthy adversary for it — but she was running like a dream, and she wasn't missing a beat.

Dave and Monty flew past the Crosby Pub, where more spectators enjoyed a pint in the warm evening sunshine, but it was all business for Dave, who prepared himself for the Crosby jump where the quicker competitors would once again feel their suspension soften.

Dave had now progressed a little over four miles and was coming up on what would arguably be the quickest point of the course, despite the fact they'd been all but flat-out for the previous two miles. Trees hung over the road from both sides, forming a virtual tunnel which only further enhanced the feeling of velocity.

A small lane on the left — flanked on one side by a modest white house — was separated from the track by a low-hanging piece of rope. Although Dave was tearing through at over one hundred and fifty, he offered a split-second wave to four heads that would only have been visible to those watching out intently for it. Those four heads on the other side of the rope, as it happened, belonged to Frank, Stan, Lee, and Stella.

"Holy fucking fuck!" screamed Lee, jumping on the spot. "That's them! Dave and Monty! Jaysus!"

Frank and Stan gave a knowing glance — similar to the one they themselves had been offered at the same point twelve months before.

Lee couldn't stand still. He was practically doing a jig.

"Oh my god, Frank! You've been going on about this place all year. But I didn't get it. Not until that very moment, just then!" He was grinning like an idiot. "Frank, Stan," he said, looking at them each in turn. "This place is completely unreal. My brain cannot register what it's seeing!"

Lee had to place his hands on his thighs and lower his head for fear of hyperventilating. After he'd sorted himself out, he stood back up, hands on his hips. He shook his head. "Frank," he said with a deadpan expression. "I actually think I've got an erection."

"You wouldn't be the first, nor the last," replied Frank, shooting a glance in the direction of Lee's groin despite himself, as did Stan. "In fact I think it's one of the reasons Stan likes it here so much," Frank added.

Stan shrugged his shoulders. "It's a fair cop," he said with a smirk.

Beyond that, Stan had the look of every TT spectator stood next to a first-time visitor. It was a face of anticipation, knowing that that person was about to enter a new chapter in their life. Once you'd seen a bike passing in anger at the TT, you would look at everything else in life with a different lens from then on.

Yes, you could *appreciate* other sports, but, with this, with the TT, you *respected* it. The riders became mythical creatures; it was simply impossible for the average man or woman in the street to comprehend how human beings were able to go at such speed on what were country roads surrounded by walls, trees, and phone boxes. Those that'd been through it just knew; there was no explanation required. TT shirts were worn the world over and for the majority wearing one, it meant that they'd experienced this spectacle for themselves. If you met someone who'd been to the TT, a simple nod of appreciation was all that was required to convey the fact that you knew. You'd had the privilege, no, the honour, to watch these sporting goliaths negotiating what was the most challenging, unforgiving test of sporting achievement anywhere, without question. There was nothing like the Isle of Man TT.

"What about you, Stella?" asked Frank. "You look like you've seen a ghost."

Stella put a shaking hand to her mouth, taking a deep, trembling draw on her cigarette.

She didn't speak at first, so overcome was she.

She gave the impression she was about to reveal the deep emotional impact the experience of the last few moments were to have on her...

Remark upon the profound majesty of the moment...

How it had affected her...

How it would change her life forever...

Finally, she spoke:

"I think I've got an erection as well, actually," she said, and she forgot, for a moment, to even take another draw from her cigarette.

Chapter Nineteen

... So make sure you tune in tomorrow for the final night of practice. Before we go, we'll hand over to Chris Kinley in pit lane to reflect on what's been another frantic practice session.

Yes, thanks, Tim. Frantic is the word. My-oh-my, what a week we're having at the Isle of Man TT. I'll be the first to admit that I thought the forecasters were being too optimistic, but the weather has been fantastic as we draw to the end of practice week.

I spoke earlier about the solo machines, and, as predicted, lap times are already approaching lap-record pace. I will not be surprised to see the outright lap record smashed in the Superbike race on Saturday.

The sidecars have really captured the imagination so far, and, oh, my, are the guys at the top of the leaderboard quick! I don't think I've ever seen them pushing that hard at this stage.

There was speculation at the start of the week as to whether lack of course experience would hamper Andy Thomas and Jack Napier, but I've been impressed. They're a little off the pace, but even so, they've dropped in the second fastest lap of the week, which is deeply impressive. They've pushed the McMullan brothers all week, and after tonight's practice session it's the McMullan brothers who top the pile with a fastest lap of one-one-five point-seven-three-two.

But the newcomers are not a million miles behind them, just over two seconds slower. For an outfit that's never raced at the TT previously, that lap time is simply stunning.

There is a chance of a few showers next week, which may impact on lap times, but regardless of the weather we're sure to have some amazing racing. I'm off to get my breath back, so, Tim, it's back to you in the studio.

The leather sofa outside Dave's awning was more than just a seat; it was an occasion. Some of the fondest of times had been shared on it — from talking through their strategy, to welcoming new friends and old, to toasting to success, or perhaps downing a few to drown their sorrows — and it was as much a part of Dave and Monty's TT experience as their sidecar.

Monty stretched out, like a cat, topless with just his shorts on, eyes closed, and with a solitary beer resting on his chest.

"What a night, Monty!" Frank called out, startling Monty from his trance-like state. "Eleventh on the leaderboard, that's unbelievable!"

"One hundred and seven-point-six-four-zero, Monty!" offered Stan, sharing the enthusiasm. "We watched you from the garden, and you boys were shifting!" he continued, expecting perhaps a high-five or some sort of reaction or confirmation.

Frank peered over from the back of the couch. "You sleeping, Monty?"

"Drunk, maybe?" suggested Stan.

Monty opened one eye — his good one — staring up at the two excitable faces looming over him. "I'm not drunk," he said. "I've only been back ten minutes, and I only have one tin during TT."

"Everything okay, Monty?" asked Frank. "I thought you'd be ecstatic. You're nearly in the top-ten fastest lap times!"

"I guess."

"You guess? You *are*, Monty!"

"Have you fallen out with Dave?" asked Stan. "Where is he?"

"He just texted me. He's in a meeting with the organisers about the big willy drawn on the race van. Seemingly there's been a bit of bad blood over it. He said I should come up as it was starting to kick off, but I couldn't be arsed."

"They know who it was?" squirmed Stan.

Monty shook his head. "I guess not, otherwise they wouldn't be having only a meeting about it. I think you're safe, Stan."

"Dave's happy with the progress of the races?" asked Frank, confused with Monty's indifference.

"Over the moon."

Frank gave Stan a glance. "Are we missing something here, Monty? You're lying there like you've got the weight of the world on your shoulders."

Monty peeled his torso from the leather surface, pushing himself into a seated position. He cupped his face with his hands and let out a sigh. "It's nothing. I'm being stupid," he eventually offered, taking a another pause before continuing. "I feel like I'm letting you boys down. I feel like I'm letting Dave down. And I feel like I'm letting the sidecar down."

Frank laughed, expecting a punchline, though none came.

"Monty, you're being serious? You're nearly in the top ten, mate. This is utterly amazing. You should be spinning cartwheels with fireworks coming out of your arse, not sat here with your face tripping you up. Fucksake, you're not letting us down in any way, shape, or form. We think you and Dave are legends!"

"Legends, is right!" repeated Stan with an enthusiastic thumbs-up.

Monty took a half-hearted mouthful of beer, which was concerning in and of itself since he never did any beer drinking half-heartedly. "I'm holding Dave back," he told them.

Frank laughed again, waiting for another absent punchline. He really needed to judge a situation with greater proficiency. "Monty, with respect, what the hell are you on about? The pair of you are flying!"

Monty reflected for a moment, taking another mouthful of beer. "Guys, that bike is too quick for me. I don't know what it is, whether it's this bloody leg injury from last year. Perhaps the crash had a bigger impact on me than I thought. Maybe my confidence has gone?"

Frank and Stan sat either side of the topless Monty, both placing a hand on either shoulder. It looked like they might start giving him a rubdown. With his free hand, Frank took his phone from his pocket and presented it to Monty. "Look at this photo, Shaun Montgomery. What do you see?"

Monty's focus, up close, wasn't razor-sharp, so he arched his neck back and looked down his nose, squinting with the one eye that would best cooperate. "It's me and Dave going past your house?" he hazarded a guess.

Frank nodded. "That's right, it's you and Dave going past our house on your way to a nearly *one-hundred-and-eight-mile-an-hour lap* in the Isle of Man TT, and it's only bloody practice week!"

Monty permitted a smile. "I know. Perhaps I'm being stupid. That engine, though, Frank, it's unbelievable. Dave, he's unbelievable. Frank, yes, we're doing that lap time. But I promise you this. Dave is one of the finest sidecar riders on that track and our outfit..." he said, scratching his head, poised in thought. "That outfit has the capability of a place on the podium. I promise you, it's that good. The problem... the problem is that I don't think *I'm* good enough for it."

"Can I get a massage next?" chuckled Dave, returning from the meeting. "I want in on this action!"

Dave collapsed into the leather seat, giving a fond nod to his friend. "Don't you just absolutely love this?" he said. "We're sat on a crappy leather sofa in the middle of a field, with close friends, you're getting a massage and I'm up next, and I wouldn't change it for the world! Well, apart from one small detail. A beer, just the one, would be good," he said, looking over to the beer fridge, then to Frank, and then looking back over to the beer fridge.

Frank was on it immediately.

"How did the meeting go?" asked Monty, which caused another chuckle from Dave.

Dave reached over, slapping Stan's leg. "Oh, Stan, that giant cock is absolutely priceless. It was on Napier's truck, as it turns out. They're all going completely mental up there. Happy days."

"They've not washed it off?" asked Stan, looking cautiously over his shoulder to make sure no one was in earshot.

"Yeah, but whatever was in the spray doesn't seem to react too well with paintwork. There's still this big outline of a huge block and tackle," explained Dave, tracing the phallic figure in the air to illustrate. "It's in the paintwork and they can't get it off. Their sponsors are going mad. Honestly. Priceless."

"What was the meeting about?" asked Monty.

"They wanted all the riders brought together as they don't want this escalating. They were asking if anyone noticed anything."

"They definitely don't know who did it?" asked Stan, nervously fidgeting with his collar.

Dave shrugged his shoulders. "Well everyone in the paddock thinks Napier's a cock. So everyone's a suspect. It'd make a really bad Agatha Christie book, actually. Or good one, depending on your perspective."

"Oohh, I know!" offered Monty. "What about, *The Case* of the..."

"Yes?" said Dave encouragingly.

"No, sorry. It's gone," Monty concluded.

"Ah," said Dave. "Oh," he continued, gripping his phone. "Oh, that's perfect," he said, suddenly struggling for breath, his shoulders heaving.

"What?" asked Frank, moving in for a closer look. "It's a picture of Tom McMullan? What's so funny?"

Dave pinched the screen, enlarging the image. "Look at what he's holding."

Monty started to laugh uncontrollably, before coming abruptly to a halt. "Nope, I don't get it," he said, the uncertainty evident on his face.

Stan moved his head an inch from the phone for a better view. The leather sofa was starting to resemble the set of a gay porn film: Frank still had his hands rubbing Monty's half-naked body, and now Stan's head was positioned two inches from Dave's crotch, and with Dave making overenthusiastic happy gulping and gasping noises.

"That's the tin of paint I used?" Stan put forth. "To make the—?"

"I know," replied Dave. "I threw it into the McMullans' garage. The fact that Tom happened to pick it up as I had my camera at the ready was a happy coincidence."

"Ah-ha!" exclaimed Monty, followed shortly thereafter with: "No. I still don't get it."

Dave, ever patient as far as Monty was concerned, pointed at the tin. "Napier and Thomas have a huge knob etched in the paintwork of their expensive truck. I've got a picture of his arch-enemy, Tom McMullan, holding a tin of white paint, and they don't need to be geniuses to jump to the wrong conclusion."

Monty raised a knowing finger. "Ah, I'm with you," he confirmed. "Print it off and slide it under their door."

"Exactly! That's the plan, Monty. Then we sit back and watch the pyrotechnics. Beautiful!"

"Should I just own up?" asked Stan.

Dave shrugged his broad shoulders. "You could, Stan. I'm guessing, a respray on a truck that size would be, maybe, let's see... carry the one, add the eleventy-seven, divide by nought..."

"How much??" Stan pleaded.

"Five thousand?" Dave suggested.

"Five thousand pounds??" said Stan, his voice rising several octaves. "I agree. We should definitely print that picture off."

"It was all kicking off at that meeting," Dave went on. "Henk was there. And the other bloke, Rodney Franks. You know you meet people who suit their name? I don't know why, but Rodney just looks like a Rodney, do you know what I mean? You just want to get him in a headlock and give him a wedgie."

"We should totally do that," said Monty. "Hang on, what happened to my shoulder rub?" he asked of Frank.

"I thought I was finished?" replied Frank.

"Did I say to stop?" countered Monty. "No I did not."

"Anyway," continued Dave, removing his own shirt in preparation for a shoulder rub on the gay porn couch. "Henk had printed off the leaderboard for the lap times and just held them in front of Franks. Whenever the officials weren't looking, he kept flipping him the bird. It was like being back at primary school. Absolutely brilliant."

"What did Rodney do?" asked Frank.

"Not a damned thing. Which is what made it especially amusing. I mean, what could he do? Henk is, what, six-foot-ten, or something ridiculous? Not to mention built like a Dutch draught horse."

"And then what?" asked Monty, expectantly.

Dave gave a shrug. "No idea, they chucked me out at that point. I wasn't actually invited to the meeting in the first place, it was only for the top riders and I just blagged along, being the nosy bastard I am. See, I only went up to throw the tin in the garage in the first place, and when I saw everyone looking deadly serious, I thought I'd head in to see what was going on. It's probably still going on now."

"We saw Henk this morning and he looked to be in high spirits, didn't he, Stan?" asked Frank.

"Sure did. So, the McMullan brothers only need to win one race and his Vincent is safe. They're pretty much guaranteed to win at least one?"

Frank nodded. "Yes, one race and his Vincent is safe. Oh, and his Aston Martin, although I still don't think he knows that's in there. The bet was about a clean sweep, so the victor has to win both races. But looking at the lap times, it would seem the McMullan brothers are going to be hard to beat in both races. In which case, Henk may well win himself a farm."

Stan appeared somewhat less than happy at this prospect. "Henk's not really the farming type," he said flatly.

"Not to worry, Stan. I spoke to Henk," explained Frank. "The only thing he's after is winning both races, regardless of any bet. And the only thing he's interested in, aside from that, is making Rodney Franks look like a tool."

"Franks doesn't need much help there, though, does he?" offered Dave, who looked around impatiently to see when his own shoulder rub might arrive. "I'm not really interested in their bet, myself," he went on. "All I care about is me and that fine specimen right there finishing in the top ten," he said, with a finger to Monty. "And seeing as how Monty is hogging all the massage action for himself just now, I suppose I'll head over to the shower block and clean myself up."

"Don't forget to print the picture off!" shouted Monty.

"On it," replied Dave. "Our top-ten finish would be a lot more achievable with the two favourites suspended for bashing the hell out of each other!"

Monty waited until Dave was out of earshot. "Don't say anything, will you?" he asked. "Dave needs to have complete confidence in me and if he thinks I'm injured or not one hundred percent, it will give him a nagging doubt."

"You'll be okay?" asked Frank.

"I'll be fine," replied Monty, rubbing his leg. "Being stuck in a metal tube going a hundred and fifty when you're only a couple of inches from the ground can cause a bit of bother when you're recovering from a leg injury. I'll be fine, though, guys. We'll get that top-ten finish."

Frank sniffed the air. "Fancy a greasy burger and a pint, Stanley?"

"You have to ask?"

The pair of them walked towards the tent at the rear of the grandstand, where dozens of people stood nursing plastic glasses, perhaps talking about the evening's practice session or more likely escaping from the noise inside.

"Good god, what on earth is that noise? Is that coming from the pub?" Frank asked.

"Is that karaoke?" rejoined Stan.

Frank put a finger to his ear. "I hope so, or I'm calling the RSPCA because there's a cat being tortured somewhere."

Ordinarily the bar would have thirsty patrons three or four deep waiting to be served, but they marched straight to the front. "That voice is doing us a favour," remarked Stan, offering a cordial wave to the barman. "Two pints, please!" he shouted over the noise, licking his lips in anticipation.

Frank leaned against a stool with a contented expression. There were a lot of similar expressions to be found in TT week — despite the present keening going on — evident as Frank looked around to the other patrons.

Stan pressed a beer into Frank's receptive hand. "You look happy, Frank," he remarked.

Frank took a sip, offering an agreeable nod. "I've got a cold beer in my hand and I'm at the TT with my dearest friend. And so I am. Say, you hear that voice?"

"Couldn't really miss that, Frank."

"Does it sound strangely familiar to you?"

"It sounds strangely. Do you know something I don't?"

"Go and stick your nose around the corner and have a butcher's," Frank urged.

Stan did as requested, and, rather than return with a grimace of abject horror regarding the mutilation of Bon Jovi's "Livin' on a Prayer," he had the visage of a man who'd just watched his first-born graduate.

Stan joined Frank back at his leaning post.

"I didn't know Stella sang karaoke?" said Stan, close to Frank's ear.

"Sing? You're being kind there," Frank answered with a laugh. "I think Stella's found her people," Frank added, that look of serenity back on his face.

"How do you mean?" asked Stan

"Look at her," said Frank, with a nod in her direction. "Stella wouldn't do that at home. Yes, she's full of bravado. But, deep down, there's a vulnerability there. She's not self-conscious, but she's been kicked that many times that it must start to hurt, eventually. Those faces," continued Frank, pointing to the crowd near to Stella. "Look at them. There's a genuine warmth. They're not taking the piss out of her at all. Just the opposite, in fact. They look like they really want to be with her."

Stan put his arm around Frank. "I don't think I've ever seen Stella smile like that, now you mention it. Well, at least not for a very long time."

"You're not wrong," Frank agreed, taking a mouthful of lager and exhaling contentedly.

"I wasn't sure about Lee and her at first," Stan added. "But look at him. I think he honestly does like her."

"Do you ever think about her?" asked Frank.

"Who?"

"Craggy Sally... Sally."

Stan smiled. "Of course. Often."

"So do I," said Frank. "She was a character. She put up with a lot, back then. We probably weren't the easiest to work for."

"I'm not sure we'd have been a fraction as successful as we were had it not been for her, having her in our lives, I truly mean that. She kept us in check, that's for certain. Well, she kept *me* in check, at least," offered Stan fondly. He looked over at Frank. "Hang on, what's this? Have you got a tear in your eye?"

"Maybe. I'm getting overly emotional lately. I'm blaming the Isle of Man beer. Sally would be proud of her granddaughter, wouldn't she!" remarked Frank, as a statement of fact rather than a question. "Do you think we've done what we promised?"

"Looking after Stella?"

"Yes."

Stan thought for a moment. "I'm not sure if it isn't *Stella* looking after *us*," he said, his eyes getting a bit misty as well. "But, yes. She's not everyone's cup of tea, but she's loyal and honest. Sally would be proud of her. Should we go and say hello?"

"Let's leave, shall we?" suggested Frank. "Leave her to her new friends? We'll finish this pint and go and get that greasy burger."

"You sure you don't want to hang around for the next song? Stella's downing her pint and looks poised for another rendition!"

Frank drained the contents of his pint, double quick. "It's a tempting offer, Stan..." he said, looking at the watch he didn't have on. "Stan, you know tomorrow, for the practices?"

Stan pointed to his ears, then indicated for Frank to hold that thought until they'd escaped the feline being tortured, so to speak, for a second time.

"Say again?"

Frank cleared his throat and looked rather sheepish. "I was saying about the practices tomorrow. Would you mind if the two amigos became three for the night?"

"Of course not, why?"

"I was going to invite Dave's mum. If you don't mind?"

"Frank, why would I mind, you silly twit?"

"I just didn't want you to think that..."

Stan slapped Frank's arm. "Think what? That we're not exclusive? Perish the thought! Frank, I just want you to be happy, and if Jessie can make you happy, then *I'm* happy."

Frank handed over a ten-pound note.

"Two cheeseburgers, please."

"You'll need more than that up here, Frank. A tenner will probably buy you just the cheese!"

"That better be some damn fine cheese, then," Frank replied with a chuckle.

Frank rifled through his wallet. "So you won't feel like a spare wheel?" he said, serious again.

Stan's expressive left eyebrow answered well enough that question on his behalf, no further words necessary. "So," was all he said, after a moment.

"So, what?" asked Frank, busying himself dispensing notes like a cashpoint.

Stan smirked. "So what does Dave think about all this?"

"I'm going to tell him, honestly! But I don't want to give him any distractions at the moment."

"That's what I always say about you, Frank, you're nothing if not considerate. One question, though, if I may?"

"Anything, old chum," offered Frank, eager to please.

"Dave doesn't have an uncle you can introduce me to, by any chance?"

"I'll be sure to ask!" said Frank with a laugh. "Now that would be an entertaining conversation to have with Dave, wouldn't it? It would definitely take some of the heat off me. And that would, I think, be a rather unique double date, Stanley."

"Unique? I think Dave would need counselling."

"You mean more than usual?"

Chapter Twenty

Friday night of practice week was the final opportunity for valuable track time ahead of the first races on Saturday. The Island had been blessed with glorious weather all week with not one practice session lost to the elements, but there was time enough to make final adjustments to eke out that extra mile an hour with the optimum set-up.

For Dave and Monty, the weight on their shoulders was lightened by having already qualified for race day by virtue of their impressive lap times in practice. They hovered just outside the top ten, but the indications were that a finish higher up the leaderboard was absolutely possible.

Dave's knowledge of the track was considerable, but he never stopped honing his skills. The ability to know where you could keep her pinned in sixth, for instance, rather than dabbing the brakes, dropping her down a gear, and losing valuable momentum into the next sector was crucial. You never stopped learning and complacency was reserved for fools. And you might be the most seasoned campaigner on the start line, but this course changed each year as well. The yellow gate you used as a braking marker previously could now have been painted red, for example, or the phone box which told you when to attack the corner could simply have been removed or partially obscured by an unkempt hedge. If you were overconfident, this course had the ability to bite back, and bite back hard.

The sun hung low in the sky and the breeze was absent, while the same, sadly, could not be said for the midge population who were in attendance, mob-handed. Stan flapped his hand like a hummingbird's wing as the little blighters locked in on his position, but his defence was to no avail.

The course was littered with vantage points, and for many a spectator a fair few hours had likely been spent deliberating over a pint as to which one was the best — but there was no one correct answer. Each and every location had its own unique charm.

Union Mills Church, in particular, gave the audience on the church lawn a view up to the Railway Inn where the bikes negotiated a sharp right-hand bend before most took to the air, landing just in time to tip her into the left-hander as you opened the throttle to gain maximum velocity into the flat-out Ballahutchin.

Stan handed over a cup of tea, "This is some spot, Frank. They've got cake and everything in there," he said, thumb pointing back in the direction of the church hall. "You, eh, a bit nervous, Frank? Only you've not stopped fidgeting since we arrived. Where's Jessie? She seems to have gone missing. She hasn't buggered off already, has she?"

"I'm fine," replied Frank, wiping moisture from his forehead. "And she's just taking a call." Frank leaned closer to Stan's ear. "I'm just a bit nervous about this whole dating thing. Which is irrational and pathetic, I know — I'm a grown man!"

"Jessie's really laid-back, Frank. She's actually pretty funny, also. I like her."

Frank nodded. "I know, I think that's why I'm nervous, because I quite like her." He shifted his weight from one foot to the other, uneasily. "Stan," he whispered. "I'm not sure I'll be able to get—"

"Say no more," replied Stan, offering a knowing wink. "Just pop along to the chemist. You don't even need a prescription now, and, trust me, they'll have you back on parade before you know it."

"Cheeky bugger! That's not it!" protested Frank, loudly at first, but then lowering his voice when two neighbouring women took a step away to distance themselves.

"Everything is working just as it should, thank you very much," he went on. "Granted, it's been on somewhat of a sabbatical of late. I just meant that– Here, will you stop looking at my crotch, Stan?" Frank protested, using his TT programme to shield from view the focus of Stan's attention. "Anyway, Stanley, you certainly seem to know an awful lot about the subject?"

Stan made a show of puffing out his chest, swelling with pride. "We all need help from time to time, Frank," he said, running a hand through his professionally-enhanced mane. "Sometimes you just need a little assistance to get your flag to unfurl."

"But... you're single." Frank shuddered, musing on the solo application.

"Always be prepared, Frank," suggested Stan, with an insightful tap of the index finger on his temple. "The Boy Scouts taught me that. Besides, you never know when your situation may change and you don't want to disappoint! Boy Scouts, Frank."

"Yeah, probably not the best context in which to reveal your Boy Scout training!"

"The sidecars are heading off in a few minutes," announced Jessie, back in the group and saving what was turning into an awkward conversation. She had a pocket radio pressed to one ear, and her outdated mobile phone was to the other. She took a position between Frank and Stan, and, once done with her phone, weaved her arms into theirs and did a little happy-dance on the spot.

"Everything okay, Jessie?" asked Frank. "Just that you looked a bit stressed on the phone. It wasn't Dave, was it?"

Jessie took her arms back so she could pull out her phone once again. "Dave's fine, he sent me a text about an hour ago saying he and Monty were having fun times, which I took to mean all is well. Who even talks to their mother like that?"

The pair of them shook their heads and tut-tutted to her in sympathy, though, in truth, neither understood what exactly the problem was.

Jessie's face hardened. "Anyway, I keep trying to reach my cousin June. I was trying to call her when Dave texted, in fact, but she wouldn't pick up. And I keep checking but she's not gotten back to me and I've no idea why. This isn't like her at all. Either I've managed to upset her somehow or something has happened."

"Ah," said Stan, with a nod in acknowledgement. Men often gave this nod as a way of saying, *I hear you and no further explanation required.* Whereas women often mistook this gesture as, *please tell me all about it, and don't leave out a single detail.* It was a balancing act for the male population; with no gesture of empathy, one was considered rude, but too much interest and you were opening yourself up to several minutes which you'd never recover, ever.

"What happened?" asked Frank, who clearly hadn't read the script judging by the angle of Stan's left eyebrow.

"Her dog died, poor dear, and quite rightly she's devastated. She's had the little fellow since he was a puppy," explained Jessie. "Anyway, after a couple of texts she called me something I don't feel terribly comfortable repeating. And then nothing since," she said, checking her phone for messages once more. "Still nothing. I don't even know what I've done to offend her!"

"May I?" asked Frank, holding out his hand to her.

Jessie handed over her phone, nodding her head. "Of course. Here you go. Maybe you can make sense of it all, because I certainly can't."

Frank scrolled his way through the text message conversation, and, in spite of his best efforts to hold it at bay, a smile swept its way across his face.

"What?" she said. "What's so funny?"

"Jessie..." Frank answered, struggling to contain his laughter. "You do know what L-O-L means?"

Jessie appeared slightly offended. "Of course I do," she replied. "It means *lots of love*. Everybody knows that."

Frank wasn't even trying to hold back his laughter once he'd reread the messages yet again. "Oh, Jessie, I'm sorry," he said, placing a hand on her shoulder. "I'm sorry, but this is absolutely priceless. I can see why she's a little cross with you at the moment!"

The look on Jessie's face said that she wasn't at all clear what the joke was about.

"Jessie, I hate to break this to you, but L-O-L means *laugh-out-loud*, and not *lots-of-love*." Frank was now wiping a tear with the back of his hand. "Oh, my," he continued. "Oh, my," he said again, and then reading aloud for Stan's benefit as well as to play the words back to Jessie:

June:	Jessie, I tried to call. Oscar died in the night. He wasn't well, but still devastating
Jessie:	Oh June. LOL. I'll phone you tonight
June:	LOL?
Jessie:	Yes LOL. My biggest LOL
Jessie:	😂
June:	Did not expect this from you

"Jessie, one more thing," said Frank, finger pointed at the screen. "You see this little thing? I think they call it an emoji."

"Yes, sad face," declared Jessie.

"Yes, well..." Frank began, trying to be as gentle as possible. "That's not the sad face, actually."

Jessie moved in for a closer inspection. "But it is. Look, there's tears on its face, it's in anguish, poor wee thing."

Frank shook his head. "Sorry, Jessie, only that's an emoji you use when's something really tickled you. They're tears of laughter, see?"

"Oh," she said. "Oh, dear."

"Yes. Your cousin told you her dog's died and you not only laughed-out-loud but added in a tears-of-laughter symbol for good measure!"

"Oh, dear," Jessie said again. "You see? This is why I don't do bloody technology. I always get it wrong!"

"I'm sure if you phone her tonight, she'll understand," said Frank, taking her arm once again.

Stan arched his neck, looking for what he could hear was imminent. "Oi! Forget all that. Here we go!"

You'd be forgiven for thinking the noise in the air was the clap of thunder, but the skies were clear and you were at the Isle of Man TT, and it could mean only one thing: machines were approaching at great speed!

Spectators who'd taken the interlude to rest their legs jumped to attention, with the first sidecar on the road approaching. If you closed your eyes, you could follow their progress with just your ears. With each approaching meter, the decibel level increased a tone as did the anticipation. Your heart rate began to increase, the air somehow had a stillness and although you were surrounded by dozens and dozens of people, nothing was said. Like a horror movie, you knew you were about to be startled when the stillness was shattered, but it was compelling, compulsive, and you couldn't take your eyes off a small stretch of tarmac where your focus was fixed.

Frank looked up towards the Railway Pub, where those enjoying a pint in the beer garden would be a visual indication of the first arrivals. The marshals stood poised, shielding their eyes from the sun, and the wildlife — sensing what was coming — either took to pad or hoof, or took to wing.

Your ears were momentarily distracted from the horsepower hurtling along Peel Road, past the Snugborough trading estate, by the *thump-thump-thump* from overhead — which felt like it was coming down on top of you. You looked up at the TV helicopter bursting through the trees, but you didn't have a chance to wave as the first sidecar negotiated the bend in front of you, the passenger performing acrobatic miracles to clamber over to the right. For a split second, it looked to those in the church grounds that it was heading directly for you, until the passenger manoeuvred swiftly to the left, ensuring the outfit carried the maximum velocity through the left-hander.

Jessie looked up at Frank and Stan and all thoughts of June's upset were forgotten in the moment.

Frank took a pause to scour the crowd, once again looking for those who might be experiencing their first TT. He smiled at the sight of a small boy, three, maybe four years of age, with ear defenders almost as big as his head. The boy jumped back in awe as the sidecar screamed by in glorious fury, and he clutched at his father's sleeve, demanding to be picked up for a better vantage point before the next bike would come into view.

"Any minute now!" announced Jessie to the others. "There's Number Thirty-Eight! That means our Number Forty-Two is coming soon!"

She counted them through, one by one, hopping on the spot in nervous anticipation, but their own outfit did not appear. "Now that's peculiar," she said. "I know they left the grandstand since I heard Chris Kinley say as much on the radio."

Frank immediately looked to the marshal's post, where the flags were fortunately fixed in a resting position — a positive sign, since flags being picked up would indicate some sort of incident.

Jessie checked her phone. "He'll always send me a text if he pulls over," she told them, but immediately shook her head. "No. Nothing," she said, fixing her eyes on the road once more. Her shoulders fell in relief when, finally, Dave and Monty appeared.

"They must have had mechanical problems?" she mused aloud. "Do they look slower than the other machines? What do you reckon?" she asked of Frank and Stan, but their blank looks in response indicated that they knew less than she did.

Jessie tilted her head, listening to the bike in question with a trained ear as Dave and Monty whizzed past and disappeared up the Ballahutchin. "Hmm. Well it doesn't sound like anything's wrong," she put forth.

Stan produced his phone where the TT app was loaded to monitor lap times through the various sectors. "We'll soon see when he gets to Glen Helen," he suggested, in reference to the official timing point on the circuit, a sweeping left-hander just over nine miles from the starting line.

"Get lively, boys!" shouted Jessie with a vigorous shake of the fist, as much a directive as cheering them on. "A good lap time tonight will give them the world of confidence for the race tomorrow," she told her companions.

Their three heads peered down on Stan's phone as the timing beam was broken by those first on the road. They saw the times for those behind Dave flash up on the screen, but not for Number Forty-Two. The McMullan brothers topped the pile by some distance, but when Dave and Monty appeared on the board, they were significantly off the pace.

"At least they're through," offered Frank.

Jessie's normally cheery demeanour was somewhat flat. "Of course, but I know how disappointed they'll be right about now. I just hope there's nothing wrong with the bike. They'll be devastated, especially as they had a fair chance of a top-ten finish."

When Dave and Monty didn't break the timing beam at Ramsey Hairpin, Jessie instinctively took her phone from her pocket.

"It's Dave," she said, but the absence of colour in her cheeks told Frank and Stan what they already knew.

Jessie put her hand to her mouth. "Oh, no," she said. "Dave will be in tatters."

She read the text aloud:

> We're fine, but had to pull over. The TT dream is over for the year.

Chapter Twenty-One

...We knew we were on track for lap records to tumble this week, after the blistering pace in practice and near-perfect conditions, but that Superbike race has left me breathless. As I look out from the tower at the Grandstand, I can see a few clouds rolling in but the rain which threatened earlier in the day looks to have missed us. With that, Chris Kinley, I'll hand over to you trackside so I can get my breath back ahead of the three-lap sidecar race in a little over twenty minutes, at three p.m.

Yes, thank you, Tim Glover. Well, what can I say about that Superbike race that's not already been said? For the thousands around the circuit and many more listening in around the globe, how about that for a starter to this year's TT? It doesn't stop there, folks. In a little over... well, eighteen minutes now, the action continues with the hotly anticipated sidecar race. A number of the machines are lining up and I can see the two favourite outfits. As we know, it's the McMullan brothers who've set the pace in practice. But you really cannot discount Thomas and Napier, who've been impressive and perhaps with more track time can really mount a challenge.

Announcer Chris Kinley now gingerly approached Andy Thomas...

Andy, the conditions are perfect as we've seen in the Superbike race earlier. Are you confident you can catch the McMullan brothers?

With that, he thrust his microphone under Thomas' helmet.

"Yes," came the terse response, followed by a long pause.

Kinley waited, in hopes for further comment, but nothing else presented itself...

Right. Okay, thanks, Andy.

Chris returned to his commentary:

I'll leave them alone. There's a lot at stake for these guys and I can see from the intensity in his eyes that he's well and truly in the zone. Other machinery is being wheeled onto Glencrutchery Road where they'll all get their chance to sit under the starting arch, waiting for the tap on the shoulder to send them on their way.

I've been doing this for years, folks, but I can honestly say I've never experienced such a sense of electric anticipation.

Ah! Now, then. There's a pleasing vision if ever I saw one. Excuse me, folks, if I can just get through? Thank you, excuse me. Okay, I'm delighted to see this man with his leathers on.

Chris thrust his microphone like a knight with a sword.

Dave Quirk! I'm delighted to see you ready for racing. You pulled in just before Ramsey in last night's practice. Everything okay with the bike? And, Dave, if you'd be kind enough, please remember you're on live radio!

Dave opened his mouth, feigning a look of insult.

"I'd never swear on live radio, Chris. I wouldn't do it to a friend like you. Yeah, the bike's fine, Chris. In fact, she's running like a dream. The problem is rather the two old codgers on board, if I'm being honest."

Is that from the crash last year?

"It is, Chris. Monty's been having a few problems — well, more than he normally has — with his leg, hip, and that. I got the tap on the shoulder last night as he was really struggling."

And you're okay for today?

"We'll see, Chris. Monty's been with the physio all morning, but we'll do what we can. If everything goes to plan, we'll be in that top ten."

I wish you well, Dave Quirk.

"Oh, Chris. One more thing?"

Yes?

"Bollocks and boobies."

Chris shook his fist at Dave, before extending his middle finger. There were benefits of being a radio commentator at times.

Well, folks, there you have it, local rider Dave Quirk eyeing a top-ten finish. And apologies for the salty language.

"Bollocks and boobies?" said Monty, once they had themselves back to themselves again. "I'd have gone for something a bit more... well, *better*, is all."

Dave pulled his helmet over his chubby cheeks. "And that, Monty, my old son, is why Chris Kinley doesn't interview you anymore. He knows I've got a touch more class, doesn't he?" he offered cheekily, whilst using his left hand to pull leather from the crack of his arse. "So how's the leg?"

"Better. Look, Dave, I'm sorry that I've been slowing you down."

Dave punched Monty playfully in the arm. But Dave's hands were like shovels, and unfortunately for poor Monty even friendly punches impacted like a wrecking ball.

Monty rubbed his shoulder, now one more injury that'd have to mend.

"You shut your cakehole, Monty, you hear me? Just shut it, mate," Dave told him with affection. "Sure, I'd like a top-ten finish as much as the next fella. But I do this because I love it. And if I didn't race with you, I wouldn't be racing at all. So, let's go out there and have some fun, right? Don't hurt yourself, Monty. And you let me know if you're struggling, yeah?"

Monty nodded, and rubbed his shoulder some more.

"Where are they?" asked Jessie, almost falling over herself.

Stan felt the pressure, holding his phone aloft in a desperate attempt to gain mobile data. They'd returned to their favourite viewing spot just before the Highlander, but sadly the dense canopy of trees was once again playing havoc with their reception. "Oh..." said Stan, watching the egg timer having a fit on the screen. "... Yes!" he shouted, punching the air. "They're through the grandstand on lap three!"

Those riders higher up the starting order had gone past their vantage point sometime earlier, but all Team Frank & Stan were interested in was how Dave and Monty were progressing.

"Go on, Dave...!" Stella called out, between sucking the life out of another fag and adding the dimp to an ever-growing pile by her foot, "... You great knob!"

"Where are they?" asked Frank, wrestling with the plastic digits on his scoreboard. Frank had been promoted to afford Dave with a scoreboard, indicating what position he was circulating in.

"Position sixteenth, Frank," provided Stan, eyes fixed on the phone. "He's seven seconds down on the guy in front."

"Roger that," confirmed Frank, poised with his scoreboard. "I can't actually believe they've got this far!" he shouted as another machine hurtled past.

Frank, Stan, Jessie, Lee, and Stella all leaned out over the rope in expectation. Yes, Dave and Monty were further down the leaderboard than they'd hoped, but a few hours earlier they didn't even think they'd be on the start line let alone looking likely to complete three gruelling laps of this majestic circuit.

"Breathe," said Frank, placing a friendly arm around Jessie's shoulder. "You'll have no fingernails left, either, you keep that up!" he told her, referring to the fingertips being nibbled in her mouth.

Jessie tucked her head into Frank's chest. "Frank, I get so nervous. TENA Lady should introduce a TT version for ladies of a certain age!"

"We should suggest it to them!" agreed Frank with a laugh, releasing his grip and leaning forward again with his scoreboard just as the big blue boiled sweet that was sidecar Number Forty-Two burst gloriously into view for the final time.

Dave, who knew they were there, lifted his left hand from its grip just enough to manage to offer a flicker of a wave as he tramped on towards Greeba Castle.

"You've got the scoreboard the wrong way round," Stella observed casually to Frank.

"Bastard!" said Frank, now frantic.

"You're a bit late now," Stella told him. "They've already gone."

Further cursing issued forth from a frustrated Frank.

"One job, Frank. One job," Stella said, with a derisive shake of her permed bonce.

"I've bloody lost it!" shouted Stan.

"I've been saying that for years," offered Stella, now on a roll.

"No, the reception's gone!" Stan replied, trying to get a signal, and windmilling his arm around like Pete Townsend playing the guitar.

"Anything?" asked Frank.

Stan mashed the keyboard. "Not a bloody thing, just this rubbish egg timer. Bloody trees!" he shouted, starting a fight with them.

Leaves rustled in the breeze, but otherwise there was no response from the trees.

"Come on," suggested Jessie. "Most of the bikes have gone through now. We can walk back to the car and may get better coverage once we're clear of the trees?"

The five of them walked along the railway line, with Stan in the lead and the others in formation behind them. They looked very much like migrating geese in their 'V' formation — all eager to look at Stan's phone.

The egg timer eventually disappeared, putting them out of their misery. Stan clutched the phone close to his chest so only he could see, keeping the others in suspense for a moment.

"Well??" demanded Frank. "We can't see!"

"Bloody fourteenth place!" Stan shouted, now leaping up on the spot.

The five of them formed a circle on the long-since defunct rail route, and in the middle of the Isle of Man countryside they joined hands and gambolled about as if they were around an invisible maypole — temporarily blocking access to the passing cyclists.

The cyclists weren't angry their progress had been impeded. They understood perfectly as this was, after all, the Isle of Man in TT week.

Frank grabbed one of the dismounting cyclists, taking him like he was offering a waltz. "Our man has just finished the TT in fourteenth place!" he gushed.

No further explanation was required, with the cyclists offering a celebratory high-five, before continuing on their way once they'd disentangled themselves from Frank's friendly advances.

Frank and the others held their arms linked as they made their way down the old railway line. There was a spring in their step as they marched with vigour, five across, faces beaming from ear to ear. They looked like they were travelling down the Yellow Brick Road, the lot of them.

Emotions were a mix of pride, admiration, relief, and several others that could ultimately be summarised in no other way than, *The Isle of Man in TT Week.*

Chapter Twenty-Two

"No way. You're being serious?" asked Frank, but before Dave could answer, Frank ushered Stan into the conversation.

"Four sausage baps and four teas," said Stan, joining Dave and Frank on the leather sofa. "Here, no Monty? I've bought him a sarnie."

"He's at the physio. But never mind that, Stan, listen to this," insisted Frank.

Dave rolled his eyes, as he'd regurgitated the story several times already.

"Sauce?" asked Dave, in regards to the food. Once that was sorted, he then took a mouthful from his sausage sarnie, creating a crescent moon in what remained.

"It all kicked off round here, last night," began Dave. "I'm surprised you didn't hear the sirens at your house."

Stan loved a bit of gossip, moving closer as Dave chewed down on his breakfast, hanging on his every word.

"Well," continued Dave, wiping flour from his cheek. "Andy Thomas was told on very good authority that Tom McMullan was the one that'd drawn the huge meat puppet on the side of his van, so he marched down to have a friendly chat with him."

"They don't know who it really was, do they?" asked a nervous Stan for the umpteenth time.

"No, you're fine," Dave assured him. "Anyway, before Andy could get a word in, seemingly Tom McMullan was in possession of a photograph of Andy with Tom's girlfriend, and it all kicked off. Tom threw several punches and got himself arrested."

"But Andy didn't?" asked Frank.

"No, technically, he was just defending himself. He managed to get a couple of punches in, as well, and cracked a bone in his hand in the process."

"One of the phalanges?" asked Stan.

"No, one of the McMullans. And Andy Thomas. I just said," Dave corrected him. "Haven't you been listening?"

Frank's jaw dropped in astonishment. "Why's Tom gone and done that? They won the first sidecar race handily. If he's been arrested, will they let him race on Friday?"

"Doesn't matter," replied Dave. "The organisers have been convinced he drew the cock on the van, or the *coq au vin*, as I like to call it. Oh, that's brilliantly clever..." he said, trailing off, and impressing only himself, before regaining his thought process.

"They've had enough of him, what with the assault charge, so they've kicked him out of the TT. Harry's furious, apparently," chuckled Dave. "So, with Tom locked up and suspended and Andy Thomas with his hand ruined, we may have a chance of finishing higher up on the leaderboard without them four tosspots racing."

"I don't imagine Henk is going to be especially pleased by this development," reflected Stan. "His sidecar took the first race at a canter, winning it easily, so chances are they'd have easily won the second? That little scuffle has lost him the chance of taking the farm from that Rodney

Franks fella. On the other hand, there's no way for him to lose the bet, either. But I'm damn sure he'd have relished beating that muppet given the opportunity."

"Ah, fuck 'em all. More money than sense, that lot," said Dave. "And here he is," he said in relation to Monty, who had successfully rooted out the breakfast sat on the table. Like a trained pig snuffling for truffles, no food-like substance escaped Monty's *au fait* snout.

"That for me?" asked a drooling Monty.

Stan handed it over. "Sure is. How's the leg?"

"You won't get all that much from him just now," Dave advised. "Let him eat, then he'll be back with us. He said he was in a bit of pain, but the physio sessions have been helping."

Frank took to his feet. "Well done, again, guys, by the way. Yesterday was a fantastic result. Top ten next Friday?"

"We'll see," shrugged Dave. "It's quite nice to know those four idiots won't be on the top step, at least. Where you off?" he added, noticing the lads were collecting themselves to go.

Frank prodded Stan. "We're picking Lee and Stella up. I said we'd take them around the course, with it being Mad Sunday today."

"Go easy out there," warned Dave. "Most folks will be out to enjoy the atmosphere, but you'll still get the odd idiot who's got all the gear but no idea," he told them, making a point to pronounce the invisible 'r' at the end of *idea*.

The blood in Stan's face drained as he checked his phone. "I've just had a missed call from Henk?"

"So?" asked Frank.

"Well, suppose he knows about me drawing the coq au vin which ultimately got his rider chucked out?"

"Ha!" exclaimed Dave, happy to see his newly-minted expression catching on.

"Why else would he be phoning me?"

"Don't be so bloody paranoid," Frank answered. "He's our neighbour, for god's sake. Perhaps he wanted you to put his rubbish bin out? It could be anything at all. Seriously, just phone him back."

Stan pondered that thought. "I'll ring him later. Maybe let him calm down a bit. I imagine he's a bit grumpy at the moment."

"Well come on, then," Frank told him, leading the way. "Let's go and discover what this Mad Sunday is all about. See you soon," he added, throwing Dave and Monty a wave.

Dave held up his hand and wiggled his fingers in cheerful reply, but there was no response from Monty as he was still immersed in his sausage bap.

Frank looked nervously in his rear-view mirror. "You're starting to scare me, Stella,"

"I bought my very own leather trousers for the occasion," she said sharply. "They weren't cheap, either. You two will be reimbursing me for them."

Stan bravely joined the fray, leaving Frank to concentrate on the exceptionally busy road. "Stella, with respect, of course. When Frank said we were going to take you around the TT circuit, at what point did you think we were going to be doing that on motorbikes? When have we ever said to you that we've passed our motorbike test or even that we own bikes? It was always going to be in the car."

"What's with this rubbish car, anyway?" she continued, still less than pleased with the current circumstance. "You pair are loaded!"

"It's a hire car," replied Stan. "We're between cars. Are you okay, Stella?" asked Stan, looking around into the rear passenger seat. "Only you're sweating a little more than usual."

"These trousers are... a little tighter than I expected," she offered, pulling down on them at the ankle. "Can you put the air conditioning on, please?"

"This rubbish car doesn't have air conditioning," said Frank, winding down the window.

"Well I think they're just grand," said Lee with a cheeky grin. He gently caressed the top of Stella's thigh for good measure. "They accentuate your curves."

As for curves, Frank approached the Ramsey Hairpin where the mountain road became one-way for the duration of the racing fortnight and those riding knew they'd not meet any traffic coming up the other way. Historically, it was just Mad Sunday that the authorities did this and attracted the name — which considering the standard of some of the riding was rather apt. The vast majority of locals and visitors rode to their capabilities, but, sadly, for a few, the enormity of the occasion often became too much of a temptation to push a little further than they should, and the TT circuit could be unforgiving as sadly many discovered too late.

"I shat myself up here, a little further on," said Stan cheerily, turning again to the back seat as if announcing an upcoming tourist attraction.

"You sound quite proud of that?" remarked Frank.

"If you're going to do it, Frank, it's as fine a place to do it as you could ever find," Stan replied. "Stella, do you want some water?" he added, seeing she was still in distress.

"I don't think these trousers were the best idea I've had," she conceded.

"You think?" replied Frank with a narrowing of the eyes.

The Ford Ka in which they were sat struggled away from the famous hairpin, through Waterworks Corner, and towards the Gooseneck, a sharp uphill right-bend. This combination placed strain enough on the engines of those racing through it, and for a subcompact with a small engine and Stella in the back, it's fair to say the poor 'rubbish' rental struggled up the Mountain Mile.

"Oi! Did you just hit me?" asked Stan, rubbing the back of his head.

"No," said Stella, struggling for breath. "The button just burst off these damned trousers. I think I need to take them off, I'm not sure I can feel my feet anymore."

"What are you wearing underneath?" asked Frank.

"You filthy old sod! You're lucky you're driving!" she admonished Frank. "Otherwise I'd—"

Frank raised one pacifying hand. "I only meant do you have anything underneath so you can take them things off and remain decent?"

"I've got my black leggings on," Stella replied, taking a quick peek to double-check.

"Oh joy," muttered Frank.

"What was that?" asked Stella, but was drowned out by the sound of a bike leaving them for dead.

"They're a bit quick, I'd say?" asked Lee rhetorically, peering out the window.

There were dozens of bikes behind in convoy, hugging the left side of the road, with many more passing by at breakneck speed on the right side of the road.

"Jaysus!" shouted Lee. "That one must be doing over a hundred and fifty!"

As soon as one bike overtook them, another and then another appeared. If you were not a confident driver, this was one place you'd be advised to avoid on Mad Sunday. The police were in position on several locations, ensuring those enjoying the day did so with consideration to the others on the road.

"You're kicking the back of my seat, Stella, and considering how busy it is up here, that's not a good idea," said Frank without daring to remove his eyes from the road.

"Well I've got to get these things off, don't I, and there's not enough room back here in this sardine tin, is there? You'll need to pull over."

"Where, exactly?" asked Frank. "I've got about four thousand bikes up my arse and we're on a race track."

"You could pull over where I shat myself," suggested Stan, as if it were the most normal thing ever.

"Right! Where Stan shat himself, it is!" Frank declared, unhappy and irritated at having to repeat the words. "And just in case you missed it, *again*, we'll be stopping *where Stan shat himself*. Stella, you'll need to hold on for about three more minutes."

"It really is a lovely spot," Stan offered, a beatific smile over his face.

Stella didn't reply, rather, easing back into her seat like she were giving birth.

"You may want to hurry that along," cautioned Lee, wiping Stella's brow.

With sporadic moans of pain and explosive motorbike exhausts, it was a miracle that Frank made it to Windy Corner, a sharp right-hand bend where the elements were ready to snap at those riders unprepared for the furious winds.

At their arrival, Stan looked back at the others once more. "This is where I—" he began, in an animated fashion.

Frank slapped the steering wheel, cutting him off. "Yes! Stan, we know! Everyone knows! I think you even put it on your Facebook status, yes??"

Frank eased into the gravelled area, which made for a spectacular vantage point with the glorious, gorgeous Manx hillside rolling in front of you, resplendent in all its, well, resplendence. Three photographers were stationed on the corner capturing those passing, as was a St John Ambulance — on hand to offer assistance should the need arise.

"I may require a bit of help?" suggested Lee, tugging at Stella's arms. "I don't think this is a one-man job."

One man became three men as Frank, Stan, and Lee extricated Stella from the car, but by now the leather had either shrank or her legs had begun to swell from the lack of circulation.

"I can't walk," said Stella through gritted teeth. "You'll need to carry me."

"What?" asked Frank. "I'm not a well man, and carrying you is not how I envisaged the circumstance of my demise. Why can't you take your trousers off here?"

"I've already warned you about your tone, you saucy old sod!" advised Stella, hobbling forward a pace. "We're right next to the road, and most of these riders haven't seen an attractive woman for days," she said by way of explanation. "So you'll need to take me over there," she said, pointing. "By the wall."

Lee leaned down, placing an arm under her right leg. "I'm here for you," he assured her, puffing out his chest. "And we'll get these trousers off of you, we surely will!"

"Remember that sentiment," cackled Stella. "Come on, you two useless buggers," she said, directed at Frank and Stan. "These things are killing me!"

They took up position, as directed, but the task at hand was easier said than done.

"I think... I'm getting... a hernia..." gasped Stan. "Or perhaps... a fractured... spine... or maybe both."

Progress was slow and painful as the three of them shuffled forward as if carrying a very heavy wardrobe up a flight of stairs.

"Everything all right, there?" called over one of the photographers.

"Marvellous!" shouted Frank. "We're actually having a wonderful day out, thank you! Beyond that, this is just a typical day for us!"

The second Stella was out of sight of the road, those gripping her legs gave up their grasp — and possibly their will to live.

Stan put his hands on his thighs, lowering his head to catch his breath.

"What are you doing? Do you think you're finished?" demanded Stella. "These trousers are too tight for me to remove alone. You're going to have to help me!"

Frank removed her shoes, taking up a position by the right ankle, with Stan positioned on the left. Lee was tasked with the area further north. With Stella's help, they all pulled on the trousers, but the leathers refused to budge.

She looked up at Lee. "Go and see if the ambulance has got something that'll help. Maybe some scissors?"

With Lee dispatched, Frank and Stan returned to the struggle, but their hearts were no longer entirely in it. Sweat dripped off the pair of them.

"They've given me this," said Lee, once returned, handing Stella a bottle.

"It's soap," she said, reading the label. "I don't need a bloody *wash*, I need these things off."

"They thought the soap may lubricate your skin and release the trousers," Lee explained, and then added with a shrug, "I'm just the messenger."

"Fine," replied Stella, lying on the ground with hands behind her head. "On you go, then," she said, looking up, but those looking down did what they could to avoid eye contact.

"I'll step up," said Lee, pulling at Stella's waistband.

He pressed down on the nozzle several times in quick succession, releasing the contents of the bottle down into Stella's nether regions. Lee then rubbed her thighs, from over the surface of the trousers, to try and circulate the viscous fluid.

"It's cold," said Stella.

"I'm not," replied Frank, all but collapsed in a heap, and happy to be able to rest for a moment.

"Is it working?" asked Stella. "Can you tug them right off now?"

Lee redoubled his efforts, but the trousers were nothing if not resolute. "The soap's starting to foam up," said Lee, braving a peek. "It's like a broken washing machine down there."

"I think I've got scissors in the car," offered Stan, with a wag of the finger.

Frank sighed. "And why are you just telling us that now? Go and get them!"

"Right-ho," Stan answered, skipping off to the car.

"We'll have you out of those right quick, Stella," said Lee, still knelt down beside her.

"Here we are!" announced a well-chuffed Stan, once returned, device in hand.

"What the hell?" said Frank, moving in for a closer look. "Those are fingernail scissors!" he declared. "What good are they going to be against a pair of leather trousers that've already bested three grown men??"

"Give 'em here," Stella said, motioning for the scissors, and, once in hand, setting upon the leather trousers with them.

"Are they working?" asked Stan hopefully, eager to accept the praise he felt he was due.

Stella didn't speak, handing back the diminutive curved scissors — now bent, with the top blade hung over the bottom like a horse's teeth.

"No," said Stella, finally. "They didn't."

"I don't mean to interrupt," said a paramedic, interrupting, who'd likely seen enough. "Only I wondered if you'd fancy the use of these shears?" he asked, presenting a formidable pair that Edward Scissorhands would have been proud to call his own.

319

Stella looked up at Lee. "When I said to see if they had something that'd help, why did you return with soap when they'd had scissors all along??"

"I must've panicked? Yes, surely that's what it was, I panicked," Lee offered. "I don't know what happened, the moment must have gotten on top of me?"

Several quick flashes of steel and the leather trousers were a threat no longer. Stella was able to stand with assistance as the blood promptly returned to her feet, circulation restored.

"I need a fag," she proclaimed, with not a word of thanks offered. She stood watching the bikes banking over to their right without a care in the world, as the soapy suds ran down her black leggings. "Ah, fresh air," she said serenely, cocking her leg, and taking in a lungful of smoke.

"Pants!" shouted Stan, pointing at his phone. "It's Henk again. Should I answer it?"

"Fucksake, Stan, he doesn't know about your big cock! Just answer his call!" replied Frank, to the confusion of the paramedic taking back his scissors.

The paramedic backed away very slowly, and, once clear of the group, scampered off back to the relative safety of the ambulance.

"Hello? Yes, Henk, how are you?"

After a moment, Stan offered a thumbs-up. *It's not about the cock*, he mouthed, helpfully pointing toward his own crotch to emphasise the point.

While Stan was on the phone, Frank took the opportunity to step away and appreciate the view. He'd only been to Windy Corner twice now, and once was when Stan had been taken short, as it were, and the other — presently — was with Stella, well, being her own inimitable self. He promised himself he'd have to make a point of returning under perhaps more pleasant circumstances.

Frank walked back to the others a few minutes later, just as Stan was ending his call. "Everything okay?" he asked Stan.

Stan nodded but sported a troubled expression. "All good. Henk was telling me about Tom McMullan being arrested and kicked out."

"That's nice of him?" suggested Frank, unsure why Henk would take the trouble to call.

"It appears it's only Tom that's been suspended, not his brother."

"And the point, please? I'm not getting any younger here."

"Well here's the thing," continued Stan. "If Henk can get another driver, then his outfit can still enter the next sidecar race. And the bet he had with Rodney Franks—"

"Fuckface," offered Frank.

"Right. The bet he had with Fuckface only covered the sidecar, not who happened to be on board. So, if Henk can find another suitably equipped driver, he can still have his sidecar race, possibly do the double with both wins, stick two fingers up at Franks, and win the bet."

"That's all very interesting," said Frank, in a tone of voice indicating it wasn't all that interesting. "What's that got to do with us?"

Stan took a moment. "Frank, as team principals, he wants our permission to approach Dave to ride his sidecar with Harry McMullan as passenger. He said the same as what Monty himself told us previously, that Dave has the ability to win a TT with the right machinery and the right passenger. Dave really is that quick."

"He wants us to break up Dave and Monty? We can't do that! What did you tell him??"

Stan shrugged his shoulders. "I told him that it wasn't really our call to make. I said we'd put it to Dave and Monty. In the end, if Dave has a shot at winning a TT, who are we to stand in his way?"

Frank looked across the road wistfully, before turning back to Stan.

"You're right, we can't stand in the way on this. But if Dave does it, Monty will be destroyed. Hell, and what a choice for Dave — fulfil your lifetime ambition, but doing so whilst kicking your closest friend firmly in the bollocks. I'm glad I'm not the one making that decision!"

Chapter Twenty-Three

It's not happening! Not whilst I've still got a hole in my arse!" announced Dave, unconcerned by those out for an evening stroll around the paddock. "I don't care what it means, and I don't care who it'll upset. It's not happening, so get that through your thick skull!"

"You told him, then?" asked Stan, cowering behind Frank. "Who's he on the phone to, Frank? Is it Henk?"

But before Frank responded, Dave hung up the phone, stomping toward their position.

"So... you decided not to do it?" asked Stan tentatively, stepping out from behind Frank's shadow.

"Hey, guys. Do what?" asked Dave, picking oily grime out from under his nails.

Frank sharpened his elbow, delivering a less-than-discreet blow. "I've not told him," whispered Frank through the corner of his mouth.

Dave's face was still reddened and angry from his call, moments before. "Do what?" he repeated to Stan, who'd now retreated once again — leaving Frank to receive the question.

Frank looked this way and that. "Monty not about?"

"He's at the physio."

"Right," said Frank, mustering up his courage. "Dave, you know about Tom McMullan being arrested," he began.

Dave's face was now returning to its normal colour, at least temporarily. "Thanks for the reminder," he chuckled.

Frank paused for a bit, then continued. "Dave, before I proceed," he said, with some trepidation. "That call you were just on. That wasn't by any chance Henk you were shouting at?"

"Why would I be shouting at Henk? No, this was that bloody fitness instructor you employed," Dave said. "He thinks it would be a good idea to lay off alcohol for one month. That, of course, will not be happening."

"Okay, anyway," continued Frank. "Henk hasn't been to see you?"

"Noooo," Dave replied slowly. "Why would he?"

Frank looked around once more, ensuring Monty hadn't returned. "Dave, before I tell you this, as your sponsors, and your friends, we're one hundred percent happy with whatever you should ultimately decide."

Dave turned up his nose. "You're not trying to fix me up with your friend, Stella, are you?"

"What? No, look. Henk phoned Stan this afternoon. Tom McMullan can't race, as you know."

"A shame, innit?" replied Dave, chuckling once more.

Frank took a step forward. He was going to place his hands over Dave's shoulders. However, considering their respective heights, and the raised elevation of Dave's shoulders, he settled for a pat on Dave's chest.

"What's going on?" asked Dave. "Why are you two acting so odd?"

"Dave, Henk wants you to take Tom McMullan's place. He wants you to pilot his sidecar with Harry McMullan as your passenger. He believes that you as driver and Harry as passenger, on that bike, can win the TT..."

Frank said all this without daring to pause for breath.

"Okay. You do know you can't just swap like that, don't you?" said Dave.

Frank looked at Stan. And then he looked back to Dave. "You can't?"

"No, of course not. You have to qualify. Henk would know this."

"Oh. So I guess it's not possible?" asked Frank.

Dave thought for a moment, rubbing his chin, which he did when deep in thought, which wasn't that often.

"It is theoretically possible, I reckon," he conceded. "You'd have to complete three laps at a qualifying time. There are precisely three practice laps next week, with two of them on Monday after the Supersport solo race, and the third on Wednesday, after the Lightweight solo race. That's also assuming the Clerk of the Course would give the change the green light, but I don't think it's been done before so I'm not sure what he'd say?"

"So you'd consider it? You know, if all went to plan?" asked Stan.

"Heavens, no," said Dave. "That was all hypothetical. I would *never* split up the dream team that is Dave and Monty, not ever. It'd be like breaking apart fish and chips. Or bangers and mash. Theoretically it could be done, sure. But what would be the point of it?"

"It's a relief to hear you say that, actually," Frank said.

"We were worried this could get very awkward," said Stan, feeling it safe to emerge from behind Frank now the crisis was over.

"I know, yeah. Don't get me wrong, it's a nice idea. But Monty and I are inseparable, as I said. So, it's a no from me. Anyway. Beer?" asked Dave, pointing to the fridge.

"Good god, yes!" replied Stan. "If you'd seen what Frank and I had to do in the name of friendship earlier today, you'd understand our need for alcohol."

After the first beer was demolished, Monty appeared, heading straight for the beer fridge himself. Monty didn't speak, draining the contents of the tin in one go, before reaching for another, and then another, and then one more.

Watching Monty down a can of beer was compelling viewing, but Frank felt the requirement to nevertheless interject. "Everything okay there, Monty? You seem thirstier than usual."

Monty collapsed back onto the leather sofa, holding his wonky gaze skyward. He didn't speak for an age. Finally, he turned to Dave. His face was grim.

"Dave, I'm not sure how to say this, but it's over for us."

"What?" laughed Dave. "Can't we at least talk about it? Is it something I said or did? I can change, you know. Monty, is there someone else?"

"I'm serious," Monty went on. "Dave, I've just been to the physio and she's told me enough is enough. The leg hasn't healed, and she said it's fucked if I carry on racing. Well, not those words exactly, but that's the general theme. Dave, if I stay on, I'll only make a dog's dinner of things, and I may not walk again. I didn't want to tell you, and I'm shattered, but... there's no other option."

Dave's jovial expression turned serious as well. He thought for a moment before speaking.

"I'm sorry about that, mate. I really am. We had a shot at the top ten on Friday, but, your leg is more important, so no hard feelings. I'm gutted, but, well..." Dave stood and gave Monty a firm embrace. "Some things are more important, Monty," said Dave, failing to hold back a tear.

Monty excused himself, likely to recycle the vast quantity of lager he'd just consumed.

Frank placed a comforting hand on Dave's. "I know this isn't the best time, Dave," he ventured. "But there is that other option. We should go and speak with Henk directly."

Stan nodded. "Frank's right, Dave. You can't give up on your dream. You've got a shot at the title, and ending it now would be a tragedy."

"It's true," Frank joined in again. "Dave, you could very well be an Isle of Man TT Winner. You simply cannot let this opportunity pass you by. Monty will understand. He'd want this for you."

Dave looked at his watch, and then to Frank and Stan. "I'd be mad not to, wouldn't I?" Dave looked down to the ground, deep in thought, twice in such a short time frame.

"Come on, boys," said Dave after a fashion. "Let's go and see Henk."

"I'll wait here," said Stan. "Maybe have a drink with Monty. You want me to mention this to him?"

"Please," confirmed Dave. "I'd have told him myself, but it's getting late and if we're going to do this we need to do it quickly."

Stan walked around the awning, caressing the oil-soaked surfaces, pondering on how this environment was now so important to him. He really wouldn't be without it.

Monty returned, clutching another beer.

"The beer's helping your leg, Monty?" remarked Stan, in reference to the absence of any observable limp.

Monty took that as another instruction to take his medicine. "It is, at that," he said, pulling up with a now visible limp, like a lame horse.

"I thought it was the other leg?" asked Stan.

"What?"

"Your limp, Monty. It seems to have moved to the other leg." Stan smiled, realisation dawning. "You've given your friend the chance to win a TT, Monty. Haven't you?"

Monty didn't react until the waterworks began. "Damn beer is playing with my emotions," he said, unconvincingly. "This is between me and you, Stan. Promise?"

Stan handed him a box of tissues. "Monty, I promise."

Monty reflected. "We wouldn't have gotten a top-ten finish with me onboard, Stan. We just wouldn't have. This is a once-in-a-lifetime opportunity for Dave and there was no way I was getting in the way of that."

"Oh, bloody hell, Monty. Now you've got me going as well," sobbed Stan. "Give me some of those tissues back."

After Stan had regained his composure, he said, "Monty, your friendship with Dave. It reminds me of mine with Frank. You're very lucky in that regard, you know, to find someone who's like that as a friend. Not everyone has that in their life."

Monty raised his beer. "Here's to my good friend, Dave. Hopefully soon to be a TT winner!"

Chapter Twenty-Four

Dutch Henk was a formidable force: built like the side of a house, and the life and soul of the party, but, if you were on the wrong side of him, you'd better watch out for he wasn't backwards in coming forwards.

"YOU VERY LARGE PIECE OF THE EXCREMENT!" he screamed, marching with vigour through the TT paddock. Those finding themselves in his way quickly made it their business to make certain they were not in his way for long.

"WHERE IS RODNEY FRANKS?" Henk demanded, looming over a grease-covered mechanic who dropped his spanner in fright (and with his bowels likely loosing next). The mechanic picked up his spanner without daring to break eye contact, raising it weakly, and pointing it with a trembling hand to a temporary office at the back of their awning. "In there?" he offered with a breaking voice.

Henk didn't wait for further invitation, rather, striding over and virtually taking the door off its hinges as he burst through. Rodney Franks pressed himself against the back of his chair, for his only exit was blocked by the hulk of a man in front of him.

Franks' chief mechanic Abe Maddocks, currently sat on the corner of Rodney's desk, stiffened up for a moment. "Are we going to have trouble here?" he asked bravely, though likely only to impress his boss.

Henk looked straight through the mechanic and pointed his index finger — which resembled a braadworst sausage — straight at Rodney, causing Franks to wheel his chair back a foot or two until it was up against the wall and could go no further.

"TOM MCMULLAN IS STILL BEING HELD BY POLICE BECAUSE OF YOU!"

Rodney raised his hands in feigned innocence. "It wasn't me who started throwing punches!"

"YOU WERE THE CAUSE OF THE PUNCHES! YOU GAVE TOM MCMULLAN THE PHOTOGRAPH OF HIS GIRLFRIEND WITH ANDY THOMAS! ANDY THOMAS IS YOUR OWN RIDER! WHY IN GOD'S HELL WOULD YOU EVEN DO THIS? YOU MUST HAVE KNOWN THAT TOM WOULD KNOCK HIM... AH!" said Henk, circulating like a rabid animal. Henk started to laugh. "AH, I SEE NOW WHAT YOU HAVE DONE!"

The valour in the mechanic's demeanour began to wane as quickly as Henk's increased. He slid over the desk trying to reach for the phone as casually as possible, but Henk's further advancement brought a halt to that notion.

Henk stood over the desk with a crazed smile on his face, saying: "YOU KNEW THAT BY GIVING TOM THAT PHOTO HE WOULD LOOSEN HIS MIND AND THAT HE WOULD BE DISQUALIFIED FROM THE RACE, OR EVEN WORST! YOU DID THIS BECAUSE YOU KNEW IF WE WON THAT SECOND RACE YOU WOULD BE HANDING TO ME THE FARM YOU WANTED SO BADLY FOR YOURSELF! YOU REALLY ARE A LARGE PIECE OF THE EXCREMENT! THE VERY LARGEST PIECE OF THE EXCREMENT! YOU WERE WILLING TO SACRIFICE YOUR OWN RIDER JUST TO AVOID LOOSING A BET??"

Henk's look of disgust was now matched by that of the mechanic. "Boss, tell him that's not true... It's not true, right, boss? Boss?" Maddocks asked, though it seemed he already suspected the answer.

Rodney grinned like a petulant child. "What can I say? The hotel I'm going to build on that farm will be worth a fortune. We're both businessmen. You can understand, surely? I'll tell you what, Henk. If you want in on a slice of the action, just ask, how's that?" Franks wheedled.

"MY RIDER IS IN THE JAIL!" Henk thundered in his inimitable Dutch drawl.

"I didn't think they'd come down so hard on him," Franks replied with a shrug and a smirk. "So that was just an unexpected bonus, I suppose." And then he laughed.

Henk flung himself over the desk, taking a grip of Franks' cravat. The very fact that Rodney Franks wore a cravat was in itself an egregious offence.

The mechanic, Maddocks, whose look of disgust intensified, grabbed Henk's arm — but not in an aggressive manner. "Leave him, Henk," he said calmly. "You don't want to end up in jail with Tom."

Henk held his grip a moment, then threw Franks back against his chair. "I WILL BET IT WAS YOU THAT TOLD ANDY THOMAS THAT TOM HAD BEEN DRAWNING THE *FALLUS* ON THE SIDE OF THE VAN, YES?"

"I should think you'd have had enough of bets, Henk?" sniggered Franks. "What can I say? If the photo didn't get them to fight, the huge cock would."

Henk shook his fist, indicating he was about to launch an assault.

"Do it, Henk!" taunted Franks, holding out the point of his chin as an easy target. "Please, be my guest."

But it was Abe Maddocks who swung into action, swiping his arm across his boss's desk, spilling the desktop's contents to the floor. He looked down on Rodney with contempt.

"I always defended you, Rodney, gave you the benefit of the doubt. Most people think you're a Grade-A tool, but I always stuck up for you. Always."

"That was your mistake?" Franks offered with a sneer.

"You know how hard me and the boys have been working on your sidecar," Maddocks went on. "But you were willing to potentially get your rider injured or even disqualified, all to win a bet? Well, you can take your job, Rodney, and stick it right up your arse!"

With that, Abe grabbed Henk's arm once more. "He really isn't worth it, Henk," Abe told him.

Henk lowered his fist. "YOU ARE NEEDING A JOB? YOU COME WORK FOR ME?" he asked.

"Sure," said Abe, flicking one final finger in Rodney's direction.

Henk took a breath for composure. "I HAVE JUST SPOKEN TO THIS CLERK OF THE COURSE, RODNEY!" he said with a smile emerging. "YOUR OBJECTION TO OUR CHANGE OF RIDER WAS REJECTED! DAVE AND HARRY HAVE NOW COMPLETED THREE QUALIFYING LAPS AND THEY ARE READY TO RACE ON FRIDAY!"

Franks shrugged his shoulders and waved his hand dismissively. "Dave Quirk?" he laughed derisively. "You've got to be joking. He's a fat grease monkey! Granted, Harry is an impressive passenger. But, Henk, Quirk is a club racer at best." Rodney reached for the qualifying timings on his desk but they were no longer there, courtesy of Maddocks. Franks carried on, undeterred. "Have you seen the timings that Quirk and McMullan have put in? They're two miles an hour slower. You haven't got a bloody chance."

"WAT DENK JULLIE WEL, VUILE TYPHUSLIJDER, DAT IK MIJN KOSTELIJKE BEDDEN DOOR ZULKE SIKRETEN LAAT BEZIJKEN!" bellowed Henk. And then, remembering to speak English: "FUCK YOU! AND FUCK..." he said, looking around the office. "FUCK YOUR BIN!" he added, swinging his leg like a pendulum, and launching the metal object straight towards Rodney's head.

"Temper, temper, Henk," said Franks as he dodged the projectile, which served only to rile Henk further.

"WE WILL BE BEATING YOU ON THE FRIDAY, RODNEY!" continued Henk, with two of his braadworst fingers now aimed at Franks like a gun. "AND WHEN YOU HAND ME OVER THIS FARM, I WILL BE BUILDING YOUR HOTEL, AND IN THE TOILETS OF THIS HOTEL WILL BE YOUR PHOTO! AND WHEN PEOPLE GO TO LEAVE THEIR FAECES, THEY WILL SEE YOUR DISEASE-RIDDEN FACE AS THEY DO THIS, AND TRUST TO ME, I WILL BE THE FIRST OF THE PEOPLE DROPPING THE VERY LARGEST OF THE FAECES IN YOUR HONOUR!"

Maddocks escorted him out, more for Rodney's safety, and to also keep his new boss out of jail.

Once clear of the awning, Henk casually turned, with full composure regained. "Was that tirade sounding okay to you?" he asked of his new friend Abe Maddocks, and with his volume level now reduced to nearly human level.

Confused, Abe held his response for a second. "Sure, I think Rodney may have pissed himself. If that's what you were after?"

"Ah, good. And what about the dropping of the faeces? English is not my first language, you see. Did I get this right?

I know how it is with the English loving to drop excrement everywhere."

"Sorry?" said a confused Abe.

"In your language," Henk explained. "You like to play with your excrement. We Dutch, however, are much more sophisticated in our cursing."

"Oh?" asked Abe, unsure what else to say.

"Yes, yes!" replied Henk excitedly, mistaking Abe's response for interest. "In the Nederlands, we use disease-related words for our cursing and insults!"

"Disease?" said Abe, at a loss again how to further reply.

"Yes!" Henk answered, animatedly. "It is a much more civilised way of speaking!" he said. "No offence to you English," he added.

"None taken?" replied Abe, uncertainly. "So, when you were yelling at Rodney, what is it you were saying, then?"

"Ah, yes! Sometimes, when I am excited, I forget to use my English! I told him, *Wat denk jullie wel, vuile typhuslijder, dat ik mijn kostelijke bedden door zulke sikreten laat bezijken!* I will translate this for you. This means, *What do you really think, dirty typhus sufferer, that I will allow my desirable beds to be pissed upon!*"

"*Em...?*" offered Abe encouragingly.

"Yes! It is very excellent cursing!" Henk replied enthusiastically. "This is proper cursing, yes??"

Truth be told, Abe wasn't sure quite what to make of this Dutch style of cursing. But Henk's enthusiasm was infectious, and he burst out laughing in response.

"Yes, yes!" said Henk, clapping a massive hand on Abe's back and joining in on the laughter.

"Excellent!" said Henk, after Abe had picked himself up off the ground, giving his newest employee a warm embrace. "Welcome to the team! Excellent! Now, there is a sidecar over there that I want you to make love with!"

"Okay?" said Abe, now taking the language differential in stride. "I'll go and make love to the sidecar, boss."

"Good! I must go and give motivating love to Dave and Harry!" replied Henk.

"Brilliant. I hope they enjoy it?" said Abe, with a cheery if somewhat confused wave.

The glorious smell of grilled meat wafted through Frank and Stan's garden, teasing the noses of Stella and Lee. "I'm wasting away to nothing over here!" Stella proclaimed. "How long for a burger, Frank?"

"She likes her meat, this girl," smiled Lee, before the expression on Stella's face saw him quickly backtrack.

"Five minutes, Stella. Though you should maybe take a moment to digest the previous two before you have another?" Frank suggested.

"Did I ask your opinion? I don't think I did. You worry about the cooking, Frank, and I'll worry about the eating," said Stella, using a twig she'd picked up from the garden to clean food from between her teeth.

Stan, ever the gracious host, returned from the kitchen carrying a trayful of exotic-looking cocktails provided in an array of different colours. "I love a good helping of Tom Collins on a warm summer's evening," he declared.

"Whut, no lager?" enquired Stella bluntly.

"Try this, Stella," suggested Stan, handing over a delicate glass that all but disappeared in Stella's mitt. She looked at it suspiciously, raising the glass to show her displeasure at the minimal volume, before draining the contents faster than Stan even had time to serve the next guest. Stella wiped her lips before taking another glass from the tray and dispatching that one just as quick.

"Stella, that was for..." Stan began. "Eh, nevermind," he said agreeably. "I'll get another one."

"Good. Don't forget my lager while you're in there," demanded Stella, handing back the newly emptied glass.

Frank arrived in short order with a platter of succulent meaty treats, fresh from the grill. "So, Lee. You've enjoyed your trip to the Island thus far?"

"Loved it, Frank. And loving it," Lee replied, reaching for a burger, but his hand was promptly brushed aside by Stella's.

"I'll take that, thanks," said Stella.

"I can see why you and Stan have fallen in love with the place," Lee went on. "It's beautiful, so it is. And as for the racing, Jaysus, I've never seen anything like it. I watched a few videos of the racing on the internet, of course, but the real thing is an entirely different animal. I think I'm going to book my ferry passage for next year, if that's okay with you both. Stella's really enjoyed it too. Haven't you, Stella?"

Stella clutched her stomach like she'd been winded. "Are you sure those burgers were properly cooked, Frank? My gut's making some noises here. Hold that," she said, handing her latest burger to Lee. "I may be some time."

Lee's smile was unwavering. "Honestly, guys, she's really enjoyed it."

Frank took a seat one side of Lee and Stan the other, with both placing a firm hand on either of his thighs and giving them a squeeze.

Lee looked uncertain as to where this was headed. He knew of Stan's persuasion, naturally, and wasn't the least bit offended, of course. But now Frank as well?

"Em, lads...?"

Frank patted Lee's thigh like a drum. "You and Stella..." he began.

"Ah!" said Lee, somewhat relieved.

"We're pleased for you both, Stan and I," Frank went on. "Aren't we, Stan?"

"Very happy," Stan chimed in.

"Lee, can we ask you a blunt question?"

Lee lowered Stella's burger. "Of course."

Frank chose his words carefully. "This isn't some sort of stupid stunt?" Right, well possibly not so carefully.

"Or a bet?" added Stan.

Rather than take objection, Lee returned the overtly friendly leg-touching. "Frank... Stan... I know how much Stella means to you both. I also know how much you mean to her. Stella's not everyone's cup of tea, I totally get that, but I genuinely like her. She makes me laugh, and hopefully she likes spending time with me as well. I promise you both that my intentions with Stella are honourable."

"I can see that she does," Stan offered kindly.

"I'll take good care of Stella, I promise you lads. I see something in her that we three can see well enough, but that perhaps most others may not take the time to see." Lee nodded his head serenely. "I've gotten to know Stella as someone very special and important to me," he went on. "She's sensitive, caring, warm, with a gentle underbelly. She's quite something."

"She is quite something," Frank agreed with a laugh. "On that we can all agree."

"My ears burning?" growled Stella, fag glued to her bottom lip. "Best not go in there, by the way," she cautioned them, pointing in the direction of the downstairs toilet. "For at least ten minutes. I'm shittin' through the eye of a needle and I'm sure it's your burgers, Frank," she said, raising the trajectory of her fag in Frank's direction.

Stella's warning was interrupted by the arrival of Dave and Monty.

"Something smells good!" remarked Monty, opening the gate.

"It doesn't in there," said Stella, pointing once again. "It won't be safe for a bit yet. Fair warning."

There was a collective hush, with Dave eager to break the silence:

"Henk came to see me earlier. He really doesn't like that Rodney Franks. Oh, and we've got a new chief mechanic, fella by the name of Abe Maddocks. Good he is, too. Reckons he can get a bit more out of the bike for us."

"A bit more," repeated Monty, for no discernible reason, for which Dave gave him a glance but let it pass.

"Anyway," continued Dave. "Henk is desperate to do the double over Rodney, as you know. Seemingly it was Franks who gave Tom the photo so Tom'd get himself disqualified. He also spread it around that it was Tom who drew the giant coq au vin."

"So," Stan interrupted, clearing his throat. "Nobody thinks it was..."

Dave shook his head. "You're fine, Stan. Oh, and guess what he's offered me? Well, offered the charity, I mean."

"He's going to give the farm to the charity," said Frank. "Yes, we already know that."

Dave lowered his head. "Oh, *em*... no. He's decided to keep it, actually, and build the same hotel that Rodney Franks was planning. Shit. He didn't already tell you this?"

"No, it must have slipped his mind," Frank replied bitterly. "But... you know, I think it was more than we could've really handled anyway," he added, trying to look on the positive side.

"Bollox, now I feel bad because whatever I say, it's going to be a let-down," said Dave.

"Let-down," offered Monty.

"Anyone eating that?" asked Dave, casually, of Stella's burger, but before he moved an inch, Stella whipped her arm out to claim it in a motion quicker than a chameleon's tongue.

"It's mine," she told him, eyes narrowed. "So don't even."

Frank and Stan stood with jaws hanging. "Dave, hello? So what did Henk say?" asked Frank.

"What's this big news?" Stan added.

"Oh, yeah. Almost forgot. Okay, well, to be fair, I did ask him to gift the farm to the charity as I knew how much it meant, but he just laughed that big laugh of his."

"That big laugh. You know the one," Monty put forth.

Dave sighed, then continued on: "What he *did* say, though, is that it's probably going to be two or three years until the builders put shovels in the ground. So it's yours — well, the charity's — until that time. And it could even be longer. And at least this way you get to see if the idea for the farm will work out. Oh, and he said the all-important words... *rent-free.*"

"What? Dave, that's brilliant!" Frank answered, the wind returned to his sails. "Imagine what we can do with the place. I can see it now, Stan!" he said, holding his hands up in the air to frame an imaginary picture.

Dave slapped Frank's hands away. "I don't mean to piss on your parade too much, gents. There is the small matter of winning an Isle of Man TT. And for someone that's never broken into the top ten, I just, you know, want to manage some expectations, yeah?"

"We've got every faith in you both," replied Frank, before realising his error. "Shit, sorry, Monty," he added, cursing his own stupidity. "I didn't mean—"

"No worries, Frank, I'm well over it," Monty assured him. "I just want this big dopey baboon to be stood on the top step of the podium tomorrow. Truly, that's all I want."

Frank raised his can of lager. "I'll drink to that. Fucking hell, can you believe that this time tomorrow we might well be having a drink with a TT Winner? Come on," said Frank, ushering his flock to follow him.

They peered over the garden wall, looking up the length of Glencrutchery Road towards the start/finish line.

"Look at that, Dave," said Frank. "Visualise yourself hurtling along here tomorrow, heading for that line, to become an Isle of Man TT winner. Just close your eyes and imagine how that's going to—"

"Right. That's been ten minutes," announced Stella, looking at her watch. "So the smell of shit should have gone by now, if anyone should need the loo."

Chapter Twenty-Five

Harry McMullan was a man on a charge. "It's not difficult, Dave," he said sarcastically. "Watch how it's done," he continued, looking back to Dave, before leaning forward to the small boy hopping in excitement. "You want me to sign that?" he asked the happy little chappy.

"Yes, please!" came the eager reply.

"How about you bugger off instead, yeah? Go on, then!" Harry told the boy, shattering the child's enthusiasm in an instant.

Granted, the walk from the paddock to the start line could be a challenge, what with all the spectators vying for an autograph or perhaps a photograph with their sporting heroes. Most, apart from Harry McMullan, were perfectly accommodating. In fact, this was one of the very charms of this event; you had the opportunity to meet your supporters, and the fans their superstars.

Dave was as happy as a pig wallowing in the muck, walking through the crowds, absorbing the positive convo like a sponge, pausing for photographs, and simply making the most of the adulation. For he was under no illusions in that, tomorrow, once the race was done, he would simply be plain old Dave Quirk once again.

"What's up with you, Quirk?" asked Harry, with no attempt to hide his displeasure. "Can we get a move on?"

"Harry, will you just shut the fu– Oh, hello, princess, would you like me to sign your hat, luv?" asked Dave, changing tack mid-sentence, ever the professional. "I'm just looking for someone, okay?" Dave told Harry once the wee one's autograph had been sorted.

"Bloody hell, now's not the time, Dave! You're moving slow as a dino stuck in a tar pit, and we've a race to start, in case you've forgotten!"

Dave continued to sign autographs whilst looking through the crowd for a particular familiar face.

"We have to go! *Now!*" shouted Harry, in between ruining another child's day.

"Okay!" replied Dave, having one last glance around. "I'm coming."

Access to the pit lane area was obtained by passing through a narrow gate at the side of the grandstand, and, at this point, passes had to be shown. Senior race day in the Isle of Man was one of the biggest events in sport and every chancer was eager to get the best view of the proceedings.

The noise of a paddock on race day was overwhelming and a true assault on the senses. There were thousands of spectators, engines revving, TV crews, radio crews, helicopters hovering overhead. There was the smell of beer, fried food, oil, racing fuel. It was easy to be overtaken by the occasion, but Dave was no rookie; he took a breath and gave those waiting by the gate the courtesy of a wave as he had one final glance around.

"Dave, over here!" screamed a voice through the din. "Dave, wait up!" the voice shouted once more.

Frank and Stan were stood at the rear of the crowd, waving furiously. "Come here!" shouted Dave in return, waving them over.

"We can't!" replied Stan, shaking his head. "There's no way thr–"

Stella rose her head and with an air of confidence borne of iron will, extended her arms like a plough. "Coming through!" she said, politely enough — in Stella terms — but with a tone which made clear that those in front best move clear. "Coming through!" she repeated, lest any doubt of her intentions remain.

Stella ushered Frank and Stan through the sea of spectators, leaving people spinning in her wake, dazed, with cries of *"What just happened?"* and *"... force of nature"* and *"I feel seasick."*

Once arrived at the destination, Frank and Stan took Dave in their arms, stopping only to look at him with an expression of paternal pride.

"You're wearing the leathers!" cooed Frank, taking a step back.

Dave fanned his hands down his body, smiling broadly. "I told Henk that if I was racing in his sidecar, then I was wearing the ones with Team Frank and Stan's Food Stamps on them. After all, if it wasn't for you two dickheads, I wouldn't be stood here now."

"It's a nice touch, Dave, thank you," added Stan.

"No, eh, Monty?" asked Dave casually, unable to hide his dejection. "Oh, bother," he said, before anyone could answer. "Is that not—?"

"Move it along, you lot," instructed Adrian. "Keep it moving here!"

"We have to go!" screamed Harry, already ahead of them. "God, this is what you get when you deal with amateurs!"

"He's a real charmer, isn't he?" remarked Frank, rhetorically, since the answer was evident.

Dave smiled. "A complete tosspot. But he's good at what he does, so, I'm smiling sweetly and going with it. Guys, I really have to go. If you see Monty, will you tell him, well, you know—?"

"Pass, please," asked Adrian, blocking the path with his somewhat less-than-considerable frame. Evidently, Adrian remembered Dave as well, and was taking no chances.

"Would you believe me if I said I'd forgotten it?" asked Dave.

"I'd suggest you find it very quickly," replied Adrian, keen to disabuse Dave of the notion he'd get in without it. "Unless you want some more of what I've got to offer, that is," warned the boy, pointing to his flexed bicep which resembled nothing more than a picked-clean chicken bone.

Dave decided it best not to test Adrian's mettle just now, opting for the easier option, raising his arm to show his wristband pass.

"Very good. Hurry along, sir," replied Adrian, eyes narrowed in an *I'm-watching-you* steely expression.

"Dave, wait there!" shouted Frank, pointing over his shoulder.

Stella's ploughing duties had resumed, as this time she moved through the crowd with Monty tucked under her arm. This display of crowd manipulation drew an admiring gaze from Adrian, who dropped his guard, allowing Dave to step back through the gate.

"Eyes off, lads!" shouted Lee over the crowd as Stella pulled away from his side, to anyone who would listen. "That one's mine!"

Once delivered, Monty was deposited by Stella at Dave's feet. "Sorry I'm late, gents," Monty offered.

"Did you get it?" asked Dave.

"Yes, here you are," Monty answered him, transferring an item to Dave's waiting hands. "Now go!" he said, holding his most sincere crooked gaze. "Off with you! You can do this, mate! I'm so proud of you!"

Dave blew him a kiss and stuffed the delivery inside his leathers, giving a final wave.

Monty, turning to the others, looked more confused than usual. "Here, you've got passes to go through?" he asked of Frank and Stan. "Pit passes are rare as rocking horse shit! But... why haven't you gone in, then?"

Frank motioned towards Lee and Stella. "We all wanted to be together, do you know what I mean?"

"I'll stay with you?" asked Monty.

"That'd be nice," said Frank.

"It'd be nice," added Stan as well. "So what did you give Dave?"

Monty's bottom lip wobbled. "It was a photo of our first sidecar race. I couldn't find it at first, that's what's took me so long, but I finally managed to locate it, in a proper place of honour, atop the beer fridge. Dunno why I didn't look there at the start. Anyway, Dave said he wanted a photo of the both of us to have with him as it's the only way he'd race without me."

"Now you've got me going again!" said Stan, rubbing his eyes. "Bloody hell, I never knew racing could be so emotional!"

"Come on," offered Frank. "Let's go and take our seats. This is going to be a proper special day."

"It'll be grand, indeed," agreed Lee.

Chapter Twenty-Six

... If you're not fortunate enough to be trackside in the Isle of Man, then listening in to Manx Radio TT around the world is the next best thing. Tim Glover here, and I'm pleased to report that conditions are perfect as I look out from the tower. It's Senior Race Day and, arguably, the home of the greatest sporting spectacle anywhere. I certainly wouldn't argue with that, at least! We're going racing in a little over twenty seconds in the second Sidecar Race and I absolutely cannot wait. Folks, this is going to be a treat!

Dave ordinarily had a little more time to compose himself. But today he was starting at the number two position, on Henk's machine as opposed to his familiar own, and with a bloke he could barely tolerate as his companion for the next three laps. He looked down at the Frank & Stan logo emblazoned on his leathers, for both comfort and motivation, before taking a final glance up to the TT Grandstand where he knew all eyes would be on him. He eased the machine forward, towards the starting arch, allowing his eyes to drift briefly to the pretty girls stood elegantly either side — positioned there, as always, to see the riders off.

The engine of Thomas and Napier's machine erupted into life as the first outfit off the mark sped away from the start line on its way to the top of Bray Hill.

This was a time trial rather than a mass start, so Dave had ten long seconds to wait until he received the tap on the shoulder. He made sure first gear was engaged, giving the throttle several quick bursts to get the oil flowing, before dropping the clutch the instant hand-made-contact with-shoulder.

He tucked himself as much as physically possible for a unit the size he was. Second, third, fourth gear... Dave was second on the road in the greatest racing event on earth. *Shit, this thing's quick!* he said to himself, before pointing the machine towards Bray Hill — where he'd once again feel like he was driving off the edge of the earth.

Back in the grandstand, Lee, Frank, Stan, and Monty couldn't take their eyes off the starting grid. "Go on, Dave!" screamed Monty, jumping to his feet. "They look bloody quick!" he offered, before taking his seat.

All eyes were transfixed on this sporting spectacle. That is, until Stella returned from the concession stand armed with a hot dog and a lager, interrupting those sat patiently as she pushed her way through unceremoniously.

"Did you not get me one?" asked Lee. "It's just that I couldn't help but notice there's only one hot dog held in your hand?"

"I did," said Stella. "But I ate it on the way back. Those stairs really took it out of me, and I needed to keep my strength up," she told him, pointing to the sweat on her face. "I ate yours, and this one was mine," she added, by way of explanation, before tucking in to the remaining hot dog.

Today they didn't need a radio as speakers the size of small cars were fixed to the wall behind them, trumpeting out the race commentary.

Frank turned to Stan, whose face was rigid with concentration. "Stan, you do know you're holding my hand?"

"Yes, Frank. I won't lie, I do."

"That's fine. It's quite comforting, actually. Have you got that app on your phone ready?"

"Sure do," Stan answered, waving his phone as confirmation.

The commentator called off the outfits, each in turn as they left the start line, as much as time would allow until having to break away as the frontrunners reached the first commentary point on the circuit, Glen Helen.

... And now it's over to Dave Christian at Glen Helen!

Yes, thank you, Tim Glover, perfect timing as ever. I can hear the roar of an engine coming up the valley and the spectators to my left are starting to fidget which can only mean one thing – the first outfit is about to arrive!

... And sure enough, Sidecar Number One and first on the road is Jack Napier and Andy Thomas, looking quick as they tackle the left-hander before heading up towards Sarah's Cottage and then onto the rapid Cronk y Voddy Straight. For relative newcomers to the circuit, they certainly came through here as smooth as you like!

We await number two on the road, Dave Quirk and Harry McMullan, but I'm counting down on my head and they seemed to have lost ground on the run in from the Grandstand...

... Yes, the gap is certainly more than ten seconds, so Quirk and McMullan have dropped time, but here they come! That engine sounds wonderful, but as we wait for the official times, I can see they've dropped back and that third on the road has actually started to gain on them...

... As I suspected, the official timings show Napier and Thomas have pulled out a three-second advance over Quirk and McMullan. It looks like the Sidecar World Champions are on a charge, and eager to avenge their defeat in the first race!

Stan squeezed Frank's hand a little tighter. "I thought Napier had a broken hand or something? It doesn't appear to have an impact on his lap time."

Frank looked down at his white knuckles. "He does, according to Henk. And I think I may have soon, Stan, as well. A broken hand, that is."

"Sorry, Frank, I'm just a bit nervous."

"You're fine, actually. The pain is taking my attention away from the race," answered Frank.

Never had Frank and Stan been so intrigued as to the progress of an egg timer. They both sat, heads bowed, staring at Stan's phone screen.

"Pants!" shouted Frank.

The app on the phone had apparently updated before the radio commentator, since it revealed that Dave had now dropped back to third place at Ramsey, trailing by two seconds, whilst Napier and Thomas were extending their lead. "Come on, Dave! You can do this!" urged Frank.

"Dave's favourite section is over the Mountain, coming up," offered Stan encouragingly.

Lee interrupted, but for good reason, handing them each a large plastic beaker of lager. "You pair look like moody teenagers Faceapping your friends, or whatever it's called. I thought a beer would release the tension?"

Stan gratefully reached out for the beer. "I knew we'd met you for a reason, Lee. Keep them coming!" he joked.

"And the hot dogs," chided Stella. "You said you were getting a hot dog."

"Balls. Sorry, Stella, I forgot."

"Don't sit down," continued Stella, with a deft flick of her perm. "You said you'd get me a hot dog."

"And so I did. One hot dog coming up, Stella," replied Lee without complaint.

Glencrutchery Road was eerily quiet in contrast to the chaos a few minutes earlier. The lower-numbered outfits had all departed and those at the front had yet to reappear upon completion of their first lap. Dave had already broken the fifth of the six timing points, located at the Bungalow section, and, as Stan predicted, he appeared to be settling into his rhythm, having pulled back two seconds on that section and promoting them into second place once again as a result.

All necks were soon arched, however, as the relative tranquillity was smashed by the noise of the engine howling their way. Napier and Thomas had turned in their first lap unscathed, but the extent of their lead wouldn't be known until the other machines broke the timing beam at the grandstand.

"They're still second," announced Stan. "But—"

"Yes!" Frank yelled. "But how far down are they?"

"Wait..." replied Stan, index finger raised. "Bugger, they're sixteen seconds down. But, their advantage over third place is four seconds. That's good?"

Monty punched the air. "Come on, Dave! I knew that boy was bloody quick!"

Frank watched Monty, who was jumping on the spot, delighted for his friend. Monty caught Frank's eye for a moment, and with a beaming smile flashed an enthusiastic thumbs-up. Not once had Monty moaned or complained that he wasn't racing, more interested was he in focussing his efforts in supporting his friend. That's what mattered most to him, and bless him for it, thought Frank.

"Have you had your meds, Frank?" asked Stan. "Only you're looking a little bit peaky. Are you feeling okay?"

Frank threw him a contented grin. "I'm feeling a bit washed out, Stan, if I'm being honest. But, at the same time, I feel more alive than I've ever felt. Do you know what I mean?"

"Good," replied Stan, waving his hand like he was fanning himself. "Because I've got a little surprise for you. It's a little bit later than expected, but you can blame the Isle of Man airport for that."

"What are you prattling on about St–?" began Frank, but then he saw what Stan had been waving for — or, rather, to. "Oh, my!" exclaimed Frank, holding his hand to his mouth. "*Molly, what are you doing here?*"

Stan pointed to the spare seat. "That's yours, Molly."

Molly took her father's hand. "I wanted to come over and support you, you silly biscuit."

Frank was left momentarily speechless.

"You've spoken so much about this place, and Dave and Monty," Molly continued. "I just wanted you to know that I was interested in your life over here, and, well, that I love you."

"I love you too, Molly," replied Frank earnestly, but also with one eye on the racing.

"Dad...?"

"*Erm...* sorry. I'm so glad you're here, honestly I am!" Frank replied. "It's just I'm a little bit distracted at the moment..."

"Enjoy the racing, Dad," Molly assured her father with a laugh. "I can see you're a tad engaged at the moment, so you can tell me what's actually going on when it's finished," she told him, giving him a quick cuddle as she took her seat.

Frank gave her shoulder a squeeze. "Perfect! Thank you so much for coming, Molly. I didn't think this day could get any more perfect, but it just did with you here with us!"

... And with that, we'll hand over to Roy Moore at Ramsey Hairpin.

Yes, thanks, Tim, right on time as usual as I can hear the sound of machinery passing through the sweeping right-hander at Stella Maris before they arrive here with us at the hairpin. I can report that machine number one is first with us and Napier and Thomas are looking very impressive as they pass us on lap two, heading up to the Waterworks where the engines will need to put in a shift.

... Next on the road is Quirk and McMullan and unless I'm very much mistaken they've eaten into the leaders, and... yes, we need the other machines to make up the leaderboard, but it looks like Quirk and McMullan are on a charge, with the lead cut to eight-point-six-four-eight seconds – we'll call it eight seconds. With third place fifteen seconds back, it very much appears the battle for the top step will be between those two machines first on the road.

Frank and Stan were coupled once more in such a way as to the casual observer must have appeared almost indecent. "Come on, Dave!" they repeated, over and over, like madmen.

"I don't think I need those tablets from the chemist," suggested Stan. "This has got to be the greatest thrill I've ever experienced!"

"Thanks for that, Stan. I mean bringing Molly over. Not that," said Frank, pointing at Stan's trouser area.

Stan turned to look at the rest of the gang. "You're welcome. I'm going to remember this very moment," he said. "Stella's actually made it onto Lee's knee, by the way."

"Is he okay?" asked Frank, giving over a concerned look. "That's not something an ordinary man would usually be able to..."

"He seems to be rather enjoying it, and I think Stella's quite taken with this racing as she hasn't even eaten her hot dog," Stan assured him. "Oh, wait, here we go," Stan said, as the necks in the grandstand were once again craned up in the direction of Glencrutchery Road.

Napier and Thomas held the lead as they tore over the start line at blistering speed, but before Stan had a chance to confirm the lap time, Dave and Harry appeared rapidly behind them on the start of the third and final lap.

"They're about twelve seconds down," said Frank, who'd manually timed the difference on his watch.

"That's amazing!" exclaimed Stan.

"It is? That's more than at Ramsey, isn't it?"

"No, no!" replied Stan. "Don't forget that Napier and Thomas started ten seconds before, so, if Dave is twelve seconds back on the road, on adjusted time, they're only two seconds down. They've pulled back another six seconds over the mountain!"

"You're sure?" asked Frank.

Stan handed over his phone. "Look at the leaderboard, mate. Napier and Thomas hold just under a three-second lead. Frank... I think... they can really do this, can't they...?"

Stan turned to show Monty the leaderboard, but the radio commentator had beaten him to it. Monty knelt on the ground, with the palms of his hands joined, offering a prayer to anything and everything that was holy, and the atmosphere in the TT Grandstand was electric.

Tim Glover gave a run-through of the leaderboard before breaking for a commercial break.

"What the hell are they going to a commercial for?" demanded Stella, shaking a fist at nobody in particular. "And I can't even bloody smoke in here!"

The radio commercial break ended with some warning about keeping domestic animals and livestock under control, but Frank and Stan were more concerned with keeping their bladders under control.

"I feel all funny, like I've been smoking weed again," confessed Stan, slapping his cheek to try and sort himself out.

Frank gave him a puzzled glare. "What? What do you mean *again*? When did you ever smoke weed in the first place?"

"It was when..."

... Let's hand back to Dave Christian at Glen Helen for the final time in Sidecar Race Two.

Yes, thanks, Tim. Bang on. The leaves are rustling, and I can hear the sound of the helicopter overhead so that can mean only one thing, and, yes, I can hear the first machinery approaching and the leader on the road is... machine number two!

Unbelievable scenes here at Glen Helen on the last lap. Dave Quirk and Harry McMullan now on top, holding the slightest of leads over, in second place, Jack Napier and Andy Thomas...

I know that Andy Thomas has been struggling with his hand, so whether that's had an impact... the strain on any injury is massive on this circuit...

Both outfits should now be heading along the Cronk y Voddy Straight, and for those sat in the hedges, look out, you're in for quite a battle!

With about twenty-six odd miles to go, I've no idea who's going to take the spoils. What a race this is turning out to be!

Monty was now joined in the prayer position by both Frank and Stan — rendering them now unable to watch the app on Stan's phone, at least for the moment.

Stan half-opened one eye, "Frank can you confirm if there's water on the floor?"

"Stella dropped some of her lager," replied Frank.

"Thank god. I thought I'd pissed myself."

Frank attempted again to listen to the commentary, but it was all muddled because he couldn't concentrate. He took to his feet and paced up and down the aisle. Ordinarily, those sat behind would have vented their objection, but it was clear to most that those idiots in front of them were cheering on the likely winners of a TT.

The blood had drained from Monty's face, and only for the efforts of Lee and Stella was he able to get back to standing position. "You can do this, Dave," he insisted, pointing skyward.

Stan's phone remained planted in his pocket. Frank and Stan stared at each other as the commercial jingle —

which they were now acutely familiar with — was drawing to a close, meaning Roy Moore at Ramsey Hairpin was up next...

> *... The first machine is coming into view and I can tell you... yes, Quirk and McMullan are still first on the road! Seven seconds the lead at Ramsey Hairpin...*

> *What a fabulous race we've seen today. Local rider, Dave Quirk, has performed heroics with his passenger to lead the Sidecar World Champions by a stunning seven seconds as they head up the mountain on their final lap...*

> *They cannot be complacent as they've still got something like thirteen miles to go and certainly anything can happen on this course, as we've witnessed over the years. After all the effort, we've seen riders run out of fuel or had their race brought to an abrupt end by something as trivial as a loose wire!*

Harry McMullan was all but hanging out the left-hand side of the bike as Dave turned into the sharp left-hander at Kate's Cottage, situated around the thirty-fourth mile of the course. Dave glanced up towards the iconic Creg-ny-Baa before tucking himself in for the long straight. The hedges were packed with an array of spectators waving their programmes, but Dave was only focussed on the right-hander in front of the iconic hotel.

The bike was running like a dream, and for all he disliked Harry, Dave knew he was something apart from the rest. Harry, like the bike, hadn't missed a beat, and the confidence Dave had in knowing Harry would be there for him propelled him onto lap times he never believed possible even in his wildest and wettest of dreams.

Dave tuned in his ears to the engine on the run to Brandish Corner, and gave the simplest of prayers that the fuel in the tank would be sufficient. He dropped down a gear, and, once again, Harry was positioned with precision to give Dave the confidence and grip he needed. He didn't dare to believe, but with Hillberry Corner approaching him at speed, Dave knew he was only a couple of miles from the chequered flag.

Henk's team had volunteers all over the course, so he and Harry were inundated with boards confirming their advantage, but Dave knew if he finished ahead of Thomas and Napier then the race was his, by at least ten seconds.

"Shiiit!" he shouted, as Andy Thomas flew past him on the inside. Dave didn't expect a pass, and his composure escaped him for a moment and he missed a gear, losing him valuable momentum through Cronk-ny-Mona. "Fuck!" he shouted at himself.

Dave was furious, but he consoled himself knowing that if he finished less than ten seconds behind them, they'd still win. The momentum they'd lost allowed Napier and Thomas to pull away as Dave opened the throttle, but as they approached Signpost Corner, Thomas was already out of sight.

Dave knew what speed he could take the precarious right-hander at Signpost, but he didn't factor in the fade on the brakes which had been under constant pressure for over one hundred and ten miles.

Dave fought with the machine but the brakes didn't slow him sufficiently, and for a moment he headed straight for the hedge.

Dave had to take it wide, which lost him more precious time.

With his heart racing, Dave eased off into Bedstead Corner and knew that the infamous Nook was ready to catch him out if taken with too much speed.

He eased through the tree-lined section, which was notoriously slippery due to the dense canopy overhead, with fallen leaves scattered about and little sunlight. He emerged back into daylight and applied the throttle, turning right onto Glencrutchery Road and on to the finish line.

Dave gave it everything and tucked in, unsure if he was crossing the finish line as the winner of the Isle of Man TT races or in second place, of which there was certainly no shame.

He couldn't hear it, but there was rapturous applause and not one person remained on their seats as he applied the brakes — this time with more success — and turned up to the return road.

Dave had only ever been used to proceeding straight on, back to the paddock, but today he was being directed towards the winner enclosure on the right. What he didn't know was which bay he'd be occupying.

He turned right, and his heart sank as Napier and Thomas were parked in the area reserved for first place, with Dave directed towards the second-place bay.

He came to a halt and allowed his head to sink down onto the fairing. He'd given it absolutely everything, and one rubbish mistake had cost him dearly. And yet...

"Fucking legend!" screamed Harry McMullan, slapping him on the back. "Dave, that performance was a pure delight!" he said, taking off his helmet. "We didn't win, Dave, but you've got some fucking talent, my lad! That display was spot-on!"

The words were appreciated, but they weren't quite enough to remove Dave's discontent.

But he had no time to dwell as several microphones were thrust in his face. Chris Kinley was first, like a Manx panther.

"Dave Quirk, you've just finished second at the Isle of Man TT! How do you feel?"

Dave took off his helmet and was blinded for a moment by the camera flashes. "Chris," he said. "I'm fucked and need a beer!"

With that, Dave leaned towards Chris and planted a kiss on his beautiful bald forehead before buggering off in pursuit of the most-deserved beer he'd ever care to pass over his lips.

Chris Kinley adjusted his rectangular spectacles, sniffed, and then called into his mic: "And there you have it, folks!"

Dave didn't have to look too far for his preferred tonic, for Stella had once again performed crowd-moving miracles as Frank, Stan, and Monty appeared at the front of the horde, and with Monty smartly armed with a beer at the ready. Stella arrived a moment later with Jessie, who'd been watching with Dave's family.

Dave fell into the throng, revived only by the beer which Monty thrust under his nose. "Dave, mate, I'm so chuffed right now, I can't even..." said Monty with a breaking voice. "That was..." he went on, but he couldn't finish as the tears ran freely down his face.

Stan stepped up. "What he was going to say..." he began, but was afflicted then by the same complaint of watery-eyes-syndrome. "Nope, here they come for me as well..." he said weakly, letting the waterworks open up.

Frank nodded in amusement. "Dave, we have nothing but pride for that performance."

"We're fit to burst!" Stan interjected.

"Well done!" Frank went on. "You truly are a legend, my friend, and one of the most outstanding people I've ever met!"

"Legend!" Monty reiterated between happy sobs.

The feeling of goodwill didn't extend over the rest of the winners' enclosure, with Andy Thomas and Jack Napier very eager to remind Harry McMullan of just who, in fact, had taken first place. And, were it not for the swift action and tree-trunk arms of Henk, then Harry would've very likely ended up in jail alongside his brother.

Rodney Franks was also on the scene, offering a cringe-worthy dance routine for the benefit of the world's press. It was uncomfortable to watch, as dancing came unnaturally to a man like Franks.

"Here!" Franks shouted to Henk. "I just wanted to show you this!" Rodney came over and stuck a drawing under Henk's nose. "This could have been yours, Henk. These are the plans for the new hotel. I'll be sure to save you a room when it's opened. Oh, and guess who's going to appear on the wallpaper in the toilets? Yes, that's right — you!"

"A bet is a bet," offered Henk with a conciliatory shake of the hand. "You won fairly and squarely, what more can be said? The highlight, for me, is this man here," he said, pointing to Dave. "That is what the TT is all about, not some disease-infested hotel. When your hotel is opened, I am going to leave a very large faeces and not flush the chain!"

Henk left Franks to his own devices in order to prevent himself from unleashing his shovel-like hands onto Rodney Franks' face. "Did that threat work?" he asked of mechanic Abe Maddocks as they walked away.

"It sounded just fine to me, boss. Just fine."

Dave smiled for the press from the second step of the podium, but the champagne didn't taste as sweet as it should have. He peered down on the admiring faces looking back at him and he knew, given time, that the sense of disappointment he was feeling — for having come in only second, and for Monty not sharing the podium with him as well — would rightly be replaced by one of elation.

All he wanted now it was all over was to get his leathers off, have a shower, and get drunk — really drunk — but as he ambled his way back to his awning, he was halted by the arm of a steward.

"Dave Quirk! I've been looking for you everywhere!" said the steward breathlessly.

"Oh, sorry. I'd made a pit stop in the port-a-loo. I was just enjoying some quiet time spent drinking a beer on the toilet, whilst having a massive—"

"Shit! You need to go back over to the post-race press conference, right now!" the steward said, offering him directions.

"Aww, bollocks. Now I've got to sit next to them arseholes? I'm absolutely knackered. Can you at least get me another beer to help me through it?" Dave asked, like a true athlete.

"Sure, Dave. I'll bring it in for you," said the steward obligingly.

"Cheers."

Dave had never finished on the podium previously, so was unsure of the exact etiquette involved. He was first of the riders to arrive, as it turned out, for all the steward's worry, and sat at the left-hand side of the table behind the slip of paper with runners-up written on it in black pen. He sat back, and if he was daunted by the attended press staring back at him, it certainly didn't show.

The illustrious Chris Kinley presented himself — being, as he was, the presenter — approaching the direction of the stage. "Dave," he whispered, taking a slight detour over to where Dave was sat. "You're in the wrong seat, mate."

Dave shrugged his shoulders, pointing to the slip of paper in front of him.

"You've not spoken to your team?"

"No," said Dave. "I was on my way back to my awning to get blindingly drunk, if you must know. In fact, I'd just been enjoying a beer while sat in the port-a-loo, having a nice long—"

"Shit!" said Chris Kinley.

"Language, Chris...?" Dave chided, managing a grin despite his fatigue.

Chris shook his head. "No, I meant, shit, you've not heard!"

"Chris, I really like you, mate, but I'm tired, dirty, and sober. Out with it."

Chris reached over to the table, swapping Dave's piece of paper with the one in the middle of the table, then leaned in further...

"Dave, I'm not sure how to tell you this, so I'm just going to tell you..."

Dave looked back at him, exhausted and his patience waning.

"... but Napier and Thomas have been expelled from the race. When their bike went through scrutineering, something was found. I've not been sent through the details, but it was summat to do with oversized pistons. Dave, they've been disqualified, so the rest of the field have been bumped up a place."

Dave stared back at him, uncomprehending.

"Dave, what I'm saying is... you're a TT winner."

"Piiiss off," replied Dave, mildly exasperated and too worn out for this sort of nonsense.

Dave looked at Chris.

Chris looked back at Dave, his expression unchanging.

"Wait... so you're not having me on?" asked Dave.

"Dave, you're about ten stone heavier than me and at least one foot taller, so, no, I'm not joking. The last thing I'd do is arse about with you, especially in regard to something like this. You've won the TT!"

"Fucking hell!" screamed Dave, his fatigue instantly dispelled.

He climbed on the table as he unfastened the top half of his leathers, took his beer and proceeded to perform some sort of happy-dance on the table, whilst singing, very badly, "We Are the Champions" by Queen.

"That's right! Dave Quirk! TT Winner! Yer lookin' right at him!" he yelled out, pouring his own beer over his semi-naked torso in delight.

Chapter Twenty-Seven

What would ordinarily have taken at least twelve beers was accomplished in only four, the evening after the sidecar race, because he was so drained to begin with from both the exertion of the race and the excitement of the result. Dave Quirk, TT Winner, sat slumped in a chair in Frank and Stan's garden. They'd mused the very night before if they would be sat sharing a beer with a TT winner, and now they knew the answer.

"You must be very proud, Jessie," said Frank, placing a gentle kiss on her cheek.

"Like you wouldn't believe, Frank," Jessie answered him, and giving him a peck in return. "And what about you, then, considering all you've done for Dave and Monty? And whilst I'm tickling your ego, I've learned some other things about which you should be proud, yeah?"

"Oh?" said Frank, blushing.

Jessie patted him on the arm. "I've been speaking to Lee. You and Stan are big softies, deep down, aren't you? He's been telling me how you both got him off the street and also about the charity. It's you two that should be very proud of yourselves."

Frank offered a bashful smile. "I've had a fortunate life, so I wanted to give something back."

Molly joined them, armed with two glasses of wine. "He's not at all bad, are you, Dad?" she offered.

"Stop it, you two, or I'll get a big head!"

Molly smiled as Jessie went off to mix with the others, leaving the two of them to talk.

"She's nice, Dad. I like her."

"What, why would you say that, Molly?"

"Dad, I'm not stupid. Well, not today, at least. If you like her, then I'll be awfully happy for you both. And it very much seems tonight like there is love in the Isle of Man air all around!" said Molly, glancing sideways.

Frank looked over at Stan, stood with Monty, and took a fright.

"No, not there," Molly corrected him. "Over *there*," she said, pointing to the porch, where Lee was presently sharing a kiss with Stella.

"She's like another daughter to me, Molly, Stella is. She may not be related, but I've known her since she was a little one. Craggy Sally would be pleased to know she's met someone nice," he confided wistfully. "I wish she could see her now."

"Jessie's right, Dad. You really are a big softie, and I'm so happy that you've surrounded yourself with good people over here."

"Ay-up, did you say good people?" joked Stan, joining them. "And what about the rest of us?"

Molly put her arm around both Frank and Stan. "I did, and I meant you included, Stan, you silly sod. It may be I've had a glass of wine or two, but I mean it when I say I love you very much, Stan. I'm fortunate to have had both of you in my life growing up. You and my Dad, I'm sure you're both going to be very happy over here," she told him, with the warmest of embraces. "Love is in the air, Stan. Hopefully it'll be you next!"

"Which man would put up with me?" he asked, flailing theatrical arms about.

Stan looked directly at Frank with a determined expression. "Frank, I know TT only finished today, but I can't stop thinking about next year. We can also put a team in for the Southern One Hundred in a few weeks."

"One step ahead of you, Stanley! We've got an appointment with Henk next morning to talk about the way forward. I didn't have time to talk with him for long today, as he was off to find Rodney Franks with a massive smile on his face. I'm not sure what he was on about, but he said something about having a shit in his toilet. I'm not sure I could make sense of it. Anyway, we've got possession of a farm for a couple of years, which we need to get Lee and the charity involved with. Hell, we're going to be busy over the next couple of years."

"And which is why I cannot afford for you to die just yet, Frank," Stan reminded him.

"I've no intention of it, believe me, though I can't promise anything," replied Frank, raising his glass. "Here's to not dying!" he joked. "In fact, no, forget that. Here's to *living!*"

Frank glanced around the garden. He was in the mood for another toast and with the rattle of his ring on his glass, the floor was his.

"Ladies and gentlemen," he announced. "First, can someone kick him?" asked Frank, nodding in the direction of Dave, in blissful repose. It took two or three firm blows to rouse him, and a further moment for Dave to realise where he was.

"Ladies and gentlemen!" Frank called out again, now that all were conscious and aware. He raised his glass. "I give you the magnificent Dave Quirk, a TT Winner!"

"TT Winner!" came the collective reply.

Frank walked over and took hold of Dave's arm.

"What, you want another cuddle, Frank?" asked Dave. "Haven't you had enough already?" he said with a jolly laugh.

"I'd never say no to another!" replied Frank, holding Dave's hefty arm aloft in victory. "Hang on," he said, something in his head clicking. "Remember when you got the tattoo? The one your mate did by picking a random picture from your phone? You never did end up showing us what it was. Let's have a look!"

"Oh, yeah. I didn't, did I?" chuckled Dave. "I really shouldn't have said I'd let him do this each year, and given him free reign. That may not have been the best idea, as it turned out. Well, are you ready for this?" he asked, slowly teasing up the sleeve of his t-shirt.

His arm revealed a full-figured lady with her skirt riding up over her arse as she struggled to mount a rodeo bull.

"Here, that's not..." Frank began. "Is it? The rodeo bull in the beer tent when...?"

"Stella climbed aboard? Sure is," chuckled Dave. "The bastard really stitched me up with this one."

Frank looked over to Stella, and then back to Dave's arm. "Tell you what, Dave, he hasn't half captured the likeness with that one," Frank remarked.

"I know," laughed Dave. "I thought having a half-naked woman tattooed on my arm would come in handy on cold winter nights, but I think I may struggle with this one."

Frank and Stan gave Dave a further cuddle, before Frank raised his glass once more between the three of them. "Can I just say it, once more?"

"Wait there!" demanded Monty, who quickly joined the circle.

Frank stepped aside and looked at Stan, Monty, and Dave, in turn. "And what a team it is. Here's to good friends, bad tattoos, and a TT winner!"

"Are we doing it again next year?" asked Dave.

"Bloody right we are!" declared Frank. "I want to see you win another TT, and, more importantly, see how on earth your mate is going to better that tattoo. Cheers!"

"Cheers!"

The End

J C Williams
Author

authorjcwilliams@gmail.com

@jcwilliamsbooks
@jcwilliamsauthor

I hope you enjoyed this book. If you did, you may also like the *Lonely Heart Attack Club* series — also based in the Isle of Man.

You may check out my amazon author page here, for all my lovely books:

www.amazon.co.uk/J-C-Williams/e/B01IRNGDNY

As well as direct links to the other two Isle of Man-set books here:

www.amazon.co.uk/Lonely-Heart-Attack-Club/dp/1548766429

www.amazon.co.uk/Lonely-Heart-Attack-Club-Olympics/dp/1976456169

And my previous book:

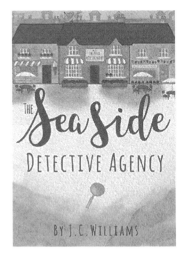

www.amazon.co.uk/Seaside-Detective-Agency-Isle-Mystery/dp/1718680333

And you might also have a butcher's at my editor's newest book, for his own peculiar (don't say I didn't warn you) brand of humour.

www.amazon.co.uk/Get-Some-Sleep-Dave-Scott/dp/1976262496